WAITING FOR A MIRACLE

Historical Novel

by

Helen (Wininger) Livnat

People will forget what I said,
People will forget what I did,
But people will never forget
How I made them feel.

— Maya Angelou

To my dear Miki
And my dear Zvika
The best parts of my life
And to the memory of my unforgettable parents,
Tizzy – Beatrice and Feby - Feivel Wininger

This book was published with the assistance of:

The Research Fund of Miriam & Dr. Michael Landau, at the Research Center of the Romanian Jews, at the Hebrew University in Jerusalem.
The Yehoshua Rabinovich Fund of Arts.
The World Organization of the Bukovina Jews.
Yad VaShem, the Remembrance Authority of the Holocaust and Heroism.
The Support Fund for the remembrance of the Holocaust survivors" books.
The Azrieli Malls Authority, Azrieli Center & IC from the Azrieli Group.

Many thanks to:

The people who made me believe in my ability to write.

The writer **Ram Oren,** for his advice, guidance, and sympathy.
Liora Zakay, for her professional help that drove me to publish the book.
Tamar Lotan, the literary editor, for her patience and her contribution to the final additions of the book.
Rony Kraft, translator, and English teacher who supported my writing.
Lihi Shahar, initial translation from Hebrew.
Francine Lashinsky for her great effort by helping me publish this book in English

I owe special thanks to the people whose vast knowledge guided me.

Professor Emeritus Nissan Rubin from the Anthropology and Sociology department at Bar Ilan University.

Professor Emeritus Zvi Yavetz from the History School of Tel Aviv University.

Dr. Aron Keidar, Jerusalem University. Director of the center that researches Romanian Jews, at the Jerusalem University.

Itzhak Yaalon, former president of the World Organization of the Bukovina's Jews.

CONTENTS

PREFACE

In a moment of enlightenment, with only a number of pages that my late father wrote and left me, I went back to the middle of the nineteenth century.

I was floating back and forth between historical events and visions I had seen in my mind's eye, story after story I had lived, every character I'd described.

I had died and been born countless times, but I never forgot my profound Jewish roots.

My father led me to the starting point of my family, somewhere in the nineteenth century in Bessarabia [Russia].

He introduced me to many Jewish people whose fate had been dictated and determined just because they were Jews.

Our haters abused us, killed and burned us, but we grew stronger, we never gave up and the proof of that is that I, a descendant of the family that my book revolves around, am writing these words with great pride and with my head held high.

Part I - Ephraim

Toward the middle of the nineteenth century, in a small house in a faraway village, on the south side of Russia, traveled a rumor that raised the hairs of all who heard it. The fear penetrated deep into the everyday life of the Jewish villagers.

In the small synagogue, at the edge of the village, the rabbi, along with the few men who prayed with him daily, would observe the tradition of sitting together on Fridays after prayer to tell stories of their wise forefathers. On this Friday, however, the rumor had gained such strength that their stories were abandoned, replaced by talk of rescue from the threatening and terrible disaster that was to take the joy from their pleasant homes.

Various suggestions were brought up. The rabbi, an elderly man, listened to the men as suggestions were made, some ideas bordering on the absurd and the irrational. He was shocked by how fear could paralyze the way people thought. How could they think of abandoning their village and homes to emigrate, with their entire family, to faraway places? Though he could not offer a better solution, he was convinced that running away was the wrong choice- there could be no chance of survival that way.

As the discussion went on, a gust of cold air blew in through a window left open, a palpable reminder of the inevitable Russian winter. The villagers knew its snowstorms and the inability to move against its harsh and freezing winds.

The evening had come quickly, and the few who remained in the synagogue were reluctant to leave. The security of the four shaky walls was felt strongly, accompanied by the fear of going out into an uncertain future.

In a small house on the village's main road, a family stood by the window, awaiting that Father would come back from synagogue, in order to partake in Friday night dinner.

The room was small and cozy, the burning fireplace spreads a pleasant heat, and was also used for cooking and baking. A fading painting was hanging on the wall. In it, an old, elegant grandfather with a long, white beard and sparkling eyes. The look in his eyes expressed so much wisdom, kindness, and peace as if to say 'Hang in there. Hang in there.'

The table was covered with a white tablecloth that had an embroidered finish. Its colors were faded a little, but my mother held onto it almost reverently. My grandmother would tell anyone who listened, that it was made by her mother before she got married, and was part of her dowry. It was a very old tablecloth.

The Sabbath candles, which were lit by my mother and grandmother, glowed and sparkled like the eyes of the grandfather in the painting. Maybe the candles were eyes too; the eyes of the Sabbath? The light flickered on the walls, the curtains, and the ceiling. The shadows were so nice. They looked like Sabbath angels from another world. Mother, with a gray head scarf, looked different from any other day of the week; so beautiful, so angelic.

This evening was especially quiet. My brother and sisters waited for Father without their usual acts of mischief. They didn't bother anyone, and where as I'd always complained about them disrupting the adults, today, for some reason, I missed the commotion all around. Was it always quiet before the storm?

I felt a need to talk and I thought I had a great idea to get my little brother to listen. I turned to him and said, "Little guy, let's see who can reach father's chair and climb it first." It was a trick we often played, and felt great about afterward; climbing on Father's chair and feeling big and important. Tonight, I got no response; he didn't even turn to look at me. He just kept looking out the window and onto the road leading to our house.

Snow started to fall; little stars that would fall lightly on your cap and coat. In moments like these, I could forget about myself, stand outside and catch snow stars. They'd fall on my sleeves and I'd choose the biggest, most beautiful one, and stare at it with admiration. It was a perfect star with perfect ribs, getting smaller and smaller until it disappeared.

The first moments of snow activated my imagination and my memories of past winters. I started yearning for pure white fields that almost never ended. Snow made the village look so beautiful; it was a shame to step on it. I felt sad every time dirt and destruction were caused to the snow by people walking over it.

There was an echo in my ears, accompanied by the march of soldiers that frightened me so. When they passed through the village, I ran home and looked for a place to hide, in which they would never find me. I had already prepared a place in my grandmother's closet; a shaky closet, with two screeching doors. I had discovered that a person could enter it from the back. A part of its back wall had fallen, and had never been fixed. Who'd find me in there?

It was getting late and Mother was starting to lose her tranquility. She rushed us to sit down at the table, claiming, it would make Father get here faster. Surprisingly, there was no argument; we all sat in unusual silence, and for a change, remembered Mother's comments about not touching anything on the table when it wasn't yet time to eat. My little brother got out of his chair, went to Mother and asked to sit on her lap. She picked him up quickly, and put him on her knees. Grandmother looked at her as if to say, 'Some days you need to be more forgiving with the little ones. They feel the tension in the air too.' Even though the room was warm, there was a feeling of a cold breeze passing from time to time.

The door opened and Father came in. No one else moved. All eyes were raised to him in a kind of prayer, wanting to know what had been said in the synagogue, what had happened. Father, as he always did, took off his cap and coat, greeted everyone, wished them a good Sabbath. I could spot a different tone in his voice, something I didn't recognize and didn't like. I felt frightened and tried, unsuccessfully, to respond to his greeting. What had happened to my voice? Words just didn't seem to come out.

Father blessed the wine and the glass was passed around the table until it was returned to him. He got up, washed his hands and greeted the bread, which signaled the beginning of the meal. Mother brought to the table a big bowl of soup, while Grandmother brought a second bowl, filled with noodles. Grandmother was very proud of the noodles she made herself on the rare occasions she could get enough flour for both bread and noodles. We'd developed a habit. Whenever we didn't have noodles we'd fill the soup bowl with dry bread, which soaked up all the soup, and we'd be left with great, moist bread. It was even better than fresh bread.

No one dared to pick up a spoon. It was strange. Usually, we'd all have our hands close to the spoons so that when the time was right, we'd leap to the bowls and forget about everything else. But that didn't happen tonight. Even my little brother, the glutton, didn't touch the food. Father raised his eyes. I could see a gray cloud covering his blue eyes. I had never seen him like that before. God, what was happening here?

"Eat children, eat," Father says.

The soup had a different taste in my mouth. It was metallic and unknown. We got a small piece of meat and a lot of potatoes. We concentrated on our plates. It was very quiet tonight; too quiet.

***

My name is Ephraim. I'm the eldest son in our family, the first born. I was born in this house eleven years ago and although I'm short for my age, I can help around the house like an adult.

Every day I go to the Heder[1] and study the Bible with the rabbi. The rabbi - teacher was very strict and always with a sad face. The children usually disturbed him just for a chance to see him get angry. He gets so mad that it looks almost as though he is dancing on the worn out wooden floor.

I envied his ability to move because he got warmer that way, while we had to sit still. My feet were always cold. I could feel the piercing cold despite the newspapers that covered my feet on the inside of my shoes. The cold was like a monster, taking hold of one finger at a time until it controlled my entire foot.

The teacher's wife was a funny, little woman; she was always asleep in her room, which was next to our room. She'd sit in a ragged armchair, her body covered with a big scarf and her snores filling the space. When we'd complain about the noise, our teacher would start jumping and yelling again. He'd let us know that we, with our wild behavior, were the ones bothering her. This routine happened every day, and I suspected it would happen at the exact time every time.

Father gave me a woolen coat. I was so happy and I didn't care if Mother had to patch it up in a few places. She did it very well, no one can see the patches without being told about them. The coat has a special smell. I love it so. When my grandfather, blessed be his memory, was sick and never left the house, his coat was passed on to my father and Father's coat was passed on to me.

The coat was long enough for me to fold my legs into when I was sitting at the Heder, and the warmth would spread to my knees. Everyone was envious of my big, warm coat. I was happy to make deliveries for my family, even when it was very cold outside because I had Father's coat to protect me.

My mischievous little brother tries to be around me all the time. He wants to go wherever I go, I try to explain to him that it's cold and unpleasant outside and that I'll be right back, but

---

1   A place little boys learn Torah

he never gives up. I love the little guy very much, but I never dare show it to him. A man cannot afford to act like a little girl, caressing all the time. Sometimes, when I finish studying, I go to the bed we share and move a curl from his forehead. It is not caressing in any way. I just don't want the curl to disrupt his sleep. I climb into bed, cover myself with the small blanket, and cover my feet with Father's coat. The nice smell of the coat helps me fall asleep quickly.

The day starts very early and, once again, I'm jealous of my brother because no one wakes him up. His time will come, and maybe by the time he grows up, we will be in a better condition. I will be working and bringing home money, and the morning will start in a warm room with the smells of baked goods coming from the oven. Everyone will have warm clothes, but I won't need a new coat because Father's coat will last for a very long time.

In the morning I'd get dressed very quickly. I had a few private tricks on how to get dressed faster and suffer less from the cold. Preparing the clothes in a specific order allows me to wear different things at the same time. In that way, I'm dressed in no time and keep the warmth I got during the night.

I needed new shoes. Yesterday, I discovered a hole in the sole of my shoe that allows water to get in. The newspapers I put in my shoe get wet, and I have to change them a few times a day. I still haven't told Mother about it. Usually, when a neighbor or an acquaintance offers us a pair of shoes that he has outgrown, and they are still in good condition, we check whom they fit. The lucky one wins the shoes. With the ones I'm wearing, I had special luck. One of my uncles left for the big city, to work for an important gentleman, and left me his shoes. Even though the shoes were a little big, I was happy to accept them. I adopted the method of putting pieces of fabric inside the shoe and it became a perfect fit. The problem is that that was two years ago, and even the strongest shoes get worn out at some point.

I still haven't told anything about my three sisters, since they are always playing together, and I don't really fit into their world. At night, they share one bed, and never stop chatting. I have no interest in their games dolls and colored ribbons.

***

There was complete silence around the dining table when Father started talking. I don't know why, but his voice was shaking. The sound of his voice cut through the silence as he tried to keep it steady. All eyes were held up to him. His face, which was usually flushed after dinner, was very pale. What if he was sick? It was the worst thing that could happen. Please, God, anything but that.

When he started talking, I realized that it was not about a disease. He just wanted to let us know, that changes would have to be made from this day on. We were going to have to cut back even more than before. If we cut back, there will not be new clothes for the holidays. Father then said, "Now, I need to ask the big children to put the little ones to sleep, as I need to talk to the grown-ups." As Father said that I thought to myself that I was surely one of the grown-ups Father was referring to. But then he said,

"Son, you go help the little ones. And from this day forward, you are not allowed to go out without an adult, not even to play with the neighbor's son. In the mornings, we will leave together to go to the teacher's house. Remember, you will not be going out alone, no matter what."

I didn't understand what I had done to deserve such a punishment. I remembered the time I'd been late coming home from Heder. It was because the neighbor's son had tempted me to go pick cherries and I'd lost track of time. Everyone had been worried and I'd had to stay home for a long time and give up the little play time I had with my best friend. At that time, I'd understood the need for punishment and I hadn't complained.

But now there was nothing to justify this punishment. I knew that saying anything at this point, would get me in more trouble. So I got up and walked to my room with my siblings.

I could hear Father saying something, but then Mother came and closed the door. This was very unusual. That door was kept open at all times because heat entered through it into our room. Something was happening; the adults were up to something that the children couldn't know about.

***

I was curious, so I tried listening through the door. But all I heard were whispers and restrained cries. Dear God, was it possible that my mother was crying? I couldn't remember ever seeing her cry. She hadn't even cried at her father's funeral. I remember seeing pale whiteness covering her face and felt her shivering. Now she was crying. Was the situation really that bad? What if I'd done something that had upset Father and he blamed her for it. I could feel my heart shrink at the thought. I never wanted to hurt them. All I wanted was for them to be proud of me. I studied many hours, so that the teacher wouldn't have a reason to be angry with me, and tell Father I was not studying properly. I must have done something really bad this time. I wish I knew what it was so that I could apologize.

Father, Mother, and Grandmother were sitting around the table. Father was speaking quietly and a terrible sadness filled his voice. He said that we are in great trouble, and that a rumor has been going around that the boys are going to be taken to serve in the Russian army. All Jewish boys older than ten years of age, are to be taken from their families to be disappeared somewhere in the Russian prairies. The fear in all the Jewish homes was great. That was the subject the men had been discussing in the synagogue, but were unable to reach any practical solution. They won't rest until finding a solution, but until then, they need to be careful, especially with their oldest son. He could disappear one day, so he is not allowed to leave the house on his own. No more fun and games, they are in a state of upcoming terror. No one knows when disaster might strike. It was also decided that nothing would be said to the children, so as not to frighten them. It was up to the grownup to watch over them in every possible way.

Mother couldn't stop crying and Grandmother, who had recently lost some of her awareness, stared off into space as if searching for an imaginary fly or a misplaced cloud.

Dear Grandmother has been walking around the house lately trying, unsuccessfully, to help my mother. Many things were spilled or overcooked and the children didn't always respond patiently or calmly. At times, we made her do things that would be fun for us to watch. If our mother caught us she'd scold us, even though all we wanted was a bit of exhilaration around the house. Usually, I'd take a book and appear busy in my studies, while the others looked for other things to do to pass the time.

It was getting late. Since I couldn't hear anything else, and I had to be up at dawn, I got into the bed next to my brother, and my thoughts started wandering. I thought about my late grandfather, may he rest in peace, and how happy I was in his arms with my head in his white beard. There I was safe and protected. I closed my eyes and dreamed about white angels, that only I could see, building his beard. I wonder why these magical moments came to my memory now.

I saw through the cracks in the door that the light was still on. That meant that they were still awake. It was late, and sleep came over me quickly.

In the morning my father escorted me to the Heder and I noticed all the other fathers were doing the same. We, the boys, looked at each other, searching for the reason for this change.

The rest of the day was the same as ever. We waited patiently for the hot soup at lunchtime. The bread served with it wasn't always edible. We learned that if you didn't eat it, you were left so hungry that the noise from your stomach could be heard all over the room, accompanied by a lack of concentration and a tendency to weakness and tiredness. A smack from the teacher's ruler would wake us up, it was an unpleasant feeling. When school was over, we had to wait for our fathers to come and get us. Sometimes we could be there for a while, suffering the orders from the teacher's wife. She always had something for us to clean or carry so that she could keep sleeping in between orders. Lucky for me, my father arrived on time, and I was glad to go home and sit by the fire.

Looking around I couldn't see any changes, but I still sensed something was different. Maybe something else was happening? I wanted to know what the adults would talk about. It was a shame they didn't share it with me, especially after Father had said I was responsible for the younger ones, and that my mother needed my help. Undoubtedly, that meant I was one of the adults. On second thought, maybe they sent me to bed with the young ones so that they wouldn't be upset that they had been sent to bed and I got to stay. Besides, my little brother needed my presence and I always made sure I was there when he went to sleep. Later I would sneak back to the kitchen where I'd be able to keep studying and keep warm. At times a piece of sweet cake or Sabbath bread was left on the table and Mother must know it disappeared into my stomach late at night.

After bringing me back from the Heder, Father left to go back to his business. I sat down, studied and waited for him to come back, hoping he'd have something to tell me while the small ones were asleep. I must have fallen asleep myself.

***

The days got shorter and the cold grew worse. I'd leave the house in the dark and get back in the darkness, accompanied by my father. When we ran into Jewish acquaintances, Father would greet them with a nod of his head and hurry forward. No polite questions or inquiries about the family's health, just a quick hello. Always in a hurry, but where to?

One night we heard a knock on the door and Father hurried to open it. Our neighbor was standing there with his face as white as snow.. After the man downed a glass of water, he asked if he could speak with Father in private. They went into the next room and closed the door.

The waiting began. I'm not sure how long they were in there, but I could see fear and concern on Mother's face.

I sat down and ruffled through a prayer book I'd taken from the table. Suddenly I noticed I'd been looking at the same page for a long time. I looked around; each one was deep in their own thoughts. No one was paying any attention to me.

The door opened and the neighbor said a quick goodbye. Before we had the chance to answer properly, he was out the door. Father left to accompany him out. When he got back, he looked at me with a strange look and said, "Stay with us after dinner tonight, Son, we need to talk."

Mother tried to catch his eye, unsuccessfully. No one dared to ask what the talk would be about.

After dinner, I stayed with my mother and grandmother to hear what Father had to say. I was proud of the fact that Father included me with the adults, with whom he could share his secret.

Father sadly said, "We are at the beginning of a very difficult time, a time we never dreamed would come. We have information from other villages about Russian soldiers going from door to door taking all the boys who are ten years old and older. The pain and grief of these families are unbearable. Many acts of desperation were made and the boys were hidden away or placed in the woods, however so they also disappeared. Sometimes it was possible to bribe the soldiers, but then other soldiers would come and take the boys. We fear our village is next and we need to do something to save our boys from this disaster."

I suddenly understood that he were talking about me and it felt as though I were sinking into the sofa, getting smaller and smaller. The sound of crying brought me back to reality. I looked at my father's face and the pain in it was clear. He suddenly looked old. I'd never seen him like that before. What did the soldiers want from us? We never did anything wrong to them. We'd done nothing to disturb them. They can take their own children; why the young ones from our village, who still have a lot to learn and understand? What is Mother going to do without me? Who will help her look after my little brother? I'm sure he won't go to sleep until I put him to bed. And who will watch over him at night? Many questions flooded into my mind, and my eyes couldn't see what was happening in front of them. For a moment I thought my father was still talking, but I couldn't hear him. All I heard was an echo, the echo of my pounding heart. Such a strong sound. I just hoped they couldn't hear how afraid I was.

I saw Mother taking out a small package from a secret place. Father opened it and started counting. It was money. Different bills in all sizes, he took a deep breath so that he could count out loud. He sadly said, "This is the amount we agreed to give and with this, we have to convince the wagon Vassily to take our boy."

Where was I being taken? Had I missed a part of this conversation? I couldn't even bring myself to ask. There had to be a mistake here. No one could take me away from my home. Again, I was reminded of the angels in Grandfather's beard. I'm sure they will come and rescue me. I'm staying here no matter what happens, I have to take care of people, especially my brother. I will tell that to the soldiers. They will understand, and maybe they too have a little brother at home.

My father called out to me, "Son." I saw his face. I could see his lips move but I couldn't hear his voice. Suddenly he started crying. That was impossible. My father couldn't cry, he doesn't know how to. The men in our family are strong, they never cry. I always say that to my brother and he immediately stops crying and smiles. His laughter sounds like tiny, delicate bells. Whenever I get sad or worried he starts jumping on one leg and makes sounds of dogs or chickens. I then forget the reason for being sad and join his game.

"Son!" Father called again. I start hearing again and my vision was less blurry.

"Yes, Father," I answered.

"Listen to me carefully. We are about to make a bold move and I know that by doing it we praise God. Our only target is saving you from the Russian soldiers coming to take you to training and the army. You will fight their war and live like a stranger in a country that is not yours. They won't allow you to keep the rules of the Bible that you were raised on. All they want is to turn you into a good soldier and ship you out to the front. Our people are not fighters and this is only our temporary country. We must save you from this fate and bring you to safety. The Jews in the village have found only one way of saving your life. They want to spare you the pain other children have gone through when they were taken."

Father stopped for a moment to catch his breath and then continued, "I think we are being brave in deciding to send you away, my darling boy. We are saving you from a cruel fate even though we don't know what the future holds. There have been talks with Jewish estate owners in Bessarabia, who have agreed to adopt our children. We still have a lot of arrangements to do so that the transfer of the children will be done the right way. We will find a Gentile wagon Vassily, who won't raise suspicion and he will take the children to Bessarabia in his wagon. We know the risk is great but we have no other choice.

From this day on, the children will stop going to school. The boys older than ten will stay home and prepare to leave. The neighbor who was here has talked with a wagon, but they still haven't agreed, the number of children per wagon and the amount of money. Each child will take a small package of food and a change of clothes. For the drive, they will wear several layers of clothes to keep them warm along the way."

Father asked me to go to sleep so that he could keep discussing this with Mother and Grandmother. I got up, my feet were like lead and my head felt hollow. I could barely move. I tried to focus my thoughts on what I had heard. Could it be? I'd be going alone and leaving my family behind? Where would I be going? When would I be coming back? Who are the people waiting for my arrival? This couldn't be real. I was just a little boy who needed his parents desperately.

I took my clothes off and got under the blanket. I couldn't feel the cold and couldn't feel my body. Suddenly, I heard crying from the next room, a quiet cry of desperation.

***

The days got shorter and the cold grew worse. I'd leave the house in the dark and get back in the darkness, accompanied by my father. When we ran into Jewish acquaintances, Father would greet them with a nod of his head and hurry forward. No polite questions or inquiries about the family's health, just a quick hello. Always in a hurry, but where to?

One night we heard a knock on the door and Father hurried to open it. Our neighbor was standing there with his face as white as snow.. After the man downed a glass of water, he asked if he could speak with Father in private. They went into the next room and closed the door.

The waiting began. I'm not sure how long they were in there, but I could see fear and concern on Mother's face.

I sat down and ruffled through a prayer book I'd taken from the table. Suddenly I noticed I'd been looking at the same page for a long time. I looked around; each one was deep in their own thoughts. No one was paying any attention to me.

The door opened and the neighbor said a quick goodbye. Before we had the chance to answer properly, he was out the door. Father left to accompany him out. When he got back, he looked at me with a strange look and said, "Stay with us after dinner tonight, Son, we need to talk."

Mother tried to catch his eye, unsuccessfully. No one dared to ask what the talk would be about.

After dinner, I stayed with my mother and grandmother to hear what Father had to say. I was proud of the fact that Father included me with the adults, with whom he could share his secret.

Father sadly said, "We are at the beginning of a very difficult time, a time we never dreamed would come. We have information from other villages about Russian soldiers going from door to door taking all the boys who are ten years old and older. The pain and grief of these families are unbearable. Many acts of desperation were made and the boys were hidden away or placed in the woods, however so they also disappeared. Sometimes it was possible to bribe the soldiers, but then other soldiers would come and take the boys. We fear our village is next and we need to do something to save our boys from this disaster."

I suddenly understood that he were talking about me and it felt as though I were sinking into the sofa, getting smaller and smaller. The sound of crying brought me back to reality. I looked at my father's face and the pain in it was clear. He suddenly looked old. I'd never seen him like that before. What did the soldiers want from us? We never did anything wrong to them. We'd done nothing to disturb them. They can take their own children; why the young ones from our village, who still have a lot to learn and understand? What is Mother going to do without me? Who will help her look after my little brother? I'm sure he won't go to sleep until I put him to bed. And who will watch over him at night? Many questions flooded into my mind, and my eyes couldn't see what was happening in front of them. For a moment I thought my father was still talking, but I couldn't hear him. All I heard was an echo, the echo of my pounding heart. Such a strong sound. I just hoped they couldn't hear how afraid I was.

I saw Mother taking out a small package from a secret place. Father opened it and started counting. It was money. Different bills in all sizes, he took a deep breath so that he could count out loud. He sadly said, "This is the amount we agreed to give and with this, we have to convince the wagon Vassily to take our boy."

Where was I being taken? Had I missed a part of this conversation? I couldn't even bring myself to ask. There had to be a mistake here. No one could take me away from my home. Again, I was reminded of the angels in Grandfather's beard. I'm sure they will come and rescue me. I'm staying here no matter what happens, I have to take care of people, especially my brother. I will tell that to the soldiers. They will understand, and maybe they too have a little brother at home.

My father called out to me, "Son." I saw his face. I could see his lips move but I couldn't hear his voice. Suddenly he started crying. That was impossible. My father couldn't cry, he doesn't know how to. The men in our family are strong, they never cry. I always say that to my brother and he immediately stops crying and smiles. His laughter sounds like tiny, delicate bells. Whenever I get sad or worried he starts jumping on one leg and makes sounds of dogs or chickens. I then forget the reason for being sad and join his game.

"Son!" Father called again. I start hearing again and my vision was less blurry.

"Yes, Father," I answered.

"Listen to me carefully. We are about to make a bold move and I know that by doing it we praise God. Our only target is saving you from the Russian soldiers coming to take you to training and the army. You will fight their war and live like a stranger in a country that is not yours. They won't allow you to keep the rules of the Bible that you were raised on. All they want is to turn you into a good soldier and ship you out to the front. Our people are not fighters and this is only our temporary country. We must save you from this fate and bring you to safety. The Jews in the village have found only one way of saving your life. They want to spare you the pain other children have gone through when they were taken."

Father stopped for a moment to catch his breath and then continued, "I think we are being brave in deciding to send you away, my darling boy. We are saving you from a cruel fate even though we don't know what the future holds. There have been talks with Jewish estate owners in Bessarabia, who have agreed to adopt our children. We still have a lot of arrangements to do so that the transfer of the children will be done the right way. We will find a Gentile wagon Vassily, who won't raise suspicion and he will take the children to Bessarabia in his wagon. We know the risk is great but we have no other choice.

From this day on, the children will stop going to school. The boys older than ten will stay home and prepare to leave. The neighbor who was here has talked with a wagon, but they still haven't agreed, the number of children per wagon and the amount of money. Each child will take a small package of food and a change of clothes. For the drive, they will wear several layers of clothes to keep them warm along the way."

Father asked me to go to sleep so that he could keep discussing this with Mother and Grandmother. I got up, my feet were like lead and my head felt hollow. I could barely move. I tried to focus my thoughts on what I had heard. Could it be? I'd be going alone and leaving my family behind? Where would I be going? When would I be coming back? Who are the people waiting for my arrival? This couldn't be real. I was just a little boy who needed his parents desperately.

I took my clothes off and got under the blanket. I couldn't feel the cold and couldn't feel my body. Suddenly, I heard crying from the next room, a quiet cry of desperation.

***

"Wake up, Son." Father, with a lantern in his hand, was bent over me.

"What happened?" I asked.

"It is time, Son. It is time."

"Time for what, Father?"

"Get up, Son." He took off my blanket, and helped me get dressed. I could barely move.

"I'm tired. It's early and dark. I want to go on sleeping."

"There is no time now, no time."

I could hear Father's voice from the shadows. He brought me more and more items of clothing, one on top of the other. I didn't object, just moved my body according to what was put on me. I just wanted this exercise to be over, so that I could go back to sleep.

"Follow me, Son."

I walked, barely; all the clothes made it hard and I was tired and sleepy. In the kitchen I saw my mother and grandmother; everyone was dressed and appeared busy. Mother was making drinks, and Grandmother was packing my bag. No one looked at me. Then Father said, "Mother, it's late. Give us something warm to drink before the wagon gets here."

Wagon? Where were we going so late at night? I was standing in the middle of the kitchen and getting sleepier. Father saw me falling asleep, took my hand, and sat me down.

"The *siddur*[2] too," Father told Grandmother. "Don't forget it." She put it in the package and tied the loose ends.

"Wait," Mother said. "I need to make a few sandwiches for the road."

Road? What road? Who was going? I woke up and looked at my father.

"What is happening here, Father?" I asked again.

He looked at me, his eyes twinkling from the light of the lantern, I felt a terrible cold go up my back.

"You are leaving, Son. It's time. Come sit next to me. I have important things to say to you."

I barely got up and moved to the chair next to my father. Mother finished making the drinks and was serving us cups of tea and pieces of bread. I could see my mother's beautiful face swollen from crying, tears falling constantly from her eyes. I looked at her in questioningly, but she looked away and the painful cry that came out of her, made it clear that things were bad, really bad.

Grandmother gave the bag to Father; she didn't look at me at all. I noticed her eyes, they were red. A terrible thing was happening in the house and I didn't know what it was. I was awake by this time. I looked out the window,. It was completely dark outside. I turned to look at Father. He was constantly blowing his nose.

"Drink up, son," he said.

I took small sips of tea. Father didn't touch his cup. Mother and Grandmother sat at the table too. The sound of their cries was the only thing that could be heard, they tried, unsuccessfully, to stop. A strong knock on the door was heard, and everyone ran to open it. The neighbor and his son walked in, the son was also

---

2 Jewish prayer book

wearing many layers of clothes, holding a package, and looking pale and confused. He was my friend, and two years older than me. Next year we would celebrate his *Bar Mitzvah*[3] and Father had promised me new pants for the celebration.

"Hurry up, Vassily will be here soon." The neighbor and his son remained standing at the door and did not come in. The neighbor turned to look at the wall. Mother came up to me and hugged me with all the strength in her. Her tears covered my face.

"Be safe, my son. I will pray for you every day. Be careful and hopeful, with God's will, we'll meet again."

Grandmother took me in her arms. She tried to say a few words but her voice was inaudible. Only a weak whimper in my ear let me know how hard it was for her, and how much it hurt. Father just kept repeating the same words, "It's late. It's late." He walked up to me, got on his knees, and spoke quietly.

"Son, it is time to move you to another area, as I explained to you a couple of days ago. You must go in order to survive. This moment is very hard on all of us, but I want you to remember your father's home, your brother, and sisters and carry us in your heart wherever you go." Father held my hand tight and didn't let go.

"My brother!" I ran back to the room.

"Wait, Son!" Father called out.

"Father, I'm not leaving without saying goodbye to my little brother. He will never forgive me if I do. He wouldn't understand why I went without him." I ran to the room and hugged him as strongly as I could. I didn't care if they thought I was a spoiled girl. He opened his big eyes and saw my face. He wondered what was going on.

"I have to go, little guy." That was what I always called him. "I'm going far away. You have to fill the place of the big boy around

---

3   A 13-years-old boy going to maturity

the house. You are no longer the little boy. Now you should watch over Mother and help her. Never forget me, I promise you that we will meet again."

I couldn't stop crying. I held him so tight, almost choking him, he didn't understand what all the chaos was about. Father was rushing me, but I couldn't break away. Being so close to my brother made me realize that I might not see him or any of my family again.

At the same time, my sisters woke up. Father told them that I was leaving. I went up to each of them and they hugged me, which was something they'd never done before. I could see the sadness in their eyes. I realized that even though they were always playing with their dolls, the bond between us was strong and deep.

I heard Father's voice saying, "We have to go."

He took my hand, pulling me after him. There was never a time of greater sadness in that house.

"Son, you are going on a long journey to an unknown place. With God's help, there will be a good Jewish family waiting for you. They will welcome you to their home and allow you to continue your studies. You must help them in any way you can. You are a good boy, almost a man. I'm sure that no matter wherever you go, you will be loved."

He put his hands on my head and said, "Blessed art Thou, O Lord, our God, King of the universe. Don't ever forget that you come from a Jewish home, and no one can take that away from you. The prayer book will be your strength for hard days and long nights. We will be saying the same prayers to keep you and us safe. May the good God bless you and watch over you. I'm sure we will see you again in good health. If we don't, remember that we will meet again in the next life. My darling son Ephraim." His voice was breaking, his eyes were filled with tears and he started crying and sobbing out loud. He held me close. We stood there, crying, forgetting there were other people in the room.

"The driver is here," the neighbor let us know. I wiped my eyes with the sleeve of my coat and looked at my family, all crying, all pale. This was really serious. I looked around me; the fire I spent many hours in front of, the dining table my family used to sit around, and I knew I would never forget the Friday nights we celebrated with songs and prayers. I had to remember these images, I must. They would have to stay with me all my life from this day on until I came back. I would come back.

The neighbor took me in one hand and his son in the other. "You must be silent all the way, you will be covered with hay and will have to obey Vasily's orders. You have a dangerous long way. He will stop in a couple of places. In these places, you need to be very quiet. There are soldiers checking the contents of the wagons. They shouldn't even suspect that you are under the hay. Vassily will stop from time to time so you will be able to stretch your legs. Your lives depend on your silence. Don't speak, stay close to each other to keep your bodies warm. We will pray for your safety." His pain finally defeated his voice. He turned away and cried silently. His son was leaving too.

Mother and Grandmother walked up to me. Mother put a woolen scarf around my neck. "I made this when I was pregnant with you. I never allowed anyone to wear it. It was probably waiting for this moment, to provide you with heat and memories."

Grandmother came near me. She held a package in her shaking hands, which she then put it into my hands. "A little bit of food and clothes from Grandmother." She couldn't say anything else. I got a great hug from this kind woman whose stories I loved hearing and who always made sure to save a piece of her bread for me. She would call me over and say, 'Quiet, quiet. Eat, eat.' Then she would put on a charming, mischievous smile as if sharing a private secret only with me.

Everyone was standing, tense, no more words left to say and no more time left for me in this warm home. We went outside. A huge wagon was standing out there, arranging some room in the big pile of hay. Father and the neighbor went and talked with him, argue a little, and then put a pile of money in his hand.

"Watch over our children, Vassily, and come tell us that they are safe the moment you get back. We will be waiting here with your favorite drink." We kept a bottle at home of a thing we called a 'Gentile drink.' We'd give some to the men who brought bags of potatoes or flour.

Vassily came, lifted me up and put me down on the wagon. He did that to the neighbor's son too. I take a last look back at the house. I could see the old tree that was next to the front door. I had spent long and happy hours in its branches. My parents and grandmother appeared as shadows standing in the doorway, standing very still.

***

"Lie down!" yelled Vassily. We both did as he said. Hay covered our bodies; our heads were still out, but I was sure he would cover them when the time would be right. I sensed the cold night air for the first time, all I could see were a blanket of bright stars over my head. I felt tired; sleep came over me and made my eyes heavy. I fell asleep quickly.

Suddenly I felt hay fall on my face. I almost jumped up, but then reality hit me. I remembered where I was and that I was not allowed to move. I opened my eyes and saw the first rays of the sun. I saw a glimpse of my friend before his face was also covered with hay. I was wide awake by that point and I realized I was on my way to a new life, a life with new people and without my family. For a moment I even missed my teacher. On a regular day, I would have been at his home now, studying.

I kept reminding myself not to move even though I was very cold. I kept guessing where we were going. I was so afraid. When my brother was afraid I would find an amusing way to get him to relax and forget his fears. What could I do now? Father said I was a clever boy and that people would treat me well wherever I went. I needed to remember that now and calm down. Father would say that God has answers, and he knows how to make the best out of everything, even if we can't see it and think our situation is bad. All we have to do is pray and God will hear us. I decided to pray.

There were stones on the road so the wagon was bumping and swaying. My hunger started bothering me. What would I have liked to eat now? I pictured in my mind our Sabbath dinners. I could even smell the food. No matter what was served, the smell was unforgettable. Those were wonderful moments of togetherness; all the family around the table singing Sabbath hymns. Sabbath is a queen. In my eyes, Mother was a queen, a Sabbath queen. After lighting the candles her eyes would sparkle as though she were crying. I asked her once if she were crying and she said no, that it was the candlelight twinkling in her eyes. She then smiled, happy that her answer had amazed me and made me smile.

So what if I were a little hungry? During school, I was always hungry. We studied from early dawn when I'd only had a warm drink and toast at home, or sometimes a piece of cake that my grandmother had hidden for me. She would wake up early every morning and made sure I drank and ate. She would walk me to the door and say, 'Be safe. Be a good student'. My dear grandmother, she must have been thinking of me that morning too, feeling sad that she had no one for whom to make tea.

I could sense the light of day increasing through the hay. I then heard dogs barking. We must have been passing through a village and we had to be really quiet. Vassily put more hay on my face. I heard people talking, but I couldn't understand what they were saying. Their voices sounded threatening and frightening.

I wanted to know if my friend were all right. Very gently I moved small piles of hay, but I didn't think I was getting closer to him. He was so quiet, and that was understandable. I moved another pile and then waited, then another pile and waited again. I was so busy I didn't notice the voices were gone; we were out of the village. If I could get closer and touch my friend we would both feel better. I was sure he was as frightened as I was and would be happy to feel my hand. I remembered the times my brother was afraid and he would cry. I would give him my hand, show him different things in the room and ask, 'Is it true that a table doesn't cry?' He would answer, 'Yes,' while crying, and I would feel his hand holding my hand tighter. That was a sign that he was still afraid. So I would ask about more things in the room and he would answer and slowly stop crying and return to his games. I made more progress in the hay but then I was shaken and pulled out of the hay.

"We will rest here until night time and then we'll cross the Dniester River, which is the border between us and Bessarabia. You can only walk in the area of the wagon and you can eat the food in your packages. I'm going to eat what I have and go to sleep." Vassily took his food out and stopped paying attention to us.

I looked at my friend, his face was gray and green and he couldn't stop blinking. He opened his mouth and, with a stammer, said, "I was afraid, very afraid. I'm shaking and I don't know if it is from fear or cold. How do you feel?"

"I'm fine," I answered. "I told myself many stories and that helped me. Now let's eat and walk around a little so that our frozen feet will function again before we have to go back into the hay."

We took out our packets. When I opened mine I saw it was divided into two. In one, I had slices of bread with pieces of cold meat. I ate a slice with meat; I wasn't as hungry as I'd thought. My friend had the same food. I didn't know when I'd get a chance to eat again so I ate another slice of bread with meat. Vassily was snoring very loudly; no one could have woken him from his sleep. Actually, we could talk without concern, but the words just didn't add up to sentences, or maybe just couldn't come out of our tense throats.

I put the rest of the food back and closed the small package. It was time to see what was in the other one. I opened it and found a few pieces of cake and my siddur and under them a new wool hat and scarf. I'd never seen the hat and scarf but I'm sure I'd seen that wool before. I tried to remember where I had seen it. I know it was in our house because I recognized the color. Suddenly it came to me; my grandmother had a big woolen scarf she always had with her. She would put it over her shoulders the moment she woke up and would tell everyone that it heals all ailments. She'd unraveled her beloved scarf and made me a hat and a scarf without anyone knowing or asking questions. She must have done it over the last two nights when the plans for my move had become certain. I held the wool close to my heart and whispered, "Thank you, my dear grandmother."

"New hat and scarf?" my friend managed to say.

"It's a present from my grandmother," I said proudly. "She made them especially for this journey." There was no point in telling him the story of the wool because I was the only one who really understood its meaning.

"I tried to find your hand under the hay," I said. "I wanted us to hold hands so that I would feel safer."

"What did you think about during the drive?" he asked.

"I prayed a little and then I remembered different stories from home. When I think of home and of the people I love I feel them close and it relaxes me. The prayers we know by heart have the power to calm me down too. I was happy I remembered them."

For a while, we walked around the wagon. We didn't speak; each of us was in his own thoughts and fears. Then I heard a horse's gallop. I ran and shook Vassily; he jumped up in a rage, ready to hit me.

"Listen," I said. "Listen."

He listened for a moment and panic was clear in his eyes.

"Get into the hay, fast."

We jumped on the wagon and were quickly covered with hay. The sounds were getting closer and closer. The wagon didn't move. The sounds got really close, and then suddenly stopped. I almost jumped out of the hay and ran to a rock on the side of the road, the one I'd left my package on. A great force stopped me and stood still. Then I heard a conversation between a number of people. At first, the voices were louder than a regular conversation, then they calmed down. Then I heard goodbyes and horses galloping away. After a few moments of silence, Vassily pulled us out and told us it was lucky that he had money and liquor for the soldiers so they didn't check the haystacks with their javelins.

"We will wait until it gets dark to get back on the road," Vassily said. I ran to get my package and placed it in the hay so I wouldn't forget it again. It started to get dark and we heard a voice from far away and Vassily showed signs of concern.

"I think those are farmers from the nearest village," he said. "They are dangerous slanderers. Go into the woods and wait for my whistle. Don't come back before you hear it."

I was scared of going into the forest. The trees were crowded and the dark was coming down quickly. I was afraid we'd get lost.

The Vassily raised his voice in anger. "Hurry! Get into the forest."

"Fill your coat pockets with hay and do as I do," I said to my friend.

We went into the forest and scattered hay as we walked. I counted ten trees and told him to stop. We sat next to each other. I explained quietly, "It is very dark in here and we could easily lose our way out. The ground here is hard and there are no leaves. If we can't see, we'll crawl, feel the hay, and it will help us stay on the right direction. I also counted ten trees, so we are ten trees away from the wagon."

"Very clever," mumbled my friend and said nothing else.

My eyes were closing despite the cold and the fear. I had to fight my desire to sleep.

"Are you awake?" I asked after a while. There was no answer. I started moving and shoving him. I was afraid to speak any louder and I don't think I would have been able to anyway. He didn't move. I put my mouth close to his hand and bit it. He jumped up.

"Be quiet, it's all right," I said. "You fell asleep and I didn't know what to do. This isn't the time for sleep. We should walk from side to side to keep awake and maybe even stay warm."

Then we heard the long awaited whistle.

We started crawling side by side. The hay on the ground was prickly and wet, but it led us straight to the wagon. It was so dark we couldn't see anything and we felt helpless. Vassily put us on the wagon and we tried to stay close together. He didn't cover us completely.

"I'll finish covering you when we get closer to the soldiers and the river. Remember that moving will cost you your lives and mine when we are near the soldiers."

We started driving again. I tried to remember a time I had been outside when it was this dark but couldn't. Once Father had come home late and he'd told us he'd barely seen the road. I'd thought to myself then, maybe when I'm old I won't be able to see the road. But that night I understood. I would have loved to tell him about it and to hear his explaining voice, starting an explanation with the words, "Listen, Son." Such warm and relaxing words.

I opened my eyes and tried to find some stars. I wasn't able to see any and that upset me, but then I remembered Mother's reaction whenever I would get upset or complain. She would say that there is good and bad in everything and that I need to find the good and leave the bad. I never took what she said seriously. In fact, I didn't understand what she meant. I understood it now. The lack of clouds was good for us because we didn't stand out and we could move unnoticed.

"We are getting closer to the border," said Vassily. "I'm going to cover you up well now. Don't move until you hear my whistle. This is the most important part, as there are many soldiers on the border pass. I hope we get past them without a problem because if we don't I'll regret this trip for the rest of my life."

I moved closer to my friend. My ears were open and I tried to hear all the voices outside. At first, it was quiet, too quiet, and frightening. After a few more moments I heard people talking. Someone was talking or maybe ordering Vassily. I could hear the word money. Vassily was yelling back and it didn't sound good. Vassily said one more thing and I could feel the wagon turning around. We were going back. My heart started pounding in fear; they weren't letting him through.

We got further away and Vassily kept swearing and cursing. I feared that my heart could be heard for miles. What was happening? I didn't dare to move. I barely dared to breathe. We were going back. Now the soldiers in our village would catch us and we'd disappear into their army. Me? A soldier? I wouldn't be able to pray and I would be treated like a slave. We heard they sent Jews to the most dangerous places, to the Russian wilderness, to the freezing cold.

Father says that when something bad happens, we need to pray and that God will hear us at all times. Well, it was time to pray. I started saying every prayer I could remember. I repeated them, and it felt like it wasn't me praying it's my heart, yelling from deep inside.

I asked, "Please, God, watch over your children, who study your teachings. You are a father to us all. Save us from a cruel fate. Bring us safely to a place where we can keep being Jews. Isn't it sacrifice enough that we were torn from our homes, our parents, and families? We are only children, your children. My father always prays to you with faith and intent and so do I. I beg of you, for a miracle that only you can do. Please."

Just like that, with my simple words, I begged for a miracle.

The wagon suddenly stopped, and my breathing did too. We were turning around again. The soldiers yelled something to Vassily. I was so caught up in my prayer that I didn't hear if the voices were calm or angry. Another conversation I didn't understand and then goodbyes and we continued driving across the border. Thank you, God, for hearing my prayer. I was choked up by tears. I still hadn't heard Vassily's whistle so we were still in a dangerous area. This was not a time to cry. I waited for the moment when I could breathe air with no hay in it.

We kept driving. I don't know for how long, but I finally calmed down because I felt weak from the tension. The fear and the effort probably made me fall asleep. The wagon stopped and Vassily pulled us out of the hay.

"We have arrived," he said. "In this place, at dawn, one of you will stay with the landowner. Rich Jews live here so we'll see which one of you will be chosen."

"We won't be together?" I asked.

"Each one of you will be in a different estate," he answered. He got on the wagon and was asleep within a minute.

I was filled with sadness. I had hoped we'd end up at the same place. We have so much in common, such as memories of the world we'd left behind and hope to one day go home. Home was not very far away, only two days and a night, and that was with a lot of stops. Maybe we could ask the landowner to take us both, but how would we explain why we wanted to be together. I was not a baby; Father says I'm a man and that I'll be fine wherever I go. Father knows what he is saying. If it is my destiny to be on my own, I'd find a way to make it until the time was right to go back home. The dream of going home was a strong man's dream and I was strong, so I'd do it. I almost had myself convinced, but then I sank back into my fear of being alone.

Daylight started coming up and we were sitting together and staring into the air. There were no words left to say and no more shared hopes. The light chased away some of the night's fears. I hoped it would help clear my mind too. I was so tired. What I wouldn't give for a hot drink and a warm bed.

***

Vassily woke up. "We are going," he said.

We jumped on the wagon, visible to all, and happy that at least there wouldn't be any more hay in our ears, nose, and mouth. We started driving. We drove through a few villages and were amazed at how quiet it was. We saw farmers in fields here and there. We passed many vineyards, and the general look was peaceful and quiet; so different from our souls.

"This is Bessarabia," said Vassily. "I've been here a few times, and there is a lot of wine, tobacco, and trees. The food is good and people live better here than in the parts we come from."

He stopped the wagon next to a wooden pavilion and tied up the horse. There were many wagons parked all around. He got down, knocked on the wooden door and talked to one of the men who told him to go around and enter a bigger building. He was gone for a few minutes and then he came back and told us to join him. We took our parcels, cleaned the hay from our clothes, patted down our wrinkled coats, and straightened our hats. We entered a big kitchen and were welcomed by pleasant heat and a smell of fresh bread. An older woman wearing an apron came and spoke to us.

"Sit down, children. I'll give you warm milk and some food." We weren't able to say a word, not even a thank you. We kept wondering what would happen next. Which one of us would stay here, and what would happen to the other? We both hoped to be liked by the people here so that they would not send us back. In the meantime, we got a big glass of steaming milk and some slices of a fresh, delicious cake. The drink warmed my body and melted my fears a little, but not for long. We ate and drank quietly, while Vassily joked with one of the workers. She brought him a bottle of wine. He drank, enjoyed it, and told jokes very loudly. Another Vassily entered from the kitchen door and joined the party. Vassily told stories. He told about paying the soldiers to let him pass. He laughed about them not even asking him what he had under the hay or not even thinking of checking. All they wanted was money and liquor. They kept talking and laughing loudly while another maid arrived, wearing a long, black dress and an apron, and asked us to follow her.

We obediently followed. We walked past a few rooms and arrived at a big hall. I had never seen such a big room. A man my father's age came up to us. A big yarmulke covered his head. He looked at me and at my friend, and then turned to him and asked for his age.

My friend said he was almost thirteen.

"You will stay here," the man said to my friend.

He turned his back and went back to his business. We kept standing in that big room, looking so small and helpless. I looked at my friend, took his hand and held it tight. I wanted to feel the warmth of his hand one more time and then said quietly, "I will see you in our village when we are older and don't forget me until then."

The maid who'd brought us in came back, and with a sign from the master, she escorted me out of that room and back to the kitchen. For me, the journey was not over.

In the kitchen, Vassily was arguing with a man I had never seen before. He was dressed like the master. I didn't understand what the argument was about. Maybe this was about me and I'd get a chance to stay here too? Could this man be interested in me? No one was looking at me or talking to me. The rest of the people, probably servants, were working hard in the kitchen and acted as if I weren't even there. I kept looking at the argument and then I saw Vassily being handed money, and I understood that it was in exchange for bringing my friend here. This had nothing to do with me.

Vassily also received two bottles of drink and some food and he then told me that we were leaving. We went back out to the cold. Snow had started coming down and I was reminded again of the games I used to play. I wanted to catch some snow stars and watch them melt. We walked to the wagon. I sat quietly beside

Vassily. Tiredness and disappointment made me indifferent but not for long. I was afraid. What if the next master wouldn't want me either? You couldn't really see how strong I was. I could carry heavy weights and do any job. I helped Grandmother bake bread and she was always pleased.

'Stop worrying,' I told myself. Stop fearing and trust in God. Father was watching over me from afar, and if he'd sent me all this way, he must have known things would work out for the best. I decided to watch the road for a while. Maybe it would distract me from my own thoughts.

We drove through villages and fields, all of them must be green in the summer. Vassily noticed that I was looking around and explained that we were passing next to grape vines. In the winter they have no leaves and are buried in snow. The snow keeps them safe and their roots warm. Come spring time they will be covered by beautiful leaves and juicy clusters of grapes. Father once told me how people make wine. At home, we had one for Sabbath, and it tasted sweet and a bit strange. One sip made me cough for a long time and I never understood what the adults were laughing about.

We entered into another village and were welcomed by small houses. The smoke from the chimneys reminded me of my village where in some houses people couldn't afford trees for the fire and their chimneys remained cold. Here it looked like they had enough trees and all the houses had smoking chimneys.

In the distance, I saw a long chain of mountains. They were tall and blue and had on white snow hats. The mountains looked as though they were trying to fly into the clouds. I remembered a trip I'd taken with my father. It was in the spring and we'd driven out of the village. We had to visit one of Father's customers and he'd brought me to help carry the wood. We'd driven through the trees—tall and green trees, with a special and fresh smell. We got lucky and we saw small forest animals. They were afraid and ran away quickly. After a while, we searched for a clear spot in the forest and opened the blanket Mother gave us, along with some food and drinks. In those happy moments, I had Father all to myself and he would tell me fascinating stories.

I would discover new qualities in Father; things I never knew. He was charmed by the beauty of nature and regretted not being able to travel more often. He told me that when he was young, he'd found an abandoned dog. It was dirty and Father was afraid to bring it home. There wasn't any hope of keeping the dog, but he decided to try. He took the dog to the river, washed it well and ran with it along the river so it would dry up. The dog was so happy with the attention that it didn't stop running and barking. They played for a long time, but then my father noticed it was getting dark. His mother had sent him to an aunt at the end of the village to get flour and eggs, but the dog had completely distracted him.

So he ran to his aunt's house with the dog following him. He got the flour and eggs and started running home. He wondered what to do with the dog. He needed to find a place to keep it for the night and then he would decide what to do with it in the morning. On his way home, he passed by the home of the village's water drawer. He was a lonely and childlike man, despite his old age. My father would sometimes sneak him a piece of cake when he brought them water.

Father knocked on his door, there was no answer. He tried to open the door and discovered it wasn't locked so he walked in and the dog followed. The room smelled of liquor, a really bad smell. Father saw the man sitting by the fire, drinking. Father said hello and then asked him if he could look after the dog. He promised to come back later with food for the dog and something for him too. The response was positive and the dog, which was very tired, lay down on the carpet and fell asleep quickly.

My father thanked the man and ran home. He was lucky that his father wasn't home yet and that he got along better with his mother. After telling a simple story that explained his delay and passing a hello from his aunt, his mother's mind was distracted and she didn't notice the time. The next day he rushed to see the dog, but when he got to the drawer's home no one was there. He started calling and whistling for the dog, but there was no response. He ran back home and there waited a pleasant surprise, the man and the dog were waiting for him. The dog ran to him. He was very happy, but wasn't sure what to do next with the dog. He tied the dog to a tree and went to talk to his mother. As he'd thought, she didn't agree to the dog. She said it would be another mouth to feed, and it was enough that they fed hungry Jewish people when they could. There was no way they could afford to keep a dog.

By that time the drawer came. He took something out of his bag and gave it to the dog. He shared his food with the dog. Father walked up to them, patted the dog, and looked at him with sadness.

"I can't keep this dog, my mother will not allow it," he said. Father then thought he would never see the dog again. No one keeps a dog unless it is for protection.

"I am willing to take the dog. You can come and visit me and play with it, and bring us some of the good food your mother makes," the man said. "I'm alone all the time and if I had a dog I'd have someone to talk with and take on walks. I might even teach it to hunt in the forest."

Father told me that if he hadn't been embarrassed he'd have hugged that man at that point. In that way, my father had a dog and the water drawer had two new friends.

The wagon stopped, Vassily took out a bag, opened it and gave me a slice of bread with smoked meat. "Eat, boy," he said to me. "We still have a long way to go."

We ate quietly. He sipped his drink and made a pleased sound after every sip. It was so easy to make him happy.

"Now I need a nap." He put a strange smelling blanket on the both of us and was snoring within a minute. I hoped to sleep for a while too but because he was making such a loud noise with his snoring, there was no chance for me to fall asleep.

Snow started coming down again. Although we were protected by a big tree, some snowflakes landed on my face. I started to move uncomfortably. For a minute I thought 'what if we freeze before we reach our destination?' With fear sneaking back into my heart, I decided to wake up Vassily.

"Look how much snow has fallen on us and on the wagon," I said.

"Yes, we need to continue," he answered. The wagon started swaying and we were on our way again.

It was getting darker. My whole body hurt from the endless drive. No matter where we were going, I just wanted to get there already. Vassily promised we'd be there soon and that gave me a brief moment of happiness. It was strange being happy at a time like that.

***

We were getting closer to the next village. I could tell by the sound of barking dogs that filled the air. I could see some lantern light coming from windows and the gray smoke from chimneys was visible. The snow piling on the road made it harder for us to move forward.

"We are almost there," said Vassily. He was impatient too and was tired of the cold. He hurried the horses, though they could barely move anyway. I remembered I needed to fix my appearance so that the people would like me. I wondered what to do first: clean the mud from my shoes or the snow from my clothes?

We entered a big yard and a few wagons were parked there. We saw a dim light from the window facing us. Vassily walked closer and someone announced that we had arrived. A fat countryman came out to greet us. He looked happy to see Vassily. They must know each other. We were invited in. The countryman called a boy over and told him to give the horse food and water. There was a big fire in the middle, spreading pleasant heat. We shook off the snow and immediately received a hot drink. The two men were quickly deep in conversation. The boy came back for more food for the horse and was told by the man, "After you finish, let the main house know a boy from Russia has arrived."

I got warmer and a little indifferent. I was tired and dirty. I sat in my corner, drinking and waiting.

The boy came back and said, "The woman in charge of the house will take care of him, and the master will arrive in the morning." He turned to Vassily and said, "You are welcome to stay here for the night."

***

I walked to the main house and entered the kitchen. It was a very big kitchen, bigger than our entire house. I looked around in amazement. Several women were doing different things. Some made jams and others sewed. Some ironed with what looked like a very heavy coal iron. My mother had an iron like that. She liked ironing in the evening, after dinner, when it was quiet. I would sit by the fire with a book and look at her peaceful face from time to time. I wondered if her face were still peaceful. I wish I could take a quick look at everyone at home and come back here. Dreaming, always dreaming. I was here and I'd be fine, and they would be fine there.

A big woman, wearing clean clothes and a big apron, came up to me.

"Come, boy," she said.

I followed her into a room that had a big bathtub on the floor. She started pouring buckets of hot water into the tub.

"Take your clothes off and get in," said the big woman. "I will get you some clean clothes," she said and left the room. I took my shoes off first. They were very heavy and almost glued to the paper that was wrapping my legs. I couldn't remember the number of days I hadn't taken my shoes off. I started taking off layers of clothes. The room was nice and warm. I touched the water and it was too warm. I looked around the room and found a big cloth on a chair, probably for after the shower. The woman came back. I grabbed one of the items of clothing off the floor and covered myself.

"No need to be shy, boy. I had four children and I washed them all."

She placed a pile of clothes on the chair and continued, "Get into the tub and wash up. I'll help you."

I was embarrassed. Slowly I put down the thing covering me and went into the tub. I didn't raise my eyes so that they wouldn't meet hers. Suddenly I felt her scrubbing my back and I smelled soap. I wanted to yell out. I was being washed. I was a big boy and even Mother didn't wash me, just helped a little. I didn't say anything.

Eventually, I grew to like it. The warm room, the hot water, and the strong scrub made me feel clean. I suffered at the thought that on the way I hadn't even washed my face.

"Get out!" ordered the woman. I came out and she covered my body with the big cloth. "Dry up and put on the clothes I brought you, then come to the kitchen and I'll make you something to eat."

I got dressed. The clothes were clean and had no patches. I felt good in them even though they were a bit big. The sweater was thick and warm and the wool was soft. The shoes were big, but I managed to walk in them. It had been a long time since I'd felt so good in dry, clean clothes and shoes that had soles. My old clothes were gone and so were my shoes. I found a small comb on the chair under the clothes. I combed my hair, put on my yarmulke, and was ready for dinner.

In the kitchen, a bowl of dumpling soup was waiting for me, which I ate quickly. The woman then said to me, "My name is Sarah and I'm in charge of the kitchen and of the staff. Would you like anything else to eat?"

I said no, I was full from the soup and started to feel tired. "I want to sleep," I answered.

"Follow me and I'll show you to your bed."

I got up, my feet feeling heavy, and followed her obediently. I couldn't wait to put my head on a pillow and sleep. We got to a small room and Sarah lit up a lantern.

"You have sleeping clothes on the bed. I'll wait until you get into bed to turn off the lantern."

I changed my clothes. The room was nice and warm, and it was a great feeling. Somehow, despite being tired, I noticed the room had a big window covered with blue curtains. I got into the bed, pulled the blanket over my tired body, and felt myself sinking into sleep.

***

Someone touched my shoulder.

"Father, just a little more sleep," I asked.

"Wake up, boy, wake up," I heard a woman's voice say. I didn't recognize it. I opened my eyes to see a woman I didn't know and had no idea how she'd got there.

"I'm Sarah, remember me?" she asked.

"Who are you? What am I doing here?" I asked in fear. "And where is my mother?"

"You are at the home of the Wininger family. You got here yesterday with the driver Vassily, and I'm Sarah. I was the one who took care of you last night. Do you remember?"

Suddenly I remembered everything. I was in a new place, without my mother and father. I was there alone. My stomach hurt and I wanted to cry. I lifted my eyes and next to me stood a strange woman with a pleasant smile.

"Come, boy," she said. "The sun is already in the middle of the sky. I wanted you to have a proper sleep and gather strength for your new life. Get dressed and come to the kitchen. The master will arrive at noon and will talk to you then."

She left the room, I felt so afraid. I couldn't stop thinking; what would happen to me now? And the master, what kind of person was he? I didn't want people to yell or be angry with me. Father never raised his voice. Even when he was upset with me he sat beside me and talked quietly. Every word he said got under my skin and I was so sorry I'd upset him or Mother. His being quiet was worse than yelling. I'd get dressed fast. I'd be swift and good. I'd promised Father to do my best so that no one would be upset with me. I wanted to show the good education I'd got at home.

I got to the kitchen and it was very busy. Four women were making food, baking bread, and cleaning. Water buckets stood in a row and were used, if needed, for cooking and washing dishes.

Many dishes were set out to dry on a wooden shelf over the fire. The kitchen was warm and the smell of food woke up my taste buds. I was ready to eat. Sarah served me warm milk, a plate of cheese, and bread with butter. It was unbelievable. The taste of bread and milk was especially good. I ate with great appetite and kept sitting and looking around.

In the days before the holidays, our kitchen had much more activity than usual. People would come to help my mother and grandmother with cooking and making special holiday treats. The house was filled with family and each one contributed different things and helped with preparations for the day's feast. I'd loved those days. When I'd get home from school, I'd rush to help the women in the kitchen. I'd run to get provisions for them. I'd get water from the well, kept the little children away, and at times fed them. The women would talk and tell stories about different things and their laughter filled the house. I didn't always understand the reason they were laughing, but it always made me smile.

A young girl entered the kitchen. She was wearing a long, clean apron and a headscarf. She whispered something to Sarah.

"Boy," Sarah said, "go with this girl. The master is waiting for you."

The moment I feared most had arrived. I asked for God's help so that I wouldn't fail. I got up and followed the girl. My head was clear of thoughts and in my heart was a prayer that he'd like me and wouldn't send me away. She knocked on one of the doors and a man's voice told us to come in. The girl opened the door, went in, and talked to the master. I couldn't hear what they said. She turned to me, signaled for me to come in, and left. I remained at the entrance, staring into the room. Like from a fog I suddenly heard a voice, and he said, "Come in, boy, and close the door behind you."

I walked in and closed the door.

"Come closer so that I can see you," said the voice. I got closer. My eyes were buried in the floor. I was afraid to look at the man and I didn't want him to see the fear in my eyes.

"I am Hirsh Wininger," he said, "and what is your name?"

"Ephraim," I answered.

"Good. Now come closer and tell me how old you are."

"I'm eleven," I answered quietly but didn't look up. This was it, now he was going to say that I don't fit in and—

"My boy, raise your eyes and don't be afraid. You are in a Jewish home with good people. We will look after you and take good care of you."

I dared to look up. In front of me stood a man a little older than my father or maybe it was the white hair under his yarmulke. I looked into his eyes, good and relaxed eyes. He wasn't going to send me away. Thank God, I was saved.

"Give me your hand," said Master Hirsh and led me to a chair. "You are a grown boy and you know exactly why you are here. The only way of saving you from the Russians was to make you a member of our family. This hasn't been an easy decision for us. We thought about it and discussed it with all of our family. We want you to feel good here and to enter the family in the right way. We took a chance too by taking you. If the Russians find out, my entire family is at risk. No one regrets the decision we made, and we are happy to save a Jewish soul and to share with you the goods God gave us.

From this day on your name is Ephraim Wininger. You are our son, who has been staying at an uncle's house across the Dniester for the last few years. Don't forget your new name. All our lives depend upon it. You will learn the habits of this place with time, along with the duties you'll have as a family member." He took a small break and then said, "I think that is enough for today. I welcome you, my son, on coming into our home. May we be as happy with you as we are with any of our children."

Tears filled my eyes. So much warmth and so much consideration. Who would have dreamed of such a wonderful meeting? And I'd thought I wasn't lucky. I was such a fool. The tears blocked my throat and I tried to swallow them and stop crying, but they were already on my cheeks and would soon wet my new sweater. The master came and wiped my tears away. I was grateful beyond words. He put his hand on my shoulder and walked me to the door.

"Go to your room for now. The package you brought is in your room. Go and relax. You can read your books and tonight you'll meet the rest of the family. Go, my son, go."

I walked away, more floating than walking. I was floating on the gentle and relaxing voice of that dear man, and the words 'Go, my son,' echoed in my ears. I crashed on the bed and a huge sob burst out of my throat. It was a wonder; my world hadn't fallen apart. I was right where Father wanted me to be. Thank you, Father.

I must have fallen back to sleep. What was happening to me? All the stress I'd gathered had made me weak. I went to look out the window. A few chickens were running around in the yard and ducks were looking for something to eat. The sky looked heavy and trees moved with the increasing wind. The snow melted and mud was everywhere.

I couldn't see other houses in the area. I didn't know if I were in or out of the village. It didn't bother me, just crossed my mind. Sarah came in.

"Come with me to the kitchen. Don't sit here alone."

"My name is Ephraim," I said.

"All right, Ephraim. Come with me and watch how I make food for the hungry people who will soon come to eat."

At the end of the kitchen, behind a low wooden wall, stood a table with a pile of plates and silverware on top of it.

"Let's clear these things up and set the table for dinner. This is where the family eats during the week. On Friday nights or when they have guests they eat in the big room."

I was happy that she was talking with me and trying to make me feel at home. She was updating me on family everyday things. These were things I needed to learn about my new world.

The table was set and ready for everyone to eat. Two girls came running into the kitchen. They were laughing and not paying attention to anything, not even me.

"Say hello to the guest," said Sarah. They stopped, looked at me with big eyes and ran out of the kitchen.

"Silly girls," she said. "They are very nice. You will have many opportunities to find that out."

I stood aside and watched Sarah and the other women at work. They were quiet and the only sound was Sarah's voice giving orders and asking questions.

Two young boys came in. They were deep in conversation and walked straight to the table. They kept talking very excitedly and paid no attention to me. I kept standing patiently, waiting to see the rest of the family. Master Hirsh arrived, accompanied by a woman and the two girls. The girls were quiet and sat politely at the table. Master Hirsh sat at the front of the table and the woman sat to his right. The boys greeted their father and went back to the conversation.

"Come sit with us at the table, Ephraim," said Master Hirsh. In slow, unsure steps I walked to the table. "This is my wife Hanna."

I looked at her. She looked at me with a small smile and I thanked her for it in my heart. She was a good looking woman and a little older than my mother.

"She is the mother of the house. Everything runs according to her understanding. She makes sure we have a nice and warm Jewish home. You will understand and know the mother better after you eat her Sabbath cooking." Everyone smiled and he continued, "Each of our children was given two names, one to be used in public between Gentiles, and another from our Bible. These are our daughters, the older one is Lanna-Lea and she is nine years old, and the young one is Rikka-Rebecca and she is six-and-a-half-years old. They study at home with a teacher who comes to teach them writing, reading, and a little math. They spend a lot of time with the mother and learn many important things from her. And these are our sons, the older one is Yosel-Joseph and the young one is Menashe. They bring us great pride, they are very smart students. Ephraim, I'm very proud of my family and I thank God for my wife and children." He looked proudly at all the people around the table and then continued, "A few years ago we lost two of our children in a plague. The pain is still strong and the sadness is deep. I hope that you can warm our hearts and become one of our children, which will make all of the family happy."

The mother put her head down; bringing up the lost children had brought great sadness to her face. She wiped away a tear and swallowed a painful sigh. I didn't know what to do so I just kept quiet.

"Hello to you, my son, and welcome to our home." A nice voice broke the heavy silence. I lifted my eyes and met the eyes of the mother, which were looking at me fondly.

We washed our hands and prayed. Bowls of food were served

to the table, some of which I didn't recognize. Sarah ran around the table filling empty plates.

"What happened at the *yeshiva*[4] today?" asked the father and the boys started telling an exciting story. For me, it was a chance to look at my new family and get to know them. The little daughter was older than my brother. I wondered what the little guy was doing right now. He probably didn't understand why I'd left. He used to wait for me when I got back from the Heder and run to me happily. Sometimes he would sit beside me quietly while I was reading. Other times we would play and run around.

The older daughter looked grown and serious. The two of them were dressed differently from the girls in my village. Lanna looked up at me. I was embarrassed that she'd caught me looking at her. I felt redness covering my face. I kept eating quietly and tried listening to the men's conversation. We finished eating, but no one left the table.

"Ephraim, tomorrow I will go with you to the Heder and introduce you to the teacher. I have to talk to you about something important and I'm glad the family is here with us." All the talks around the table stopped. All were waiting for what the father had to say.

"After we made the decision to take you in, we told our friend here that you are our returning son. I repeat that so you know how important it is. We've all talked about it a number of times. We cannot make mistakes in speech and let anyone know you were smuggled across the river. That would hurt us all and we don't want a disaster. You need to memorize again and again, until it becomes a part of you, that your name is Ephraim Wininger. No matter who asks, that is your name. I am about to say a very

---

4   An institution to study Torah, according to Jewish tradition

harsh thing, but for all of our lives depend on it, I will say it and demand it. You need to forget your old family name. When you wake up in the morning the first thing you have to tell yourself is your new name."

Silence spread around the table. Everyone was looking at me. I felt ants crawling over my numbing feet. My heart was pounding so strongly. To forget my family name? I missed them so much and I couldn't even say it. I loved my family. And Father, what would he say? And Grandmother, who always had an answer to every problem, what would she say? And then I understood it. I had no choice. I had come here to live with these strangers and live with them for many years. This is my fate. I had to smile, say I understood and thank them for having me. I raised my eyes to the father and all I could ask was, "And how do I call you, master?"

"I am not your master, Ephraim, and we will talk about it another time."

The mother got up and took her daughters, and the men were left at the table. I sat quietly as they discussed different verses and sayings. I tried to listen but was so far away in my thoughts that none of the words made sense to me.

"Ephraim, you can go to sleep," I heard a voice say to me.

I got up, said a quiet thank you and almost ran out of the kitchen. I got into the room, my room. In a second I was in bed, praying that I would be successful in my way. There were so many things I didn't understand, so many things.

***

"Wake up, it's time to go to the *Heder*."

"Mother, give me a few more minutes," I responded.

"I'm not Mother, it's Sarah," the voice answered.

"Not Mother?" I said. "Where is my mother?"

"You are in your new home, Hirsh Wininger's home."

"Who?" I asked. A hand patted my head.

"Everything will be fine, Ephraim. You will get used to the new situation. Now get dressed and a warm drink will be waiting for you in the kitchen. Today the master will drive you in his wagon to the Heder. I prepared clothes for you. It is very cold outside. Next to the door, you will find boots so that you don't drown in mud."

I was awake at that point. This was the second morning I'd responded like a lost boy and it had to stop. I got dressed quickly and went to the kitchen.

"Good morning, Master Hirsh."

"Good morning, Ephraim," he answered. "Please don't call me Master in front of other people, it sounds suspicious. We will talk more about it in the evening. For now, you are Ephraim Wininger. We'll have time to talk about names and manners in another time."

The two boys walked in. After saying good morning they sat down and drank the drink Sarah served them. I had a feeling they were ignoring me. I realized I was a stranger to them and it would take time until they had processed my presence. One of drivers came in and asked the young masters if they were ready to go. They put on warm coats and a hat and were on their way.

It was quiet and warm in the kitchen. Back home Father had probably left on his business after Grandmother had prepared his drink and some food for work. My brother and sisters were probably still asleep; maybe dreaming of me? I was thinking about them all the time and their faces were so clear to me. I thought of Mother and felt a sting in my heart. She must have been sad and missing me and I knew exactly how that felt. I used to ask her for a smile whenever she looked sad. I wanted to see her so much and Father too, and Grandmother, all of them. It felt like I've been away from home for such a long time and the yearning was so strong.

"We are leaving, Ephraim."

I looked around and barely remembered where I was. I was far away from there in my mind, and close to my family. Sarah handed me a coat and a hat. It wasn't my coat, but it didn't matter. I put it on and we were about to leave.

"Just a moment," I said. I ran to my room and took out the scarf my grandmother had made for me. I put it around my neck and felt the touch of my dear grandmother. I could hear her say, "It will be alright, my boy."

I ran to the kitchen quickly and was out on the wagon with the master in no time. I relaxed and felt a lot better, maybe because of the scarf.

***

The wagon was very comfortable. We sat on the bench behind Vassily. The bench was upholstered with nice furs. Vassily covered our legs with warm blankets. We had a sort of shade to keep us from the rain and snow. I had never seen such an elegant wagon before. I felt comfortable in my seat and looked around. We left the yard. The road was muddy; piles of snow covered the sides of the road. I loved the cool and fresh air. It was not yet the terrible cold of winter, but the cold air was felt in my lungs. Coming out of the yard, I didn't see the chickens that had been running around outside my window.

"Where are the chickens?" I asked innocently.

The master smiled and said, "Don't worry about them, son, they are probably hiding from the cold. Did you have animals in the yard back home?"

"No," I answered, and realized my question had been silly. From now on, I decided, I would keep my mouth shut and stop making a fool of myself.

The master turned to me and said, "Listen to me carefully, Ephraim. In the next village, where we are headed now, there is a good teacher with students from all the villages in the area. We take care of him and he takes care of our children, teaches them reading and writing, the Torah[5], and the prayers. My boys studied with him too, and today they are in the yeshiva; very smart students. I talked with the teacher and told him that we would be arriving today. I told him that you are our son. He will prepare all the books you will need and with God's help, you will be a good student and bring us pride. One of the drivers will pick you up in the evening. Don't forget your new name, what is your name, son?" he asked to my surprise.

"I, I'm win... win... Wininger," I stuttered.

"You need to memorize the name," he said.

It isn't my name, I wanted to shout. It isn't my father's name or my grandfather's name. But I didn't dare to open my mouth and say the words. For now, I was Ephraim Wininger, just for now. I would play the game the way these people wanted until I get back home. I wanted to look at the road, but I was busy learning my new name, and everything else was blocked from vision.

Snow started to fall, a thin snow that marked the beginning of winter. Like a thin fur, it sat on the driver's back and hat. Back home, when winter would start, we'd take advantage of the cold being bearable and run around outside. In fact, we didn't feel the cold, we were too busy running down the street, making snowballs to throw at each other. This was after we'd returned from the teacher's house in the evening. When it got dark I would go home, take off my wet coat and sit in front of the fire. My little brother would come and pull me to play with him, which I'd do happily. When we'd get too loud Mother would remind us this

---

5   The Jewish religious literature

was a house, not a yard. When Father was home we would find something quiet to do.

"We have arrived," said the master. He got down and helped me. I followed him to the little house at the side of the road. We entered a big room with little tables and chairs. The Heder was lit with many lanterns. It was warm and pleasant. When I got in, a few pupils were already there, studying. The master walked up to the teacher and I followed.

"Come here, boy," said the teacher.

I did and he gave me a few books and asked, "Can you read?"

With my eyes down, I said, "I can read, Rabbi." I just hoped he wouldn't ask for my name. I wasn't ready to say it yet. I decided to practice at home before I went to sleep.

The teacher took my hand and sat me in one of the chairs.

"This will be your regular seat," he said and went back to the master. They talked for a few minutes. The master took out a small package and gave it to the teacher. It was clear that he was grateful. The master took a quick look at me and left the room. The teacher walked up to me and opened one of the books for me.

"The new boy's name is Ephraim and he will begin the reading."

I looked down at the book and decided to read as though I were reading for Father, as I'd done many times at home. Father would then sit at my side and would be pleased with my reading. He rarely had to correct me and when he did it was calmly and with understanding. I read the chapter the teacher asked for and had no problems so he gave me a few more to read. He didn't stop me or comment on it. He was pleased with my reading.

"Very good," he said and started explaining the chapters I'd read. He didn't ask me anything else that day and I was starting to feel comfortable in my new environment.

In the late afternoon, a Vassily came to take me home. It was dark and all I could see were small houses spread into the distance. It wasn't like my village where I could call the neighbor's son from the window of my room or talk to people walking past my house leaning on the kitchen window. Here the houses were separated by fields. It had snowed again while I was inside and it was colder. I was covered well and the cold didn't bother me.

At the master's home, I saw Sarah.

"Dinner will be ready in a little while. The master left for the big city and will be back in a few days. The boys won't be returning today either, so you will be eating with the girls and Lady Hanna."

That made me feel a little uncomfortable. I had spoken with the master and knew him a little, but I haven't exchanged a word with the girls, and their mother was a stranger to me too.

"I'm not really hungry," I said, trying to avoid dinner. "Maybe I should go to my room to sleep."

Sarah stopped preparing the table and sat down. She said, "Sit next to me and let's talk."

I sat down and she said, "Look, Ephraim, you can't run away. You need to understand that this is your home. The sooner you get used to it the better you'll feel. The people here are very nice. This is a good Jewish home and we are trying to understand you too. The master talked to us about your arrival and this is a new situation for everyone. I can see that you have gotten a good education at home. That will help you adjust and we all will find a way for this new life to work."

Sarah spoke to me with a nice and soft voice. I wanted to tell her I probably wouldn't be here for long and that I have a family waiting for me. I knew this wasn't the time to talk about it so I just said, "Thank you, Sarah. I'll wait and eat with everyone." I felt a big, warm hand on my head, that gesture almost made me cry. I took a deep breath and was relieved when Sarah went back to work.

The mother and her two daughters came in.

"Hello, Ephraim, how was your day? Come sit next to me and tell us. Come now, girls, let's hear what Ephraim has to tell us."

We sat at the table. The girls laughed and pushed each other as part of a game.

"Everything was fine at the Heder," I said with my eyes down. In the meantime, Sarah served food and I was happy that everyone was busy eating. I ate with great delight. The food was warm and tasty.

"Ephraim, I want to talk to you," said the Mrs. "It is hard for me to talk to you about this but I have no choice. I've explained it to the children so after dinner the girls will leave and we'll stay and talk."

Dinner continued for a while. I wanted it to last forever. What was the new thing waiting for me? There were surprises all the time and not the kind I liked. The girls finished eating, said goodnight, and left the kitchen.

"As Mr. Hirsh told you, you're joining us demands a serious change in our family. Suddenly we all have a new family member, someone to accept as a son and brother. We don't have a lot of time to get used to the situation. We live among Gentiles, and even though we have a good relationship with them we have to be careful. They are not our brothers, only our neighbors, and not once have they expressed envy of our achievements and our financial status. I would have preferred it if Mr. Hirsh was here for this, but he will be away for a while, I don't know how long, so I decided to bring this up with you. Because you leave the house every day and walk among people, and at times people come into the house, your behavior and ours are very important."

I paid close attention to what she was saying.

"It is very hard for me to ask you what I must ask. I know you come from a warm home and parents you loved, but I have to ask that you call me Mother."

The room got quiet. My face was buried in the empty plate and my heart was racing. I have only one mother. I can't call another woman 'mother'. This cry was held deep inside of me. I had never thought of a situation like this. The next step was calling the master 'Father.'

"I know how you feel. But we adopted you. We accepted you as you are. We are happy to have you. You are a brave boy, a dear boy, and we will treat you as one of our children, our boy. We will be a close family." She put her hand on my shoulder and brought me closer to her. I could feel myself shaking under her touch, lost in this awkward situation.

"Cry, my son. Cry for this cruel world. And then bless your brave family who knew how to save you."

I burst into tears and held on to this woman, who from now on I would call Mother.

The next night was filled with dreams. I saw my mother talking to me, asking how I was, and then the face changed and the face of my new mother appeared. I yelled, 'Mother!' and saw them both reaching out for me, calling my name. I stood in front of them, small and scared, and said, "I want my mother", and they both answer me together.

"What is wrong, Ephraim?"

I opened my eyes. Sarah was standing over me with a lantern in her hand, wearing a nightgown and a woolen shawl on her shoulders.

"I dreamed of my mother; both of my mothers. I must have spoken from my dream. Thank you, Sarah, for waking me up. I just didn't know which one to choose. They were both calling me. Now I know that my mother was passing her job to my new mother. They stood in front of me together, like old friends, and they both wanted me. Now I have one mother in my heart, a treasure to keep and remember always, and another mother to look after and take care of me for the one in my heart. I talk too much for this time of night. I'm fine now and will sleep peacefully." Just then I raised my eyes to Sarah, who was standing quietly, listening to me talk. She smiled and said, "I'm here too, child. Sarah is here for you as well." She turned away and quickly left my room. What were her eyes saying? I turned to the wall and a quiet sleep came over me.

The next few days passed without problems. I went to the Heder with a driver, and studied well. In the Heder, everyone was wearing good clothes and the teacher was a kind and pleasant man.

When I got back on Thursday, I walked into the kitchen as usual. A warm drink was waiting for me there and so was Sarah. She said to me, "I prepared clothes in your room. Those are clothes for Sabbath or holidays. Try them on and I'll come and see if they need to be fixed." I walked into the room and Sarah followed after me. "Put them on," she repeated. I was embarrassed to take my clothes off in front of her. I didn't have a reason to be, after all, she'd scrubbed my back when I first got here, but still, I was embarrassed. She felt it and turned around.

"No need to be shy with me. I had four children you know, a girl and three boys. One of the boys was your age. He was thin and small like you. He was very hard working. He helped his father whenever he could. He brought pieces of wood home and carried buckets of water from the well. He was always ready to help his younger brothers and sister. He was my firstborn." Her voice was cracking. "I'll tell you the rest another time. Now let's see how you look."

Except for the pants, which were a little longer, everything fitted perfectly. Sarah didn't look at me, but I could see tears in her eyes.

On Friday, I got home early from the Heder. Coming in, I noticed a lot of activity and more women. Some were cooking and others were cleaning the kitchen. The smells were great; they reminded me of smells from a small house in a different place.

***

The girls went running through the kitchen and called me to follow them. Finally, they'd acknowledged my existence. I was happy with their daring approach and hurried after them. I entered a big room with full light. In the room stood two beds covered with colorful fabric. The room also had a small table and two chairs. On the carpet that covered most of the floor, were a few toys and a basket full of wool in different colors. They sat on the carpet and started dressing the dolls.

Lanna turned to me and said, "Sit and look at how many dolls we have. Mother made them clothes and today we are changing them to Sabbath clothes," I smiled. Girls and the things they have on their minds.

The young one, Rikka, had trouble dressing her doll. She put it in my hand without a word, as if asking for my help. I took the doll. My sisters had a few dolls. I never played with them and they were made out of old fabric my grandmother kept. I finished dressing the doll and gave it back to Rikka. The charming smile on her face was a great thank you for my help.

"Do you like dogs?" asked Lanna.

"Yes, very much," I answered and almost told them Father's story.

"I really want a dog, but I don't dare ask Father about it. No one we know has a private dog. Many have guard dogs in the yard, but they are big and filthy, not the kind I want. We had a Vassily once who had a dog that followed him around everywhere and even slept with him. Once, when no one was looking, I went to the driver's room. The dog was outside, getting warm in the sun. I looked around and after I made sure no one was looking I patted it a few times. The puppy was very happy. I hurried to get away from there and get home, the dog followed me. Lucky for me, Vassily came and called his dog. Those were a few moments of real fear. The memory of that dog stayed with me."

I was happy that Lanna had shared a personal experience with me. Then we heard the master's voice.

"Father is back," said the girls happily and ran to greet him. I got up slowly and followed them.

"Hello, Master... hello. And welcome back," I mumbled.

"It is good to find the family in good health and especially good to be back home. How are my daughters? And my sons?" I assumed he was referring to me too. Mother came and everyone sat in the big room to hear stories from Father Hirsh's trip.

"I will have a drink and go get ready for the Sabbath. I will tell you all about my trip the first chance I get."

Sarah came in with two girls to prepare the table in the big room for Friday night dinner.

"Ephraim, we are leaving for synagogue soon. It will be just the two of us going; the boys won't be back before next Friday," said Father Hirsh and left the room.

I entered my room and only then noticed how clean it was. On a chair, in a corner of the room, stood a bowl and next to it a fresh bottle of water. Clean clothes were hanging there, to be used after I washed up. The bed was in order and my sleeping clothes were folded neatly on the pillow. On a chair were the clothes I'd tried on yesterday. It was obvious that someone had done it while I was at school. On a small table were the books I'd brought from home and a new prayer book.

I washed up and got dressed. I noticed the pants had been altered and were in my size. I took my coat and scarf, and my siddur*, and headed for the dining room. Mother and the girls were helping to prepare the table. Two *challah*[6] breads were covered with an embroidered napkin. Shining candlesticks stood on the table and Mother was placing the candles. We stood around her. She covered her head with a big shawl, lit the candles, covered her face, and said a prayer. Her voice reminded me of the voice of my real mother. Despite the many lanterns that were lit in the room, the light from the Sabbath candles was different and special.

"Good Sabbath," said Mother and we all answered. I noticed that the mother and her daughters were wearing festive and elegant clothes. The girls' hair was combed and tied with ribbons. Father Hirsh looked refreshed even though he'd returned from a long trip just a few hours previously.

"I'll return from synagogue with two guests. They are passersby who will spend Sabbath with us and will continue their journey tomorrow night," announced Father.

We put our coats on, said, "Good Sabbath," to everyone and left for synagogue.

The sky was clear and despite the cold air it was nice to take a walk together, me and this man who I hadn't even known a few days previously and who today was my father. I had to remember to be especially careful among people to not call him master. I decided to look only at my prayer book and not to talk. I thought we'd get a chance to talk on the way but, as we left the house, we met more people who were on their way to the synagogue, and all were greeting each other with good Sabbath, good health and more. Most people brought their children, who ran ahead, talking and playing. I wanted to stay close to Father Hirsh so I

---

6   A braided bread traditionally eaten on Shabbat and holidays

reached for him with my hand and he took it with his big hand, held tight and didn't let go. I felt good in his hand, safe and comfortable. We arrived at the synagogue. A few people had got there before us and they welcomed us. Father had a regular seat and had people clear a seat next to him for me. I had the feeling I was being watched, I didn't raise my eyes.

The prayer began. I was deep in the book trying to follow the rabbi's exact words. After the prayers, he made a Kiddush and passed the wine glass to the people.

"Come, my son, I want to bless you on returning to us," said the rabbi. A little push on my shoulder made it clear he was talking to me. Father Hirsh led me to him. He put his hand on my head, blessed me, and everyone in the room said 'Amen.' I returned to my seat. Sabbath hymns could be heard throughout the synagogue. There was real Sabbath joy.

On the way home, Father Hirsh was busy talking to the two men he'd told us about. Snow started coming down. I raised the collar of my coat and tightened the scarf around my neck. The snow didn't disturb me and the way home wasn't long.

At home, we were welcomed by the light of lanterns, the Sabbath candles still struggling to survive, and the smell of food. The men and I thanked the angels that accompanied us on the way and finished by saying, "All his angels be ordered to keep you on your way. God watch over your comings and goings, from now until forever."

Father Hirsh poured wine into a cup, raised it, and said a prayer. The glass passed from hand to hand and everyone drank from it.

"It is a wine from our vineyards," said Father, while looking at me. The meal was served and its taste was amazing. Our guests told us stories from the road and I listened with great attention. They came from the other side of the Dniester, from the area I'd come from. They said that the Jews were not doing well and that they kept getting new taxes and were forced to give larger parts of their incomes or crops to the Russian government. They said that there were robberies on the roads so they tried to move in the day and hide in villages at night. They traveled without revealing that they were Jewish. They looked like Russians.

One night they arrived at a small village and couldn't find a place to sleep, even though they were willing to pay people to take them in for the night. It left them with no choice. They decided to sleep in their wagon at the village's edge. They settled in and fell asleep. In the middle of the night, they heard some noise and woke to find a few of the village's young men circling the wagon. They were forced to give away their money and the liqueur bottles, they'd brought to keep them warm. They were actually pleased because the men didn't hurt them. They stayed awake the rest of that night worrying about the fact that they have a long way to go and had no money.

"So where are you going?" asked Father Hirsh.

"We are on our way to Kishinev. There is a big yeshiva there and we are hoping to be able to study the Bible. We also heard, from a family member who was there, that we might also be able to find a job. Since we've been robbed, we need to find work in your village and get more money to keep going."

"My sons have mentioned that yeshiva*. They might be going there soon. You can stay in our home for now and after the Sabbath, we will talk with the rabbi to find a way to help you," said Father. The two men were very thankful and blessed Father and all the people in his home.

After dinner, the men started talking about the Bible. I was very tired, so I was happy when they sent the girls and me to sleep.

***

When I opened my eyes Sarah was standing beside my bed, changing the wet cloth on my head. I felt bad and my entire body was hurting.

"Thank God you are awake. I was so afraid until I saw your eyes opening. All kinds of thoughts ran through my mind. You didn't wake up to go to the synagogue, so the master sent me to see what was wrong. I touched your head and you had a very high fever. You were burning up. It is the afternoon now and you've only now woken up. I think your fever is down a little."

"I'm very thirsty," was all I could say. A cup of tea appeared instantly and I drank it with delight. "Why did you get so worried?" I asked. "I would get a fever at home too, and my grandmother would sit beside me until I felt better."

Sarah started crying. I didn't understand what I'd said that made her cry. She left the room, trying to control her tears, and came back after a while with a fresh cloth. Then she told me.

"Remember I told you that I had a husband and children? A few years ago a plague started in our village and many people got sick. It started with a high fever and strong body pains. My entire family was sick, including me. No one came in to help because they were afraid. After a few days, people started burying the dead. I fought the illness while taking care of my family, but one day my strength ran out; my body couldn't fight the disease and I collapsed. I don't know how much time passed before I woke up, but when I did, I lit a lantern and went to check on my husband and children. They'd died while I was asleep or collapsing. I didn't even have enough power to scream from the pain. I buried them the next day. I didn't think I'd have the power to survive and handle the pain. All I wanted was to die. I blamed myself, thinking that if only I had been awake, I could have saved them. There was no point left in my life. I still had a high fever. I stopped eating and only drank water. One morning I woke up and my fever was down. I was able to get up and walk around.

I went out and saw my neighbors. Some of the families weren't hurt while others had buried their dead. The plague was gone and I was all alone, a grief-struck, lonely widow. The Wininger family took me into their home and by doing that, they saved my life."

Sarah raised her tearful eyes and looked as though she were coming back from another world.

"I don't know what I'm doing, telling you this story. I must be out of my mind." She touched my forehead. "You are doing a lot better, son. Sleep some more and you will be strong and healthy in a couple of days." She changed the cloth on my head again and left the room.

Later that afternoon, Mother came to see me. She sat next to me and said that they were very concerned about my fever. The girls weren't allowed to visit me, for fear they might catch something. My eyes closed and I heard her quietly leave the room.

After a few days I felt much better. I stayed at home all week because of the stormy weather. I spent a lot of time with Mother and the girls. I brought my book to the girls' room and read, and they were sewing, with the help of their mother. In the afternoons we played a little and often visited the kitchen to take baked goods or spoons of jam from the jar that stood on the table.

One evening I was sitting in the dining room reading quietly when Father walked in.

"Hello, my son," he said to me.

I answered as he took off his coat, shook his hat and sat beside me.

"We have many things to tell each other," he said. "I want to tell you a little about the things we have here at the estate. At Friday dinner, I told you that the wine we were drinking was our own. Our family name also comes from the word 'wine,' Wininger. We have vineyards on great tracts of land. In the spring I'll take you to see them and show you how wine is made. You will get to see the big barrels we put our wine in. Later on, it is sold to inns and pubs in the area or the farmers. We also make liqueur from plums that grow in the area."

I started laughing. "We call that *Reque*, or Gentile wine," I explained. Father smiled.

"I like that expression; it suits the wine's purpose."

Father took a short break and asked for some tea. Then he continued, "We have a big stable and we raise horses. Some of them are used here on the estate and others are sold. A special foal was born a few months ago. His color is brown, but one of his legs is as white as snow. If he survives the cold winter we'll keep him for ourselves. We are expecting a very cold winter."

We stopped talking and drank the tea.

"I would love to see this foal," I said enthusiastically.

"I'll take you with great pleasure."

I continued with my studies in the Heder and my life went by with no surprises. My interaction with people in the house was nice. We all tried hard. The boys didn't come home frequently. They were busy with their affairs and spoke with me infrequently. I was most comfortable with Mother and the girls, especially Lanna, who became my friend. I would tell her stories from the Heder and about things the other students did. We told jokes and laughed at the youngest daughter's tricks and at how we would slip away from her to the kitchen and talk.

***

One day, in the late afternoon, I was studying in the kitchen, my favorite place.

"Come quickly," Lanna called, pulling my sleeve. I got up and followed her.

"Put on a coat. We are going outside," she said.

We put on our coats and sneaked out from the kitchen door. She kept looking from side to side, afraid that we would be seen. Lanna ran to the big warehouse that was across from the kitchen and I followed. We went in. I had never been there before. Lanna started moving things in search for something.

"What are we looking for?" I asked.

"A small, brown dog," she answered.

"A dog?"

"Stop asking questions and find the dog before people notice we've left the house."

We looked at the piles of wood and hay, but he was not there. We climbed up the piles and tried to see the dog from up above, but no dog could be seen or heard. Then I remembered that my father had told me that the first thing he brought the dog he'd found was food and water.

"Let us get some food from the kitchen, some sort of meat, put it on the floor, and hide. Maybe the dog is hungry and will come out to eat."

"Wait here, I'll be back," Lanna said and ran off. In the meantime, I kept searching, unsuccessfully.

Lanna returned with a piece of cold meat. We placed it on the floor and went to a distant corner. We then sat down and waited. After a few minutes, we saw him, a small and brown creature that looked frightened. He snatched the meat and went back into hiding. Now we knew where he was and we slowly walked closer to him. The dog kept eating and didn't even try to run away.

"Ephraim, from this day the dog is ours. We can come once in a while to bring food and play with him. He is so small and cute. Touch him and see how soft he is." A light of joy sparkled in her eyes. "Now we share a secret." She smiled at me and happiness showed on her beautiful face.

"A dog doesn't sit in one place, waiting for people to come and play," I said. "He will probably leave soon."

"If we adopt him, the dog will not leave," she said. The word adopt was like a fist in my stomach. The dog would be like me, adopted. I banished the thought. Basically, I was happy, and that meant that my parents were at peace.

"Maybe if we bring him food and water every day this place will become home and he will stay here. This place is safe from snow and rain, and the hay will provide heat. I wonder where he came from. We need to make sure no one finds the dog or that we are stealing food for him. This is a great secret, Lanna. I'm happy you found him," I said, and I was really happy with the present we'd received. We patted the dog, which looked happy and full. We got out, looked around, and ran to the house.

"Children, your faces are red and your eyes are shining. I hope you aren't getting ill," said Sarah when she came into the kitchen, a few minutes after us. We laughed and ran out of the kitchen, to avoid more questions.

Our story with the dog lasted a few months. We left the house every day and the dog welcomed us with obvious joy. First, he would eat the food we brought and later roll around and jump from one pile to another and we'd follow. When he'd get tired we'd sit beside him, and pat his nice fur. One day we came and didn't find the dog. We left the food in the usual place and when we returned the next day it was clear that the dog wasn't there. We feared we wouldn't see him again. We tried looking for him for a few days and then realized it was over. We were both very sorry.

***

Days and years passed, and it was two years since the day I'd left my first family. One night I realized that I was thinking less of my old family. I started feeling guilty. A few days before that I dared to ask my father if I could go to visit my family. He had many wagons and I was sure that he could spare one of his drivers, and let him go with me. Father looked at me and said, "I would be delighted to send you to see your family; I know how much you miss them. I wish I could make it happen. The roads are very dangerous now, and you know that only here in Bessarabia you are protected by law from going to the Russian army. Nothing has changed in that area during the past years. Once you cross the Dniester River, soldiers can stop you and take you away. You would disappear and we would never get to see you again. You are very important to us and we couldn't allow anything bad to happen to you. Maybe one day Jews will be able to drive safely from place to place and at that point, I would be happy to let you go and see your family."

I knew Father was right, but I couldn't have kept the question inside.

My *Bar Mitzva* celebration was coming up. I started learning the *Haftara*[7] with the rabbi. Our house got busy too, in preparation for the event. Guests were coming from a few villages in the area and we were all hoping that the older sons, who'd moved to the city to study, would come too. The matchmaker found them appropriate wives and Father was pleased with the families of the future brides.

Mother was nervous too. A few years had passed since the boys' *Bar Mitzvahs* and everyone was excited about the celebrations. For days, the girls followed a seamstress around who'd come to

---

7   Verses that are read on holidays and Shabbat

prepare the clothing for the event. They used the opportunity to get more new clothes for themselves. Lanna was much bigger so she got a whole new wardrobe. The seamstress also made new dresses for Mother; so everyone had new things. Men were absolutely forbidden in the room where the seamstress worked, except at times when I was asked to try on a shirt or a pair of pants that she made for me.

I saw Sarah in the kitchen and she came and gave me a hug. She said, "You've gotten so big and tall. Only yesterday you arrived scared and fearful and today you are almost a man. I am very happy that you're here. You gave back to me what God took away, the privilege of looking after you and taking care of you as if you were my own son. You are a good boy, Ephraim, God will give you all that you deserve. Everyone in this home is happy with your presence, and they are lucky that you are who you are. I know all the hard nights you have had, especially when you first came here. I heard you crying at night and I cried with you. I didn't come in because I had no words of comfort for you. Some types of pain can't be comforted and I know that better than anyone. We both learned that time covers our wounds and pushes them to a distant corner of the memory. They will never disappear; we will carry them inside for the rest of our lives."

I loved that woman. It takes so much strength to go through what she did and still remain pleasant, understanding, and thoughtful. Sarah got up and returned to her work, but I could still hear her blowing her nose several times.

The boys arrived and there was great happiness in the house. In their first evening home, we gathered around them, wanting to hear all about the school they were going to and about the big city. Father was the only one besides them who had been to the city. They told us about a secular Jewish school that had opened there. They explained that in addition to Bible studies, they teach general things like history, geography, mathematics, and languages.

Father was shocked by the story and said, "Jews sending their children to study subjects the Gentiles study? How can that be? And wasting time that could have been used to study the Torah. God save me from these sinners."

The boys kept telling the story, saying that Jews, especially wealthy merchants, had decided to give their children a secular education. The business connections of these merchants with other countries forced them to learn other languages and professional business management. These Jews spent great amounts of time with Gentiles, studying their habits, and learning general subjects so they'd have conversation topics and would be able to strengthen their connections. We were surprised. We'd never heard of such things in our village or in the villages around us. It appeared that you could find all the new things in the big city. We sat quietly and listened to the boys' stories. When the report ended, Father had something to say, "My sons, I know you don't belong to that group of Jews and I am proud of you for that. I have been thinking that it is time you started working with me, alongside your studies, so that you will learn the job and will know how to run the estate with or without me. Business is very good, thank God, and I need your help."

The boys didn't look very happy with what Father had to say. I knew I wasn't at a good age for business but I wanted to work with Father.

Sarah came in with a cake and hot drinks. I noticed that the boys hadn't answered Father yet. In fact, I knew that the decision wasn't theirs, that Fathers' offer was a fact that was to be obeyed.

The big day arrived. I woke up very early when it was still dark outside, and I thought of my distant family. They must have remembered that I was turning thirteen that day. A family always waited for its firstborn to have his Bar Mitzvah. I wondered if they were awake and thinking of me.

I decided that on that special day they would be with me in my thoughts. I was even thinking about them while I was reading the Bible in the synagogue. They would be a treasure in my heart. At times I wanted to tell stories from the place I once called home, but I knew I wasn't allowed to talk to anyone about it. At that time I didn't even cry when remembering my family. Something had changed in me. It was a part of my growing up. I tried to picture my loved ones' faces and it was hard to do.

Then, finally, morning came. There was a big commotion in the house. People were getting dressed in a hurry to get to synagogue on time. Sarah made sure that I dressed properly and brushed my hair. She was wearing something new too, and formally announced that she would be with us in the synagogue and would hear my voice from the court of women with Mother and the girls. She didn't even try to hide her excitement.

Mother came up to me, held me close to her heart, and congratulated me. The boys did it with a handshake and the girls came close and whispered congratulations. Rikka smiled shyly at me and ran to Mother.

The synagogue was filled with more people than usual. Everyone congratulated me. The regular prayers passed quickly and I found myself in front of the open Torah with Father and the rabbi at my side. It was quiet all around me as I started reading the *maftir*[8]. The sounds that came out of my mouth were floating in the synagogue. My hands were sweating and my eyes became moist. It was a good thing I knew the *maftir* by heart.

I had no mistakes, thank God. My father, with a big smile on

---

8   Matifir - reading chapters in the books of the Prophets

his face, said, "*Mazal tov*[9], my son." I felt another pair of hands, hugging me but I was the only one who knew who they belonged to. I was a man. I was thirteen.

After the Sabbath prayers and songs, we went out to the great hall. A number of women were setting the table, putting out cold food and drinks. From the women's court came Mother, the girls, Sarah, and a few more women. I could see the happiness on their faces. I received many compliments about my reading. I was happy and excited, and a little confused.

The men gathered near one of the tables, eating and drinking wine, all in a good mood. The women, at another table, were also eating while congratulating Mother and wishing her joy from all of her children. Mother was shining with happiness.

My day was both happy and hard. I would have loved to have my far away family with me, today of all days. I thought of them again on my way home. If the celebration had taken place in my old home, my little brother, who was probably much bigger now, would have been around me constantly. I imagined my mother and grandmother's excitement. My father would have been so proud. He was proud of me every time I came back from the Heder and told him about a new thing I had learned. I pictured my sisters, wearing new and beautiful dresses and walking proudly beside Mother. I wished I had spent more time with them when I'd had the chance.

"Ephraim," Father called me as I woke from my daydream and walked toward him.

"The rabbi was very pleased with you. He said that I was blessed to have a son like you. I was very proud, my son." Father placed his hand on my shoulder and we walked together the rest of the way home.

***

---

9   A blessing for a happy occasion

A year after my Bar Mitzvah, as I was coming home in the evening, I saw Vassily, the wagon Vassily. He ran toward me and hugged me. I was surprised and happy to see him. We went into the house and I was excited to hear about my family. Vassily suddenly turned serious, looked down and started talking, "As you know, Ephraim, I used to come to your house often to help your family, and you were always kind to me. Lately, your father had had many health problems so I helped the family as much as I could. The last time I went there I was surprised because no one answered my knock at the door. I tried to open the door and it eventually opened. I had a bad feeling. I went in and no one was home, which was unexpected.

I went from room to room and all the furniture was in place, only the closets were open and it looked like things have been taken out. I had heard that Jews were being harassed and humiliated for no reason. There were stories of abuse and beatings of Jews. The farmers were angry that the Jews were more successful in their business, and soldiers were encouraging plundering and violence." He took a short break and continued, "I went back to the kitchen and noticed a small package on the table. An envelope with a note in it was attached to the package. In the note, your father wrote to me that they needed to leave because their lives were in danger. He asked me to give you the package on one of my trips. He even left me some money along with some grateful words. Even in those hard moments, he didn't forget the help I had given the family all these years."

I couldn't believe what I was hearing. Such a cruel fate was pushing my family further away from me. I didn't know where they were. I looked at Vassily. He couldn't look at me. Maybe he wasn't telling me everything. Maybe he knew more and didn't want to burden me with more pain. Then he said in a broken voice, "Ephraim, take the package that I found. Your father badly wanted you to have it."

All that time his hand had been stretched out with the package in it. Sarah came and brought us drinks and something to eat. She placed the food on the table and walked away.

I took the package in my shaking hands. Father had packed it with his own hands. I wondered what had been going through his mind. I couldn't imagine what he was thinking. Mother was next to him, or grandmother, or my brother and sisters? I would never know.

I didn't have the courage to open it.

"Vassily, how did everyone was when you last saw them? And Grandmother, how was she?"

Vassily didn't answer, he couldn't even look at me and that was my answer.

"She is gone?" I dared to ask.

"Gone," he answered. "Last winter she developed pneumonia. The doctor couldn't save her."

I felt choked, but couldn't cry, something was blocking my throat. There were no words to express my feelings. There was only pain.

My fingers untied the cord from around the package and inside was a letter; a letter from Father. My blurred vision made it impossible to read so I just sat there, staring at the paper.

"I have to leave before it gets dark," said Vassily. He wanted to get out of the uncomfortable situation and had nothing more to say. I placed the letter on the table and got up.

"Thank you, Vassily." I wanted to ask him so many questions, but I couldn't think of anything. All I had was emptiness and weak knees. He shook my hand warmly and in a quick walk, almost running, he left the kitchen.

I returned to the letter and read,

"To my dear son Ephraim

We must leave the village as soon as possible. We might be leaving tonight with several other families. This place is no longer safe for Jews and staying here might cost us our lives.

I want to tell you a story that I never told you. It is very important to me.

My grandfather, rest his soul, was a very religious Jew and a wise man. People from all the villages around us would come to him for advice and a blessing. He was very special and we were all blessed by his knowledge and his warmth and understanding.

He looked a lot like the painting in our house, a grandfather with a long, white beard and loving and wise eyes. When I was a young boy I loved listening to his stories and I enjoyed learning with him.

One day he left the house as he usually did. He used to sit in the synagogue and help people who came to him with their problems. At night we were all home waiting for him, but he hadn't returned. At first, we assumed he was delayed at the synagogue, but the more time passed, the more we worried.

I was seven years old at the time and I asked my father to go with him and search. We left the house following the path Grandfather took to the synagogue. We passed by the forest and heard a voice moaning. We ran in. After a few steps we found Grandfather lying on the ground. Only when we got home, we saw how bad Grandfather's condition was. The doctor told us that there was not much chance for him to recover.

I hurried to see him. I loved him a lot. He was a friend to me. I lay down beside him and held him tight with my small hands. He told me that a few of the villagers' children attacked him with sticks and hit him without mercy. They kept yelling, 'The Jews take all our work. Leave this place.' He could barely speak. I saw he had something important to say so I got closer.

"Listen to me, my beloved grandchild," he said. "I know it is my time to go. I am old and tired and I have lived a lifetime. All I had to give to you I did in our talks and in the stories that I told you. Despite your age, you were a loyal and patient listener and bless you for it. I have a small treasure that I received from my father for my Bar Mitzvah. I would like to give it to you for safe keeping and to your sons after you. It is an old Bible, the entire Torah on one scroll. I carried it with me wherever I went. Please, take it and look after you."

It was a big effort for him to say so much. His voice got weaker and the pain was visible on his face. I couldn't move. His eyes closed and his grip on my hand got weaker until it was gone. I hugged the Bible and kept it until today.

I don't know what will happen to us or where we are going. I need to follow his request and pass this to you. Take it wherever you go and pass it on to your sons.

We love you very much. We talk and think about you all the time. May God be with you forever. Amen."

I could tell from the writing that he was in a hurry. Maybe his hands were shaking.

I took the little Bible and kissed it. I walked to my room with weak knees and tearful eyes. I put it among my belongings. It would be with me for the rest of my life.

Thank you, Father.

***

In the following years, we celebrated the marriages of Yosel and Menashe. The joy at home was great. We were awaiting the birth of two grandchildren. Lanna had grown up to be very beautiful and we have remained good friends, sharing our secrets.

Yosel and Menashe were working with Father, helping in the business. Their opinions mattered a great deal to Father and he allowed them to make important decisions in the estate management. Father would take me on long trips, explaining to me about running a business in general, and ours specifically. He told me about his relationships with customers. A number of pubs in the area were run by Jews with whom Father has a special connection and mutual trust. At times these trips took days and I enjoyed them greatly. Aside from stories of the business we talked about issues in the Bible and the Talmud. Father was a wise man and a great storyteller. I got to know him in time and I had to admit I was fortunate. All family members thought of me as a part of them. At times I would wonder whether they'd forgotten that I'd only joined the family a few years previously.

***

By the time I turned eighteen, my life was running smoothly. I studied and helped around the house whenever needed. Everyone knew I was unfailing and that I had good hands. Mother and Father had gotten older and were working less. Sarah was getting older too, and relied on young women to do the house and kitchen work. The matchmaker visited our house often with matches for Lanna but not one that would satisfy Father.

One evening, Father and the boys arrived home and they looked troubled. During dinner, everyone was unnaturally quiet and I noticed that Father was eating very little. Every once in a while he sneaked a sigh.

"After you put the babies to sleep, I would like to talk to the entire family," he said and didn't explain. The women hurried to put the young ones to sleep; Sarah's assistants cleared the table and served tea.

It looked like a regular evening at our house.

"I have been hearing rumors from nearby villages and from Kishinev that the situation for the Jews is getting worse," he started after the women returned. "We can feel it in the business too. Lately, the Gentile buyers take more time to pay their bills and their attitude toward us has changed for the worse. A few customers that aside from being our business partners were our friends for many years are speaking in a different tone. They've stopped being polite and they postpone paying their debts without explanation. I have seen a number of estates offered for sale at low prices but no one buys them. Do you remember what we heard about Jews, mostly in Kishinev, who learned the local language, customs, and way of dressing? These Jews sent their children to secular schools and universities.

They did everything to resemble Gentiles in order to be accepted and to have good business connections. Surprisingly, these Jews today are in the worst state. They trusted in their connections, loaned money, allowed others to run their businesses, and now they are treated with disrespect. Encouraged by the authorities, some families were banished from their homes and all their possessions were taken, under the claim that their stay was illegal because they didn't have permanent residency documents. The Russian government's anti-Jewish policy has gotten much worse." Father stopped, he looked tired and worried. Yosel continued, "On our last trip we arrived in villages and saw that many Jewish families had disappeared and no one could tell me where they went.

The Jews' pub licenses were taken so they left everything and disappeared. Among them were people who owed us money and we can safely say that the money is gone. We were told that many Jews received deportation papers with strange reasons. Jewish farmers couldn't meet their costs due to the drop in prices. They left their farms and moved to the city. Very soon we will have to decide what to do with our vineyards and with the wine production. The amount of wine in the store is growing and we don't have enough buyers. We just wanted everyone to know that we are headed for uneasy times, which might be followed by hard decisions."

We were all quiet. I wondered what he meant by hard decisions, but none of us knew. Yosel kept talking.

"There is something that I have been feeling and don't know how to say. I have only told this to my wife so far, but I have been in contact with a group of people from Kishinev and we might be joining them."

Father's eyes opened wide and he looked frightened. We were all looking at Yosel, as he said, "We feel there is no future for Jews in Russia. The situation is getting dangerous. We hear about new laws and punishments every day. It is better in our area, but I fear it is only a matter of time. I waited until now to say this because I had hoped it would get better. I knew how hard this would be for you, Father, and you, Mother. It is difficult to say, but the moment of truth has arrived."

It seemed like everyone was waiting for him to say more. It looked as though the next thing he had to say would be hard for us all.

"Whenever I would go to Kishinev on business I would meet with a number of friends who were organizing in order to leave Russia and settle somewhere across the sea. They have been reading about immigration opportunities and there are long waiting lists for several places. The preferred place is America and some families talk about going to Palestine."

The silence in the room was heavy; a cloud of sadness came over us. No one spoke. I feared looking at Mother and Father, but I could hear Mother crying quietly.

The main thought in my head was: my family is breaking apart again. It had taken me so long to get used to this situation and now it was over.

I had to stop thinking about myself; there were parents whose family was falling apart. At that moment I heard the noblest thing I could imagine. Father, a man who in his greatness knows to accept difficult situations in a graceful way, turned to Yosel and said, "My dear son, I understand your concerns and fear of telling us this. I appreciate the fact that you didn't make this decision lightly and that you share your thoughts with us. Up to this day, I had much to give for our family's welfare and I'm aware that will change. I don't have much power and wouldn't be able to start over.

All I want is for you, my sons and daughters, to find your place in this world; a world in which we don't know what is waiting around the corner. If you think that leaving is the right thing for you, with all the pain of saying goodbye to you and your family, I cannot stop you. The one thing I can do is give you my blessing and hope that our love will be with you wherever you go. I know that we will meet again, in this world or the next. We... we..." At that point his voice broke, he lowered his eyes and tears came down into his gray beard. My eyes were full of tears too. I had known the pain of separation.

In the following days, we barely spoke, as if nothing had been said on that difficult evening. No one mentioned it again. Everyone made an attempt not to be heard or noticed.

***

The matchmaker kept persisting about Lanna. He had a new match every day.

One evening a man was coming as a match for Lanna and to meet Father. The excitement of his arrival dimmed the sadness for a while and kept the minds of everyone from the problems. The meeting was for Father, and the man alone. Lanna wasn't even allowed to peek.

There was a knock on my door. It was Lanna!

"I am so excited because I've heard stories about the man the matchmaker is bringing today. He is from the big city. He studies at the yeshiva Odessa. It is far away from here. I haven't even been to Kishinev. Imagine if I have to move to Odessa. I don't know what will happen with Mother and Father. Yosel will probably leave soon so if I leave it will only be the three of you here with them. Who knows how long it will be until you leave too. I would really love to live somewhere close. This family is all I have ever known and I love all of you. I cannot imagine living in a different place, with new people, and a new family. You know that I think of you as my brother. My other brothers were always too busy or too far so I had only you close and I could talk with you about everything and take you along on my games. Do you remember our dog? You know, I think about him at times, wondering what happened to him. Am I going to have to think about my entire family that way, guessing what happened to them? I'm talking too much. I just wanted to ask, in the evening, when the man comes, could you take a look at him and at least tell me what he looks like? I couldn't ask that of anyone else, not even my sister."

Lanna stopped talking and took a deep breath, smiled at me, and left the room before I had a chance to answer.

That evening we all left the big dining room to avoid running into the matchmaker or the man he was bringing. That was the rule and we all kept it. I thought about Lanna's request, I knew that if they will see me, I would be in trouble. I wasn't a young boy who could make silly mistakes. I was eighteen and close to being matched myself. That was a strange thing to think about. Some nights, when I couldn't sleep, I thought of Lanna. I knew it was impossible because it was understood that we were brother and sister. I knew the truth in my heart. Under different circumstances, I would have wanted to be her partner. She was a girl with such good character and very pleasant looks. I had to stop thinking about it; there was no chance for it. I wondered what to do about her request; she was expecting me to do it. I didn't want to disappoint her. She had asked so little of me, how could I not do it? I decided to try.

I heard the guests arrive. There were the usual greetings and then the matchmaker's loud voice filled the house. After a few minutes, a different voice could be heard; Lanna's possible match was talking to Father, but I couldn't hear what they were talking about. I had an idea. I went to the kitchen where Sarah was making sure her helpers were doing everything right. I asked her to call me to carry the tray of tea and cookies to the guests.

"Sarah, I'll be in my room and you call me loudly to come and help. That is the only way I can think of to see this man," I said. Sarah looked at me as if I were losing my mind.

"What are you up to, Ephraim?" she asked.

"I worry about Lanna; you know how important she is to me. I only want to take one look at this man. I'll help you with the tray to the door and you will take it in. It will look natural." I tried my luck. I was using Sarah's innocence a little.

"We'll see, Ephraim. We'll see. Now leave because I need to prepare food for the visitors."

I left so I wouldn't upset her and hoped that my plan would work. I sat in my room with the door open and I waited. A long time had passed and Sarah hadn't called me. I laughed at myself for my silly plan. I kept thinking, what do I tell Lanna? That I tried to use Sarah but it didn't work? I pulled up a chair and sat closer to the door.

Time passed slowly and I was getting sleepy. Then I heard Sarah's voice, "Ephraim, I need your help." I jumped up. I always hurried to help Sarah, especially those days when she had gotten older and was often complaining that she was tired.

"I served the food a long time ago, with the help of my girls. I sent them to their rooms because it was late and since I want to clear the dishes I need your help."

"Are the guests still here?" I asked.

"Of course," Sarah answered and winked with a smile.

I followed her and stood at the door to the big room. Sarah went in and left the door open.

"Would anyone like more tea?" she asked.

"No, we will be leaving soon," answered the matchmaker.

"Come, Ephraim; take the heavy tray to the kitchen."

I almost jumped to the table, and sent a quick look at the man. I said 'hello' and left the room with a tray filled with glasses. Sarah left after me and closed the door slowly. We talked in the kitchen.

"Did you see?" she asked.

"Yes, I did. He looks perfectly fine. I assume Father thinks the same or he would have said goodbye a long time ago."

"I think so too. I'm tired. I'll go to sleep. The girls will take care of the glasses in the morning. Good night, Ephraim," Sarah said and left the kitchen with heavy steps. It was not the Sarah I'd met when I'd first got here.

I didn't get a chance to talk with Lanna until the following evening. She was nervous and anxious to hear what I had to say.

"Father said he approved the match and that they will set a date for the wedding soon. The man wants the wedding ceremony to be held in Odessa but the trip will be hard for Mother and Father. His parents are still young, so it is possible that we will have the wedding here and his parents will give a party for his family in Odessa later. Now tell me, did you see him?" Her cheeks were red. Excitement, curiosity and even a little fear were showing on her face.

I looked at the lovely girl before me. She was leaving too, and I would not see her anymore. It was such a cruel world. I would miss our talks and the moments she'd sit across from me at the dining table and I was able to look at her beautiful face.

"Ephraim, answer me..."

"I did see him. You can relax about the way he looks, he looks nice. About the rest, Father could probably tell you more because they talked for hours. Congratulations, Lanna," was my answer. She looked at me and I could see that in her thoughts, she was already far away. She left the room without another word.

The next morning I went to the kitchen and found Father there, talking to a man I had never seen before. I wanted to sit in a distant corner so that I wouldn't disturb them but Father called me over to sit with them.

"This man is a Jew called Moshe. He comes from Gura Humorului in Bukovina, an area that is a part of Austria. He is going to try and help us sell some of the wine that we have stored. I would like for you to go with him, meet the new buyers, and be in charge of the sales there. According to Moshe, there are many towns in the area with pubs run by Jews. I hope this will help us during this hard time. The wine will be placed on wagons today. You will take all you need for the road and will be ready to leave at dawn tomorrow."

We left the village at dawn, in the direction of the Austrian border, to Bukovina. The drive took a few days. We used daylight for the drive and at nights we found places to sleep in Jewish homes. We didn't want to risk driving at night. Moshe was filled with stories. Apparently, he was a merchant, a matchmaker, and a money lender. He told me about the area we were going to as if we were on our way to paradise. The best part of his story was the one about the best way in which Jews were treated. The Jews there did many things, had different jobs, were allowed to own pubs and run their own businesses without harassment from local farmers or authorities. Compared to the new situation we had back home it really sounded like paradise, but no one knew for how long. Back home in Bessarabia things were good too a few years previously. Jews had been doing well and had privileges, however, within a few years it had all changed. The latest stories threatened the existence of Jews in Bessarabia.

We reached Gura Humorului in the evening. I was invited to Moshe's home and was received well by his family. They gave me a warm meal and a clean and comfortable place to sleep.

"Tomorrow we will begin the work," said my host Moshe.

I said, "Goodnight," and was asleep before my head even reached the pillow.

When I awoke, a beautiful morning was waiting for me. After a light meal, we headed for the pubs to meet with merchants and try to sell the wine.

We started with Gura Humorului, which was a lovely tourist town. We sold most of the wine there and the rest of it was sold in Vama. I was happy to have succeeded in my business dealings and that everything had run without problems. I imagined that my father would be proud of me and would send me in the future too.

In the first place we'd visited, I'd felt that the merchant was being extremely nice. At the end of our long conversation, he invited me to his house that evening. Moshe encouraged me to go with a wink of his eye. I didn't understand why, but I accepted. When we left that place my host explained that the merchant had a daughter and that they have been looking for a match for her for a while. No man was good enough in the father's eyes.

"It is a great honor to be liked by him. He owns much property and many men try to be his daughter's match. His daughter is very beautiful and hard working. I've known her since she was a baby. That man has had a lot of sadness in his life. His wife died giving birth to his daughter and he has stayed alone ever since. He's made sure his girl got the best nannies and teachers. It is said that she will be a great housewife. There is no other woman beside her in the house so she takes care of her father and she is very devoted."

"I don't think it's my time to be matched yet. I am far too young. And I have to first talk with my father about the subject," I answered.

"You don't have to decide anything yet; all you need is to hear what the merchant has to tell you. You will come here again, God willing, and if he likes you he'll give you time to think and decide," said my host.

That evening I went to the merchant's home and we sat and talked for hours. He told me about his life, about the disaster, he'd experienced and the best businesses he'd had. We discussed the Bible and the Gemara and I saw that he was pleased with my knowledge. Later he told me about his seventeen-year-old daughter, how good and hard working she was. He didn't forget to mention he was getting old and that it was important to him that the man who marries her would continue running the business after him. He wanted to know about my family so I told him about my married brothers and about Lanna, who would soon be married. I told him I had another young sister who spent most of her time with our mother. I was served very good food and my host made sure to say that his daughter had made it all. I got tired so I got up and thanked him for his hospitality. I promised to come visit him the next time I came back to the area, and I imagined it would be soon.

***

The trip home was pleasant. Even though I had no wine in the wagon I made sure to go back to the place I'd stayed the first time and not risk driving at night. I had a large amount of money from selling the wine and it was better to be safe than sorry.

On the road, I had time to think about the merchant's offer. I felt too young to take on the responsibility of a family. My brother Yosel planned to leave home and go across the ocean. Lanna was getting married and leaving for Odessa. I couldn't leave too. I was afraid that this would add sadness to my old parents. I had to consider whether or not to tell Father. I didn't want to do anything that would cause him or Mother more pain.

I looked around. The road between the villages was beautiful in spring. Everything was green and blooming. The wildflowers were in full bloom in all the colors of the rainbow.

Bird songs escorted me and every once in a while a fox ran across the road. The trees were covered in green and the universe was renewing itself. There was a time for everything. Even the Torah tells about the rules of nature. There was no way to stop the wind, or the rain, or the growing of trees. Then maybe it was time for me to start a family? That was an interesting thought. Was I starting to like the idea I'd rejected a minute before? The girl sounded nice and the match seemed good. I figured I should tell Father and I'd know what to do from his reaction. My other brother, Menashe, was staying with our parents so that they wouldn't be left alone. The business wasn't very good and this way Father would have fewer people to take care of.

I kept thinking of reasons both for the match and against it and they all seemed right. I decided there was no point in thinking and that the match might add up to nothing. Maybe the merchant hadn't made up his mind yet.

I arrived home in the early evening. It was strangely quiet in the house. Mother hurried to see me.

"Sarah is very ill. The doctor was here and his opinion was not encouraging." Mother looked concerned. I understood that the situation was bad.

"I would like to see her, if possible," I asked.

"You can go in quietly, my son. The room is dark and she is having a hard time talking," she replied.

I took off my hat and coat quickly and went into Sarah's room. The room had only one lantern for light. I walked to her bed.

"I'm here. It's me, Ephraim," I whispered.

She signaled with her hand for me to sit on the bed. She reached out and I took her hand in mine. I'd never noticed how small her hands were, so unfitting for her large body. She was trying to tell me something.

"Don't talk, Sarah. The doctor said you must rest. I'm right here. I'll hold your hand like you held mine when I first got to this house. You were the closest person to me. I remember wondering every day how you managed to clean my room without me seeing. You always made sure I had clean and ironed clothes. Every evening when I got to my room, I felt your touch. I was embarrassed to thank you with words, but I did every day in my heart. Do you remember the time I had a fever and you sat beside me day and night, nurturing me back to health? You were like a mother to me, you must know that."

I stopped the flow of words. A tear rolled from Sarah's eye to the pillow. I knew she could hear me and she was still with us. I prayed to the good God to help and make her all better.

I sat beside her quietly. Her hand was loose inside mine and I listened to her breath becoming rhythmic and relaxed as she fell asleep. Mother came to the door and I signaled that Sarah was sleeping and that I'd be staying there. I fell asleep next to her bed.

In the middle of the night, I heard a noise that woke me up. I slept lightly, ready for any request that might come.

"What is it, Sarah?" I asked in fear. She opened her eyes, reached her second hand to me and with great effort managed to say, "My son. My son." Then her head dropped to the side and I couldn't hear her breathing. I'd lost an important, loving part of my life. I'd lost Sarah.

The next day we buried her in the Jewish cemetery. Sadness filled my heart. The entire family, the girls who worked with Sarah, and a number of the village Jews accompanied her on her last way. I asked to say Kaddish for her. I wanted to and I knew she would have wanted it too.

It was a different kind of goodbye, a kind I had never experienced before. Goodbye forever. I didn't know whether I'd get to see my old family again, but a spark of hope remained that they were still alive and that I might get to see them. I still had the hope in my heart even though I rarely thought of them.

Death was such a frightening word. It is the most final state possible and everyone said it was a part of life, but it was a part I couldn't comprehend yet. I knew that the dead, the ones who were good people and followed the rules of the Bible, would go to heaven. Sarah must be among them, but I still dreaded the word death. We didn't talk about it and I couldn't ask the others how they felt. The world was full of people and every person dies in the end. So a circle formed; a circle that had existed since the beginning of time.

The day was beautiful and so unfitting to my mood on the way home.

We went into the kitchen and the first person I expected to see there was Sarah. I would forever miss her; in fact, the entire family would. There wasn't a person in the house who hadn't respected her and who hadn't admired her dignity, her calmness, and the warm attention she gave everyone. Blessed be her memory.

Father followed me to the kitchen. I gave him the money I'd brought back from my trip.

"We'll talk about it tomorrow," he said while putting the money in his coat.

Only the next day did I remember the merchant from Gura Humorului. I decided to give Father the full report of my trip, including, if I had the courage, the match.

In the early evening, I sat in the dining room and prepared the papers with my sales. I figured I'd sit with Father after dinner. The first one to enter the kitchen was Lanna. Her face was flushed with excitement.

"In the days you were away we talked about my wedding," she said. Suddenly she felt as if she shouldn't be happy. "It's a shame that Sarah won't be at my wedding. She has been in our house since I was a baby, you know. I was used to her. In fact, sometimes I even called her Mother."

I knew exactly how she was feeling.

"I'm happy for you, Lanna. You must be happy about your wedding. You know that is what Sarah would have wanted. Before I left, she told me how happy she was that you'd found a good man and that you were going to have a family of your own. She reminded me of what we did when I wanted to see your future husband. She was a special person and was willing to do anything to make us happy. A loved person doesn't disappear with death. They stay to be with us in all our joys. Don't forget that, Lanna, and be happy in your new life." I tried to keep a confident tone in order to convince her. I'd decided I loved her as a brother and all of my guilt was gone.

One by one, people arrived at the dining room. I knew it would take a while before we would enter that room without looking for Sarah. The girls served the food. We weren't very hungry and almost no one spoke. We had so many things on our minds on top of Sarah's death, and I still hadn't added my story to the mix.

"I would like to sit with you and go over the report of my trip. I have new buyers to tell you about and what's going on in that area." I tried to talk about other things, to maybe lighten the air.

Slowly the room cleared, only Father stayed and waited to hear what I had to say.

"As you know, I sold all the wine, and I have more orders. In one town they asked me to come every month with supplies. The Jews' condition really is better there. They can own pubs and sell a lot of liqueur, in some places even homemade pastries. Jews told me that Gentiles visit their pubs and there is no sense of tension. Here is a list of all the sales. Since I didn't know these people, I asked for upfront payment. I promised them that in the future we could give them the wine and collect the payment on our next delivery. Moshe was a great host and he gave me warm meals and a comfortable bed." I finished my report and still didn't have the courage to tell the rest of the story.

"You did a good job, my son. I trust you," he said. "If there is nothing else I'll go to sleep. These last few days have been hard for me."

"There is another matter I wanted to discuss with you but I'd be happy to do it another time," I said sheepishly and was happy when Father got up and went to his room. I was relieved.

***

A few days passed, the wedding preparations were at full speed and Father forgot about finishing our talk. The seamstress made a beautiful wedding dress for Lanna. The first daughter in the family to get married needs to have a good dowry that includes clothes, tablecloths, and napkins. I watched Father and Mother discussing the dowry with great care. The wedding brought a special feeling to the house; it felt like a holiday. The in-laws were coming with their children so the sleeping arrangements had to be made. I decided to wait and talk with Father after the wedding.

Yosel, our oldest brother, announced that after the wedding, he would be moving to Kishinev with his family. Lanna and her new husband planned to stay with us for a few months before moving to Odessa.

The wedding helped us all to forget our troubles and share happiness with the new couple. The bridegroom's parents turned out to be very pleasant people and they showered Lanna with affection. I was happy about that. The most important thing for her was to feel good among them given the fact that she would be spending all her life with them and away from her first family. No one knows how important that is more than me.

One evening Father came up to me and asked, "Do you have something more from your trip to Austria to tell me?"

"Yes, Father," I answered as my confidence faded. I hadn't thought about the subject for some time. I had been focused on the wedding. The truth was that I was nervous to talk about my match offer and everything that was happening had helped me postpone it. We sat at the table with a couple of hot cups of tea. Father looked eager to hear my story.

"During my trip, I was invited to a merchant's house for dinner. He told me about his business and his life story. His intention was to tell me about his daughter, for whom he was looking for a husband. I hadn't yet thought of starting a family of my own and certainly not in Austria. I was bewildered and I didn't know what to say. I don't want to leave you. I am sure I'll find a good match here in the village or in the villages around ours, and this way I will be able to stay close to you and work with you for as long as you need. You and Mother took me in as your son. You gave me a home, a family, and love. I could never repay you. The one thing I can do is stay close to you and support you as you get older."

I said all that was in my heart. I said what I was feeling. I wasn't trying to make anything sound better. Father looked at me for a moment.

"Listen to me now, son. I have known you for enough years to know that you are an honest man and a family man. I know you worry about your mother and me and that you would do anything to be good to us and help us, and God bless you for that. It is going to be hard for me to say what I am about to, but I have to say it because you are so dear to me." He stopped talking and drank from his cup of tea. I would never forget the eyes of this good man.

"Before I say anything about what you have just told me, I have something to share with you. During the time you were in Austria I sat down with my son Menashe and we talked about the future of the family. In light of the fact that Yosel will be leaving in a few days and Lanna is moving to Odessa with her husband, we decided that Menashe and his family would stay here with us and with young Rikka, of course. Things here are getting worse and it is possible that as a small family, we will be able to spend the rest of our lives here with enough livelihoods. It was before I heard your story so we counted you too. We plan to sell some of the vineyards and keep only a small part. We will keep making wine with the grapes we'll gather and hopefully we'll sell that too. With a smaller property, we will be less noticeable and we might not suffer at the hand of the Gentiles. You know I believe that God knows the best way for our lives to go, even if we cannot see the reason. Maybe all the changes that cause us great pain now will be for the best later. My point is that you can see that we can age with dignity and we won't be alone. With this long story, I gave you my opinion on you finding an appropriate match and follow the path God gave you."

I could hear the tiredness in his voice; he hadn't made a speech this long in a while. He got up and went to his room. I sat for a long time, thinking about all the recent events. Only Father Hirsch could have such a dignified answer to such a painful topic. I have such respect for that man. I know he later had a conversation with Mother about this and that he put her mind at ease with his persuasive arguments and his calming voice. I cherish him with all my heart. Him and the quiet and always supporting Mother Hanna. I truly love them.

I went to my room and tried to calm my roaring soul.

***

I was looking forward to my next trip with Father. I had many ideas for ways to ease my leaving if the match take place. I was restless with that subject. All the recent changes made it impossible for me to talk with people who used to be my confidants. Lanna and her husband were in a world of their own. And Sarah, how I missed her; I could tell her anything and get her advice or at least an ear that listened without comments or criticism.

The only solution was to talk to Father, tell him what was in my heart, and ask for his advice.

The opportunity came sooner than I had thought. We took a drive to some villages nearby. Father sat next to me on the best wagon we had and said, "Ephraim, my son, I plan to join you on your next trip to Austria. I would like to meet the new buyers and go with our merchant/matchmaker Moshe to meet the man who is looking for a match for his daughter. That is the way we always handled matches. Some things need to be said before the match takes place, and that is the job of the groom's father and the bride's father. Don't look so upset, this is, after all, a good thing. Your mother understands that you need to find a good match and live your own life."

Father was calm and happy, and his relaxed voice helped me to feel better.

"Father, if you approve of the match and it happens, I would still like to do the trips with our wine to my new home in Austria. It will be a good way to see you every month or two, and I will be helping to sell your wine."

"I am very happy with your offer. Long trips aren't for me anymore. I think that this drive to Austria with you will be my last one. Menashe will have to go in my place, even though I'll need him for other things. I like this offer. It is important to keep selling in new areas." He smiled at me warmly and I was reminded of how lucky I was.

I found myself thinking a lot about the match. I felt great anticipation about going to Austria but I didn't know why. I knew they wouldn't let me see the girl and that I wouldn't have Sarah and Lanna to look for me. I kept myself busy with work. I helped in the business, which gave Father time to plan the sale of the vineyards. It wasn't simple, Father sat many hours with potential buyers but nothing happened.

Mother wasn't at her best and I was concerned about her health. I had a chance to talk with Lanna about it. She said that there was no need to worry and that Mother was weak from all that was happening in the house lately. Lanna didn't seem at all worried. I wasn't sure I could trust her judgment because she was preoccupied with her own things.

I decided to mention it to Father during our drive to Austria.

Everything had been arranged for the trip. Barrels were loaded on the wagon and one of the girls made us food for the road.

The driver who came with us was a quiet young man who only spoke Russian so we were able to speak Yiddish without worry. But we didn't talk much. On the subject of Mother, Father reassured me that her weakness was only temporary.

We arrived at Gura Humorului and Moshe welcomed us and offered his home for us to sleep and eat in. Father was very tired and as soon as we arrived at our host's house he asked to take a nap. He had something small to eat and I didn't see him until the next day. I talked with Moshe until a late hour. He made sure to remind me of the match and that the merchant was still waiting to meet my father and set the terms.

The following day we managed to sell all the wine we'd brought. The buyers were happy to meet Father and told him that his wine had sold quickly.

Our host told us that the merchant would be happy to meet with Father that night. The two of them left; I was alone and tried to read. My mind was distracted with different thoughts. I remembered what Father used to say, "If something works out it means that it was God's will. And if it doesn't, God didn't want it to be."

It was late and despite my wanting to wait up I was too tired and went to bed.

The next morning we began the drive home.

"Ephraim, I think we have a match." He sounded pleased. "The man has money, which is good for the future. He lives by the Bible and despite being a merchant, he seems dependable. According to him, his daughter was a good homemaker and a quiet and polite girl. Even Moshe had only good things to say about the father and his daughter."

Father slept a lot during the drive, and I had time to myself. I daydreamed of being in my old parents' home, telling them that I was getting married. I could feel Mother's arms around me and see Father's eyes shine. My old home seemed so real as if I were standing in the kitchen. I could even see the big tree in front of the door.

"Ephraim." Father brought me back to reality.

"Yes, Father," I answered as if waking from a dream.

"We will have the wedding at our house. I have spoken about it with your future father-in-law. We have celebrated every wedding there and we will do the same with yours. We will make it a beautiful wedding; trust your father." He started getting excited. "A wedding like we held for Yosel, Menashe, and Lanna. Can you believe Rikka is the only one we have left to marry off and then all of our children will be settled? It is a great feeling for your mother and me. What more could we want?"

"Father, don't get too excited, I can't forget your heart. You need to be happy and calm for bringing all of us to this place. All of your children are good and satisfied."

"Yes, son, you are right," he answered as a smile spread across his face.

***

Time passed too fast for me. Yosel left with his wife, and his beautiful children. It was very painful for Mother. Even though we had known it was coming, it was still hard. Lanna left a short time after that. We drowned in a sea of tears, hugs, and best wishes. Lanna promised to come and visit once she'd had children.

The house became very empty. The dining table became too big. I took on Yosel's entire job to make it easier on Father. Menashe ran the business well. I spent most of my time with him, working and learning a lot. Father sold some of the lands and was feeling better.

My wedding date was set. We were to get married here and then leave for Austria. I didn't allow myself to think about leaving. I was working all day and studying all night. In that way, I'd get to bed so tired that I had no time for thoughts.

The time of the wedding came. I saw my bride, Feige, for the first time. She was a beautiful girl with big and innocent eyes. If our lives looked as good as my bride I would be very happy.

***

Many Jews were leaving the villages in the area. We weren't getting along with the Gentiles like we'd used to. Lanna and Yosel, who had left a short time previously, weren't able to come to my wedding. Lanna told us in a letter that she was in the first few months of pregnancy and that she wasn't feeling well. From Austria, only my bride and father-in-law came. I wasn't sorry for not having a big wedding. I knew that the size didn't matter and would have no influence on the rest of my life.

My father-in-law left the day after the wedding because he had to return to his business. Feige stayed in our house because I wanted us to have time with my family. In the hours I wasn't home, Mother spent a lot of time with Feige. She taught her how to make food that I liked and I told her about the rest of the family, where each one was and what they were doing. Rikka and Feige formed a warm friendship. I often heard them chatting and laughing. My heart was filled with joy that my wife was becoming part of the family so quickly. Menashe's wife was always busy with her babies and very often my wife would go into her room and help feed and change them. I was sure Feige would be remembered by my family as a hard-working, efficient, and smiling girl.

No one mentioned our approaching departure. We were behaving as if we were not leaving soon. We also tried not to think about it, in order to make our remaining time in the house pleasant.

In the evenings, when Feige and I were alone, we would talk a lot; it made us feel like we'd known each other for a long time. I was pleased she knew how to read and write, and that she read her prayers from the book, like Lanna and Rikka. Girls at that time were taught by teachers who came to their homes. Many families could not afford such an expense, but mostly they didn't understand why girls needed to know such things. In most people's opinions, women were only needed for housework, taking care of a husband, giving birth, and taking care of children.

Feige told me that from time to time a Yiddish newspaper would come from the big city. Her father, who would bring it home and allow her to read it. In the newspaper, there was news about Jews from the area, and articles written by known rabbis. She told me she'd read about emigrating from Russia to countries across the sea. I couldn't believe my ears. That quiet girl knew more than me about everyday news.

On the evening of our departure, Mother made a special meal. The table was set as if for a holiday and a bottle of Father's special wine from a very good year was placed on the table. We stayed at the table long after we'd finished eating. We wanted to have a few more hours of being together. We went to sleep very late. Feige fell asleep quickly but I stared at the ceiling almost until dawn before falling asleep.

Ever since I was eleven years old, having to say goodbye broke my heart. I was now saying goodbye to many people who were very significant in my life. First, there was Yosel and his family, then Lanna, Menashe and his family, my little sister Rikka, and my mother and father.

Our boxes, with things Mother had prepared for us, were loaded onto the wagon. Father gave me a wagon with my favorite horse, which had been born shortly before I'd got there; the brown horse with one leg as white as snow.

Feige hugged Mother and Rikka. She said goodbye to Menashe's wife and her kids. Father and Menashe wished her health and a good life and said they looked forward to seeing her again. It was then my turn to say goodbye.

"I'll be back in a month to take wine and I'll stay for a day or two, so it isn't really goodbye, it is more a 'see you soon.'" I wanted to be strong and convincing but my voice betrayed me and gave away my feelings.

Hugs, blessings, and some tears and we were on our way to our new home in Austria.

***

It was the end of spring; a little cold but the skies were bright, and they gave a great feeling of newness. I was young, I had my whole life ahead of me, and I wanted to do well and give my wife a good life and treat her well. That's what I saw in the two houses I'd grown up in, respect between men and women, never a loud word or an argument. Women knew their place and made sure to keep the house pleasant and clean and the children were well educated and taken care of.

"Ephraim, what's on your mind?" I didn't know how long I'd been detached, but I suddenly realized I was no longer alone and that from that day on I would have to pay attention to my bride.

In the short time we'd been together, I'd discovered she was mature, interesting, and curious about her surroundings.

It was getting dark, so we started looking for a place to spend the night. We stopped at one of the villages in front of a house I'd stayed in before. People were gathered outside the house and were talking. I got off the wagon, walked up to them and found out that a family member had been beaten badly by a group of men and was in bad condition. When I asked how it had happened, they told me that he'd gone to a nearby village to buy flour and potatoes and as he was coming back, he'd been attacked, beaten, thrown off the wagon, and left by the side of the road. A wagon had happened to pass by and they'd picked him up and brought him home. They told me they had been searching for the doctor for two hours with no luck. I realized that there was no way we could stay there for the night so I asked around and found a neighbor who said he'd be happy to take us in for the night.

I started feeling worried. Feige and I were alone on the road and it sounded dangerous. I didn't know if I should tell her what had happened, but then I realized they might talk about it at the house we were going to. I needed to find a way to get my wife home safely. I knew we couldn't get back on the road without protection. The doctor arrived, and everyone quieted down and cleared a path for him, and he entered the house.

I tried to think. I knew I had to come up with a plan to tell Feige regarding what had happened. I couldn't think of anything. I wished I had Father with me as he always had the right answers. I knew that if we kept going we had another day and night before we arrived at our destination. Another option was to turn and go back.

The doctor came out without a word then and shook his head as if to say no. We understood that he meant he had no way of helping. Loud voices came from the house. I couldn't think there so I returned to the wagon. Feige looked at me and waited for me to explain.

"A family member has died," I said. "A neighbor has invited us to stay with him for the night. His wife is home so we can go there now."

We stopped the wagon behind the house. I made sure it wasn't visible from the road and that I didn't need to take everything from it. Inside the house, lanterns were lit and it was warm. We introduced ourselves to the woman and told her we were newlyweds and that we appreciated their hospitality. The woman hurried to make us something to eat and started talking.

"Have you heard about the disaster that happened to our neighbor? Things are getting worse with every day that passes. There is no safety on the road. Those people get brave and now they steal from us without shame. They steal chickens, goats, and tools we leave outside for the night. What have we come to? We used to be good neighbors and help each other. Should we be afraid to leave our homes?" The woman's face got red and her voice became hoarse. That was the last thing I needed. I couldn't afford Feige getting afraid too. She looked at the woman, not really understanding what she were talking about. I thought I might be able to hide the tragedy from her.

"Ephraim, what is she talking about?" Feige asked me. The woman didn't even give me a chance; she started talking as if she'd just been waiting for the sign.

"You don't know? They are killing us, simply killing us. Do you know why? I don't know either. We got letters from family about pogroms they did to Jews in southern Bessarabia. Can you believe that it's our faith here too? After what happened to the neighbor I'll believe anything. If you want more details my husband will arrive soon and he knows more than me." Her talk was cut short when the door opened and the husband entered.

I looked at my wife; her blue eyes were wide open and so was her mouth. She looked so strange. Her pink face had turned to a shade of yellow. She didn't move. She sat as if paralyzed.

"Feige, are you alright? It was only one incident. It is very sad, but you know that in Austria things are better and that is where we are headed." I tried to get her thinking; she looked at me and said,

"And how will we get to Austria?"

That was the one question for which I had no answer. I didn't expect such a reasonable question from Feige in her state of shock.

"Woman, did you take good care of our guests?" said our host to his wife. "I hope you didn't exaggerate as usual with your storytelling. We can't think that this is our future because if we do, we might as well pack our bags and go wherever the wagon takes us."

The man looked around to see the effect his words were having and I decided to help his point.

"You are absolutely right; one incident doesn't say much about the rest. It is true that what happened was horrible and God save us from such things. Not all Gentiles are like those ones, and after all the men who did this will be punished and no one will dare hurt us again." I was happy with my speech.

I looked at my wife. The color of her face had returned to normal and she seemed less terrified. I took advantage of the opportunity and suggested to her to get some rest. She followed the hostess to a room. I stayed with the man.

"My name is Motale," he said. "With everything that has happened, I forgot my manners and didn't introduce myself. My wife's name is Mina."

"I'm Ephraim and my wife's name is Feige. She is from Austria and that is where we are headed. I would like your advice about the rest of our drive. The truth is I am worried because the situation is difficult. We both know that the authorities won't do anything to find the men who did this; we will have to defend ourselves somehow. I have money and I'm willing to pay for protection for the road to Austria. Do you have a way of helping me with this?"

Motale took a moment to think and then said, "There are some good boys in our village, sons of farmers with whom we live in peace, and it is possible they would be willing to escort you in return for money. The fact that they are with you will help, and hopefully, you won't be attacked. What do you think?"

I hesitated. There was the chance that those farmers' sons would do the same to us as was done to that man who had been killed. I had no other choice, though, so I hoped that the men Motale was suggesting would be willing to escort us.

"I think it's a good solution. Will you talk with the boys?" I asked.

"I see them every morning on my way to work. I'll talk with them and send them here. Where are you coming from?" he asked.

At this point, the conversation moved to different areas. I told him about the village we'd come from and about the troubles near the Dniester River area. I asked him not to talk about things like these near Feige because we had a long drive and I had enough worries.

Motale took out a bottle of red wine and we kept talking until we heard his wife yelling about how late it was. I thanked him for everything and he showed me to the room. It took me a while to fall asleep.

Knocks on the door woke me up. I jumped out of the bed and hurried to the kitchen. Mina was in there making breakfast. She rushed to the door. Outside stood two big guys who said:

"Your husband sent us, about a drive to Austria," they explained.

"Come in, come in." Mina invited them and then said to me, "They are good boys."

I turned to the boys and explained my request. They were willing to follow us in their wagon. We settled the money issue and I asked them to be back in an hour with the wagon and be ready to go.

"I heard voices," said Feige as she entered the kitchen. She said hello and sat at the table. "I am very hungry," she explained. She cut a big slice of bread, covered it with butter and looked like she was enjoying it. I placed some money on the table hoping that Mina would see it. She did, but then acted as though she hadn't. It was as I wanted. I had no desire to embarrass the nice couple who had been perfect hosts to us.

The two boys returned to their wagon. They told us they had food and drink for the road and that we should hurry so we wouldn't waste time.

We said goodbye to Motale and Mina after promising to visit if we ever pass through their village. We got on the wagon and got on our way. Feige didn't really understand why the boys were following us. I told her I'd hired them as escorts to make us feel safer. I tried not to get into details and she accepted my explanation. During the drive, she told me about acquaintances and family members I'd meet in Austria.

When night fell, we stopped in a village that I'd stayed in before. The people I knew there were happy to see me and meet my wife and they took care of the boys too. We went to bed early; we both needed a good night's sleep.

On our way to the border my young bride surprised me again by saying:

"Ephraim, you are going back to your parents' next month. I would like it if you had someone to escort you in this area. Maybe these boys would be willing to meet you at the border on the day you tell them and stay with you until you get back to the border? If you can agree on a good price, then I won't be so worried."

I couldn't believe my ears. That woman understood more than I realized. She knew exactly why we were being escorted.

"You are right," I said. "I'll talk with them and if they agree we'll set a time for them to wait at the border."

We reached the border in the early afternoon. We had enough time to get to Gura Humorului before night time. I spoke with the boys who were very pleased with their new work. I found out they were brothers who worked with their father in the field. They said it wouldn't be a problem for them to meet me. We said goodbye to them and returned to the road.

***

After several knocks, my father-in-law opened the door. His eyes were bright with joy.

"I didn't know when you were coming. I've been waiting for you since the day I arrived. It is so good to have you here; the family keeps asking about you two. So how was the drive? I'm sorry for talking so much, please come in. I am so happy I got confused. Forgive me, please forgive me." He finally moved away from the entrance and allowed us to come in. He called the man who worked for him and asked him to take care of the horse and luggage and then he prepared drinks.

"So tell me about the road? And how are you? Ephraim, how are your parents? Are you hungry? I keep asking questions. I'll be quiet now and let you answer."

Feige did her best to calm him down, "Father, we are fine and so are the in-laws. The drive was good and now we are tired." Hot tea and baked goods arrived. I still hadn't said a word. My father-in-law just kept on talking.

"The aunts arranged your room. I. I didn't want to be unprepared. The entire dowry was sewn and is inside the big box in your room. I'm so happy you're here, I've said that already, haven't I?"

We started laughing and he joined us. The tension was gone. We were home.

I started working with my father-in-law. He took me into his business and the experience I had helped me fit in. In the evenings we went to the synagogue and after praying we stayed and studied. As for Feige, she ran the house with great efficiency.

I returned to Bessarabia as planned to get wine. The buyers asked me to bring a larger amount. The two boys joined me at the border and they accompanied me to my parents' house.

My family was pleased to see me. I told them stories of my new family, my father-in-law, Feige's aunts, and my new job. Mother looked tired. She told me that she was spending most of the time resting. When I had some time alone with Menashe I asked him about her. He told me they were all worried and that the doctor didn't know what was wrong. In fact, the doctor said it was just longing for her children. The next day, when Father and Menashe left for work, I sat with her and we talked. I told her I was worried about how weak she was.

"My son, I am no longer a young woman. I have raised my children, I've run the house, I enjoyed my grandchildren, and I have said goodbye to them. I did everything a mother can do and now no one understands that I am just tired. My body is not as it was and all I need is to rest quietly."

"Mother, your job isn't over yet, you still have my children to enjoy." I looked for something that would give her hope and a desire to live.

"Should I be congratulating you?" she asked as a light came on in her eye.

"Not yet, Mother. But with God's help, I'm sure it will be soon." Father came in holding a letter.

"A letter from Yosel," he said. Menashe and Rikka followed in after him. We were all listening as Father read the letter.

"My dear father, mother, Rikka, Menashe, and Ephraim." He stopped and looked around. Then he said, "A nice beginning isn't it?"

"Just read." Mother hurried him.

"Both we and the children are feeling good. We are still in Kishinev. We are in a group that leaves for America next month. We've heard only good things and I have a good chance to find work there. A number of Jews will be waiting for us there and will help us get settled. Two groups left a few months ago and from their letter, we gather they are very happy. I wanted you to know we are looking forward to going. We'll write to you from America.

I wish you all good health and hopefully, we'll meet again. May God be with us, Yosel."

"Amen," we all said together. It got quiet. I didn't know if the letter was good or bad. Father had taught me that if you didn't have anything good to say, don't say anything at all.

"Mother, what do you think of our son going to America? America is an advanced country, I'm sure Jews won't have problems there."

"Good for them. May they travel safe and arrive safe," she answered. Then she turned to me and said, "Ephraim, maybe you'll come and spend Passover with us. You can bring your father-in-law and we'll have a big celebration?"

"I like the idea. I think we'll come."

"Ephraim," Father started talking. "Who are those boys who came with you?"

"We were told it wasn't safe to travel alone on long journeys, so they will escort me here and back every time I come. I don't want Feige to worry."

I stayed one more night and left the following morning with a wagon filled with wine barrels, food and drinks for me and the boys. As I left I promised to see them all soon.

I arrived home safe and sound. Feige was alone in the house. She was lying peacefully in our room and looked as though she were taking a nap. I turned around to leave the room, but she woke up and said,

"Ephraim, welcome home. I'm so happy you are back."

"Hello, Feige. Everyone back home wondered about you and they send all their love. Mother sent something she made for us. Where is your father?"

"I haven't been feeling well since yesterday. I didn't want to worry Father so I got up this morning as usual and waited for him to leave on his business, then returned to bed. You know I'm not simply being lazy. I can't remember even once taking a nap in the middle of the day. I've barely made something to eat and I've been in bed for hours. Every time I try to get up I get dizzy and my stomach turns. I haven't eaten all day. What do you think is wrong?"

Whenever someone would get sick in my house I'd just shrink to a corner, totally helpless. Now I needed to take action.

"Maybe you ate something that is making you sick. Come with

me to the kitchen and we'll eat something. I'm sure you'll feel better."

Feige got up and held my hand.

In the kitchen, I placed a pot of food on the table and as soon as I opened it Feige ran away and I could hear her throwing up and moaning. I followed her with a glass of water. She drank a little, washed her face and went back to our room.

"I feel so bad. Maybe you should ask Aunt Sally; she always took care of me as a child."

I left immediately to Aunt Sally who lived across the street.

"Aunt Sally, come with me, Feige isn't feeling well. I don't know what to do."

"What is she complaining about?" Sally asked while still eating her bread and meat peacefully.

"She is dizzy and nauseous and she hasn't eaten all day." I started to get upset. Feige wasn't feeling good and Sally didn't even care.

She started laughing, stronger and stronger every second. I stood in front of her, feeling foolish, and she just kept laughing. I felt my face getting red and all she said was, "Well, Ephraim, congratulations," and kept laughing.

It was all too much for me so I turned around and went back home. I rushed to the room to tell Feige what an aunt she had. I decided to tell her that it wasn't her who needed a doctor, but the aunt, because she'd lost her mind. Before I ever opened my mouth Sally came in, went up to Feige, hugged her and said, "My dear child, you are going to be a mother."

The two of them started crying and hugging. Neither of them noticed me. I just stood there, looking at them.

"Ephraim, why are you standing there like a log?" Sally said to me. "Do you see there is a good reason for Feige to feel sick? The best reason in the world."

I carefully got closer, sat on the bed, and held Feige's small hand. My heart was beating faster and all I could think was, "I'm going to be a father."

My father-in-law loved the news. He promised to order the baby's crib in the best carpentry shop. He said he'd invite the entire village and would give a big donation to the synagogue. All this of course after the baby was born safely.

I had to give my parents the good news. It was especially important to me that Mother heard it. I so wanted to raise her spirits. I decided to write a card and find the quickest way to get it to my village.

***

In the following months, Sally spent most of her time in our house. She took care of Feige and made sure she didn't work too hard. Feige's mother had died while giving birth to her so Aunt Sally took it upon herself to raise Feige. She was never married and Feige was her whole world.

Feige started feeling better and she started getting round. She was in a good mood, her cheeks were always flushed, and her blue eyes had a wonderful spark.

I received an urgent letter from my brother Menashe. He wrote that Mother was sick and said that by the time the letter reached me she might not be among the living.

I read the letter over and over. I knew she hadn't been at her best the last time I was home. But from that to death was a long way. She'd promised to wait for my children; she couldn't have forgotten something like that. I decided I had to go and see her. Maybe Menashe was wrong and her situation wasn't as bad as he thought. I had to see it with my own eyes to believe it. I had to go.

I found my father-in-law and showed him the letter.

"I have to see my mother," I said. "I'll tell Feige I'm worried about Mother and that I have a bad feeling about her health. I don't want her to see the letter so that she won't get upset."

My father-in-law looked at me and said, "You are a wonderful man, Ephraim. I am lucky to have you as part of my family. Go in peace and return in peace. She will be in good hands here."

It was clear he was trying to get me to forget my worries. My concern for my mother was hard enough. I couldn't let my escorts know so I decided to go alone. I told Feige I needed to visit my family because they didn't answer my last letter, in which I'd written about the pregnancy.

I started preparing things for the drive; food and water for the horse. As I was packing some food for myself a messenger came with a letter for me. I put everything down and rushed to open the letter. I'd recognized Menashe's handwriting on the envelope. My heart started pounding, my hands were shaking and as I read the first line I knew – my mother had died. Menashe wrote that it had happened shortly after the first letter had been sent. In her final moments, she'd mentioned all of her children, including me. I tried to keep reading, but my eyes were filled with tears. I felt a great emptiness inside of me. I don't know how long I sat there with the letter in my hand. I was so tired. With great difficulty, I raised my hand to keep reading.

The second part of the letter was in Father's hand, writing, "My dear son, Ephraim. We lost Mother, may she rest in peace. I can sense your pain and the pain of all of our children. She loved you all so much and that love will go with her to heaven. I'm sure you wish to be with us at this difficult time and despite the fact that it is hard for me to write, I knew I was the only one you might listen to. Don't come now. Bad things have happened here. The violence towards Jews gets worse every day. Until a more peaceful time, I won't be able to bear the thought of you on the road. You are with us in every moment and every situation. Watch over Feige for us and hopefully, we'll find a way to see each other without risks. Bless us in your prayer. Bless you, my son. Father."

I heard Feige's voice calling me, like in a dream. I gathered all of my strength, got up and walked to the room she was in. We cried together.

I took my Bible and left for the synagogue early. There was a small number of people there. I sat in a distant corner and my thoughts took me far away. I closed my eyes and prayed. In my mind, I saw my two mothers. Then I understood; they'd met each other in heaven. They were both gone from this world. I couldn't mourn for my first mother because I didn't know when she'd died. I couldn't mourn for my second mother because she hadn't given birth to me. All I could do was pray. I prayed like the boy underneath a pile of hay, praying for the wagon to turn around.

I felt a hand on my shoulder. I opened my eyes to find the rabbi standing next to me. I took his hand and held it as close as I could.

***

The years passed very quickly. I went to visit my father and my family at least once a year. Rikka got married and was living close to my father's house. Father was no longer working. He passed time at home with his grandchildren, and the oldest one would read chapters from the Bible for him. He was going blind and spent most of the time napping.

My father-in-law passed all the business to me. He too was getting old. We didn't have as much money as we'd had before, but we were holding on and supporting our six children.

Feige took care of the house, our children and her father, and on occasion did some sewing work for the village women. I learned to sew too, and we earned more money that way.

We kept having more babies. Once a year or a year-and-a-half we had another child to feed. They filled the house with noise and happiness. Feige was pregnant again, this time it was a difficult one, and the doctor told us there was more than one child inside her.

That winter was more difficult and many people were ill. The winter took people from our home too. One of our sons died after we couldn't lower his temperature for a long time. We also lost both our fathers; their bodies couldn't handle the winter illnesses.

Feige wasn't doing well, her stomach was very big and she could barely move. I had one of the women in the village stay with her during the days.

My eldest son Moshe worked as an apprentice to a blacksmith in Vama. He was a quiet and modest boy. The matchmaker followed him around for a long time but Moshe refused to be matched.

The twins, Nathan and Berl, worked in a village close to ours, one as a tailor's apprentice and the other in a mill.

My daughter Sima stayed home and did sewing and embroidery.

My son Shlomo left for Vienna. He was our educated son; we made a big effort to allow him to get out into the world. New winds were blowing. It wasn't the world I'd been raised in. Trains were driving, factories were producing steam. Ships were more developed and many boys left home for the big cities, to new lives and new adventures.

Our two young sons were studying in the village Heder (a place little boys learn Torah) and we had a baby named Hanna crawling around the house.

I was worried about Feige. The midwife ran around the house, giving orders. The delivery was sooner than expected. It was one more thing to worry about.

We were up all night. Feige went into labor and I waited for the right moment to go and get the midwife. Everything was ready for the delivery; it had been less than seven months since Feige had gotten pregnant. People said it was bad and that she should have tried to hold on for another month. I sat beside her and prayed that she made it through the night and for the delivery to be delayed as long as possible.

Our lives passed before my eyes: the wedding, the calm beginning, Feige's devotion to the children. She'd always say that all people needed was their religion and work. She needed very little and gave everything. She knew to accept the difficult times and the painful moments too. When work was low she never complained, she would just say, "I'll sew more at nights."

"Ephraim, get the midwife," she yelled. I ran out and got the woman. There were chaos and loud voices for a while and then complete silence. Those moments scared me more than others.

"Ephraim, get the other midwife."

I ran as fast as I could to the other side of the village. One of her children opened the door and told me his mother wasn't home. She'd left to deliver another baby. I hurried back. I prayed to God to please not forget me. I ran into the street like crazy. I saw a wagon driving in my direction. The second midwife was on it. I couldn't speak; I just pulled her off the wagon and dragged her to my house. She knew the situation with my wife. I sat on one of the chairs outside and tried to steady my breathing. The midwives went in and out, bringing hot water, clothes, and ignoring my questions.

From time to time there were moments of silence. The women stopped running around. I was afraid to go into the room, I couldn't stay outside. One of the women came out, her hair was a mess and her clothes were full of blood. She stood in the doorway with her eyes on the ground.

"You had a boy and a girl. They were too small and didn't make it. Feige lost a lot of blood and energy. You need to pray for her recovery. We'll clean the room and leave. She will need a lot of attention and rest over the next few days and may God help you." She never looked at me. She went back to the room and closed the door.

Thank God that Feige had made it, was the first thought that came to my mind. I would make sure she rested and recuperated. I couldn't think about the babies who didn't make it. I sat on the chair, closed my eyes, and prayed.

Feige was asleep for many hours. I checked in on her on occasion, to see if she was awake. I needed to tell the children what had happened. It was good that they weren't home yet. The young ones were at a neighbor's house and the others didn't come back from the yeshiva or from work until the evening. I knew how disappointed they would be as there was always anticipation before a new baby came.

"Ephraim, what happened to the babies?" Feige, in a weak voice and shut eyes, was trying to find out what had happened. I hadn't thought of that part. I had only thought about what to say to our children because I didn't realize Feige wasn't aware of what had happened.

"Feige'la," I started. When I called her that, and I rarely did, it was a sign of bad news. She was lying there, so pale and weak, I was afraid her heart wouldn't be able to handle the sad news.

"Feige'la," I tried again. "Your life was in danger. You lost a lot of blood and that is the reason for your weakness. You know you are more important than all the babies in the world. The babies who were born were very small, even the doctor told us that if the delivery was too early there was no chance that they would survive."

She started crying. I suddenly realized what had happened to us. While telling her what had happened, I realized I had lost two babies, two of my children.

I sat on the bed beside her, hugged her and together we cried. There was nothing left for me to say. I suddenly felt the pain of loss. I felt helpless. All my desire to explain and comfort was gone. I needed to calm down before Feige got too weak and fell apart.

"Feige, this was God's will and you know that it was meant to be. God gives and God takes away." I tried to believe in what I was saying.

"Oh, Ephraim, I really wanted those twins," she said and her voice broke. I needed to find a quick way to make her calm down.

"Feige, listen to me." My voice was firm and steady. "We need to be strong so that the children won't suffer from this. If they see us lost or if we aren't the same with them, we would have to worry about them too and we have no energy for that now. You get some more sleep now and I'll go ask one of the neighbors to take care of food for the children and us. Do you want to get stronger and take care of your children?" It was a silly question but I would have tried anything. Feige surprised me with her wisdom.

"You are right," she said. "I feel very weak. I can't even get out of bed. I want to return to taking care of the house and the children and there is only one way to do so. I have to accept what happened as God's will and get stronger." She put her head on the pillow and went back to sleep.

I left the room and sighed heavily. I needed to pull myself together. I had to take care of my wife and children. I left immediately to find a neighbor willing to help.

***

Feige never really returned to her old self. The doctor told me that her condition worried him and that I needed to behave as though everything was fine.

I wanted Feige to live to see at least one of our children get married. I needed to talk with Moshe; he was twenty-three years old and kept avoiding the matchmaker. He was weak in his studies and preferred going to work. He was a hard-working and devoted worker and his boss was pleased with him.

I asked the matchmaker to come to our home on Friday after Moshe returned from work. I wanted the matchmaker to talk to him and try to convince him that it was time for him to start a family. I promised to talk to him too, and maybe hint that it would make his mother happy.

The matchmaker came running on Friday.

"Moshe isn't home yet?" he asked.

"He won't be back for at least two hours," I explained.

"I need to talk with you, Ephraim. That is why I have come now."

We sat in the kitchen with a cup of tea and I waited for him to give me his news.

"I think I've found an appropriate match for Moshe," he said with excitement. "First, I need to tell you a story." He positioned his chair so he could see me better and began, "In the village of Vama, not too far from where we are, lives a widow called Henia Zisman. Her sister died eleven years ago, a widow as well, and she left a five-year-old daughter. Henia took the girl in, raised her, allowed her to study reading and writing, taught her housework and acted like a mother to her. Henia never adopted the girl on record so she considers her an illegal daughter. At the time, when her sister died, she didn't think of it and it was forgotten. The girl's name is Frida." He took a break to see my reaction and to drink.

"Well, Ephraim, don't you think this could be a good match?" He almost decided for me.

"I will talk with Feige, tell her the story, and of course I need to ask Moshe. I will try to get him to at least see Henia and Frida. Today it's different than in my days, I only saw Feige at the wedding."

"But what do you think?"

He was special, trying to convince me at any cost. His job was so extraordinary.

"Why don't you come back at noon and talk to Moshe. By then I'll have told Feige the story and maybe we'll have a match. You know I really want him to find someone to spend his life with." I got up, he followed, and, with a promise to return at noon, he left.

"Feige, the matchmaker was here and he has a match for Moshe." I didn't tell her that I'd initiated the meeting to speed up the match. She was so weak. I prayed that she would make it to the wedding.

"A match for Moshe?" she asked and I could see the happiness in her eyes. I knew how much she wanted to see our boy married. "I hope we know the girl's family."

"We don't. It's a girl that has been living with her aunt since the age of five. They live in a village called Vama, not far from here." I told her all the details the matchmaker had given me. She was pleased to know that the girl had received a good education and could read and write.

Nathan, Berl, and Moshe came home for the Sabbath. They went to see their mother first. Feige looked forward to those moments. She welcomed them smiling, and asked each of them to tell her about his week. There was very little to tell. They worked from day to night and then went to study the Torah and the Gemara. But Feige was satisfied with hearing their voices and she didn't really care what they were saying.

After a while, she said, "I'm going to rest for a while and we'll talk later." She fell asleep quickly. She was getting weaker every week and the boys expressed their concern.

"Moshe, I want to speak with you," I said in a serious voice. "The matchmaker was here, and he will probably be back soon. He has a match for you and your mother and I would be happy if we went to see the girl and her family. The girl's name is Frida and she lives in the village you work in, Vama." I feared his reaction. He always rejected offers to be matched. He never wanted to see the girls and always asked for more time.

"All right Father, we will go together to see the girl and her family," he said very seriously.

I was surprised. I was happy I didn't need to give the speech I had prepared to convince him it was time to start a family.

There were knocks on the front door and then the matchmaker came in like a storm.

"Did you talk to Moshe? What did Feige say? Can I take you there next Friday? I will talk with Henia. Congratulations."

"Dear matchmaker, calm down." I stopped his flow of words. He'd asked, decided, and arranged the match before I'd had a chance to speak. "We agree. We will go next week."

"Ephraim, do you want me to talk to Moshe?" he asked in disbelief.

"There is no need. I have spoken with him. We will be waiting for you this time next week. Have a good Sabbath." He looked so happy. He left the house in what looked like a dance.

We had a match. Even though the girl had a modest dowry, we knew her aunt had given her everything that was possible for a widow who barely had anything to give. The girl was nice and quiet. She was a good fit for Moshe.

The happiest was Feige. She waited for me in our kitchen, which was a thing she hadn't done in months.

She wore the blue dress that I liked and had colored her cheeks in red. She waited for Moshe and me impatiently.

"We have a match," said Moshe with a big smile on his face. I hadn't seen a smile like that on him for a long time. Thank God he could smile too.

That Sabbath dinner was more special. Feige never stopped talking. She was planning what to do and how. She was happy; it was our first child to get married. I looked at her and felt such pain in my heart. I couldn't believe I was going to lose such an amazing creature. I was mad at myself for thinking that, this day was for celebration, not sadness. Even though, I knew something no one in the family could imagine.

"Ephraim, where did you go?" teased my Feige. It was a question that was asked whenever I would drift away in my thoughts. Feige waited to hear what I was dreaming about. I wasn't about to share the thoughts I just had.

"I was listening to you talk." I smiled. She smiled back at me. Suddenly she got paler. I helped her get to bed and quickly called the doctor.

"It isn't good, Ephraim, not good at all. I can't get her on her feet. I don't know what else to do. The wedding must be soon, very soon." The doctor looked at me with sad eyes. He'd known Feige since she had been a child and had a special affection for her. I saw it was painful for him too.

***

We set a date for the wedding. Feige and I spoke about the event a lot. I noticed that those talks lifted her spirit and helped her forget about her weakness and her problems.

We agreed on a small wedding so that we could use the money

and get the young couple a place to live in the village Moshe worked in. He didn't make a lot of money, but it was enough for the two of them. The bride had a small family and we invited only the family and our closest friends.

Feige wanted a bigger wedding but she understood we had better things on which to spend money. On the day of the wedding, the doctor gave Feige an especially strong medicine.

"To help her handle the excitement," he explained.

All the guests arrived. They all went first to Feige. I hoped she didn't notice the surprise on their faces as they saw her. She was extremely thin, and she looked pale and faded, even with all the color she'd put on her face.

During the marriage ceremony, I stood close to her. I feared she would collapse. I looked at Moshe as he raised the veil from the bride's face; he looked like a child opening a present. Feige cried and so did other family members and neighbors.

A month after the wedding I buried the woman I loved. The sky was heavy and gray. The rain didn't stop falling and my tears were mixed with tears from above. I felt like I was burying a piece of me with her, burying my soul.

In the last few years I married off the rest of my children, all matches went well and my house was almost empty of children. Moshe had a son named Herman and two daughters, Metta and Mina. Since they lived in a village not far from mine, they came every two weeks to visit their grandfather. They loved my stories of grandmother Feige. I described her beauty and wisdom with great love.

I told them about the village I came from in Bessarabia, about the special horse I had and about the dog I shared with Lanna. I loved those hours with them. They took me back in time to places I loved and to people I was missing. I was happy to think and talk about them.

***

I was tired. I felt like I didn't have the power I used to. I barely got up every morning and I got tired quickly. Maybe it was my time to go? The thought that my end was near caused me no fear. So many people I loved were waiting for me in a better world. My life without Feige had no meaning or purpose. I worried about my children and enjoyed my grandchildren, but my life had very little happiness after she was gone. I tried to think about whether I had anything I needed to do before my time came. Then I remembered; I had a treasure that I'd kept all my life and that I haven't thought of in years. I got up and started looking for it.

Inside the closet where I kept the holy books, the Tefillin and the *Tallit*[10], was a small package, wrapped in the same cloth it had been when I'd got it. The Torah from my birth father; the only thing I had from the little house in a village from which I was torn when I was a child. The most important present I had to give, but who could I give it to?

I had to decide who to give it to; to pass it along with my life's story.

I gathered the yellow pages on which I'd written my story and placed them with the Torah. I hoped that someday my story would be passed on, on fresh white paper, and maybe someone would find it interesting to read.

Moshe came to visit with Frida and the children. They brought joy and happiness into my house. After sitting for a while with the young one I asked Moshe to follow me to my room.

"Son, I would like to give you my life." He looked at me questioningly and I continued. "When I was eleven years old, something happened that changed my life. I was taken to a new home and environment and I needed to get used to a new world with strangers who weren't a part of my old life. I was a young

---

10 Tallit and Tefillin – Traditionally men religious garments

boy, a little sensitive, and afraid. From the moment I arrived at the Wininger family house, I adopted a friend to pass life with. He suffered with me, was happy with me, and knew everything in my heart. My friend was this pile of papers I wrote on every night before falling asleep. There were nights when I had so much to write that I slept very little, but the writing gave me the energy to face a new day."

I stopped talking. I was tired. I felt excited and my heart was beating so fast, I needed to rest. Moshe sat beside me in silence. He didn't understand what I were talking about. He waited patiently for me to recuperate and finish my story.

"This was my life's secret. No one has known about it until now. My friend is this pile of yellow papers written in Yiddish, my mother's language." I gave them to my son, such a big pile. I'd had a long and eventful life. To the papers, I added the little Torah and said, "I put my treasure in your hands; an old Torah from my parents' home and the pages with my story. My wish is that they will be passed on to the last son you'll have. If you have only girls, your son Herman will receive them and he will know what to do with them."

Moshe looked at the pile and the small Torah in amazement.

"I have never seen these things," he explained.

"Of course you haven't. No one has ever seen them. You are my first born child, and that is why I decided to give them to you. Take them for you and your family, my son."

I felt like I'd done all I needed to do in this world. I was very calm and happy to have gained many things, some of them so well, in this world.

Thank you God.

Part II - Feivel

The twentieth century started with an eruption of inventions and innovations. The world was so different from the one that my father Moshe lived in. My father never stopped marveling at all the new things, and yet kept on telling us how things used to be. Because of the stories I'd heard from my father, I sometimes thought that I'd lived through those times myself.

My father's name is Moshe. He is an industrious and pleasant man and dedicated to his work. He remained a reliable tradesman his entire life. My mother, Frida, is very different. She is a woman who studies all the time. Any written scrap of paper is a treasure to her. She just has to read it and will not skip a single word. Her hunger for knowledge was a treasure for the family. Any new thing she learned or heard of she'd tell her children right away. We are six children in my family and I am the youngest one. My name is Feivel. I have an older brother, Herman, and four sisters.

I was born in Gura Humorului, a beautiful part of Bukovina. I am the naughty one in our family. My sisters spent their days whispering among themselves and sending me to do their errands. I didn't mind; that way I was free to roam outside at will. I am fascinated by nature and I especially enjoy listening to birdsong.

***

On one of my walks, I found myself outside the village and into the great fir woods. From the moment I reached the clearing, I plunged into a world of marvelous sound. The wind was whistling among the tree branches, the birds sang their songs and this harmony was joined with the sun, peeking through the clouds, creating a marvelous play of light and shadow to the rhythm of the trembling leaves. The twittering, the wind and the lights made a world of music; my own magical place.

I must have fallen asleep. As I woke up I was still in the woods, but the place around me was too quiet. My first thought was that the birds must have gone to sleep already. I have never heard such silence in my wood. I was frightened, I was only seven years old and I was really scared. My mother must have been worried by then as I was always home before dark. I tried to find the right direction. I had been here so often that I was sure I'd find the way out. A growl made me freeze on the spot. What could it be? I started shaking. I hid behind the next tree. The place was still unnaturally quiet. I raised my eyes to the sky and wondered to where they had vanished. The darkness was threatening.

My brain started working again. I had to get home, I had to. Suddenly I could see everything; a faint light filled the wood clearing. This was my chance. I chose a direction and pushed through the trees. I was soon covered with cuts and scratches all over. I didn't care about that. I was going home. I started wondering where the light was coming from. I hurried to move before it disappeared. My steps got longer; I pushed branches aside as a warm liquid streamed over my face and back.

There was another frightening howl, but this time I didn't stop. I had a goal: getting out of there quickly. I was finally out of the woods and found a small and well-lit house. My legs carried me there. There was still a little bit of light. I tried to find out where I was but I couldn't. I didn't know that area. I raised my eyes and saw the faint light, smiling at me – the moon.

I knocked on the door. A young girl opened the door, jumped back and yelled,

"Mommy, come quick, there's a boy here covered in red."

I stood at the door, I felt the tears about to spring from my eyes and that girl was stopping me from doing so. I refused to cry in front of a girl no matter what. Her mother came running.

"Boy, you are wounded. What happened to you?" she said and her frightened voice scared me too.

"Come in and I'll clean up your blood."

Blood? I was sure I'd pass out if I saw blood. I remembered my big brother Herman coming home from a fight with one of the boys in school. Blood was flowing from his mouth, and straight away, I felt bad and fell onto the floor. Later when we talked about it my mother said I felt like a sack of potatoes. I was really offended but I said nothing and I decided it would never happen again. The woman brought a bowl of water, sat me down, and started cleaning my face and my arms. The girl stood next to her and watched. I was really uncomfortable. Suddenly it came to me; I jumped aside so that the woman remained standing with the rag in her hand and I yelled,

"Mother! I must go to my mother."

"What's your name, Boy?" asked the woman and started cleaning me again.

"I am Feivel Wininger of Gura Humorului," I answered shakily.

"Get the boy a glass of water and stop staring at him," she told her daughter.

"You look much better. Lucky your mother didn't see you the way you were when you got here. Your village is on the other side of the woods. I'll ask my husband to take you home in his wagon."

The girl brought me a glass of water. I drank it all in one gulp and tried to take a deep breath. I thanked the woman and quickly got into the wagon. I kept very quiet and never said a word on the way. The man tried to talk to me but my fear of my mother's reaction and worry that my father might be already at home tied my tongue.

***

I saw my home from a distance.

"There is my house!" I rejoiced. "I'll get off here and run home. Thank you, mister. Thank you very much." And even before he could stop I was off on my way.

My courage left me once I stood in front of the door. I stopped and started thinking about what I should say. That I was kidnapped and managed to escape? I remembered mother telling me of a Jewish kid from a nearby village who was caught by two Gentile boys who took his bag of groceries, beat him up, and wouldn't let him go home until it got dark. Perhaps such a story could serve me as well?

As I stood there lost in thought the door opened. My brother Herman stood there and shouted, "Where have you been, Feivel? I went out to look for you twice. Mother is here worried and you are running around alone in the dark?" Suddenly he started laughing and his laughter got louder and louder.

"Look at the shape you are in."

I was so worried about Mother's reaction that I didn't even answer my older brother when he was trying to provoke me.

"Five, is that you?" Mother came running from the kitchen, wiping her hands on her apron, and still, I stood outside waiting for an attack.

"Come in, my son. I almost went crazy with worry." She spoke without anger and I thought I could hear the relief in her voice. "Your father is also not back yet. I don't know what's with you all today," she said while pulling me in and only then did she notice my wounds.

"Who hit you?" she asked, and I could see her fists tightening. "And where have you been running so late?"

The kidnapping story was ready on my lips. I had a large crowd; my sisters–all four of them—stood at the other side of the room and waited for the show to begin. The truth was that whenever they were angry with one of them, I always tried to be around and on my best behavior. Sometimes I was even taken as an example of a good and polite child. That was the day of their revenge. I would never give them the satisfaction. I was about to tell such a special story that they would be sorry for me and commiserate. Mother went on watching me and waiting for an explanation. I decided to put up the full show.

"I fell asleep in the woods and I lost my way." That was all I managed to come up with. My sisters' sneers only made it worse.

"Come with me," said Mother and went to the kitchen. I followed her with downcast eyes.

A new fear rose up. I really didn't want them to send me to school in the city. Mother told us that some Hasidic courts would take children and teach them the Torah, and in return, the children would work for the older Hasidim. I really didn't want to leave my home.

"Feivel, what were you looking for in the woods?"

My mother surprised me with her question.

"Mother, I really love being there." I felt my heart beating faster. I was happy to describe my magical place. "There is a clearing in the middle of the wood, and I just sit there and listen to the bird songs. Do you know what marvelous music they make? I could listen to them for hours." I felt I was getting excited, and went on even though I knew that my late return was inexcusable.

"Mother, you know this never happens to me and I'm always back on time." I had to get back to my special place, my mother's watchful eyes took me there. "Have you ever heard the music made by the wind? The wind and the birds sound like a fiddle. I heard a fiddle at Uncle Berl's wedding and ever since then I love anything that reminds me of that marvelous sound." I felt I was getting carried away and that Mother surely had no idea what I was babbling on about, but at that moment I was in another place, a magical place with sounds I loved so much. I could not stop.

"Did you know that all that great music comes from only four strings? So many sounds from such few strings. The birds too can make so many sounds from their little throats, I just love it." I stopped. I looked at my mother. I hoped she didn't think I was mad because that would be a good reason to send me away. I remembered a few times that I had skipped school to go to my special place – Mother surely hadn't heard of it yet.

"You are a special child, Feivel," I heard Mother saying. I was overjoyed. "Go wash and we'll sit down to eat once Father gets home." She turned around and went back to preparing dinner. I was amazed. Was I going to get away with it so easily after what I had done?

I must be dreaming. I figured that the scandal would be on once Father gets home. Mother would tell him of my latest mischief and then it would start. I imagined that first, they'd shout at me and then would come my most hated sentence, "You are not allowed out until Friday." It was always that long. For me not going out after coming home from school was the worst punishment. I needed open air, the woods and the birds twittering, and I would never be able to explain that to Father.

After washing up, I sat down in the kitchen with a book; the very model of a good and industrious child. Not much later, Father came home from work and Mother called us all to the dinner table. After the blessings and the ritual washing of hands Father noticed I was scratched all over.

"What was it this time, Feivel?" asked Father and his voice sounded threatening. I wanted to answer, but Mother was quicker.

"Moshe, the boy was naughty and he has already been punished, as you can see. Plenty of painful scratches." Herman was sitting next to me and smiled happily at me, seeing I was about to get away with it.

After this incident, I tried to always stay in school until the end of classes like everyone else and to study whatever I had to do. It was an effort and I had to try and stop daydreaming too often.

Sometimes I would come home with my brother. My brother was seventeen at the time and I was very proud of him. He was industrious and responsible—all that I had yet to learn to be. He thought I should study for as long as I could. What could he mean?

The truth was that I was not happy to becoming an adult. The responsibility and the homework did not really interest me. It was great being the youngest at home.

After a while, I started improving in school, much to my father's joy, and more so my mother's. She had suffered more from my lack of interest in school than from my naughtiness.

***

On Fridays, Father usually returned home early and he would pass by the post office to get news from our scattered family. We had family members in different cities and countries. Receiving the mail was a special ritual. More than once, I had a chance to go with him. Father would get there and wait for his turn. Since everybody knows everyone in our village the clerk and Father had a regular conversation.

"How many letters would you like to receive, Mr. Wininger?" he'd ask Father.

"Many, and from many places," would be Father's response. The man took out one letter and gave it to Father. Even if he knew he had no more letters for him, he would check again until Father would get tired of waiting and would say, "I will settle for this letter for today."

He'd thank the man and leave.

One day I met father outside the post office and went in with him. The clerk took out a big envelope and handed it to Father.

"Who is it from?" asked the clerk as he always did.

Father turned the envelope over and looked happy. "It is from my big brother Shlomo. I haven't heard from him in a long time." Father answered beaming. I think he was stroking the envelope.

"I have another one here," The clerk announced and submitted another envelope.

"Who is this one from?"

"This one is from Bessarabia, from my uncle Menashe. But the strange thing is that this isn't his handwriting. Is there anything else?" He held the two envelopes and waited. Father's appetite grew from envelope to envelope.

Maybe someone else had remembered him.

"Come back next week and I'll try to save a few more for you." The clerk smiled kindly.

We said thank you and hurried home. Father always opened his mail with Mother. It was a known family routine. Father went into the house filled with importance and sat in the kitchen. He placed the two envelopes next to each other on the table, so that Mother would see them. Then Mother washed her hands, took off her apron, and sometimes it looked as though she was fixing her hair. She sat down beside him. He looked at her and she signaled yes to him. He took one of the letters and carefully opened the envelope. The letter was pulled out and was handed to Mother.

During this ritual, no one was allowed to speak. Whoever was not silent would need to leave the kitchen. I stood still, eager to hear.

"Well, read it to us," Father rushed her.

The first letter opened was the one from Uncle Shlomo, from the big city Vienna. The round and small handwriting looked perfect. I loved Uncle Shlomo's letters. He wrote beautifully and with big words, which Mother sometimes had to explain to us.

"My dear family." That was how my uncle began each letter. Father sat and smiled, unable to hide the happiness he felt about the letter. Mother continued, "I hope this letter finds you all well. I am sure you want to know what is new with me. Well, I have yet to finish my studies and I am working hard on writing articles for several newspapers. The situation in Vienna is very bad for us Jews. I experience anti-Semitic outbursts every day. It is seen in arguments at the university, in groups on the street, and in articles in the Austro-Hungarian journalism. It is especially hard when it comes from our own youth, and I have witnessed some shameful behavior. This youth grovel to the Gentiles, and are ashamed of being Jewish. There are anti-Semitic groups forming from within our people, our brothers, our flesh, and blood."

Mother stopped for a moment, moaned, looked at Father and kept reading. I realized that this is where I needed to take action.

This thing is burning in my soul. I decided to write with great pride about all those great men of prominence, writers and poets, artists and creators, wise scholars, and men of science. We were blessed with many men like these. I understood that the youth were filled with feelings of inferiority and with my writings I could give them all the arguments to make them stronger and restore the honor they shattered themselves.

Many articles published lately have our family name on them. I was shocked to find anti-Semitic words with my name on them. I added some of those articles with the pages I sent to you.

In Vienna lives a Jew called Otto Wininger. In fact, he is a former Jew that converted his religion and his life's purpose is to prove how much he hates Jews and how Gentiles are superior to us in knowledge and in spiritual wealth. Otto is a philosopher driven mad by hatred.

Instead of studying in peace I have to fight and I do it with all of my power. While collecting information on the great Jewish men in the past and the present, I found hundreds of names of our people and I decided that if it will be in my power I will publish an encyclopedia that will be full of those men. This work fills me with joy, even if I only get three hours of sleep a night and even with that I feel like I'm losing important time.

The concern in my heart is about the size of the movement of the young men that accept Otto Wininger's opinions. I try to appear in the same newspapers and magazines as Otto and I emphasize my name and my religion so that no one would think I had anything to do with that man and his foul words. The payment for my work is very small and that is because the editors know I will fight for my name and that I would agree to any fee to get published.

I need to end this letter. I am pleased that I was able to share my feelings with you. I would like to add something happy. I have met a girl who is helping me with my fight. Her name is Eva; I believe that with time I will find out I love her."

Mother stopped, smiled at Father, and gave him the letter.

"There is a line you didn't read," Father complained and gave the letter back to Mother.

"Give hugs to the children and goodbye, Shlomo."

Mother put down the letter.

Father sat there for a while, thinking about what we had just heard. Mother took the pile of articles that were with the letter and put them aside. We knew she'd read them when she had the time and would fill us in. Mother got up, put her apron back on, and went to make dinner.

"There is another letter," Father reminded her.

"Today is Friday and I have to prepare everything before lighting the candles," Mother explained.

"All right. We'll read the second one later. Shlomo's letter was long and I am still thinking about it." Father opened the next letter, prepared it, and went to get ready for Sabbath.

After eating Sabbath dinner and singing Sabbath songs we stayed at the table. Father got up and gave the letter to Mother.

"A letter from Bessarabia from Uncle Menashe," Father explained to everyone and looked at Mother.

"This isn't Menashe's writing," she commented. "He writes much bigger," she said and started reading.

"To Moshe and the family, hello. I am sad to say that my father, Menashe, has died. He has been coughing since last winter and had fever and chest pains. All the doctors and healers we had couldn't help him. He died of old age, but we still find it hard without him. We buried him in the family plot, next to our mother. As you probably understand, I am Yehuda, Menashe's firstborn. Father must have written and told you that I am married and have four children. I have written to America to Uncle Yosel but we haven't heard from him in over a year. If I hear anything I'll be sure to let you know.

I hope that one day we will be able to meet. I keep making wine in small amounts. We live humble but sufficient lives, thank God. If you could answer this letter I would be honored. May God be with you, Yehuda."

Mother finished reading.

"It is the way of the world," said Father. He took the letter from Mother's hand, folded it carefully and put it back into the envelope. I knew where that letter was going. Father had a box in which he kept each letter that he received. There were some old letters that were read several times and Father knew them by heart.

**

The last period passed without any special events. My eldest sister, Metta, was always excited and smiling. She spent a lot of time talking alone with Mother and it seemed strange. I couldn't imagine something interesting happening at home without me knowing about it. I waited for an opportunity when Mother was alone in the kitchen; I sneaked in and tried my luck.

"Mother, what is happening with Meta? She has been so happy lately."

"Have you seen Salo, the boy who arrived from Chernovitz?" she asked.

"Sure, I have. He told me great stories about the city. We talked about schools there and about going to the university. He studied at the university for two years and now he is thinking about going back there and finding a job."

Mother, as always, was surprised at how perceptive I was.

"You have seen and heard more than me," she said and smiled at me. She was so beautiful at those moments. I loved her so much. She was always understanding and always treated me like an adult.

"What does that have to do with Metta?" I insisted on getting a clear answer.

"We might have a wedding in the near future," She said with satisfaction.

"Will there be singers with musical instruments there? With a violin?" I asked with excitement.

"With God's help, there will be. Salo's family is wealthy so we can expect a big wedding with many people and a large band. Feivel, imagine having a married sister. What do you think of that?"

"It is wonderful," I replied, and added jokingly, "there will be more space in the house." I laughed. "If they'll live in the big city I could visit them and see new things."

Quickly, I returned to the topic that interested me most. "At the wedding, I'll have a chance to sit close to the violin player."

Mother's smile was her approval of what I had said.

The house was a mess. My mother and sisters got new dresses made for them. The bride got a dress that was ordered from the city. Even I got new clothes. Father was going to wear a suit that he'd received from Uncle Shlomo. It was sent from Vienna a year ago, but he didn't want to wear it without a special occasion.

In our village lived two of Father's brothers, Uncle Berl and Uncle Nathan. Uncle Nathan was handicapped and Father always made sure to fix his roof and to clean the gutters before each winter. I visited his house often and helped his wife with the shopping and with cleaning the yard. Nathan's wife didn't talk much, and especially not with me. Every request that she had, she told my uncle and he would tell me. We got along very well. My aunt is a little upset with the world and Mother told me she probably had a good reason.

Uncle Berl was very friendly. I often played with his children and two of them went to the same hedder as I did. They had a nice house and they had a few chickens and two goats running around the yard. We had fun running around with the animals, but we were able to do it only when my aunt wasn't home. She would say we are keeping the chickens from laying eggs. I thought they were enjoying my games and they just couldn't tell that to my aunt.

All of the uncles and many of our friends from our village and around it were invited to the wedding. The groom's family arranged everything. The plan was to take the train to Chernovitz and spend the night there, and then the wedding would take place the next day.

I was very excited. I had never traveled so far away, and especially to the big city that I had heard so many stories about. Everything was set. Metta had left early and planned to stay with cousins in Chernovitz. She would have time to meet Salo's family and get used to a new place.

We were scheduled to leave in two weeks.

***

A week before the date of the wedding, something unexpected, cruel, and disappointing happened.

Recruiting orders appeared in all the public places in the village. All men must report to the gathering place—as it states in the notice—anyone above the age of seventeen, not old or handicapped, will be drafted without any possibility of appeal.

We were shocked. We didn't know who was fighting who or why. Mother read the news in a German newspaper. The Austro-Hungarian heir, Frantz Ferdinand, had been shot and killed by a student in Bosnia. Austria-Hungary had declared war on Bosnia. This changed our lives completely.

My father and my brother Herman enlisted immediately. Father's attempt to explain to the officials that he was the only provider for a family of seven fell on deaf ears. The men were given forty-eight hours before leaving.

A quiet sadness fell on the house. Mother and the girls prepared warm clothes for Father and Herman. Each item of clothing needed to be planned. It was July and there was no chance that they would return before winter. On the other hand, it was forbidden for them to take more than one bag, which needed to be small or else it would be tossed out and they would have nothing.

I wandered around the house trying to find ways to make it easier for Mother. Schools were closed and transformed into drafting places. Mother tried to appear calm, despite the fact that in a few days she would become the head of the family. If only they had left Herman home it would have been easier for Mother and there would have been someone to help support the family.

Early the next morning we said goodbye to Father and Herman. Mother kept asking to make sure that no one had forgotten anything.

Suddenly she stopped and a gasp that sounded like a shout came out of her mouth. "The wedding! Metta, Salo! What about the wedding? How will we let our girl know what is happening?"

We looked up at her in astonishment. We were all in shock. How could we have forgotten? Father was the first to respond.

"They probably know what we know. If they are drafting here they must be doing it there too. The city is big and many would be drafted. This wedding is so sad."

The word sad was too small to describe what was happening. How quickly we had gone from happiness and anticipation to fear and despair.

"They will probably have a quick and modest wedding. Hopefully, joy will return to us someday." Mother summed it up.

The girls stood next to Father and Herman. They were pale and frightened. Mother asked us not to cry. She said it would be a short time apart. She kept thinking about what to do next. She needed to make quick and right decisions.

"Let's sit together and think. Who knows when we might get a chance to sit like this. We need to find a way to leave this place soon. According to the newspaper, the Russians will immediately go to war with us. People say they are very cruel. We live very close to the border so we need to leave. Moshe and Herman, you'll send mail for us to Uncle Nathan's house. He wasn't drafted. You two will look after each other and I'll take care of the children." Mother stopped talking, took a deep breath, raised her head and said, "Let's finish packing the men's bags and start on ours."

I went to Father and took his hand in mine, and said, "I have decided to come with you and Herman. You two will fight and I will take care of everything else." My offer was honest. Everyone smiled and I think that they were amused by my offer. I was happy to be able to put smiles on their faces.

Father hugged me and promised, "We will be back soon with many interesting stories." He went to Mother and whispered something in her ear. He said goodbye to me and my sisters and left. Herman took a second. He looked around, hugged Mother, waved at us, and then left in a hurry to catch up with Father.

We remained standing as if we had nothing more to do. The door opened and Father ran in.

"I forgot the most important thing," he yelled while running to the bedroom. He returned a few moments later looking pleased. "Thank God I didn't forget," he said, and before we could ask him anything he was gone.

We gathered around Mother, each of us trying to hold her and be held, to feel safe.

"I am going to talk to some families and arrange a trip together. Every hour we stay here is a danger to our lives. We have a wagon and two horses. They will be our legs for now. Prepare only things you must take with you," She said and left.

I went to the window to watch as she left and I saw the trees and flowers in the yard. It was such a beautiful time of year in an ugly world. I felt better thinking of Father's promise that we will return soon and I would be able to play in the yard again.

It would be over three years before that promise came true.

Mother returned after a few hours with a boy who we didn't know. He was big, his hair was messy, and his clothes were torn. We gathered in the kitchen.

"Listen carefully," mother began to explain. "We decided, together with several other families, to leave tomorrow night." She added something to the boy and went on, "The group of Jews we are joining is going to the city of Olmitz in Moravia, and each of us will pack up our bags and be ready to go."

We looked questioningly at Mother and then at the boy. She understood and said, "The long road would be difficult without a man to drive the wagon and take care of the horses. At first, I thought I would do it, but chance, or luck, made it so that I don't have to." She stopped to give the boy more bread and continued, "On my way home, I saw two soldiers hitting this boy. They asked for his age and when he said he was fifteen-and-a-half they kept hitting him and asked to know where his family was. He tried to explain that he was an orphan with no family.

I stopped and saw the whole thing. They tried to force him to say he was eighteen so that they could draft him. It was as though a strange hand forced me to step in. I walked up to the soldiers and told them that I knew the boy. I tried to stand as straight as I could appear taller and more forceful. I said he is fifteen and told them to leave him alone. They stopped for a moment, looked at each other and then at me. They said something I didn't understand. One of them gave the boy one last kick. He dumped him on the road and they left. I stood for a moment to calm down and at my feet was this boy. I felt bad for him so I helped him up and here he is."

Mother sat down. I could see that telling the story had taken a lot of her strength.

"Do you want something to drink?" I asked her.

"Water," she answered.

"Maybe I could be of help to you. I won't eat much and I will sleep wherever you say," said the boy. We all looked at him. Then Mother said, "Do you want to be our Vassily to Maren?"

He looked happy. "I would be glad to leave this bad place. I got beaten here enough to last all my life. I will stay with you for as long as you'll need me and then go on my way." He was just what we needed.

"As I said, we leave tomorrow night. Be ready. What is your name?"

"My name is Gorki but everyone calls me Guri," he answered with a smile.

"All right, Guri. You are coming with us. Come with me and I'll give you some clothes and you could start loading food for the horses on the wagon. Later we will put our belongings there." Mother sounded pleased.

We, the children, didn't really understand what was happening. We were too young, so the burden fell on Mother.

On the last night before we left, I heard Mother moaning. I couldn't help her and didn't know what to do. The next day my sisters did everything to help Mother prepare the house for our absence. There wasn't much to do because we were already packed. We took with us a bag of potatoes, sugar, and flour for the winter. Mother also decided to take smoked meat so that we would have something to eat at the beginning of our stay at the new place.

We left at dawn. The families that left with us that morning were mostly women, old men, and children. Families on full wagons were leaving everything behind and going. It was a long line of worried and sad people.

***

The summer weather made our journey easier. After a few days, we arrived at Olmitz. It seemed like a good choice. The place was far from the route of the Russian army. The people came and offered us cheap rooms.

We stayed at the home of one of the local families. We were given a large room and the ability to use the kitchen. The family we stayed with had only four people so it worked out well. The wife and her two children were always home and the husband worked far away and would seldom return home.

On the first night, we asked the woman to allow Guri, who really was a good boy, to sleep in their barn. We let him use the blankets we'd brought and Mother explained that she would only need him for a day or two more until she'd sold the wagon and the horses. We desperately needed money. We hoped to get enough from the sale to pay our expenses and to pay the rent for a short while. If the war was short, we could return home this winter and reorganize, with Father and Herman, of course.

The next day Mother and Guri wandered around looking for buyers. People there were afraid to lose money too. No one knew what the future held or how the war would turn out. No one wanted to buy.

"Madam Frida," Guri turned to Mother. "I could use the wagon for deliveries and give you the money."

Mother thought about it for a moment and said, "While you

are out there keep looking for someone to buy it or at least one of the horses. I would really like to sell them before the winter."

Guri made a very small amount of money from the deliveries. Mother was worried by the fact that she had no buyers, until one day Guri came home happy.

"There is a buyer for the wagon and the horses." He announced.

Mother, Guri, and my sister Anna went to meet the buyer. I was left at home.

After a while, I saw them walking back. I tried to guess if they were happy with the amount that they'd got. As they got closer and I saw Mother's face, I knew she was disappointed.

We were left without a wagon and horses, with very little money, and we had to send Guri away as we'd agreed.

In the meantime a school for refugee kids formed in Olmitz. My two younger sisters, Dora and Mina, went there willingly. I didn't want to go. I was the only man in the family and I needed to help Mother. I was sure Mother would be upset and force me to go to school.

"Feivel, I would be happy if you chose to go to school." That was all she said. I understood the decision was mine and I was proud of that. My big sister Anna didn't fit the system that the school offered so she stayed home with us.

***

Like the rest of the women who came with us, Mother also struggled to find work. Very few found work and Mother was worried. Time passed and there was no sign of the war ending. Our money was running out and caring for four children was a heavy burden.

Since I'd decided it wasn't time for school, I wanted to help earn money. So I would wander around the market trying to work for change. At times I would get lucky and get loading jobs. I would run home happy and give the money to my mother. She looked at me with sad eyes.

One evening, after we ate, I saw Mother talking to the landlady. I listened to them.

"I can bake good bread and small personal rolls. I can also bake good cakes and great kigels[11] . If you are ready, we'll do it together. You will prepare the necessary ingredients and I will bake them. I will work at night and in the morning I'll take my eldest daughter and sell them. I saw a place near the market that might be good for it. My people walk past there and hopefully, we will sell."

"I like the idea, let's try," agreed the woman.

The next day, the kitchen was filled with flour, sugar, and eggs and after a short while, we could all smell bread and fresh cake. We were asked not to go into the kitchen unless it was necessary.

Mother made the baked goods and my sister helped sell them. I was glad to take part in the family effort and as much as necessary. I carried boxes to the market, helped arrange the patisseries and I was there for Mother's every request. From the sales, we were able to pay the rent and buy enough food. Not many families had such good conditions. When we returned to our room we ate quickly and went to sleep.

My sisters shared one bed and I slept with mother in another. She would get to bed many hours after we did. She stayed up to bake for the next day. Her life was tiring and hard, but we never heard a word of complaint or dissatisfaction.

We asked Uncle Nathan, who'd stayed behind in our village, to pass on to us every piece of information he got from Father and

---

11 Kigel is a baked casserole, Ashkenazi Jewish dish

Herman. Near the place where we lived, was the Grimmenstein Castle, in Olmitz, Moravia, which was overcrowded with refugees. All the mail for the refugees came to that place. We let them know that we would come on occasion to check for mail. They wrote our name and promised to save our mail for us. We sent Uncle Nathan a postcard to let him know the address of the castle.

After eight months of concern, we received a letter from Uncle Nathan and enclosed was a postcard and a picture from Father.

Father wrote, "To Frida and the children, hello. This is the first postcard I have been allowed to write. After two weeks in the army, Herman and I were separated and I don't know where he is. I asked my commander to help me find him and he promised to check where he is. I still haven't gotten an answer and I won't give up until I know where he is and what happened to him.

Our army was fighting along the river Prut and was defeated. Luckily, I'd left the area a short time before it happened.

I am worried about you. I want this nightmare to end. I am tortured by the thought of how terrible it is that a father and his son are fighting a war for strangers. I have never felt so out of place as during this war. This forced draft did something to my soul. In the little time I get to sleep, I can't stop thinking about all of you and about the house we left empty.

Dearest Frida, to be away from the family in this difficult time is a horrible punishment for me. I wonder how you are handling the children and the new place. You are a wise woman, but I know you are not in perfect health and I can't wait to return home and free you from your burden.

I promise to let you know as soon as I have news from Herman. There is no way to write to me because I keep moving from place to place.

Goodbye Frida, my good wife and my dear children." He signed it Father.

We sat quietly as mother read the letter. I didn't know what to expect, but after hearing the letter we knew one thing for sure, we'd lost track of Herman. Father didn't know where he was. If he was well he would have let us know.

"No news of Herman." Mother summed up the letter. "Where can my son be?" she asked. She closed up in herself; her eyes were open but not seeing. We sat beside her in silence.

Suddenly she jumped up, "We don't have bread for tomorrow. I'm going to bake."

I watched her go into the kitchen, a little down, her feet were heavy and I knew she wouldn't be able to carry this burden for much longer.

***

It took a long and troubled time for a letter to arrive again. We gathered around Mother and waited impatiently for her to open the letter with her shaking hands. She ripped the envelope carefully so as not to hurt the letter. Inside was a torn and stained piece of paper filled with words. The handwriting was small; we recognized it as Father's.

"Frida and the children, hello. Two days ago I received my first news about Herman. Frida, don't get worried, he is fine now. They told me he was injured shortly after we were separated. His condition was bad, so they took him to a hospital in Vienna. I was told that he received special care and that is why he is alive. I tried to figure out what happened, where and how he was hurt, but no one knew. I do know he is still in the hospital and as soon as he gets back on his feet they will send him home. I am very happy to give you such good news. I am excited about the news and about writing to you. I only write when they guarantee that the mail will be sent. I am holding on and hoping to return home soon. Signed, Father."

Mother and my sisters cried. It was a cry of sadness and concern. All I could think of was that Herman will be coming back soon and Father will arrive after him and we will return to our little home and the routine of our pleasant life in our village.

Another year passed, during which we received only one postcard from Father. It was really short; two lines in which he wrote that he was still fine and that he hoped Herman was already home. We hadn't heard from Herman.

In a conversation between Mother and the landlady, I heard Mother complaining that she was not feeling well lately. She was very tired and her feet were swollen and hurt.

They talked about our home and Mother expressed her concern for the way that she would find it when we returned. She told the landlady that she read in a newspaper about how brutal the Russians and the farmers were toward Jews. They were taking people out of their homes, abusing them, and sending them to Siberia. In another newspaper, she read that they burned villages and destroyed homes. Mother didn't notice that I was listening and not sleeping. I saw in front of me a fragile and hurting woman and it was the first time I ever heard her complain about her health. Maybe if I were older than nine years I would have known how to help.

***

On Friday night, Mother was exempt from baking, because on Shabbat[12] there was no selling. Even during this difficult period

---

12 The seventh day of the week, the day of rest for the Jews

of our life, mother made sure that on Friday evening we would sit together in the light of the candles and sing Sabbath hymns, just like we used to sing with Father.

My sisters and I have beautiful voices and Mother encouraged us to sing. I couldn't tell who was the bigger hero, Father who was fighting in the army, or Mother, who fought to preserve human dignity, to support a family with four children and to observe the Sabbath eve as it is?

A letter from Uncle Nathan surprised us and made us very happy. Attached was a long letter from Herman. We were surprised that Mother read it quietly to herself and did not share it with us. We stood quietly around her and waited.

"Thank God, my boy is coming home soon," Mother said with relief. "Herman writes from the hospital in Vienna. He says that his condition is much better and that he will be able to leave soon. He is very happy with the treatment he received and he misses us all. He asks about Father and hopes to see us soon."

One morning we rushed to the market with the bread. We stood in the usual place and during the entire day we only sold four loaves of bread. Everything else was left untouched.

"We will try to sell the cakes tomorrow. They will still be fresh." Mother tried to lift our spirits. We knew that we would have to pay the landlady back for the flour and the eggs and that we would be eating stale bread for the rest of the week. On that day there was no school so my sisters wandered bored around the market. I stayed with Mother. It was getting dark; we never stayed at the market so late.

"Maybe more hungry people will pass by," she explained.

We stood and waited. Suddenly my sister Mina came running.

"Two guys are bothering Anna. They will not let her go." Mina's face was red and she was barely breathing.

"I am coming," I said with such confidence that I almost believed that I could face those two guys.

"Feivel, you stay here next to the merchandise. I'll be right back." Mother and Mina walked away quickly. I watched them until they disappeared into one of the alleyways. My heart was full of worry.

A very elderly woman, with a wrinkled face, dressed in rags, stopped and stared at the pastries.

"I am so hungry; I haven't eaten anything in two days," mumbled the old lady. She didn't even see me. Her look shifted from one pastry to another. I was embarrassed. I have seen people like that every day since the war began. I tried not to worry about it. There were days we went to bed with empty stomachs too.

That old woman did something inside of me. I felt sorry for her and without a second thought I took one of the loaves of bread and gave it to her. She snatched it from my hand and before I could see what was happening she started eating. She gave me one more look and disappeared.

My mother and sisters returned safely. Anna, my beautiful sister, was sobbing and her hair was a mess. Mother tried to calm her down. Mother took one look at the food and I heard her say happily

"Good, Son, you managed to sell one more loaf of bread." I lowered my eyes. We, the poor, give bread to others? Even I couldn't understand why I did it.

"I gave bread to an old and hungry old woman," I managed to say, I did not dare look up and waited for her sharp reaction.

"You did a good thing, Son. You are very noble. Sometimes we need to give even if we don't have what to give from."

It was dark and there were no people left outside. We gathered our boxes and hurried home. Not another word was said about what happened at the market. Mother's words were engraved deep in my soul. Nobleness of mind at such times.

***

The First World War was over. We knew that Father and Herman would arrive straight back at Vama and would stay in the house we had been forced to leave behind. We packed all of our possessions, which weren't many, said goodbye to the family we'd stayed with and paid our debt. We rented a wagon with another family and we finally headed home.

The road seemed longer than the one we remembered taking over three years ago. The weather was bad and unpleasant. Strong winds flogged us without mercy. Mother wrapped our heads with pieces of cloth and old shirts. We passed through many villages on our way. Some were completely abandoned. We used places like that for sleep. The empty buildings were filthy and had bad odors.

One morning we woke up to find that a few of our bags had been stolen. Those bags had all of our belongings. We ran out to make sure the wagon was still in place. Fortunately, Vassily we'd hired was a responsible man and he slept in the wagon.

"They could steal our cart, horse, and coach," I said, trying to be amusing and change the murky atmosphere. No one paid attention to me, there was no reason to laugh.

We continued on the long road leading to our village. On our way we saw wagons filled with wounded soldiers or families with children, all emigrating from place to place. The feeling was that the convoys, in both directions, were of lost creatures with no tomorrow, no future, and no purpose.

My little sister Dora started feeling ill. Mother asked Vassily to stop in the nearest village. In the late evening, we stopped next to the first house, at the edge of a village. Mother got out of the wagon and walked up to the house. She knocked on the door, but no one answered. She tried to open the door and it wasn't locked. She asked Vassily to come into the house with her and we waited and hoped outside that they would return with a doctor's address. Meanwhile, my feverish sister began to hallucinate loudly. I panicked. The other family members who were traveling with us were silent and were not ready to move. I was getting worried and decided to go get Mother.

I ran into the house and found mother leaning over someone. I got closer and to my amazement saw a mother and her baby on the floor. Mother and Vassily were trying to take the baby away from the mother, but couldn't, despite the fact that the mother had passed out.

"Feivel, get water, quickly," Mother yelled to me. I ran to find the kitchen, got a bucket of water and returned to the front room. Mother took the bucket, took off her headscarf, dipped it in water and wiped the woman's face. Suddenly the baby started crying.

"Feivel, go see if there is anything to eat in the kitchen, look for bread or milk."

There was a groan and then a faint voice, "What happened to my baby girl?" The woman woke up, she didn't notice the baby that was crying in her arms. I returned with a bowl of milk.

"Mother, there is some milk here, what should I do with it?" I asked.

"Get it warm," she said and turned to Vassily "Help me pick them up. The floor is cold and it will be a miracle if they haven't gotten pneumonia." They lifted the woman, with the baby still in her arms, and placed her on the bed.

I returned with warm milk, Mother got a spoon and started feeding the baby. The woman opened her eyes and whispered, "Water..."

"Feivel, warm up some water." Mother was in control of the situation, but it looked as if she'd forgotten about my sister Dora.

Mother gave the woman the water, Vassily took the baby from her mother and Mother gave them both drinks. The driver lit another lantern and we were able to see the mess all around us.

"They tried to take my baby," the woman cried. It seemed her power was back; at least her voice was. "They took my husband to take care of them on the way. I held my baby tight so that they wouldn't take her. My husband said that he would do whatever they wanted if they leave me and the baby unharmed," she started crying. "My husband was like a doctor. He knew how to take care of all illness and I used to help him before the baby was born. When the wagon with the wounded soldiers passed through the village, they were told to come to us for help. The moment they arrived was the moment my world ended." She dried her eyes and asked, "What about my baby? How is she?"

"She is fine now. She'd probably not received any food or water for a long time and she became very weak. She looks relaxed and happy now."

"Good people, how can I ever repay you for what you did? Without you, we would have been gone."

"I have a sick girl in the wagon outside, can you help her?" Mother asked hopefully.

"Bring her, I want to see her," said the woman as she sat up. "It's late, you should stay here for the night, and we will find room."

"There are more children and two women outside."

"We will find a way," the woman insisted.

I hurried out to get everyone and Vassily carried Dora. The woman came and touched her forehead. She asked her to stick out her tongue and said, "The child has a high fever. Let's hope it is food poisoning and not something worse."

She went into the kitchen and returned with some medicine. After Dora took it, the woman brought a bowl with water and vinegar and changed compresses on Dora's head for a long time. In the meantime, Mother found everyone a place to sleep. The house was warm from the fire so our coats were enough to keep us very warm. The woman took her baby, changed her diaper, fed her, and put her to sleep. Mother sat with Dora for another hour before going to sleep.

Mother woke up early in the morning and hurried to see Dora. She found the woman there, feeding her with a strange mash.

"Her temperature is down. She will be alright," the woman said.

"Thank God," said Mother and asked to warm water for everyone.

"I will take care of it," the woman answered. "You finish feeding Dora and I'll make you breakfast and a package for the road. I'm happy to be able to do something for you."

We ate well that morning. We had warm milk, bread, and butter. Then we had to say goodbye to the nice woman. She hugged mother and said, "May you stay healthy, you and your family. I will never forget you."

***

We got deeper into Bukovina. The air was filled with dust and a bad smell. It took us a while to recognize the smell. It was the scent that is left after a fire. We entered a village. The houses on the main road were burned and people were running around. They looked terrified as if they were afraid of us. Mother looked around with horror in her eyes. "I just hope we have a home," she whispered.

***

As we got closer I could see a look on everyone's face; a look of fear combined with anticipation. It was the look of people who don't understand, or maybe don't believe, what they are seeing. I looked around and thought I was in a story that did not belong to me, unbelievable and impossible. When we drove away from Olmitz the sights had been completely different. Where had the tranquility of the villages disappeared to? Where were the well-kept houses proudly carrying the red roofs?

Once I'd asked Father what the difference was between heaven and hell. I still remember how he explained to me, with a smile on his face: the Garden of Eden is easy to describe because it must be like our village, but all its inhabitants are rich, beautiful, and happy. Hell also has the same things, but you cannot reach them because they are burning with bad fire. The people there are dressed in rags and running around in desperate attempts to escape from the fire and the heat. The description had startled me and I'd asked him to stop his story. Now I understood exactly what hell was, and only hoped that our village looked different from the shocking sights we had discovered on our way.

We stopped on the way to stretch our legs and Mother gave us some of the food we'd received from the woman who had taken care of Dora. It was hard for me to swallow and as I looked at everyone I realized that the lack of appetite was shared by all.

Our despair was stronger than hunger. We drank water and returned quickly to our places on the wagon. Vassily finished eating and we returned to the road.

From different roads, we saw wagons filled with people. We recognized some people from our village. We exchanged looks, but no one said a word. No one could hide the deep freezing in our souls and our fear of finding out in the next few minutes what had happened to our homes.

"I have often thought of Metta, my girl. We haven't heard anything from her since the war began. I don't know what happened to Uncle Nathan, who stayed in the village. The last letter we got from him was a year ago. And how could I forget about Uncle Berl? With all that happened, I almost forgot about him. He disappeared the day the draft began. His wife Lilli took the children and went to her parents' house in Romania. And Aunt Sima, I wonder what happened to her family. As I get closer to the village they all come up in my memory. I am afraid to see; afraid to hear. I am so tired and all I want is to rest."

I am not used to hearing Mother speak so much. For a moment, I allowed myself to believe that the end of the road would be the end of our troubles.

I was before my Bar Mitzvah and I had been through difficult things and days of hunger that made me feel like an old man. I remembered Father's story about his father Ephraim, who at the age of eleven had had to deal with a new family and a new life in a different place and that it made him grow up fast. The same thing happened to me.

The feeling of being an adult and being in charge followed me since we'd left our village. I forgot my childish behavior, and the days I would disappear into my favorite corner and I would do as I pleased. Where are those distant days? Will they ever come back? For a moment I allowed myself to hope that the end of this road would also bring an end to our prohibitions. But I was in doubt. Could it be possible?

***

All eyes were fixed on the first houses of our village. A wagon laden with people stopped in front of us so we had to stop too. I jumped out to see what had happened. I ran to where the wagon had stopped. I couldn't see any reason for them to stop. I raised my eyes to the couple on the first wagon. Their heads were turned to the right and their eyes were wide open. I recognized them as the couple who lived in the first house in the village. I turned to look at their house and I understood everything. Instead of a house there stood a pile of burned wood. There was nothing left of the beautiful wood house that had stood there previously. It was a shocking sight. They needed to be moved to the side of the road. The wagons crammed with miserable people who have come back from such a long way cannot wait indefinitely. I had to act.

I went to the horses and pulled them a little to the right. I think that the woman in the wagon fainted. The horses started moving. I pulled once more and the road was clear. I couldn't look at the people on the wagon. I ran back to our wagon. I still didn't know what was waiting for us at our home.

What happened?" asked Mother.

"The horse must have been scared by something," I lied and looked the other way. Mother kept looking at me with distrust. I didn't dare to meet her eyes.

***

Uncle Nathan's house was on our way.

"We will first go home and drop the bags and then we will check on Uncle Nathan's house. I hope that Father and Herman are there waiting for us." Mother decided.

I was afraid of the moment Mother would see our house. I had to stop her before she saw it. I needed to check it out first.

Perhaps I was afraid of meeting with the family. The faces of the neighbors who looked from the carts to the village frightened me. And what about those who would not return? Until this moment, I had not dared to think about this possibility. There are so many people I love and fear for their fate. My brother Herman and Father. Have they returned? How are they? My sister Mata, the aunts and their children; who knows what awaits us in meetings with them. How would Mother stand up to all this? I was afraid for her.

"I am sure Father and Herman are here," I said. I looked for help from my sisters but they were apathetic, curled up next to each other unusually quiet and dozing. I understood that I had to take the initiative and told my mother firmly, "You go down here to Uncle Nathan's house. You deserve to meet them first. We'll go home, take the bags down, and come." I tried to sound convincing.

The tiredness and the desire to see her loved ones after more than three years overwhelmed the scales. She took out the bag with the little money left, paid the coachman with a trembling hand, and nodded to the other family. I helped her out of the wagon.

She turned to go to Uncle Nathan's house that looked just as it had when we'd left. We continued on the road to our house.

The lack of knowledge about the fate of Father and Herman and the possibility that my mother would be disappointed had clouded my spirit and frightened me.

The other family left on the second street after Uncle Nathan's house. We asked Vassily to keep going to our house. My sisters and I sat up. We were nervous to see it. The wagon stopped in front of the house. We looked and remained paralyzed at the sight in front of us.

Vassily became impatient and angry, disappointed by the amount he had received.

"First, I wasn't paid enough and now you are wasting my time?" Vassily lost his patience. He jumped out of his seat and started throwing our bags to the side of the road. I felt like I was losing control of my nerves. I jumped at him, grabbed his coat, and started yelling like crazy.

"You will not touch our bags!" I felt the blood rushing to my head and my face was burning. My sisters hurried to get the rest of our belongings off the wagon and jumped down. Anna walked up to me, grabbed my coat, and pulled me aside.

"Everything is fine, Feivel, don't get so excited. Come and help us get the bags into the house. We've got everything." Anna spoke in a calming voice. I realized I was still holding the driver's coat and that my other hand was in a fist.

"I'm all right, Anna. I will be right there." I left his coat. We gathered our things in front of the gate. I took a second look to make sure we hadn't left anything on the wagon. Vassily was still not moving. He was so shocked by the way I'd jumped at him that he forgot his intention to leave.

"You may go now," I said to him and turned to look at the house.

***

The gate and the fence around the house were completely destroyed. Father was very proud of that gate. He'd worked on it for a long time. It was broken and leaning to the side. I used to love to hang from it. The few times Father had caught me doing that I would be yelled at and be given a lesson in behavior; how to treat something that took many hours to build. I would also get a lecture about how it wasn't built to carry my weight.

My sisters were as shocked as I was.

"I hope that the inside is not as bad as the outside," I said. I took two of the bags, walked into the yard, and up to the front door. I didn't look to the sides. I'd already seen that all of Mother's flowers were gone. The flowers weren't important, and neither were the gate or the fence. The important thing was that we were home.

I put down the bags and tried to open the door, it wouldn't budge. In another attempt, and with a push of my shoulder, I managed to open only a narrow slit. My sisters came too, carrying the rest of the bags in their hands. "Something is blocking the door from the inside," I explained.

"I will go around and try to get in through the kitchen," said Anna. To my delight, Anna had taken the initiative this time.

After a few minutes I heard Anna yelling and the voices of men answering her. I didn't understand what was happening. I dropped the bags and ran around to the kitchen entrance. The door was open so I followed the voices. Anna was standing in the middle of the kitchen, surrounded by three men in uniforms.

"What are you doing here? This is our house!" I raised my voice and was noticed by all.

"You have nothing to do here," said one of them. "This is our house now. At least until we find a way to get home."

I didn't know what to do. Anna sat on the floor and started crying. I felt as if Mother's anxious eyes were following me, urging me to find a solution. The three soldiers started making jokes and paid no attention to me. I looked at them. They looked pathetic despite the uniforms they were wearing. The clothes were torn and dirty and their shoes were old. Suddenly an idea came into my mind.

"We arrived here on a wagon. The driver is going back to Maren. He might take you with him." They stopped laughing and looked at me seriously.

"A wagon? Where?" they asked with interest.

"If you hurry, you might catch him. He was going in that direction." I showed the direction with my hand.

They rushed to one of the rooms and came back with their bags. They moved Mother's box that was blocking the door and ran out.

Anna sat on the floor and looked at me with her mouth open. Did I see admiration in her eyes?

Through the door, which had been blocked by the soldiers, now entered Dora and Mina dragging the rest of our belongings on the floor. It was time to see what had happened in the house and prepare it for Mother's arrival.

We started checking around the house. First, we discovered that the kitchen had no windows. The glass was shattered and pieces of wood were blocking the light. The house used to be so beautiful and big. There used to be six large rooms and a kitchen that was the center of the house. The kitchen was always heated and in the middle of it stood a table big enough for the whole family.

I ran to my room, but there was no room there. The outer wall, or what remained of it, had been burned. A wind blew in without impediment. I went from room to room; the whole area of the house was burned. We were left with the kitchen and with two rooms. In only one room the windows haven't been smashed, but it was full of stench and dirt. I realized that it was where the soldiers had been staying.

The stench and grime dominated everything. I didn't know where to start cleaning. I returned to the kitchen. My sisters started picking the dirt up and piling it into one spot. The kitchen looked so big and then I realized that the table and the chairs were gone. The only room that had any furniture in it was Father and Mother's room, where the soldiers stayed.

"We need to run over to Uncle Nathan's house. Mother must be worried," Anna said. "Feivel, why don't you go and we will keep on cleaning."

"What should I tell her?" I asked. They looked at me for a moment and then returned to work.

I quickly went to the road that led to my uncle's house. The things I saw on the way were hard to bear. Most houses looked like they had been through a storm of fire and wind. I met people who were going back to what used to be their home. I could barely recognize the people I saw. They looked slim and sad. Old age had overtaken them.

As soon as I entered the house I saw Herman. I didn't even say hello to my uncle and his wife. I immediately ran to Herman, shaking and happy.

"Herman, my big brother," I said and started crying. I hugged him tightly.

"Feivel, be careful, my whole body still hurts." Herman's voice hadn't changed. I stepped back and looked at him. His head and his legs were in bandages. Next to him were two support canes.

"You've grown up," Herman said, looking at me. "You really are a big boy now." There was sadness in his voice or maybe over-excitement. After the joy of the meeting had passed, I noticed how terrible he looked.

"Herman, what did they do to you in the war and how do you feel now?" I asked anxiously and immediately went on. "And Dad, where's Dad?" I looked around and realized he was gone.

"We received a postcard from him a month ago, and he will be back soon," replied Uncle Nathan. I went over to him and his wife and hugged them.

I turned to Mother, lowered my eyes, and said, "Remember you told us that the most important thing is to be home, no matter what we find?"

A silence fell and Mother said nothing.

I tried my luck again. "Mother, we have Herman here and Father will be here soon. We can all build the house up again together. We have survived so many difficult days so far and we still made it home."

"How big is the destruction?" Mother's voice was calm and without drama as she asked a simple question.

"Anna, Mina, and Dora are already cleaning the house. Some of the rooms were burned down. We have much work to do before the house will return to what it was. But tonight, on the floor, covered with our coats, we will be sleeping in our house." I said this with good intentions, but I couldn't get the images of our house out of my head.

My aunt brought out some sandwiches and something warm to drink. Only then did I remember we'd hardly had anything to eat. I thanked my aunt and said, "We still have food from the road. I will eat with my sisters."

Mother fell asleep while sitting down.

"It would be good if Mother could spend the night here. It is best that she doesn't see the house today. I think that everything that's happened has taken all of her powers. I will return in the morning."

"We have blankets and tools here that belong to you. When you left, the farmers started emptying the Jews' homes. I went to your house and filled a wagon with everything I could carry," Aunty said and left.

When she returned I took the blankets. Then I hugged Herman and whispered, "Big brother, you owe me a lot of stories."

Herman smiled a tired smile. We had a long way to go to full recovery. I arrived home to find my sisters sitting and eating. "We left food for you and Mother," said Mina.

"I have blankets. Herman is back. He is still weak and bandaged. Mother fell asleep while we were talking so she will stay there for the night."

I looked around and was surprised.

"The house looks a lot better. You've done a great job."

Anna started blushing and I didn't understand what I'd said that made her blush.

"Anna, what happened?" I asked curiously.

"Chaim was here. He helped us clean up. He brought a wagon from his sister's house and we cleared all the dirt." Mina answered me.

"Who is Chaim?" I asked.

"He is Anna's suitor. Before the war, they went to school together in Campulung Moldovenesc," Dora teased Anna.

"No, he is not. We were just friends."

"How did this Chaim get here?" I asked.

"His sister returned with her family. Her husband is still in the army. Chaim came to help her. He has been here for over a week. Since he knew where I lived, he checked if we'd returned. He found us today and was happy to help." Anna summed up.

I took my food, sat on a pile of blankets, and slowly chewed my first meal at home, after such a long time.

***

Loud knocks on the door woke me up. I opened my eyes and needed a few seconds to remember where I was on the floor, covered with a blanket. I was … home.

I went to the door. Outside stood a man in uniform, with a bag on his shoulder and a bearded face and suddenly I recognized him.

"Father!" I called out loud and jumped on him. My sisters came as they heard me yell.

"Children let me take this bag off my broken back," begged Father. We helped him put down the bag. We went into the house. The floor was clean, but the house was empty. I saw Father's eyes checking everything. He hugged us again and asked, "Where is your mother?"

"We arrived yesterday and she stayed at Uncle Nathan's house for the night," we answered together.

"Herman?"

"He too is with Uncle Nathan."

"Is there any news from Mttetttta?"

We shook our heads. There was a moment of silence. Dad looked around. "They robbed everything?" he dared to ask.

"The aunt managed to save a few things before the Russians and the farmers came," I reported.

"Wait for me here. I want to see the rest of the house." Father started walking and I ran after him.

"I want to do this alone, Feivel. Wait for me in the kitchen."

I didn't understand his reasons, but I respected his wishes and returned to my sisters in the kitchen. After a few minutes of tension, Father returned with a smile on his face. We looked at each other with concern. Had Father gone crazy after seeing the house half burned?

"I found it. They hadn't discovered where I hid it. I am so happy." Father's eyes were shining and we stood around him, trying to understand him. He saw the question in our eyes and explained, "On the day Herman and I were drafted I remembered I had a small package that my father had given me. I promised him to keep it as safe as I could. That is why I returned after Herman and I left. You must remember. I went to the room that the package was in and hid it under the roof in our bedroom. I believe that package kept the room safe."

With shaking hands Father opened his package and took out an old Torah. He kissed it and gave it to me. I brought it close to my mouth and kissed it. A chill ran up my back. I was kissing a hundred-year-old Torah that had saved half of our house from burning down. I believed that with all my heart. I gave the Torah back to Father carefully.

"What else is in there? I see a lot of pages," I asked.

"One day this package will pass on to you. Before he died, my father asked me to give it to my youngest son. I remember he told me that my son would know what to do with it. A day will come that this treasure will be yours." Father gently opened the package.

We couldn't take our eyes off it.

"Father, do you want me to go and bring Mother here?" I asked with hope.

"No, my son. We will all go to see Herman and we will return home with him and with Mother," Father decided. We picked up the blankets quickly and went to Nathan's house.

Mother saw us approaching, hurried toward Father, and fell into his arms half-unconscious. I hurried to get a glass of water. She recovered and we all crowded into Uncle Nathan's kitchen. The girls' meeting with Father and Herman was very emotional. Questions were asked, but no one was waiting for answers and new questions chased the old ones.

"Calm down," said Mother. "Herman is still weak and Father has just returned from a long drive. We are taking a few things and going home. It is time to get our lives back to normal."

"I will ask the neighbor for a wagon so you will be able to take your stuff home. I also collected bed covers and some clothes you'd left. You will find everything in the warehouse."

Father and I went there and the neighbor came too and was ready to help.

We put everything on the wagon. We decided that Herman should stay for a few more days at the uncle's house. Our parents got on the wagon and my sisters and I walked. We arrived shortly after them. The neighbor helped my parents take it all down in front of the house.

"Children, give me a few moments, children," I heard Mother say. "I need some time to get used to the way our house looks now. Wait here, I'll go in with your father. Don't look so worried. I promised you that no matter what happens, we will build everything back to the way it was. Didn't we say that?" Tears were coming down from her eyes, she took Father's hand and they opened the door together. They went into the place that was once was their beautiful and organized home.

We, the children, who were outside, seemed to be staying there too long. What was there to see? Two rooms with broken windows, a kitchen, and a ruined garden?

"Maybe something happened to Mother?" Anna started worrying.

"We are waiting here. We need to respect Mother's request," said Dora. We waited. A few more minutes passed. The door opened and Mother came out wearing her old apron.

"Look what I found, my old trusted apron. Children, get these things inside and we will start organizing the house."

This wonderful woman again surprised me and in this lean body. We have a tremendous vitality.

"We'll get wood and build beds for everyone. The roofs need to be fixed before the winter. Judging by the roof and gutters I saw on my way, I am about to have a lot of work to do. I will go to the place I worked in before the war. If more people have returned, we might be able to start working immediately and we will have money to live comfortably."

Father sounded optimistic and full of energy.

"Feivel, you can work with me and help support the family."

"Sure, Father, of course," I answered enthusiastically.

My aunt arrived with two loaves of bread and some letters.

"I forgot to give these to you; they arrived while you were away. I have brought bread and salt. Welcome home."

A good person doesn't change. I remembered Mother's words. 'Sometimes we need to give even if we don't have what to give from.'

The smell of fresh bread drove us all crazy and it went perfectly with the butter Father had bought from the farmers.

***

Father quickly found work. All the houses in the area were covered with tin and that was Father's speciality. People kept coming by and asking him to fix their roof.

Herman came home after two weeks. He was able to walk around without crutches and he wasn't wearing his head bandage. He had promised to tell us about what happened to him in the war and in the hospital in Vienna. But every time he tried to he would get tired and ask to postpone the story for another day.

Mother told Father about what she did in Moravia and decided that, with the help of the girls, she would cook bread, rolls, and cakes here too, and sell them.

It was Friday, the first Friday at home. Father built a table for us. Mother found a white sheet and spread over it. It's the first day since we came back that there's a smell of food at home. Up until that day, we'd only had bread and potatoes.

Wooden boxes were covered with pieces of cloth and served as chairs. We sat at the table and had a proper Kabbalat Shabbat, with Shabbat candles and challahs—as before, as always.

We arrived at the Sabbath songs. Father and Herman began singing and my sisters and I joined them. The singing began hesitantly and grew louder and louder. What a strange world: between planks and crates, in a half-burned house, we sit and sing songs, singing hymns for the holy Sabbath.

***

Mother got up and brought several envelopes to the table.

"Letters that arrived while we were away," Mother explained. I wondered if they still remembered our ritual for reading letters. Father had already opened the envelopes so that they would be ready to be read on Friday night. He gave one of them to Mother.

"A letter from Metta," Mother rejoiced. "Let's see what my girl is writing."

"Our girl," Father corrected her. "And read it slowly."

"My dear family, Salo and I worry about you a lot. We hear of terrible things that happen in your area. People who arrived here told us horror stories about the things the Russians have done. We were lucky. Salo's family live outside of Chernovitz in a secluded place and soldiers didn't get here.

A few months ago our son was born. We named him Freddie. He is a cute and chubby boy, very alert; I wish you could see him. We plan to return to Chernovitz soon. I promise to write as soon as we get there. Once the trains start operating you could send my sisters here. I miss them. I could get them into school here.

Write to me soon about each and every one of you. We are waiting for that letter.

Love you, Metta, Salo, and little Freddie."

In an excited voice, Mother turned to father and said, "Moshe, we have our first grandchild, and it turns out that if you stay alive, there is more hope for joy."

"We survived and we came to this time," said Father, and

I took part in the general joy.

"Hey, I'm an uncle!"

***

Herman was very quiet and alone. He would answer of our questions with short sentences and still refused to tell us what had happened to him during the war. Father decided to get him out of the house by claiming that he needed his help fixing roofs. After a few days of work, Herman said he wasn't feeling well and returned to stay at home alone and hidden in his corner.

One evening we all huddled in the kitchen. Mother made supper and helped set the table. Only Anna had not come yet. I needed those common evenings. The long period that we'd lived without Father and Herman made me anxious that I would lose them again. Every evening like this I would rediscover them again and my heart would overflow with joy.

Anna burst in, red-cheeked, with a broad smile on her face. "Anna, what happened?" I asked curiously.

"Someone is waiting outside, he is ashamed to enter."

"It must be Chaim." I spoiled the surprise. "Mother, he is a nice man and he helped us clear the house on the day we arrived from Moravia."

"Anna, let the boy in. Where are your manners?" said Mother. Anna opened the door and called Chaim.

"Hello, I'm Chaim Grosman," he introduced himself.

"Where are you from, Chaim?" Father was interested.

"My family lives in Chernovitz, and that is where I was born. We left during the war, and returned a few months ago. I came here to help my sister settle in. She lives in Frasin not far from here. In a few days, I am going back home to finish my studies at the university."

"The girls told me that you know Anna from the school in

Campulung," Mother said. Anna went over to her and whispered a secret to her.

"He needs to talk to Father about that." Mother reacted.

"You need to talk to me in private, Chaim?" Father asked.

"Yes, if possible," Chaim answered shyly.

They went to the other room and talked for a long time.

"What are these secrets, Anna?" Mina asked. "Are you keeping something from us?"

"We want to get married and go to Chernovitz together."

Mother wiped her hands on her apron, sat on one of the boxes, and sighed.

"The nest is emptying, and with it the soul. The truth is I know that a time comes when the young people go and the old ones are left alone. In my time we would stay in the same village, the whole family, and the connection would not be broken. Times have changed and for me, it's hard and sad."

My old fear that we were moving apart returned. At that moment I decided that I wouldn't ever leave my parents, no matter what.

***

Father and Chaim returned, smiling.

"Mother, what do you think about our Anna getting married soon?" He looked pleased. Mother didn't answer. Chaim looked embarrassed.

"It is late and I have to go. Goodnight," he said and left. Anna wanted to go after him but Mother grabbed her arm and stopped her.

"Anna, you hadn't told me anything. You make plans and don't share them with your family. What's happened to us all of a sudden? What has changed in our feelings and in the relationship between us?" She sounded offended.

Anna hugged her and said, "It all happened so fast that I had no time to realize it myself. When Chaim told me he was leaving and that he wanted me to come with him I told him that I was afraid to tell all of you. He volunteered to come and talk with you. I never meant to hurt anyone. I would really like to get married and go. I have nothing to do here. Even if I wasn't getting married, I would still want to go to my sister in Chernovitz."

"It would be best if she leaves married, wouldn't it?" Father tried to help Anna.

Mother raised her tired eyes, looked at each of us, and nodded.

The wedding was modest. Our family, Uncle Nathan, and a few neighbors. After two hours I had another married sister. Mazal Tov.

***

Father tried again to convince Herman to help him, but Herman kept complaining about different pains and stayed home. I asked Mother for permission to go in his place. I might be of use.

"We need wood for the oven. We do not have any wood for the oven. You'll come out of the village, into the cut-off trees, and maybe you'll find dry twigs at least," Mother said. I took an ax and a rope with me and left.

I found myself in the pine forest. I walked to my familiar clearing. It was autumn and a cold breeze started up. I stood in the middle of the clearing and waited to hear the birds. The wind was blowing angrily. I had waited and dreamed of that moment for three years. In Maren, during difficult and sad moments, I would close my eyes and hear the birds and the wind. They would make such a beautiful melody together. Where had they gone?

Angry and disappointed, I started collecting wood. I walked among the trees. I didn't care that I was getting scratches. I made a pile, tied it up, and headed home.

Suddenly, my ears caught a familiar sound. I stopped and listened. That was the voice of my favorite bird, the one who could whistle many different sounds. I stood, fascinated. I felt like throwing the bundle of twigs, but I stopped myself and put it down slowly, careful not to make a noise or to scare the bird away. I stood listening to the wonderful melody. The sounds played and my heart echoed. I felt tension in my vocal cords and started whistling, just like her, and the bird answered and increased its chirping. What wonder was happening here?

I returned to reality. I quietly lifted the pieces of wood and hurried home. I whistled all the way there. I paid no attention to people I passed on the street. I was deep in my world of sound all the way home. I placed the wood in the backyard, entered the house, and kept whistling. Mother stopped working and looked at me.

"Feivel, you don't whistle inside a Jewish house!" Only then did I realize I was inside the house. I immediately stopped whistling. I was embarrassed.

"What was that, my son?" Mother asked.

"mother, it's not a whistle, it's the wonderful tones I learned from the bird. You know, mother, the bird answered me and we whistled together a wonderful tune."

My mother's eyes looked at me and I wondered if she understood what I were talking about.

"Like the sound of a violin?" Mother surprised me. "Like in the forest?"

I hugged her warmly.

***

I went in to check on Herman. He was lying in bed, staring at the ceiling.

"Herman, tell me how you were injured in the war," I asked. He sat up. I sat beside him and I was eager to hear the story.

"As we arrived, we got uniforms and weapons and they taught us how to use them. I saw Father almost every day. We took part in four fierce battles against the Russians. Once, one group had been cut off. Father had moved with them in another direction and I had not seen him since then. At first, I was worried and then had no time to do so. We had other companies. Our aim was to cross the Prut River and hit the Russians who sat across it. The battle was hard and cruel, there were many casualties around me. I saw endless scenes of horror, I knew that I had to fight and survive. If I make it out of this war alive, I told myself, this country won't see me again. That promise gave me strength."

I couldn't move. I waited quietly for him to recover and continue to tell the rest of the story. It was hard for him to talk.

"At some point, I felt a strong hit and I flew back. I can't remember any more. When I regained consciousness, I was told that a round of bullets hits and I flew a few meters back. The soldiers kept going and the wounded were cleared later. I was hurt badly so after the initial treatment I was transferred to the hospital in Vienna."

Another break. I silently begged that he wouldn't stop.

"I was told, that for months I went from consciousness to unconsciousness. I can't remember that time. One day I opened my eyes and saw an angel in the shape of a woman. Ocean blue eyes and bright hair. The angel wore a white robe and smiled at me. I was conscious enough to think I was in heaven and I thought, 'If this is how an angel looks like then heaven isn't a bad choice.' The angel looked at me and started talking. I couldn't hear a word. I just saw lips moving, talking and smiling. It was too big of an effort for me so I passed out again."

I was very nervous. Herman was tired, and I didn't speak because I worried that I would confuse him.

"After a while I regained consciousness. This time someone supported me into a sitting position. I looked around and saw I was in a hospital and that I was in a room with many other men. I looked for my angel but with no luck. I didn't know whether I'd dreamed it or I'd visited paradise I did not calm down and did not give up. Food was given and someone helped me eat. I couldn't chew so I drank the soup and went back to sleep.

The next morning I heard a gentle voice speak to me, 'Today we will try to get up and wash.' I opened my eyes and did not believe the wonderful sight before me: the angel. Just as I'd remembered; a blonde with blue eyes and a divine smile. 'It's not an angel, it's a nurse,' I explained to myself.

'What is wrong with me that you can't take your eyes off me?' I heard her voice saying.

'Are you my angel?' I asked and immediately felt that I had said something foolish.

'I've been here for three months now. Every day I took care of you. You were the worst casualty who came to the hospital, and I decided I would do anything to help you live.' I felt as though she had tied her fate to mine and together we fought for my life.

'You see? It was worthwhile. You see? We succeeded?' she said.

I asked her for her name and she told me that everyone called her Countess because she came from a family of nobles. From that morning she came every day and took care of all my needs. She wrote me a letter for Father, and brought me reading material, and when she saw that it was hard for me to read, she would sit next to me and read to me aloud. She took care of my body and made me happy, and I owe her my life."

Herman paused and still I did not move. Maybe there's something else he wants to tell me. I had no desire to go. I wanted to hear more about the Countess, but his eyes closed and he fell asleep.

***

Father forgot to take his lunch bag to work and mother sent me to bring it to him. I was happy to go to his workplace and had hoped that he would ask for my help. I took a different road that time so that I wouldn't get bored. I mostly didn't want to see people who would ask me questions I wouldn't want to answer.

Suddenly my ears caught the sound of a violin! It was impossible. I'd never heard a violin playing in the village. I was drawn magically to the house from which the notes came. The window was open and I was getting closer to the sounds, almost touching them. I sat on the ground under the window, closed my eyes and floated with the music. I heard happy sounds and sad sounds. With joy, I smiled and with the sadness, I almost cried. Suddenly the music stopped. I did not move, I waited for it to continue.

"Boy, what are you doing here?" someone shouted from the window. I raised my eyes and I saw a shaking beard and heard a grumpy voice.
I jumped up and started running.
"I know who you are, Boy. I'll talk to your mother." The man called after me as I was near the corner of our house.

I got to our door and breathing heavily, I realized I still had Father's lunch in my hand. I turned around and took a different road. Father was happy to see me, but couldn't stop asking what happened to me and why I was upset. I didn't share my secret with him. That man's promise to come and talk with my mother still bothered me.

***

Late at night knocks on our door woke up everybody in the house. The knocks were loud and frightening. I thought it must be the man with the beard. I let the others answer the door.

Outside stood my uncle Berl. The one who'd disappeared the day Father and Herman were drafted and hadn't been seen since. No one talked about it, but everyone believed he wasn't among the living.

"Let me in," he called. "I came at this hour because I didn't want any of the neighbors to see me. I came to say goodbye. I am starting on a journey to Poland tonight. I don't want to stay here. If they start looking for runaways I will be among the first to be arrested." He looked awful. His beard was gray and messy, his hair was long and his clothes were dirty. Mother quickly went to get him something to eat as he kept talking.

"During the war, I lived like an animal. I wandered in the woods and ran from populated areas. I lived in terrible fear. I was afraid of my own shadow. The obligation to go to the army must have driven me mad. I can't say now whether I made the right choice."

He looked miserable and confused.

"Why Poland?" Father asked.

"It is the best place to live. They told me that people do not ask questions there."

We didn't want to make it more difficult for him so we stopped asking questions. He sat down, ate, and asked Mother to pack food for him for the road.

"Tell Nathan I was here," he asked. We promised to do that. The relationship between the three brothers had always been tight. It was surprising that in difficult times he chose not to ask for his brothers' help or at least tell them what he was doing. He hugged

Father, said goodbye to all of us and left. We knew that was the last time we'd see that uncle.

Anna, Mina, and Dora were getting ready to go to Chernovitz. They were cheerful and happy and were looking forward to life in the big city. Metta knew they were coming and was looking forward to seeing them.

Another goodbye, more tears, and they were gone. Father escorted them. Mother and I stayed by the door and watched them leave.

"When will I see my girls again?" Mother painfully asked. I wished I had an answer to give her.

***

Since they'd left, it had become very quiet at home, and mother had changed too. She was not the same as before and that was worrying. She walked slowly and felt the need to rest often. From time to time she held her left side and complains of heartache. She eats very little and explains that she has no appetite.

A knock at the door made me think. I jumped up in alarm. That must be the man with the beard. I was sure he was coming. I sweat with fear. I would not forgive myself if Mother gets mad.

"Feivel, see who is at the door," Mother asked. I feared to open it because he might catch me and hit me. I had no choice. I opened the door and ran inside.

"Are you alright, Feivel?" asked the man from the post office. "Did I frighten you?" He had a letter in his hand.

"No, I wasn't frightened at all," I said. In fact, I was relieved to see him.

"The stamps are from America," he said. "Please try not to rip them when you open the letter, I would really like to have them. That is why I came here to deliver it. He placed the letter on the table, repeated his request and left.

"Who is it from?" Mother asked. I turned it over and on the back was the name Jacob Wininger.

"Do you know anyone called Jacob Wininger?" I asked.

"We will need to ask Father. It doesn't sound familiar to me." In any case, I knew that letters only only got opened when Father was at home.

Father and Herman arrived. They both looked happier than usual. In fact, Herman's mood has generally been better. He went to work every day and Father was pleased with his help.

"Uncle Nathan told us some nice jokes about Russian soldiers," Herman explained. Suddenly he saw the letter on the table and all he could say was, 'America.'

Father sat up and took the letter beside him. Mother dried her hands, took off her apron, and sat down too.

"Moshe, do you know, someone named Jacob Wininger?" Mother tried to find out.

Father took the letter out of the envelope. A few green bills fell out of it. He stared at them in surprise.

"Dollars," Herman said, bent down and picked up the money. He spread them on the table and couldn't take his eyes off them.

We looked at the unfamiliar notes. We couldn't imagine where we'd got that treasure from. Mother recovered from the shock first.

"Moshe, are you going to hold that letter in the air for long?"

Father handed her the letter but his eyes remained on the money.

"Herman, how much money are those green notes?"

Shocked, Herman paid no attention to the question.

"It is time to read the letter." Mother sat up, placed the papers in front of her eyes and started reading.

"To my cousin Moshe and his family, hello,

My name is Jacob Wininger and I'm the son of Yosel, may he rest in peace. I have wanted to write to you for a long time to hear what happened to you during the war. Life here isn't always easy, so I didn't have the time until now. You must wonder how I received your address. My cousin Yehuda, son of Menashe, writes to me often and reports about all the family. I am very grateful to him for his actions and I am happy he sent me your address.

My father had a little small wares store and I, his eldest son, stayed with him and we worked together. In the years before he died, Father spent very little time in the store and I did all the work. Today I run the business alone.

Instead of asking how you all are, I want to tell you my troubles. I also have happy things to tell. Two of my sons study at the university and my two girls go to a Jewish school. They study general subjects and also religion. This school is a new concept and many Jewish families are trying it now. My wife is still raising our youngest daughter. I am very proud of my family.

I am sending some dollars for you to buy things you need. It isn't much but it is all I have. If you ever need anything else I will be happy to help. My family sends you a blessing.

I wish you all the best and may God watch over all of you. I would love to hear from you.

Yours sincerely, Jacob Wininger.

"That long letter made me tired," said Mother.

"I could help him with the business," said Herman with dreamy eyes.

"What business are you talking about?" Father jumped up. Mother lowered her eyes.

"Mother, I know what you must be thinking. Another child is leaving you. I understand your pain but I have nothing to do in this country. I went to fight for people I don't even know. I was injured and spent months in a hospital with no hope for my life. I vowed that if I survive that war I'll jump on any chance to leave this country."

He breathed heavily and sat down to rest. Mother lowered her eyes. I went up to her and held her hand. Her hand was ice cold, lifeless.

I looked for a way out of the heavy distress. "What can we buy with the green money?" I asked.

Mother turned to look at me. "What would you like, Feivel?"

"I do not lack anything. It's worth saving money for difficult periods." I remembered the days of famine during the war, and I did not want them to return. Father took the dollars and promised to hide them in a secret and well-guarded place. Mother put on her apron and turned to the oven, distracting herself by baking.

Herman went to his room and I followed him.

"What are you planning, big brother?" I asked worriedly.

"Do you remember telling you about the Countess, the angel in white? I often dream about her. She gave me my life as a gift and her memory does not allow me to waste them in this wretched country," he replied excitedly. "I feel as though I have been ordered to enrich my world and rebuild it." His eyes glowed with enthusiasm, and he sounded full of hope. "You will see. I will succeed there and bring all of you to me."

From that day on, Herman wandered around the house like a lion in a cage, lost in thought and planning. Meanwhile, he continued to work with Father. I did not get to see him again happy and enthusiastic.

***

For the time being, I forgot about the man with the beard.

One day Mother asked me to help her. She made the dough for rolls and bread and I developed a quick method for rolling rolls. We both worked quietly when there was a knock at the door. I shook the flour off my hands and went to open the door. At the door stood the man with the beard, a large parcel was wrapped in his hand. He had a severe look on his face that made my heart sink.

"Hello, Mrs. Wininger." He turned to Mother. He was so upset with me that he didn't even say hello to me. I needed to find a reason to get out of there before he started telling Mother what I'd done.

"Do you want me to go and get more flour?" I asked.

"We don't need more flour. We have enough here," she said.

"There must be something important your son needs to do," hinted the man. Mother understood and sent me to Uncle Nathan's with four fresh rolls.

I grabbed the rolls and ran out. I decided to stay behind the door to listen to what was going on inside. I figured that at least I wouldn't be there while he tells her what her son did.

***

"Mrs. Wininger," the man started his story. "A few weeks ago I took out my violin, which I hadn't played in a long time, and started playing." He stopped for a moment, took a deep breath, and continued, "My youngest son was very talented and I started teaching him how to play the violin at the age of four. His violin was a bit too big for him, but it was the smallest one I could find. When he played the heavens cried and laughed. He would make sounds that even I, an old and experienced violinist, couldn't believe was possible. Well…" he stopped talking, took a piece of fabric from his pocket and wiped his eyes. His heavy breaths were heard over the silence in the room.

"When the war began we ran. We were chased away from place to place. My child got ill and I couldn't find a warm place to stay in. We definitely couldn't afford medication. You look so pale, Mrs. Wininger. Maybe you should sit down?" He helped her sit.

"This is hard for me to talk about. I lost my boy in the war. I returned home and couldn't even look at our two violins together. I wrapped the two of them in a blanket and stored them deep in a case.

On the day I want to tell you about, I was missing my boy and felt that only by playing the violin I could express my longings. I took the two violins out of the case. I lovingly wiped the small one with the same lint my boy used, and then placed it on the table. I took my violin and started playing. The music went from my heart to my hand and I couldn't stop. I felt that my boy was smiling at me happily and my heart was beating very fast.

Suddenly I felt like I wasn't alone. I knew the house was empty and would be for a few hours. With great effort I stopped playing and went to the open window and what did I see? A boy sitting under the window, listening to every sound. I saw his face and couldn't believe it. They had the same heavenly joy I would see on my son's face whenever he would play. The boy saw me looking at him and ran away. Do you know who he was, Mrs. Wininger? Your son, Feivel. Do you think he would want to play the violin?" In his voice were hope and desire combined.

Mother sat quietly, trying to absorb the sad story she had just heard.

The man continued, "Don't worry about payment, we will work it out. Most important for me is to be able to teach and in return…" then he saw the bread and rolls on the table. "And in return, you'll give me some fresh rolls and maybe a meal from time to time."

I could hear the happiness in my mother's voice. I was sure that she was smiling at him.

"If you offer Feivel all that is beautiful and expensive in the world or offer him to play violin I have no doubt what he would choose."

The man said, "I have the small violin here with me."

It was long enough to get back from the uncle's house. I opened the door. At a glance, my eyes caught the violin on the table. I did not see the man or Mother. I saw a beautiful shiny violin lying quietly on the table.

"A violin." I could barely breathe. Then I said, "And a bow too." Only then did I look up to see a kind smile and the look of a man that was happy for me. They were the eyes of the bearded man.

"Your mother told me you wanted to learn to play the violin. My name is Idle and I will be your teacher." He reached his hand out to me. I stood there, not knowing what to do. I took his hand in such a clumsy way that I slipped and fell to the ground. I sat on the floor and looked up at my mother and at Mr. Idel with great affection.

I had a violin and I was about to make sounds that would make a bird proud. I stayed on the floor and feared to get up. I feared that the magic would pass and I would find that it was only one of my dreams.

***

I started taking violin lessons. I practiced so much that my arms and my neck were sore. There was something magnetic in that instrument that made me play on it whenever I could. I gave up sleep and time with friends. All I wanted was to play my violin. Mother would send my teacher fresh rolls and at times some money, for which he was very grateful.

***

Herman took the initiative and wrote to his cousin Jacob in America, in New York, Brooklyn. In the letter, he asked for legal entrance and a boat ticket. Herman read his letter to us. We sat around the kitchen table that had gotten so empty of people and listened to him quietly.

"Next, I wrote, without a legal entrance I wouldn't be allowed into the country. As for the price of the boat ticket, I promise to work for it, for as long as it takes, and pay you back. I don't want to burden you by coming. I would be happy to work with you there but if you don't need me, I will find a different job. Thank you for your help and blessing for your family. Herman Wininger.

That is the whole letter. Wish me luck," asked Herman and looked at Mother.

"You know, son," Mother started talking. "A mother can wish her son only luck."

***

We were doing well financially. Father had work and the addition of the money Mother was making allowed us to buy wood and make new furniture. On Sundays, Father and I made closets and beds for everyone. We replaced the boxes in the kitchen with stools that Father designed. The kitchen table was reduced in size, and received a new wooden top.

Mother wanted a business of her own. Selling bread and rolls from our kitchen brought different people into our home, sometimes at uncomfortable times. The old man who was selling alcohol in our village became ill so Mother decided to buy the liquor license. That way she would still sell bread but also serve drinks and would have her own business. The problem was the location of that business.

My parents decided to rebuild the walls that had been burned down. The little money we'd saved was enough to fix the walls. A window from one of the rooms was changed into a door. In this way, Mother had a small place from which she could exit the house, but customers would get in from the street. It was a kind of pub. We had long tables and benches, a counter with bottles and baked goods and that was the business. Mother and Herman worked during the day and Father helped in the evenings.

I didn't have time. I started working hard at school and I kept playing the violin so my days were full. I practiced the violin more and more and, when I would get tired of the melodies that my teacher made me play, I started making up new melodies. At those moments I was separated from the world and taken from rhythm to rhythm. When I would open my eyes, the place that I was at would surprise me.

One day, a letter came from America. Herman was nervous and excited to hear the answer from Jacob. Father opened the letter and handed it to Mother.

"Herman will read to us this time," she said.

Herman grabbed the letter and read eagerly, "To my cousin and his family, hello. I have received Herman's letter and request. I am doing everything possible to get all the legal paperwork we need. This will take some time, but I decided to write to you so that you would know I am doing all I can. My wife and children send their hellos and best wishes. We are happy to help Herman and hope he will find his place here," signed Jacob Wininger.

Herman looked a bit disappointed. "That's the whole letter," he announced. He'd been expecting a visa and a ticket already. We did not know whether to be happy about his upcoming trip or not. Time would tell.

***

A silent movie theater opened in the village. We would get movies every once in a while and the people of the village would go and watch the new wonder.

My violin teacher told me he was playing during the screening of a movie. He explained that the people on screen would move, but there was no sound, so they would invite someone to play and keep the audience from falling asleep. My teacher tried to be funny and I believed him. One day he told me that the owners of the cinema had agreed to have two violinists and that he wanted me to play with him.

"You will be the first violin and I'll accompany you," he explained to me. "You will be at the front of the stage and I will be at the side. You'll find a chair there; sit on it quickly so you won't block the screen. You can play any melody you like."

I ran home happily and told Mother that I had found a job at the cinema. It took me a while to explain the cinema to Mother and to explain what my job would be.

"My teacher said it will be a good experience for me. I can play in front of people and earn money." I was sure Mother would be happy but I was wrong.

"You need to study and have a profession. You need to go to school. The violin is for the soul not to make money. I wanted you to play so that you would have something that you love, to which you could go back to when you are happy, or, God forbid, sad. Feivel, school is first."

"Mom, I'll only play in the evening once or twice a week and

I'll continue to study, and I'll make sure that it won't bother my studies at all."

The evening of my first performance arrived. I wore my best clothes. They were a little small and tight but didn't care. I took my violin and hurried to the cinema.

"You go on after the lights go off," my teacher explained.

I waited impatiently for the lights to go out and then I went on the stage. The screen was lit and I could clearly see the chair. I sat on it with my face to the screen and played happily.

When the movie was over, the lights were turned on and the people in the crowd applauded me. Very naturally I stood up and took a bow. Then I heard laughter and realized I had been sitting with my back to the audience. I'd bowed to the screen and the audience saw the less beautiful side of me. I hugged my violin and went off the stage. It was the first and last time I was with my back to the crowd.

The money that I made I gave to Mother. I kept studying and playing my music. At night, before going to sleep, I would put the violin in Mother's room. I don't know why.

The distance between the villages in the area was small and on Sundays, I would go from village to village with some friends. I met two musicians; one played the bass and the other played the trombone. We decided to form a band and play together. We needed a place to practice. After a lot of begging, Mother allowed me to use the warehouse in our yard. We gathered a group of friends, cleaned up the place and used it to rehearse.

Herman was still waiting for his papers and tickets. He was anxious and impatient. He was helping Mother without really wanting to.

My Bar Mitzvah was approaching. I studied my Haftarah with

the rabbi of the community, and at home, preparations began for the ceremony.

We wrote to my sisters and invited them with their children to the celebration, and we hoped for a happy family reunion. The answer was not long in coming.

"We wish our little brother happiness and health … The trip to you is long and expensive, and we will have to postpone it for a better period..."

I found it hard to accept the disappointment. I missed them. I wanted to be the reason for a full family reunion for all of us, which for so long had not happened.

One Friday evening, Mother started talking about my upcoming Bar Mitzvah and asked Father to talk to the rabbi about preparing me for it.

My Bar Mitzvah was held in the small synagogue in our village. We invited very few people. Uncle Nathan and his wife, a few neighbors, and Herman. There were also the regulars from the synagogue.

Father stood by my side the whole time. When it was time for me to read, he walked me to the the stage on which was the Torah. The rabbi showed me where to read from. I started reading in a faint and weak voice. With a small push from Father, I raised my voice. It was a special feeling for me. I didn't fear the people who were around me, I didn't feel them and I read as loud as I could so that Mother and the women would hear clearly too.

I was congratulated from every direction. Father and Herman stood next to me and praised my reading. Mother waited for me outside the synagogue. Her eyes were red from crying and she was looking at me with love. I hoped her tears were happy ones. My aunt and the neighbors also showered me with love. I was grown up and I needed to remember that every day.

***

The letter Herman was waiting for arrived a few months later. A short letter, legal papers, boat ticket, and some money. It was all that was needed for my big brother to leave us and go to America.

One night my sleep wandered. I heard a little noise in the kitchen. My brother sat at the big table and sipped some tea.. I went up to him.

"It's hard for me, Feivel," he said. "It's so hard to say goodbye to all the family, but you know, Brother, maybe there's a confirmation of my decision from an unknown source." He smiled to me, and I saw him sailing far away.

Herman arranged his things, said goodbye to Uncle Nathan and his wife, and after a whole night of sitting and talking, it was the moment to say goodbye.

Mother spoke very little and kept repeating the sentence, "Take care of yourself and do not forget to write." She looked very pale, and when we went out to accompany Herman, she leaned against my father.

Herman left us on the threshold, facing a new and unknown world.

Despite the cold wind, we could not and would not go into the house. We stood and waited. Maybe it would turn out that it was all just a hallucination and we'd find out that we were not the only three of us left at home from our whole big family.

***

Driving distance from our village was a bigger town called Campulung Moldovenesc. In that town was a school of commerce and children from all the villages in the area went there. Before the war, my sisters had studied in that town. The families there allowed students to sleep in their homes in return for a small fee. The children then didn't need to return daily to their village.

Mother noticed that I was paying too much attention to the violin so she decided to send me to the commerce school. I packed up some things and the agreement was that I would stay in Campulung during the four days of school and return home every weekend. I packed some clothes, some books, and my violin and headed for Campulung Moldovenesc.

The family that rented a room to my friends and me had a beautiful daughter called Rikka. She was older than me and I sensed she was interested in me. We were four boys in one room. Two of the other boys played string instruments. After school, if we went to school, we would play together.

Rikka would knock on the door and ask if she could sit with us and listen. She spent most of her time with us. Her parents worked long hours and arrived home late at night. Our days were spent playing music and drinking a little. We had fun and it was hard for me to return home on weekends.

One weekend I decided to stay in the room. I asked one of my friends who lived in my village to tell my parents. Rikka was happy I'd stayed and we spent a great few days together. I felt guilty for not studying as I should and that it was costing my parents money. My parents weren't happy about the way I felt about school and about my view of life. In my mother's opinion being a musician was disrespectful for a boy who in her mind was smart enough to study and get a profession. The nightlife of being a musician and being near people that drink and party bothered Mother very much.

Music was a principal part of my life. I barely spent enough time in school. All I wanted was to play music. I played at parties and weddings and made money to buy more instruments. I replaced the small violin with a full-sized one, and I also bought a viola and a cello.

During the summer, I went on a long trip with some friends. We traveled on bicycles for four weeks and carried our instruments on our backs. Those were crazy and carefree days. We played concerts on the road and made money to continue traveling.

Everywhere we played, there were girls who were interested in us. From time to time some of them would join us and we believed life was a big party. We didn't think about our parents or about our commitments. The vacation was almost over and we all had to return home. I said goodbye to my friends and to the girls and headed home.

Suddenly a wagon filled with young people showed up behind me. They were singing and shouting very loudly. They were on their way to a wine celebration. They noticed my violin and offered me to go with them and play. I explained that I had to get home, because my family was waiting for me, and they would be worried if I didn't arrive on time.

"You should want to come with us," said one of them. I understood that if I didn't want broken bones I should go with them. I ended up in their party and after an hour they were all drunk and some of them scared me. They placed me on a pile of hay and made me play. Every once in a while one of them would come and give me something alcoholic to drink. A shadow clouded my mind.

I remembered that my bicycle and clothes were left on the wagon. I needed to find a way to get to my things and run away from that strange party. My bicycle looked to me like a last resort. I kept playing the same thing over and over, but no one noticed. They were singing, dancing, and drinking. I felt disgusted. I remembered the parties that my friends and I had and I hoped we hadn't looked like that. In fact, I wasn't sure. Drinking turns people into creatures without control and misery.

I had to concentrate on one thing now: how to get out of here as quickly as possible.

Up until that point, I hadn't noticed that there was a cute girl standing near me and looking at me admiringly. I smiled at her and then thought of something. I stopped playing and started talking to her. Everyone was so loud that they didn't even notice that I'd stopped playing. I suggested to her to go outside because we wouldn't be able to talk in that noise. I placed my hand on her hips and complimented her beauty. I didn't need to do anything else. She pulled me out and jumped on me with hugs and kisses. My eyes were looking for the wagon.

"I'll go back to get my violin and then I'll play something nice for you in the moonlight." She almost fell into my arms with joy. We ran inside and took the violin. No one paid attention because I was with one of them. I played a quiet tune and then asked, "Maybe you should get us a bottle of something while I finish tuning the violin and we'll have a private party." I hadn't even finished speaking and she was on her way.

I had a few moments to run to the wagon, take my things off it and tie the violin to my back. Then, without looking back, I started riding my bicycle at a crazy speed. I didn't care that I came close to falling twice.

I arrived home early in the morning. I was dirty, sweating, and tired. The house was dark. I went to the back, hoping the door was open and then I saw a little light from the kitchen. I tried to open the door, it wasn't locked. I went in and walked to the kitchen. Mother was sitting there. She knew I was supposed to return that day so she'd stayed up to wait for me. I stood there with eyes on the floor. I didn't know what to say. She got up, took another look at me, and said, "We will talk in the morning. I'm tired." She went to her room.

I don't know how long I stayed there. I felt ashamed. In fact, I was flooded with shame for everything, for the past month, for my reckless decisions, for wasting time at school and mostly for not thinking about my worried mother. All I could think of during that time was myself; where would I play tomorrow, and which of the girls to seduce? I quietly placed the violin on the table. That was the only time in my life I was mad at it too, for dragging me into such a different world.

I lay down on the little bed in the kitchen while the first light was showing through the window. I was dirty in body and mind. Tiredness won and I fell asleep.

The next morning I woke up at noon. I hurried to wash up and change my clothes. No one was home. I didn't know how to show my face after the long time I'd spent away from home. I didn't know how to justify my behavior. I hurried to Mother's shop to help. She wasn't there and the door to the street was closed. I ran to Mother's room. The door was open, the room was dark and mother was in bed, asleep. I didn't want to wake her up. I was terrified.

When I turned to leave, she called out to me, "Feivel you can come in, I'm just resting." I came in and sat on her bed. "Business has been slow so I only open in the afternoon and stay open until the last of the drunks leave." She spoke very quietly. I could barely hear her voice.

"Mother, I am sorry for being late last night and for prolonging my vacation." I started explaining. She held out her arms and hugged me. I wanted her to be angry with me; I wanted her to tell me what a bad son I was. I wanted a chance to apologize, explain, and promise. Mother didn't say anything about it.

"A girl came by to find out about violin lessons," she said. "She will probably come again to speak with you." She went back to regular life as if nothing had happened.

"I would love to teach violin." I didn't want to tell her about the band I'd started with my friends in Campulung. There was a guitar, a saxophone, and a violin in the band. That band was my pride and joy. I wanted to tell Mother very much, but I knew it would only hurt her more. A 'musician' wasn't what she thought I would end up being. I preferred to stay quiet.

***

My friends and I planned to return two weeks before the beginning of school and tour the resort towns looking for places to perform. I had ten more days to spend at home. I had one more difficult year in order to finish school, I wasn't sure how I would do it.

I promised Mother that I'd help her in the evenings and night and that I'd spend my days studying. I promised to only play music in the time I had left.

It was noon, Mother was making rolls for the evening, and I went into the kitchen with the violin.

"Mother, I would really like to play for you."

"I would love to listen to you play," she answered and kept working. It had been months since the last time I'd played at home. I stood in a comfortable position, and started playing. A strange thing happened to me. The melodies that came out were beautiful Jewish tunes I had heard on different occasions, at weddings or gatherings. I had never played those melodies in front of an audience. People usually wanted to hear music that they could dance to. I knew most of Strauss's waltzes; I knew tango beats and folk songs.

I played in front of Mother, and was surprised by the sounds coming out from my violin. The violin seemed to sing in Yiddish, singing songs that mother had sung to me when I was a little boy. Yiddish songs that were more than music; they were the soul of the Jewish people.

I followed them up with chapters of singing I had heard in the synagogue and with songs we sang on Friday nights. I couldn't stop playing. My fingers were shaking on the strings. I was sweating despite the cool air and my bow was moving up and down. The violin had never sounded better. I had a magical violin. That is what was going through my mind. Melody after melody. My eyes were closed. I was floating around and the sound was dancing around me. Music notes were smiling at me. Smiling notes? I could see them, but couldn't stop playing. Between sounds, I could hear a crying sound. I didn't open my eyes. Was the violin crying? My head was spinning and I swayed a little. I felt I was about to fall. Only then did I open my eyes.

Mother was sitting in front of me with her eyes looking deeply at me, smiling and crying at the same time. I gently placed the violin on the table. Mother walked up to me and hugged me with both arms. She pulled me close and kissed my forehead. Moments like those burn like fire in a person's heart. They never return, but they are never forgotten.

"You know I was playing just for you." I tried to explain how I felt.

"Yes, I know. I've never heard such wonderful music before. Never."

***

The girl who wanted violin lessons returned. She was about my age and very attractive. I liked her immediately. I promised to teach her during the breaks I had from school. She wanted to start right away so we agreed that she would come the next day for the first lesson.

We taught each other many things; one of them was playing the violin, which was my specialty. We spent every day together. I promised not to charge her for the lessons but she explained that it wouldn't look good to her parents. She said that if I didn't want money they could send chickens, flour, and other things that were valuable to us. Mother was happy with that arrangement. I didn't care about it.

I had a lot of fun with my new friend. We were young, beautiful, and talented. We laughed a lot together, and we forgot all the troubles of the world around us. It was a shame to leave, but my friends from the orchestra had already arranged performances for us. I parted from the girl and promised to return whenever possible. I managed to teach her to play some melodies and prove to her parents that I was indeed a worthy teacher. The ten days in the house passed much faster and much more pleasant than I'd expected.

I had a great vacation.

**

My friends were waiting for me. They'd arrived days before me and the violin had been missing in their rehearsals. Our mood was high and the music flowed in our veins.

We organized and headed for the town Vatra Dornei. It was a beautiful spa in Bukovina. The man in charge of entertainment hired us. He explained that the people who came there were wealthy and came to have fun. He said that if they will like us, we could play there for the rest of the season, which meant for two weeks. He also said that happy clients leave big tips. We received a big room for us to sleep and rehearse in. We started preparing for the first show.

We wore white shirts and black pants. We wanted to look like a professional band. We made sure our shoes were shined. One of us had a greasy cream to put on our hair, to keep it neat.

We tuned our instruments professionally and during that time guests started arriving. That was a night of dancing, singing, and drinking. In a short time, the place filled up with people celebrating. We got the signal to start.

We played different background melodies and tried to get over the noise of the crowd. We looked at each other thinking we were just a sad background there, that no one noticed us. Different drinks and snacks were served. We knew we had to change something in the music or we would lose the job. We were very flexible; a sign from one of us was enough to get all of us to change song or rhythm. I signaled them to let me lead in another direction and started playing Monti's Csárdás. My friends looked at me like I was crazy. The risk was great. If that hadn't gotten the audience's attention I didn't know what would have. I played with a lot of feeling and let high notes follow low ones. I hope I played it the way it was written.

I was playing alone and while I was playing the room got quiet. People turned around, sat down and listened. I made my friends join me and we created an unusual sound together. I was a first and only violin, this time with my face to the crowd and with daring and boldness. The people loved it. Loud applause filled the space. We had won. From that moment on it went smoothly. We changed to dance music and the crowd refused to let us stop until the early morning hours. It was a great success.

People went by to thank us for a great evening and made sure to leave a big tip. The manager paid us generously.

The stumbling block happened after six days of playing and drinking that swept the crowd and us. On the seventh night, I saw a familiar woman in the crowd. I couldn't say where I knew her from. I was busy playing and a bit drunk, so I wasn't bothered by it. I spent the next day sleeping. In the afternoon we were preparing for the show when the man in charge of us came in.

"Which one of you is Feivel Wininger?" I turned to look at him. "Someone is waiting for you outside," he said and left the room.

My friends started teasing me, "You have a girlfriend and didn't tell us?"

We would always report our girls to the rest of the group.

"I really don't know who he is talking about," I said. I finished dressing, put some of the greasy stuff on my hair and went outside. I was walking through a long hall when my vision got black. Mother was standing right in front of me with her eyes burning like fire. Her voice was cold and angry as she said, "You are coming home with me right now."

"But, Mother—" I tried to speak.

"No 'but, Mother.' I'll wait for you to get your things. If this is the school you said you were going to. I have a surprise for you."

She was so mad at me. I had told her that school was starting two weeks earlier than usual. This time I'd really hurt a woman I loved so much.

I turned to go back to the room. My friends were waiting with big smiles. I walked into the room in a terrible mood and announced, "My mother is here. I have to return home with her."

They quickly wiped off their silly smiles. They realized I was serious and that they had to start thinking about what to do without me. I didn't bother to worry, I was angry and upset.

I gathered my clothes and my violin and said, "Explain to the manager that I had an emergency at home and that I had to go. You will know what to say." I left my room with my head down. I was ashamed. The biggest shame wasn't because of my friends but toward my mother who had to come and rescue her son from the nightlife and the alcohol.

I can't describe the way I felt on the way home. Mother didn't speak, which was fine with me. I didn't have anything to say or any explanations to give for my lies and my irresponsible behavior. Suddenly, I realized I had another thing to face; Father was waiting at home. I didn't know what Mother told him about the sudden trip she had to take. She would rarely leave our village even to buy things she couldn't find close to home.

Only then did I realize that Mother couldn't have known where I was unless someone had told her. I wanted to ask who it was but I couldn't. I started analyzing the situation. My friends, who knew where I was, wouldn't dare to tell my mother. We knew to honor each other's secrets. We didn't tell anyone else about our destination. Then I remembered the face I saw in the crowd. Who was that woman? I needed to know who'd got me into such trouble.

By that time we'd arrived home. I went into Mother's room and placed my violin there. Mother followed the violin with her eyes.
After a short silence, she said,
"Take the violin to your room. I don't want it in mine."
I went to the violin slowly, hoping she would regret it and stop me.

I was hurt. It wasn't the violin she was wounding, it was my soul.

*****

I thought a lot about Herman, my beloved brother. So many days had passed since he'd left, and I was not used to his absence. I heard Father say, trying to reassure Mother, that Herman had not forgotten us. "It takes him time to get along there, and soon he will write."

The only dinner we had together was Friday night. Father would come home early and Mother wouldn't open the business. The evening started very uncomfortably. I saw that both my parents were waiting for an opportunity or some courage to start talking. Mother took initiative.

"The business has been making very little money lately. Many people go out of the village to get drunk. I don't know how long I can keep it operating, and for another reason too. I haven't been feeling well and I get tired easily. I don't know what has been happening with me lately." She moved slower and rested a lot. She kept speaking.

"Father gets very little work and he is thinking about looking for something else. There are many wood mills in the area and they need people. The work isn't easy, so I don't know how long your father can keep working."

Father tried to make it sound better, "I'll try looking in other villages for easier work, the kind of work I usually do. The mills won't pay much because it is unskilled work." Then he turned to me and asked, "Feivel, what do you plan to do?"

"It is time for me to take a part in supporting the family. On Monday I will start looking for a job."

Mother wanted me to finish school but she didn't say anything about it. I knew that the situation must be worse than they'd described.

"I am already eighteen years old and it is time for me to take part in the family's livelihood. I will try to get a job at the lumber mill." mother wanted me so to finish my studies, and since she did not respond, it was a sign that things were very difficult. "Should we stop selling pastries and sell only liquor? If they are not sold immediately they at least do not spoil after two days," I suggested.

"I think Feivel is right. I'll make bread for regular buyers and in the business, we'll only sell drinks."

I was pleased that Mother was willing to do less.

**

Mother would often send Father to check for letters. When asked whom she was waiting to write she said she just had a feeling that an important letter was coming. We were looking forward to that letter not knowing who it was from.

Father and I both found work. Mother baked bread during the day and opened the pub at night. After work, I went to the pub so that Mother could go and rest. I stayed up late and closed after all the people left. I would stand long hours in the pub and realized what unpleasant work it was. In the past, most of the men who came were from our village. There were very few strangers, so even when they were drunk they still treated Mother with respect. After a while, people we didn't know started coming, probably from other villages or new workers from far away. Mother had to put up with rude jokes and wild behavior. Mother shouldn't be around people like that. I wanted to open the place after I returned from work so that Mother wouldn't have to be there at all. But she explained to me that we needed to open early or people would go elsewhere. The little money we made there was crucial to us.

The work at the sawmill during the day and at the tavern in the evening kept me away from my beloved violin, my friends, and the girl I taught to play. All were neglected and disappeared from my crowded daily schedule. I was sad and tired. Maybe this was the price of excessive debauchery?

***

Mother's moans at night tore my heart. I knew something was bothering her, but she refused to talk about it. I assumed that she missed her children.

One Friday, the man from the post office came to our house. Mother ran to him as if he were someone she'd waited her whole life to see.

"From America?" she asked with hope.

"From America," he answered. "Don't forget about the stamps."

I didn't think anyone heard him. Mother took the letter from his hands and didn't even wait for Father to open the envelope. She cut it open with a knife. She even forgot to take off her apron. She sat down, raised the letter to her eyes and didn't say a thing. Her face was completely pale. She sat there without moving, but then she fell back and lost consciousness.

"Feivel, run and get the doctor," Father shouted and rushed to wipe her face. I ran like crazy, and went to the doctor's house. He was an old friend of the family, and all I could say was, "Mother."

The doctor grabbed his bag and said, "Come on, let's hurry."

I ran ahead and the doctor, an old man, was trying to catch up with me. I couldn't wait for him anymore, so I ran to see what was happening at home. When I arrived, I found Mother in her bed and Father was sitting next to her.

"Frida, what happened to you? Scaring us like that. We were waiting to hear what was written." In a different situation, Father's attempts to cheer Mother up would make me smile, but my mood wasn't fit for it. The truth was I felt terrified. I worried that Mother had had a heart attack.

The doctor entered.

"Everybody out, I need to check my patient."

We went out to wait in the kitchen. The letter was on the floor. I picked it up and placed it on the table. I didn't dare read it. That was Mother's job.

"Why is the doctor taking so long? I hope Mother will get better soon." I tried to start a conversation with Father. I couldn't stand the silence.

"Yes, Feivel," Father said. He could have said more. I was sure that talking would be good for him too. It got quiet again and the doctor was still in Mother's room.

The door opened and he finally came out. He placed his bag on the table and sat down with us.

"I don't like the situation her heart is in. I injected her with something and she will need to take some pills. I will leave some here for you and we will see what happens. I'll come back tomorrow to check on her. She needs to rest and stay calm. She told me several times about her son Herman, that he is in America and that a letter came from him. I asked her what he wrote, but she didn't know. She doesn't remember what happened to the letter.

She will be sleeping for a few hours. She can eat lightly and rest a lot. There is no cure for a Mother's broken heart." He picked up his bag and left.

We folded the letter and placed it inside the envelope.

***

Our whole way of life changed. I would get up early to prepare breakfast for Father and me. I also made porridge and something to drink for my mother. Father would come at noon for half an hour, to see how Mother was doing and to get her something to eat. We didn't open the pub and we considered selling our license to someone else. Mother hardly left her room, complaining of dizziness.

The doctor came again after a week and said: "She is still weak, but the medication helped. Don't expect big changes. You will need to live with this new situation. Mother is sick in the heart. All of you will have to live with this." He gave us more pills and promised to visit often.

Another week had passed and then Mother asked to read the letter. We waited for Father to return from work and then we sat down to read the letter. We sat next to Mother while she was holding the letter and waited.

"Dear Mother, Father, and Feivel," Mother started reading in an excited voice. Her face gained a little color.

"A long time has passed since I left you and I have been busy getting settled. Jacob and his family took me in very nicely and I am still living with them. The family lives in a small apartment and I sleep in the hallway between rooms. I am very lucky to have a place to sleep. I am working with Jacob in the business, but I still don't know if the money we will make will be enough for his family and for me.

He pays me half a salary and the other half goes for paying my boat ticket. I pay them a small amount for food so I have a little left to save. America is different from any place I have ever seen. I thought it would look like Vienna, but I was wrong. Everything is bigger here, the houses, the streets, the stores. I don't dare to go to the center of New York alone. I was there only once when one of Jacob's children took me. I was frightened by the size of everything, I didn't like it.

I wanted to tell you about my job. Jacob and I leave home every day at seven, go on a train and arrive at the street where the business is. The streets here are very long, so we need to walk another twenty minutes to get to the store. We open the entrance to the store, which is closed with an iron net for protection. We stay there until the evening. At night I try to learn some English; it is very important here. Jacob can't leave me alone in the business because even though many people who speak Yiddish come in there are people who don't. I will learn more of the language and then I'll be more helpful.

I wrote so much about myself. I wanted you to know everything about where I am.

I would love to hear about the things that happen at home. I hope that money is good and that you are all healthy. I ask you to write about each of you and don't forget to report about my sisters.

I can see you in my mind, sitting around the kitchen table, close to Mother, who is reading this letter after taking off her apron. The truth is I miss all of you very much and I think of you often. I don't know where I found the courage to get up and leave. I must have been desperate and the trauma of war was affecting me.

It is after midnight here, I should finish writing and go to sleep. Soon I have to go to work. I bless you and hope to hear from you soon.

From your loving son and brother, Herman."

There was silence. Mother kept looking at the letter as if she were hoping to find something else in it. Finally, she gave the letter to Father, who put it back in the envelope and placed it very gently on the table.

I felt my heart contract with longing. I wanted to be with Herman, to consult him, to share my life with him, but he was so far away.

Mother began to speak quietly as if to herself. "I hope my son will be all right there. When the girls left I suffered, but I knew they would be a train-drive away. When Herman went so far away, he took a piece of my heart with him. I didn't want to talk about it or to cause more pain. I would lie at night, choking on my tears. What could I tell you? At first, I was afraid that something might happen to the boat. Later I started fearing that I would not see him again. There is no greater pain for a mother than saying goodbye to a child." She took the letter, held it close to her heart and rushed to her room. She didn't allow herself to cry in front of us.

***

We received a long letter from my sisters. They wrote that Paul Tregerman asked Dora to marry him and that Anna was about to give birth to her first child. They asked us to come and visit them. There were many reasons to be happy. Metta and Salo said that they would pay for the trip.

"Mother, you are about to have another grandson or maybe a granddaughter. And there is Dora's wedding, a chance for the whole family to be happy together. I am happy we are all going to Chernovitz." I jumped up in happiness. I had never been to that city.

"It is a shame that Herman can't be a part of the celebration. We need to talk with the doctor before planning this vacation," she said.

"Is there something you are not telling us?" I asked in concern.

"We will tell the doctor about the trip and see what he thinks," she said again, not paying attention to my question.

After talking with the doctor we realized there was no way Mother could make the trip. The road was long and tiring and the excitement there would be too much for her. Mother suggested that I should go alone but I didn't agree. We wrote a long letter to my sisters explaining why we couldn't come. We told them about Herman's situation and about Mother's health. We wished them well and finished the letter by saying that if in the future we wouldn't go to them, they could come and visit us.

Father got a job in Vama and he decided that we should move there.

One evening I saw Mother knitting.

"I haven't seen you knitting in a long time," I said in surprise.

"It is for my grandson, and when I'll know if Anna is having a boy or a girl I'll knit for him or her too. They need to have something warm from their grandmother." Her eyes were shining in a way I hadn't seen in a while.

"Mother, have you been feeling better lately?" I asked.

"I have, my son. I haven't been doing much except resting. Running the house isn't hard these days when only you and your father are here. I don't really miss the pub. I just thought of something. Our financial situation is better, so maybe it's time for you to finish your matriculation exams and complete your professional studies?"

"I would love to go back to school." I looked at her and added, "I am done fooling around. I won't run away from school to play music."

After thinking for a while I said, "You know, I will keep playing and if I get a chance to earn money from it, I will. I promise not to do it instead of studying. And I promise that when I do it you will know about it."

We smiled at each other with understanding.

***

I completed my studies as promised. I had a chance to meet with many of my old friends. I also persuaded them to finish the exams. We sat in the evenings and studied. In order to rest from our studies, we played for our enjoyment. The atmosphere was pleasant and we behaved responsibly and maturely.

Our entire group consisted of Jews. One evening our guitar player arrived with his face burning, and very excited. We realized that something special had happened to him, but he could not talk about it. We sat around him and waited. We even brought him some water and it seemed to give him back his speech.

"I want to go and live in Israel," he said. We looked at each other and decided that the guy had lost his mind. Who went to live in Israel? What was he looking for there? We'd heard about families leaving to go to America, but to Israel? To the desert? To a place ruled by the British? Who was crazy enough to go there? We asked him all those questions. He just sat there with a smile.

"Have you heard about Zionism?" He felt more knowledgeable and wise than we were. The truth is that we really knew little about Zionism. "I will tell you about it. We Jews have our own place in a distant land. It's true that it is occupied by others. It's true that life there is hard but the place is ours." There was an infectious enthusiasm in his words.

We finished our exams and decided to speak with a Zionist emissary from Israel to hear how we could take part in the Zionist enterprise. Suddenly everyone was talking about it. Only a month earlier we had attributed no importance to that little country, and here we were drawing on every shred of information with infinite thirst. I went home and decided to tell my parents about my plan. Then I decided to wait a few more days and find a suitable moment.

Mother was happy that I'd finished school and that my diploma was on the way. In the evening I went to my room to get my violin and couldn't find it. I ran to the warehouse hoping I'd left it there. It was not there either. I didn't want to tell my parents about it. What would I do?

Meanwhile, mother made a good mamaliga [corn porridge] with a lot of butter, the way I loved. It was a food that was served everywhere I went, even I could make it, but Mother did it in a way that made it a special delicacy for me.

"Would you like to repay me for the mamaliga?" she asked me seriously. The question embarrassed me. What could I answer? I smiled and decided to joke, "In what currency do you want the payment, Romanian or American?"

Mother smiled at me and there was a mischievous glint shone in her smile

"I would like to be paid in sounds, something happy in Yiddish. Is that too expensive?" she asked and looked at me with kind eyes. I'd been caught out. I had to tell her I didn't know where the violin was.

"If you are looking for a violin you can find it in its old place." I ran to Mother's room and found the violin and the bow there, covered with fabric. I took the fabric off and noticed that it was Mother's good dress. I knew she only had one—the dress that had been made for Meta wedding and had never been worn. I folded the dress gently, took the violin, and returned to the kitchen with it in my hand. I felt that the privilege of playing in front of Mother and making her happy was like a wonderful gift for me.

***

After a few days, a letter from my sisters came. Anna had her first son, Uri. A grandson for my parents and a nephew for me. We were very happy with the news.

"I need more wool to prepare another sweater," Mother announced.

Now that we were all in good moods it was time to tell them my news.

"I want to tell you about my plans for the near future." I started working my way to the heart of the story. "During school one of our friends brought to our attention a movement that was getting ready to leave Romania and go live in Israel." I stopped to check their reaction. They were looking at me, waiting for me to keep talking. I didn't notice any recoiling so I kept talking.

"People come here from Israel and they train people who want to go and tell them about life there. They teach us how to work the land and teach a little Hebrew. The truth is I never thought about it before. The talks we had made me love our country. Do you know it is the place that the Bible talks about?" I asked innocently as if I had discovered the connection between the Land of Israel and the Land of the Patriarchs.

"Of course, I knew about it. But I'd heard that the English don't allow Jews in the country. And there are all the wars with the Arabs. Is that a place you would want to go? Wasn't the war we had a few years ago enough for you?" Mother's logic could be clearly heard in her voice, or maybe it was the fear of losing me too.

"We are not safe here. This is not our country. We are only good to them when they need soldiers. They abuse us and chase us out whenever they can. I feel that this is my chance to live a new life in a country that is my birthright." I said the words of someone else but I kept on talking.

"If I have to fight, I'd rather do it for a country that is mine. If I have to work a land, I'd rather it was my land. I will go there first and later I'll bring you too." That was most important to me. I needed them to know I wasn't planning on leaving them, that I was just going first.

"So what is your plan?" Mother asked.

"We are a group of forty guys and two girls. In a large estate near Chernovitz is a camp for working and learning about Israel. We will learn to work the land and study Hebrew. The camp runs for six months. An Israeli man will stay with us and guide us. He explained that after the camp we need to be ready to leave quickly. That man will take care of all the details of our trip there." I took a deep breath and then summed it up, "You know that someday we will have to leave Romania. This just feels like the right time for me."

"You should do what your heart tells you to do, my son," Mother said. She got up and fixed something warm for Father to drink. Father was silent throughout the whole conversation. He looked as though I were talking about a different family.

We started hearing about riots and anti-Semitic acts more and more. Jews thought that if they didn't pay attention to it that it would just go away.

I left with my group for the camp. They called it 'training.' We learned about the land during the days. In the evenings we would hear lectures about the country, the history, and the geography of Israel. They taught us Hebrew. After studying, we listened to Israeli music and danced to it. Even though we were tired we didn't want to stop dancing.

It was a challenging time for me. Suddenly my life had meaning. It was like a new love, with excitement and doubts. The six months flew by and we were about to return home. We were assigned to collect money for the trip to Israel. Each of us returned to their village and the Israeli man promised to return in a few months to arrange the trip.

I said to my friends, "Do you know how I feel? I'm about to go to my country. I'm about to go home." Everyone clapped his or her hands. The smile and glittering eyes confirmed that they felt just like me.

***

I was appointed as a guide and responsible for the fundraising in my area of residence.

At first, we'd thought that the organisation from Israel would fund the trip, but our guide explained to us that the country is poor and there was no money to bring us. We would need to use donations from Jewish communities. They made me a guide and we divided up the group so that each of us got an area that included a few villages around their homes.

In my village, Vama, there were fewer than 400 Jews. A few kilometers away was the village called Gura Humorului. Both of the villages were on the same river, the Moldova River. In it lived about two thousand Jews. I learned my role as a guide, and as soon as I arrived, I went looking for help in raising funds.

The first girl who agreed to help me was Beatrice Doliner; an energetic girl whose help proved to be most helpful. She was blessed with great persuasion and grace that opened all the pockets generously, and we collected a considerable sum.

We spent a lot of time together. We took notes and made calculations so that everything would be ready when our guide returned.

Whenever I arrived at Gura Humorului, I went first to Beatrice's house. With time I got to know all the members of the Doliner family; her parents and three brothers. She was the youngest. There were times I arrived at dinnertime and was invited to join them. I felt good with them.

One evening, I told Mother about the money we raised and about the girl who was helping me. I must have been talking about her with excitement. Mother stopped my speech and said, "I think you are in love with this girl. I would like to meet her."

Was I really in love? With everything that was happening, I hadn't noticed, but I really had fallen in love with her. It was strange that it was Mother who'd realized it and wanted to meet her. With how I described her, Mother must have started liking Beatrice. I decided to bring her home with me the first chance I had.

My behavior during the next encounter with Beatrice was more romantic. It was all flowing very naturally and there was an undeniable feeling that we were meant for each other. I asked her to come and meet my parents. They loved her from the first moment.

It was a wonderful time. We chatted, loved, and dreamed. I called her Tizzy as a nickname, played her love songs on my violin, and she loved my music. We also told her parents, Rachel and Yehuda Doliner, that we wanted to immigrate to Israel together, and they trusted me and did not object.

Was everything really perfect? What happiness we had! The messenger was about to arrive soon and we talked about meeting him again.

I ran home happily. I wanted to hug the whole world. I felt I was smiling at everyone I saw.

I entered the house with a smile and ran into the family's doctor. I almost knocked him to the floor.

"What happened to you, Feivel?" he asked. "Your mother is very ill and you are running around smiling?"

"What is wrong with Mother?" The smile faded from my face all at once and all the blood left my face. I felt an emptiness in my stomach.

"She isn't doing well, not well at all. She collapsed again. The medication isn't working anymore. Her heart isn't well and her longing for Herman is shortening her life. You better get your brother here before it is too late."

A few brief moments separated my great happiness from my terrible anxiety. Of course, if I have to, I'll make sure to bring Herman. I went into mother's room. Father sat next to her with his head bent and motioned me to be quiet. I tiptoed to the kitchen and sat down to write to my brother.

I realized that all my plans were gone. There was no chance that I was going to Israel. I discovered that life can't be planned. Single moments can change everything.

I had to let Tizzy know what had happened and give her my job as a guide so that she could meet the man from Israel. She had all the money and the notes we'd made. I figured that she would probably go with the group to Israel. Losing her was to me worse than not going to Israel.

I finished writing to Herman about everything that was happening. He was old enough to be told the truth and make his own decisions. I wrote that if he decided to come he should write to let us know when so that we would be able to prepare Mother. I ran to the post office and the letter left. I never told Mother about it. I promised the postman the stamps, provided that the letter he received would be delivered only to me. I was afraid he would bring the letter home as usual and the excitement would again endanger Mother.

On Saturday, when Father stayed home, I went out to see Tizzy. It had been two weeks since our last meeting and I'd had no way of telling her what had happened. Maybe she thought I'd run away from her. The meeting was hard for both of us.

I passed on all the material I still had, and the authority on finances. I explained to her that if she wanted to go I would not stop her. Judging by her reaction I could tell she wanted things to be different too.

"Do you have anything to offer me instead of Israel?" she asked in a sweet way.

"Will you marry me?" I asked very seriously. I didn't even think about it. The words just came out of my mouth. I really wanted her to say yes.

"Certainly, Febi." That was how she called me when we were alone and she wanted to make me feel that I belonged only to her.

I felt her heartbeat converge with the beating of my heart, and a wonderful sense of joy overwhelmed me after all. I had won the best thing of all, the love of my life. I had won Tizzy.

***

A letter from Herman came. He apologized for not answering sooner. He explained that he'd wanted to give me the exact boat he was coming on so that the doctor could prepare Mother for it. He gave all the details and from them, I realized he was already on the way. I told Father and showed him his letter. He was happy about what I'd done and only said, "I hope this will help Mother."

Father wrote a short letter to my sisters telling them about

Mother's condition and about Herman's visit. He left them to decide if they wanted to come.

I hurried to the doctor and told him the story. He promised to speak with Mother.

"Frida, do you know anyone called Wininger in America?" It was a silly question because Mother was the one to tell him about her son going to America. He had no other idea about how to get to the subject.

"Why do you ask, Doctor?"

"I have heard that there is a man called Wininger on a boat that is arriving here from America soon," he explained.

"We have family there. And my Herman, too." Mother didn't notice that the conversation was strange and she answered very seriously.

"Well, Frida, we have to prepare for a visit from America, one of those you mentioned will probably come soon."

"My heart tells me that it is Herman."

Who can argue with a Mother's heart?

On the day my brother was scheduled to arrive, I told Mother I was going to the train station to pick up our guest. Mother tried to get up and get dressed, but she couldn't. Father convinced her to stay in bed.

I rushed to the train station. They announced that the train would be late. I waited impatiently. Time was moving very slowly. I heard a train and tried to see it coming closer. Among the first to get off the train was my brother. I haven't seen him in years. He'd grown up. I ran to him. We hugged and cried like two kids who had missed each other.

"How is Mother?" he asked in fear.

"Not good. Don't be scared when you see her. She has lost a lot of weight. She had no appetite. She was so weak that she couldn't get dressed up for you."

"I dread that first moment of seeing her," he said.

"The doctor promised to be there. He is a nice man and very devoted to Mother, but he has nothing more to offer that will help her."

During the conversation, we'd arrived home. Herman stopped for a moment, took a deep breath, raised his head and went straight into Mother's room. The doctor sat there talking to Dad. Mother saw us, tried to say something, and her tearful eyes said it all. We stood around the bed and we all cried, even the doctor did not hide his tears. She held up her hand, held it out to Herman, and he went up, took her hand in his, held it to his lips, and did not let go.

"Mother needs to rest." It was the doctor's voice. "You're leaving here and I'll stay a few more minutes," he added. Herman put her hand on the blanket and we left the room.

A few days later, it seemed that a miracle had taken place. I went into mother's room and could not believe my eyes. She was sitting up and eating. Lately, she would only agree, at most, to drink some soup and eat some porridge. And suddenly she was eating and there was even a trace of a smile on her lips. Our doctor's diagnosis had been accurate: it turns out that one can get sick from longing to see someone.

Herman devoted all his time to Mother. He told her about New York, about the lives of the people there, and about the family he lived with. She swallowed every word he said, asked questions, and took an interest in everything. I got back my alert, curious mother, who wanted to know everything right away.

The next morning my sister Mina arrived. She was the only one who was not yet married. I knew she would be happy to stay with us and take care of Mother.

Tizzy used to come to our house often. She brought dishes that her mother Rachel sent, and drank thirstily every word Herman said. I was happy that my brother had met my betrothed. In the evenings, Father would join us, and Herman's stories had no end.

Time ran too fast. It was a week before Herman would leave again. Meanwhile, he sat next to Mother. He was sorry for every moment that he was not there. He knew he would never see her again, and gathered the moments of grace in her memory. I was afraid of leaving him. How would Mother stand up excitedly? How do we prepare her?

I took the initiative and started a conversation with Mother. "How good it is that Herman could come. You see, mother, you can come from America anytime. Do not forget it tomorrow when Herman leaves." I wanted so much for the separation to not hurt her.

I managed to calm her down, and Herman's departure went well and left her hoping for his next visit. We all knew that Mother had not much time left but we hoped she was not aware of it.

Mina decided to stay for a while longer, and it made all of us happy. The house did not empty again at once and Mina took care of all of us.

***

Our doctor sometimes went to Campulung Moldovenesc. He had medical friends there, and I asked him for help and advice. He promised that on his next trip he would see who could help. When he noticed my impatience, he added, "I will be back in three days. I know how urgent it is." I knew he was there for us and I was grateful to this dear man.

The doctor, on the way back and straight from the train, stopped at our home.

"The manager of a big hospital in Campulung Moldovenesc is a heart specialist. My friends say that he is the best." He gave me the doctor's name and the name of the hospital where he was working. He hesitated, but said, "You should know that the doctor is known as an anti-Semite and he charges a lot of money for his counseling. My friends say that in your condition it would be a waste to go to him. I'm going in to see your mother." He turned to go to her room. I thought about what I had just heard. My rage was burning up inside of me. The conclusion I was supposed to make was that because I was poor and a Jew, I shouldn't waste my time trying to live. I couldn't accept it. I knew that his warnings wouldn't stop me.

The doctor came out of my mother's room, and I saw in his expression the severity of her condition. "Your mother is calling you." I hurried into her room. She moved her lips but I could not understand what she was saying. I put my ear to her mouth to hear her request. "I feel like I'm sinking," she said in a whisper as she breathed hard, and the effort was evident on her face. "Bring me the director of the hospital from Campulung Moldovenesc." Her eyes closed with exhaustion.

Despite our poor financial situation, and despite the attitude of the hospital director to the Jews, I had no choice. I'd go to him. I knew it was a crazy act, but my purpose was clear, at mother's request.

***

I left the next day. I was worried and concerned. I feared that the doctor would refuse to come and see Mother. I knew that it would be a death sentence for her. I didn't want to think like that.

I couldn't lose control and do something stupid. I needed to stay calm and not lose my head.

I arrived at the hospital. It was a big place so I had to walk for an hour before I found his office. A serious-faced secretary received me in front of his door.

"What do you want?" she asked as if I were some youngster coming to beg for charity.

"I need to speak with the doctor," I answered. She started laughing.

"You want to see the doctor? Who are you?"

All the blood was rushing to my head. I was standing there arguing with a secretary when every moment was crucial to me. My hands closed into fists. I told myself to calm down, that I wasn't there to fight, but to save my mother.

"I really need to see him, please," I asked again. She gave me a disrespectful look.

"He isn't here yet." She looked away and went on with her business. I stood at the door and waited. At noon the secretary left the office and I stayed alone. I started suspecting that the doctor wasn't coming. I had no choice but to stay and wait.

"Could you move away from the door?" said an unfriendly voice. "I want you to leave right now."

By the bag in his hand, I assumed he was the doctor. I hadn't said a thing and already he was yelling and throwing me out.

"Doctor, would you—" I tried to speak.

"Go away before I throw you down the stairs," he said clearly, went into his office and slammed the door angrily. I remained standing outside. I didn't go all that way to not get a chance to speak. I gathered all my courage and went up to his door. I knocked lightly and since there wasn't any response I knocked harder.

"Come in," he ordered in a threatening voice. I opened the door. As soon as he saw me he jumped up, ready to hit me.

I pulled back so he stopped and started yelling.

"You are so rude. Telling you once to leave isn't enough?" He raised his hand. I didn't mind him hitting me as long as he was willing to go and save my mother. He lowered his hand and came closer to me. I couldn't stay calm anymore. I got hysterical. I started crying and shouting. I lost all control. I was breathing quickly and I couldn't control my voice.

"You can kill me. I am not moving until you come with me to save my mother. I beg of you. Please, I'm begging. Please, I'm begging." I didn't know what else to say. My body was shaking. I stood in front of the man who held my mother's life in his hands and I had nothing more to say. I tried again with all the power in me. "I'm not leaving without you, Doctor. You are Mother's last hope."

I could not see the doctor anymore. My eyes were unfocused and I kept talking to myself. "My mother is so sick, and I love her so much …"

I felt a heavy hand on my shoulder.

"Sit down and relax. Tell me about your mother." His voice had changed from the voice of a monster to a human voice. I opened my eyes widely to make sure I wasn't dreaming. He pushed a chair in my direction and I sat down.

I told him everything about Mother's illness. He listened quietly. He didn't answer right away. I sat there waiting for his verdict. A few moments passed and he still hadn't said anything. I didn't know what that meant. I didn't want to ask whether he was coming with me or not. I knew that now I had to be patient and be quiet too.

"Be here exactly at one o'clock, with a taxi."

I wanted to shout, "Thank you!" and kiss his hand. I was willing to do much more, but I was tired from the fight I had just gone through. I said goodbye and left the room.

At exactly one o'clock I was outside his office and a taxi was waiting outside.

In the taxi, I shrunk myself into a corner. I wanted to give him as much space as I could. He started asking me questions about Mother and later about myself. I told him about my school and during the conversation I mentioned that I played several musical instruments and that I'd just received a new cello from my brother. It turned out that he played too, and our talk focused on music.

"After I see your mother and hopefully be able to help her, I would love to hear you play."

"I would be happy to play you anything you'd like," I answered.

***

Father and Mina were in Mother's room. She was in bed looking almost lifeless. She weighed barely forty kilograms and looked bad. The doctor asked everyone to leave and closed the door. He stayed there for a long time. My thought went from hope to despair. A good doctor and a miracle were a good combination at that time.

The doctor left her room and came to sit with us.

"I gave Frida an injection. I waited and saw that she was responding well. She started talking and told me about the treatments she'd received in Vienna. That information was important to me. I have a clear diagnosis of her illness. I hope that with the new medication I work with I will be able to help her." Then he turned his eyes to me and said, "I would be happy to give your mother back to you." He smiled an almost paternal smile to me. I was amazed.

"Do you remember to keep your promises?"

At first, I didn't understand what he meant, but then I jumped with joy.

"Music! You must want me to play for you."

"Let's go see how your mother is feeling and then you could play something special for me."

We walked in and were surprised to see Mother sitting up with color in her cheeks and very alert eyes. She asked my sister to get her some food. I knew that the doctor and the miracle were in the right place. They'd saved my mother.

"Bring your cello and play for me the music that Jews play on holidays," the doctor asked. I hurried to do as he asked. I closed my eyes and in moments I was gone. I allowed my soul to play like I had never played before. I put all my gratitude into the music. I was shaking and crying. Sweat was covering my face and neck. It was the music of thanks, to man and to God. I was playing the prayer of Yom Kippur[13], the 'Kol Nidrei[14].'

When I opened my eyes, they met the doctor's eyes. I couldn't swear to it, I thought I saw a tear in his eye. He turned away and wiped his nose. I will never know what was going through his mind in those moments. He came up to me, hugged my shoulders, looked at Mother and said, "You have been blessed with a good and loving son. I have met many people but have never seen such dedication." He turned to me and said, "That instrument is my weakness. Your playing gave me a thrill I've never experienced before."

"Doctor, how much do I need to pay you?" I had a little money; I gathered all the money in the house to pay him. He smiled and said, "Are you sure you have enough to pay me?" Then he said that I'd to go back to the hospital with him to give me all the

13 A day for soul-searching and forgiveness
14 Day of Atonement

medicines Mother needed. I went back with him. Because I felt we were becoming friends I dared to ask,

"Doctor, how did you make such a miracle that made my mother feel better in an hour?"

He didn't answer right away; he thought about it and then said, "I gave her a drug that had only two results, life or death. I gambled on it and was lucky to be able to give her life."

How glad I am that I am not a doctor! I could never do such an experiment in humans.

In his room, the doctor filled a box with all sorts of pills for me and prepared a letter to the family doctor with a detailed explanation. "Keep my business card, in case you need me. I'd be happy to help." A slight pat on my shoulder made it clear to me that he meant every word he said.

My mother's condition had improved beyond recognition. She began to walk around, and within two months she was functioning normally.

I was the happiest person.

***

Because of my mother's illness, I did not announce at home that I had decided to get married. During this time, I'd continued to meet with Tizzy. We talked about our lost plan, and more than once I asked her if she was not sorry that she stayed with me instead of emigrating to Israel with her friends.

"Dreams come true," she replied, "even if it seems to us that they are too late".

A warm and pleasant season came. We went on a hike in nature, immersed in the pure waters of the Moldovan River and enjoying our love. One morning I took Tizzy to my lovely corner of the wood. We decided that the birds there would sing songs for us, especially for young couples in love. We laughed a lot and the world seemed perfect again.

One day Tizzy asked me to tell my parents about our desire to get married. I promised to talk to them that evening. "I like the snow. Let's get married in December, on the twenty-fifth of the month." She was happy, bouncing and dancing like a little girl, and I loved her every move.

Mother was in the kitchen making something to eat. Mina had gone to visit Uncle Nathan and his wife and Father had yet to return from work. I was happy to be alone with Mother and share my secret with her.

"Mother, how would you feel about your youngest son getting married?" I thought she would be surprised but she wasn't.

"Tizzy is a great girl. When do you want to get married?"

"In December. We want a lot of white snow, like a wedding dress spread all over the world."

"You look happy, Feivel. You make me happy." After a short silence, she added, "I would like this time for it to be a wedding with the whole family. Of all my married children, I never got to have a real wedding. I am getting excited. It's a shame that Herman cannot get here. You can schedule a meeting with your bride's parents," she suggested.

***

The house was full of happy people. My sisters came with their children. Something wonderful happened; we were all together again like in the good old days. We planned for the wedding to be in Gura Humorului, which was a short distance away. It was all arranged in good taste. My bride's parents, Rachel and Yehuda, took care of it. The two families mixed together perfectly. There were two bands. It was a celebration that lasted two days. The bride wore a beautiful white dress and a long veil. My friends from my old band kept everybody dancing. At some point, they called me to the stage and I took out my violin from hiding. I happily played with them. I thought that if that was how our life would look we had nothing to worry about.

Outside were endless white surfaces, just as we expected. I had never had such a pure and charming winter.

Mina stayed with us. Tizzy lived with her parents in Gura Humora and I was called to serve in the Romanian army. In the Zionist group that I participated in, we would dream of the chance to have a Hebrew army, so that we would not fight and die for strangers. Now I had to wear the Romanian army uniform. What an irony of fate.

Mother was also angry at the draft, but that was the law and there was no choice. She asked me to come with her to the rabbi. "He will bless you to have an easy service and come back quickly and safely home."

"Mrs. Frida, you have nothing to worry about," the rabbi promised. "Your son will have light military service and he will return home before the official end date."

My mother calmed down and hoped it would be so.

They gathered the Jewish men and moved us in trucks to a military base. Stables were turned into beds. After two hours they called us to a specific area and started asking for personal details about our lives and professions. Most of the people were merchants or students.

When it was my turn, I announced that I was a musician. The officer asked me to his chamber. I was happy. I took my violin with me because he'd asked me to play for him. I did and he was happy, he asked me to get my things from the stables and come with him to his house. I was the only soldier that spent his first night in the army in a normal bed.

I told the officer that there were other men that were in my band. He called all of them and made sure we received special conditions.

My service started on the right foot. All of us in the band were allowed to return home often and while others were practicing marching, we were playing music.

The celebration lasted three weeks. One day we were asked about who had finished school. We hoped it would improve our situation so we told the officer that we all had. We were wrong. We were twenty guys. Except for me, they were all sent to work in another camp, and only I remained in the office of a notorious and anti-Semitic major in the camp, who was known for his cruelty.

In fact, I received a fair treatment from him and felt no hostility at all. Two weeks later he invited me to his house to play with him. He played the piano and I played the violin. His family welcomed me, and I was kindly invited back there.

I missed Tizzy and my family. I told the officer that I had been married for a short time and that I had barely been with my wife. He smiled and promised to give me frequent vacations, and so it was. After a year I finished my compulsory service and went home.

When I returned home, I saw that my family was packing. My parents told me that they were emptying our village, Vama, of Jews.

In order for my parents to sign documents certifying that "the house was sold voluntarily," they were paid a ridiculous amount of money. We loaded all our belongings and transferred them to a village nearby, to Gura Humorului. Tizzy was waiting for us there and helped us to move into an apartment that belonged to my grandmother Feiga and my grandfather Ephraim. So we returned to the apartment we'd lived in many years ago.

All the while I kept thinking about my friends who had emigrated to Israel. How good it was for them not to have to leave their home and spare themselves from expulsion and contempt. I assumed they had already come to rest and land.

In the meantime, I was hired to work in a mill in Niagra-Lisa, about fifty kilometers from our home. Because of my experience, I was given the job of running the mill. I was happy with my work. We moved in with my wife's parents. We had a big room there, which would make any couple happy.

Tizzy was waiting for me at home with a happy smile, her hands on her belly, and we hoped for the best. At night I felt her swollen belly and felt the baby running wild in her womb. We laughed and enjoyed the little warrior who was about to emerge into the world. We were excited about the birth and thought it was all we needed in our lives to be perfect.

On the fifth of June, my wife gave birth to a sweet little girl. We couldn't stop being amazed at the little crying miracle we had got.

A year-and-a-half later, our world began to collapse, and sweep us into the arms of mass extinction.

The Holocaust.

Part III - Survivors

Helen - The author

In the ghetto   Before 10.1941

I ran up the street. I passed all the houses I knew very well. The wind at my back strengthened and pushed me forward.

I passed next to the synagogue, it was completely filled with people praying and masses of people gathered in the doorway. Even on holidays, there was no such density. To my right were shops all along the road. I could see the shop owners; they stood outside and didn't even greet me. The wind kept pushing me. Then I saw Tizzy's parents; they too were standing outside their house and ignoring me.

My mind was racing, what was happening? What were my two brother-in-laws and their wives doing on the street? Everyone was standing outside and staring at me. My legs kept pulling me forward; the wind kept pushing me mercilessly. I wanted to stop, but I couldn't. The road kept leading up and the wind didn't care about my hurting feet. My father stood there with his head down, reaching out his hand to help me stop. His hand wasn't long enough; he didn't reach me. My mother was covered with a gray headscarf; she was very thin and weak and reaching out with both hands. I noticed her too late and within a second I was far away from her. I felt a burning pain in my back. I started smelling burned meat. At that point, I saw my wife holding our child in her arms. There was a look of horror in her eyes. She yelled out, "Watch out for the fire! You are burning up. You are covered in flames."

As I passed her, she reached out her arms, trying to catch me, at that moment our baby fell to the ground. I held my wife's arms and dragged her with me. I saw her beautiful curly hair go up in flames. We both started shouting, "Helen, Helika, our girl, we left her behind!" The fire had a hold of my wife's clothes and her eyes were staring at me in terror. I flew in the air holding her burning body. With the last of my strength, I cry out, "What happened to the girl?" And the two of us were thrown onto the cold ground…

Someone shook me. I opened my eyes and saw my father bent over me.

"Feivel, stop yelling! Wake up, wake up. A messenger is spreading strange messages out on the street. I do not understand what they say."

I touched my aching body. I could still smell the burned flesh. My body was covered in cold sweat. My breathing was heavy. I tried to gather my thoughts. I looked at my father. He was still leaning over me and he looked panicked and strange. I wanted him to let me recover from my dream, but he just kept yelling, "Come and listen to the announcement. We have to go. I don't know where to. I don't know what to do."

I thought that my father had had the same dream that I'd had. I sat up, but my father kept shaking me. Almost in anger, I jumped up. He rushed to the window that faced the street and I followed him. As I looked out I saw that many people were standing there. Some of the Jews we knew, were crying. The rest, our Romanian neighbors, were happy. I opened the window and heard calls of banishment that very day by trains. I couldn't believe my ears.

If I thought that the nightmare in my dream was the worst thing I had ever experienced, it soon became clear to me that the road to hell was just beginning.

***

We did not have much time to savor Helika, the wonderful baby we had. All around, strange and incomprehensible things began to happen. Every day brought a new shock. Hitler conducted his campaign of incitement against the Jews. We heard about his conquests and hoped that he would fall long before he reached our area, Bukovina.

Our town, Gura Humorului, young men in black uniforms decorated with swastikas, shouted, "Heil Hitler!" with a salute. There were rumors that the Czech Republic no longer existed and Poland had been devastated and shattered. We refused to believe it.

My sister Mina returned to Chernovitz. We asked her to write to us as soon as she could, but a letter from her never came. The atmosphere in the village was strange. All of our Gentile friends treated us like we were strangers. Friends, who only a short time before had invited us to their home to sit, drink and laugh, had suddenly turned their backs and ignored us.

In the mill that I managed, we had a lot of work. The unofficial rumor I heard was that the Germans were buying an unlimited amount of wood from the Romanians. Most of the workers in the mill were Gentiles and they stopped sitting with us at lunch. They stayed away from us as if we were lepers. I tried to talk with one of them and asked for an explanation. He looked around and said, "Everyone talks about how you Jews are the reason we are having a bad time. You are our enemies. It is hard for me to say this to you, but we were ordered to humiliate Jews and that would add points in our favor.

Everything you have will soon be ours." He tried to avoid looking into my eyes and kept talking. "You know that I won't cause any harm to you or your family, but I can't be seen talking to you." He turned his back to me and left.

Things got worse and worse and I felt my work at the sawmill was coming to an end. We wondered whether things were better in other places where I remembered my group of friends had lived. I decided to visit the next day to see what was going on. Maybe I'd look for work there. I announced my decision to the family. Early in the evening, we gathered in the kitchen with Tizzy's brothers, Max and Yosel, and their wives, and my in-laws. Tizzy was sitting beside me with the baby wrapped in a huge feather pillow. Everyone looked at me in surprise, not understanding what I was talking about.

"Don't you feel that wherever we go they treat us differently? We've forgotten that we are strangers here and that we are unwanted. We've already been through one war; we were banished, we were killed, our homes were burned down. I won't go through another war like that," I said.

I was annoyed at the conversations at work and all I wanted was to take my wife and child and run away.

"And what will happen to us?" asked Yehuda Hemi. I had not thought about that. He was right. I was responsible for the whole family - for them and of course for my elderly parents. All Jews have the same fate. "I have to think, maybe I will postpone the trip until the situation becomes clearer."

There was a knock on the door and my parents arrived with a letter. After the usual greetings, my mother said,

"You know the Augur family who lives across the street from us? They have always been good neighbors to us and we have helped each other a lot. Lately, the young ones have stopped saying hello to us, and when they walk past us, they pull faces and laugh.

Today a horrible thing happened to me. I went out to the back yard to hang the laundry and one of their sons came up to me with a stick in his hand and said to me, 'Stinking Jew, stop hanging your disgusting laundry in front of our yard.'

He stood in front of me, a big man with great hatred in his eyes. He raised his stick. At that moment, his mother came out into the yard and shouted at him to leave immediately before she called his father. This time I was lucky. Before he turned to go he said, 'You're going to be out of here soon. Hitler will slaughter you. All your possessions will be mine. Heil Hitler!' His poisonous laughter still resonates in my ears."

I helped mother sit down. Tizzy walked over and sat down next to her with the baby. The little girl began to make happy noises in honor of her grandmother. There is no better medicine than the gurgling and smile of a baby. My mother looked at her and her face immediately softened but the sadness remained in her eyes.

"I will go and speak with that family and I'll warn those boys not to look for trouble with us. We can use weapons too."

I was angry and upset by Mother's story and I wanted to show some power against them. But lately I, too, had felt that everything that belonged to the Jews, including their lives, was in the hands of others.

One of my friends owned a radio and from time to time he was able to hear the BBC. Yesterday he told me about the horrors that were being done to Jews all over Europe. I didn't dare tell my wife about those things. It was good that she and our parents didn't see many people, so they avoided hearing the stories about things done to our Jewish brothers.

I tried to change the subject, "I notice you are holding a letter. Who is it from?" I hoped that the stories in that letter would be more pleasant.

"I almost forgot about the letter. It is from Uncle Shlomo in Chernovitz." Mother took the letter out of the envelope and began to read. "To my brother Moshe and his family, hello. I received the letter in which you told me you were moving to Gura Humorului. I understand that it was an elegant banishment. At least they paid you for leaving.

I met my nieces. They invited us to their home for a nice dinner. We had fun. I got to meet your two grandchildren, Freddie and Uri, they are cute and cheeky. Metta and Dora are doing well financially and they are happy to make it easier for Anna and Mina. Chaim Grosman, Anna's husband, is a knowledgeable man and a good man to speak with. We promised to meet again soon and have a long talk. I promised my nieces I would write to you and now I am doing just that.

As you know, we are now "owned" by the Russians. We might be lucky that the Romanians didn't agree to the Russian ultimatum in which they were asked to take back the north of Bukovina and Bessarabia. The hope is that we are safe from the hand of the Germans and their Romanian supporters. I hope that the racial violence and the anti-Semitism will end soon and I can go back to writing my encyclopedia. I am happy that my daughters and yours are living here and are able to live a normal and a good life.

Two weeks have passed since I started writing this letter and only now have I found time to finish it. It turns out that the first part of my letter was too optimistic.

At first, the Russians only took large factories and lavish apartments for themselves. I was calm. We were all living in small apartments and live well but modestly. A few days ago, men from the 'new order' knocked on my door. I have to say I was surprised by the visit. They said that they were there to check whether I was a "provocative element," which would determine if I could stay in my apartment. They found me working on my encyclopedia and the room was filled with piles of drafts and articles in different stages of preparation. Finished volumes were in my bookcase. I'm sure I don't need to tell you about the low level of our Russian friends; they almost leaped up in awe at my work. One of them opened the volume T and found the biography of Trotsky. He asked me to remove that volume immediately. But later he showed a willingness to help me advance the rest of my literary work. The most important thing is that I was able to stay in my apartment and keep working. My wife, Eva, and I live our lives almost as we did and hope that our children won't be harmed.

One of the men who were in my house sent several Soviet scholars who expressed interest in my work. I took advantage of the opportunity and asked them to find for me some biographies of important Russian Jews in all areas. They promised to help me and in that way, I was able to make the best out of the situation.

From what we know about the German army, they appear to be far away from South Bukovina. Let us hope that it stays that way. Congratulations on the birth of your granddaughter Helika, daughter to Feivel and Tizzy; may there be many more. Goodbye and may God take care of all of us, Eva and Shlomo Wininger."

We were happy to hear that my sisters were well. My mother gave the letter to my father and there were no signs of happiness on her face. Her encounter with the neighbor's son must have strongly affected her.

"There is a demand for apartments or rooms for rent," Father said. "I met some people from villages in the area and they told me they have to leave their home in a few days. There was a government order that all the Jews who live in the villages must move to the towns. They have been ordered to move to Gura Humorului. They are gathering us in centers so that we will be easier to handle," he said in anger.

"I think that you are too frightened. It will all be over soon. How long can Hitler keep fighting the Russians, the French, and the British?" said my optimistic father-in-law. I wanted to believe that he was right.

"We need to take care of food for the winter. I will take the wagon tomorrow and buy everything we need. We need a lot and I have to buy things for Uncle Nathan too," I volunteered.

"I'll go with you," said my brother-in-law, Yosel.

Each of us went on with their business. We were troubled. Everything new we heard made us worry more and we didn't know where it was leading.

Autumn dominated everything. Leaves in shades of brown covered the side of the road. Trees were naked in preparation for the winter. The air was so clear and yet why did I feel like I was suffocating? I went to play with the baby. It always made me feel better.

***

Several hundred people came to Gura Humorului from close-by villages. Most of them were in good financial state and they settled quickly in the new place. Their move felt temporary, just until the anger was over and they were allowed to return to their homes. Very few of them looked for work. Some of the local Jews were fired. I knew that my time at the mill was limited. I was still thinking about Campulung Moldovenesc and wanted to go after the holidays.

Each year at that time we would gather all of our relatives and prepare good food for the holidays. That year we barely spoke about the holidays but I still wanted all of us to be together.

On Rosh Hashanah, the synagogue was completely full. People that hadn't been there in years came. They were all there to pray and it wasn't hard to guess what was in their hearts. My mother and mother-in-law sat in the women's area. The sounds of prayer and crying that were heard from there were different than in years before. A black and threatening cloud hung over us and we didn't know what to do. All we could do was to pray and hope that the cloud would pass without harming us.

We passed Yom Kippur in prayer too. We spent the whole day in the synagogue. We waited for the Shofar to help our prayer reach heaven and make God spare and save us. We knew whom we needed to be saved from, we just didn't know how.

A few days after Yom Kippur, I sat on the back porch of my father-in-law's house, a place I was particularly fond of. In the inner yard, chickens were pecking and crowing. A small goat would nag them from time to time and they'd spread their wings and hurry to the other side of the yard. Opposite were the stables. We had only one horse and it was rarely used. The silence around and the trees in the autumn complemented the pastoral scene. My wife and my little girl were spreading corn seed in the yard. If it had been possible to freeze this picture and live in it forever, I would have been the happiest person.

I wanted to examine various possibilities in case I was removed from the sawmill and decided to consult with David, an acquaintance and a friend who had returned from Campulung Moldovenesc the day before.

His wife opened the door and I saw that something terrible had happened. "Come in, Feivel. Maybe you can help get David out of his room. He came back from Campulung yesterday in a terrible mood and is not willing to talk to anyone."

I knocked on the door.

"David, it's Feivel. I need to speak with you," I said in a determined voice.

"Feivel, go home. It will be best if we don't talk. It is the end for all of us. Go home."

David sounded completely desperate. I decided to take a different approach.

"David, listen to me. I am going to Campulung Moldovenesc tomorrow to see our friends; they will tell me what happened. I think it will be better if I hear it from you."

"You are not going anywhere." It wasn't an order, it was a heartbreaking cry. The door opened immediately and David came out. He wasn't shaved and his clothes were wrinkled. He jumped on my shoulder and started crying like a child.

"You are not going to Campulung Moldovenesc. They will kill you like they killed the rabbi. They kill Jews like they are dogs. Don't you dare go there."

He cried as he spoke, he wiped his nose and eyes on the sleeve of his shirt, sat on the floor and started telling me what had happened.

"I was in Campulung Moldovenesc for Yom Kippur. I went there between Rosh Hashanah and Yom Kippur to visit my parents. My mother didn't feel well and asked me to stay longer so I stayed for Yom Kippur. That morning we went to the synagogue together. Everyone there was dressed in white. We prayed very loudly and with great faith.

You know that nice rabbi and his two sons. While we studied there the boys were still young. Well, during the prayer two large men walked into the synagogue, grabbed the rabbi and his sons, dragged them to the basement and forced them to take out the barrels and bags. Their wagon was standing outside. They made them load everything on the wagon. We stood around and our hearts were breaking. For a moment, I thought we needed to do something, but there were so many people around that were ready to kill us if they got the chance.

We thought it was over and we got ready to go back inside the synagogue, but those men had different plans. They released their horse and tied the rabbi in his place. Our rabbi, still wearing his Talit was harnessed to a wagon. Can you imagine it?" He broke down in tears again.

I sat beside him and cried with him. I felt the shame and the pain. He kept talking, "After that, they sat his sons in the driver's seat and forced them to hit their father with a whip to make him move. The old man collapsed after a few meters." He stopped talking. He was breathing deeply and I could see that he had more to say, but then changed his mind.

"David, what else happened?" I asked.

"Feivel, my heart won't bear to see a thing like that again. I can't close my eyes for a moment without seeing that terrible vision. Don't go away. Don't leave your family alone. The way things are going you might be stuck there with no way of returning. You can't go. Please hold me. I am so afraid of tomorrow."

I hugged him. His heart was racing. I didn't have the words to comfort him or myself.

I parted from him and went out into the clear autumn air.

I took a deep breath, but couldn't purify my thoughts and my fears. I wondered where we were all headed.

I hurried home. Everyone there was busy. Tizzy was ironing. I couldn't talk with anyone. I didn't want them to know what I knew. It was hard enough for me to deal with it on my own. I went into the room my little one was in. I looked at her angelic face, so small and pure. There was such calmness in her face. What could I offer her? What crazy world had I brought her into? I took her little hand in mine, a perfect hand. Suddenly she opened her eyes and looked at me with big green eyes and smiled. She looked so beautiful, so happy. I kissed her white forehead that hadn't yet known sorrow wrinkles. She smiled again and returned to her dreams. I stayed at her side for a long time. I didn't want to leave. It was a calming moment with the purest creature nature had to offer. She kept smiling in her dream. I was happy she didn't know what I knew.

The violin stayed with mother; a good reason to go there and play a little. How long since I had taken it out of its case? I was amazed that I had not even thought of it.

The house seemed unusually dark. The front door remained open, in accordance with the new law: The Jews were not allowed to lock their front doors so that the authorities could follow their actions. I'd heard that in Bucuresti there was Hitler's adviser who dictated these decrees and the authorities here welcomed them. It was clear that Jews were no longer welcome in this country. I went into the house and looked for Mother. No one was home. I decided to wait. I knew she didn't leave the house these days unless she needed something urgently.

Suddenly a stranger burst into the house.

"Come quickly! The doctor asked me to call someone. The old woman is there!"

I hurried to the doctor's house. It was our doctor from Vama, who had been exiled here with us.

"Hello, Feivel, come in. Mother's condition has already improved a little."

"What happened?" I asked, worried.

"I injected her with medication, her pulse stabilized, and she slept."

"What made her faint?" I asked.

"You know how her heart is, I'm afraid she'll have to lie down again and avoid any effort. The drugs I have are not good enough for her, but there's no choice. The delivery of drugs that should have come from Campulung Moldovenesc was lost or stolen on the way." After a bit of thought, he added, as if to himself, "I would be happy to consult with the doctor from Campulung

Moldovenesc but it is dangerous to travel on the road these days, and who knows if he is still working in the same hospital?"

"Feivel, my boy, what are you doing here?" Mother opened her eyes. "And what am I doing here?" She was surprised.

"You fainted and the neighbor brought you in. Do you remember what happened to you?" I asked.

"I was outside hanging laundry. Our neighbor came home and yelled something at me. I don't remember what. I got dizzy and I don't remember anything from that moment."

"What did he say?" It was important for me to know.

"I don't remember a thing," she said again. There was no point to keep asking.

"Mother, your heart is making trouble again. You must not make any effort. We will not allow you to do anymore work like washing and hanging up the laundry. We will come to help, and you rest and keep your strength up." I knew she hated being waited on but it was the only way to keep her alive.

"Feivel, wait outside while I check your mother." The kind doctor came into the room and spoke in a reassuring voice. I left the room and sat outside. I tried to guess what the neighbor had told her, or whether she had just fainted. From the thoughts in my head, my blood pressure rose and thoughts of vengeance darted through my mind. After the doctor finished examining her, I took a cart and brought Mother home. She got into bed without resistance and soon fell asleep and slept peacefully as a baby. I stayed to watch her till Dad came back.

**

I heard, from outside, an announcer's voice accompanied by clapping and cheering. I jumped up and ran out. I wanted to make him lower his voice so he wouldn't wake up my mother. It was the first thing I thought of. On the street, many people followed the announcer. I knew something special must have happened because nothing less could make Gentiles make such a noise. In all the chaos, I managed to hear what he was saying.

"All the Jews, of all ages, must wear a yellow patch in the shape of the Star of David twelve centimeters square big. Any Jew caught without it will be arrested. This way, every innocent Christian will be able to recognize the true enemy."

Their inventions never ended. I knew we hadn't heard the last of it. The Romanians who heard the message laughed and yelled loudly, "Dirty Jews, all our troubles are because of you. The war is because of you too." Curses and derogatory words filled the street.

I went right back into the house. On days like this, it was better to stay out of sight. It was still early and I hoped the crowd would disperse by the time my father returned. I went into mother's room. She had, of course, already woken up.

"What's happening outside?" she asked.

"They decided to put signs on us so we wouldn't get lost," I tried to sound amused.

"What do you mean?" She tried to understand.

I told her about the yellow badge. "Soon we will have to grow horns, so they will really recognize us from a distance." I had forgotten that I had come to play the violin.

Meanwhile, Dad arrived. He, too, saw the mob on the way and heard the cries of hatred. Fortunately, they were content with curses and did not raise their hands at the Jews who passed through the street.

We talked about the un clear and unsafe situation we were in.

Father called me to the kitchen and told me the latest news about what was happening to the Jews under the German occupation; ghettos, deportations, hunger, and torture. People who managed to listen to the radio reported contradictions and confusion about the victories of the German army.

"Feivel, I just hope they do not get here."

Someone knocked softly on the door, and we both jumped up in alarm. On such days, anyone might lose their confidence. "Should I open?" Father asked with fear in his voice.

"I'll open," I said, and went to the door. It was late and it was dark outside.

"Hello, Feivel. How is your mother?" It was our neighbor Augur, the one who'd brought Mother to the doctor. For a moment, I was surprised to see him outside our house. He pushed me a little, came inside and closed the door after him.

"So that no one sees me here," he explained. "Your mother was hanging laundry. I saw her when I arrived home and I tried to tell her that I was sorry for what my son did.

Suddenly I saw her collapse to the floor. At that moment I didn't care if the neighbors saw. Before all of this started we were very close and Frida helped my wife many times. I jumped over the fence, picked her up, and took her to the doctor."

The three of us stood there looking at each other. Our relationship had changed so much in that year, but weren't we the same people? Endless questions ran through my mind and I had no answers.

I recovered and then said, "Thank you, Mr. Augur. I know you risked yourself to help and possibly save my mother. You are a good man. Maybe we will have sane times again and we will be able to spend time together like we used to."

He lowered his eyes and said, "I am sorry about the new generation and ashamed of them. We have no control over them. I would never hurt you. You must know that." He turned to the door. He opened it carefully, looked around, and only then, very quickly, left the house.

***

I was away from the sawmill for a few days. They actually asked me to "take a break" until after the holidays. I was worried about the reception awaiting me when I returned, but I had to go back. I arrived in the morning with all the other workers and went into an office that I had in common with two other clerks. The relationship between us had been good throughout my time there. At my desk, sat a man I did not know. I went over quietly and said, "Excuse me, sir, this is where I work."

The man stood up, inflated his chest and in a loud voice said, "Jews don't work here anymore. This is my space now." He jumped up like a rooster ready for a fight. I wanted to slap his face. The two co-workers suddenly seemed to be very busy and absorbed in the papers in front of them.

"I have wanted to leave this place for a long time. Any other place would pay more and for fewer hours. I have other offers. Now I have to decide where to go." I was happy that I had control of my voice. I could hardly believe that I was the one speaking. I turned to the rest of the men in the room and added, "I feel sorry for you for losing your personalities and becoming the monkeys of the government."

The two of them jumped to their feet. I was a little frightened, Maybe I'd gone a bit overboard. I raised my head and left the room triumphantly.

It was only when I was away from the factory that I allowed myself to vent my anger and hit the wall with my fist until it bled.

***

It was a very long night. I sat with my wife and we had a long talk. We tried to support each other and chase away our fears and the pain that was building up inside of us.

We couldn't talk about it in front of our parents. We wanted to protect them so they would not panic. The truth was we felt weak and powerless. Everything made us jumpy. Whenever our little one, who slept in our room, made a sound, our hearts would shrink with worry.

The days of our happiness and careless youth seemed so distant now. Tizzy reminded me of my magical place in the forest. It seemed like a thousand years ago. Those birds must have flown away; war wasn't a place for their music.

We hugged and swore to stay together forever. The word "forever" took on a frightening meaning.

Our little one was one year old. She was a naughty little creature. She went everywhere and touched everything. We couldn't leave her alone. Wherever there was something to carry, move, or spread around, she was there. One thing she wouldn't do willingly was to eat but my wife found a way to handle that too. Every lunchtime, my wife would take her out to the back yard, and there, between the animals, she was so happy she was willing to open her mouth at every request. At one point a little black-and-white cat joined the animals and she became my girl's favorite. Every time my wife would look away, she would take food out of her mouth and give it to the grateful cat. My wife ignored it; there was enough food for both of them.

I stood on the veranda looking out at my beautiful vegetable garden. Suddenly I heard someone on the street crying for help. I ran to the street. An old man was sprawled on the path with two thugs standing over him. As soon as they saw me, they quickly ran away and their evil laughter echoed all around. I helped the old man up. I knew him. He was our neighbor, who had been a clerk at the court. I helped him to his house. His leg was bruised and painful.

"They kicked me. Do you hear what they did? They kicked me." He was shocked and couldn't calm down. I got him a glass of water and raised his leg onto a footstool. A huge blue stain had spread along the leg. It could have happened to my father too—the chilling thought crossed my mind. The lonely old man was frightened and looked up at me in a plea for consolation, but I had no words to comfort him.

***

Toward evening I went to visit my parents. I took the little girl with me to see Grandma and Grandpa. My mother could not leave the house and I tried to visit her every day. I had plenty of free time since they'd thrown me out of work. I used the time to organize the warehouse in my father-in-law's back yard, and stored some winter supplies there; a few barrels of wine, bottles of beer, and sacks of potatoes. Many businesses were closed. All Jewish employees had been laid off and the streets were full of people in despair.

"Father, see, a flower." I was so deep in my thoughts that I didn't notice my little one running up the narrow way to my parent's house. She sat on the wet ground and looked at a flower. I picked it for her and lifted her into my arms. She held the flower to her nose and smelled it with pleasure. Tears choked my throat. How could there be, in the world, the innocence of a child with a flower and the horrors of war?

A group of young boys walked near us. I held the little one close to me, almost crushing her. They noticed our yellow patches and they started cursing and throwing fists. My girl, in her innocence, waved to them with a sweet smile on her face. Suddenly, they stopped talking, lowered their fists and waved back to her. What was going through their minds? I was shaking.

I started walking faster and arrived at my parent's house.

Helika ran to her grandmother and gave her the flower and my mother's face lit up. Mother took out a white coat made out of sheep's fur on the inside. The little one jumped up with joy and gave an order, "Wear, now."

She came back and said with a laugh, "I have a little cat." She corrected herself. "I am a little cat."

She touched the inside of her coat with pleasure. We laughed and for a moment we forgot all about our troubles. She ran to her grandfather, jumped on his lap, took his big hand and placed it on the fur.

"Happy birthday, Helika. You are one year old." My mother completed the picture.

"I one hour old, Helika is bigbig." She twisted the words that were said as she jumped on her grandfather's lap.

I turned to my mother, "I hope that next year you will prepare delicacies for our little girl's birthday, but especially that the mood will be much better."

My mother's health and the murky atmosphere around ruined every desire to celebrate.

"Feivel, of all my children you are the only one who stayed with us. Not a day goes by that I don't think about it. I regret the fact that you didn't go to Palestine when you had the chance. I had a part in that too. As a mother, I always want to give my children the very best and at times I found that I was holding them back."

There was such sadness in her words so I had to say, "You know I stayed because I wanted to. You never asked me to change my plans. I love you both and to love means to give. You taught me that to love means both accepting and giving. To be away from you when you needed me would have broken my heart."

By that time Helika had found something new to do. She was trying, unsuccessfully, to take my father's watch out of his pocket.

When she gave up, she tried explaining what she wanted in her cute but limited vocabulary, "Helika clock." She looked at her grandfather and didn't think he understood so she added, "Tic Tac."

My father took out his watch and a light turned on in her eyes. She placed her ear on the watch and laughed.

"Feivel, play something for us. The violin is just gathering dust." My mother asked. I couldn't remember the last time I had played.

Standing, as usual, I tuned the strings, closed my eyes and played the song I loved so much, A Yiddish mother. My tears dripped on the violin and the strings and the sounds played and expressed all the love and respect I had for the wonderful woman in front of me. Even our little girl sat quietly and listened.

**

One morning we decided to visit Uncle Nathan. I took Helika's hand because she insisted on walking. She also insisted on taking the overcoat her grandmother Frida had given her. It was a bit warm, which was regular weather for the end of June. My wife took some food she'd made and the three of us started walking. Suddenly the bells of all the churches started ringing. It was an ordinary day so there was no reason for the ringing. We stopped walking and I picked up the little one, despite her objection. People started coming out of their houses, curious to find out what had happened. After a few minutes, we heard the news. Germany had declared their invasion of Russia.

The Christians in the crowd got to their knees. We started hearing shouting against Jews.

'Death to all Jews!' and 'Your God is responsible for the war.' We backed up against a wall of one of the houses. The gate was open so we walked in and tried to find a place to hide. I didn't know the people in the house we were entering but hoped that no one would go out to the yard and would want to hurt us. I had to decide quickly what to do. The crowd was getting angrier and I was getting more afraid. I worried most about my wife and child. I held the baby in one arm and with the other, I dragged my wife across the yard to the back wall. Lucky for us the wall wasn't high. We jumped over it and found ourselves on a side street. We gave up our plans for a visit and hurried home.

A group of young men appeared in front of us. I had to protect my family because the situation didn't look good. I recognized a man from the mill in the group. While we'd worked together we'd had a good relationship and I'd helped him when he had trouble with his family. I would ignore the times he came late to work and allowed him to leave in the middle of the day. Our eyes met and he hesitated. I didn't look down, it was the only weapon I had. He stopped the group and said something I couldn't hear. They came closer to us as the blood in my veins froze. I almost started saying a prayer as they suddenly went around us as if we were a tree in their way. The baby started crying and only then did I notice I was crushing her in my arms. My wife took her from my hands and with shaking legs we went home

Rumors started coming from different places in Bukovina and Bessarabia. All the stories seemed like horror stories. They were killing Jews everywhere. They were kicking them out of their homes. Jews were moved by trains like animals until most of them died of suffocation. Letters that were smuggled out by Jews who managed to escape the places where the horror took place told of hair-raising things.

People in Gura Humorului decided to go and talk with the authorities. The heads of the Jewish communities started collecting money in order to obtain information about what would happen to us next. They also used the money to ask them to leave us in peace.

We would secretly listen to the news on the radio. The information was general; they didn't say anything about specific areas. We tried to live for the day, not to think about tomorrow, and only hoped that the war would forget us. But fear lay above us like a dark heavy cloud.

Early one Friday morning, the loud voice of an announcer was heard to say, "All Jews must come to the center of the town."

We hadn't expected anything good, but what we got was the worst. We decided that only the men would go to the square to hear the news. I went there with my father and brothers-in-law Max and Yosel, while the cries of the announcer and the thunder of drums continued to echo throughout the town.

We received a terrible blow as we heard the news. All of the Jews, men, women, children, old men, sick men and impaired men had to be at the train station by two o'clock in the afternoon. All the Jews who were in hospitals had to be taken out. No Jews are allowed to stay in town. The instructions were clear; each person was allowed to take only what they could carry.

We had to take bread and water for the road. We had to give away all of our valuables, gold, silver, jewelry, and money to the police and get a receipt for them. We were reminded to give away our house keys too. Anyone who did not show up at the train station or who tried to escape would be shot.

The messages continued to tear up the air. We realized that we had to hurry up and prepare for a nightmare that began that day and would end who knew when.

We hurried home. I decided to take command, otherwise, we could not organize properly at this fateful hour. On the way, I asked my brother-in-law Yosel to buy bread, as much as he could afford. At home, the women sat together in the kitchen and waited for us. I told them everything we'd heard.

"We have no time to cry, we have to leave this place in less than four hours. We all have to gather up our valuables and sew them into our clothes. We have to take warm clothes because the winter is coming and we don't know where they are taking us." All of their faces were pale and they looked at me with eyes wide open. I realized they didn't understand what I was talking about. I had to go and get my parents and Uncle Nathan ready to go. I started worrying about Mother. How would I take her if she wasn't able to walk? Thoughts were going through my mind like crazy. What about our little girl?

The thoughts ran through my mind at a crazy pace. I turned to my wife. "Tizzy, take the warm clothes for us and the girl. We'll take as much food with us as possible..." I felt my head explode, I could not remember what I wanted to say. I glanced at the people around me and realized that everyone had frozen and no one had moved. I lost control of my nerves, and shouted like a madman, "Hurry up, or we'll be lost! Move! Do what I say. Within an hour you will be standing here with ready packages and bottles of water for the way." I do not know exactly what they understood from my shouts but they all ran off.

My brother-in-law came back with several loaves of bread.

"You wouldn't believe the things that happened in the line for bread. People pushing other people; people stealing. It was good that I went there immediately or we wouldn't have had any bread." He placed the bread on the table and went to his room to see his wife.

I told my wife I was going to bring my parents to our house so we could all leave together. I ran through a short cut, over fences, and across yards. The world seemed to me to be uncontrollably cruel. It held no future, and for us Jews, it had lost all meaning. I reached my parents' house and found them all packed and ready to go. They didn't have much. Mother was giving orders to Father from her chair.

"I came to help you finish packing and to get you to our house. It is closer to the train station. Take warm clothes and hide your gold in your clothes. We are not giving anything to our enemies; every piece of gold is important." I saw that my father was only packing necessities.

Mother turned to me, "Feivel, my son, I want to stay here. I am tired and weak. I won't be able to survive on the road. The last time I did it, in the First World War, I was much younger and healthier. Today, I know I will only burden all of you."

I looked at her sad face and her skinny body and I knew that there wasn't a thing I wouldn't do to save her, even if that meant having to carry her on my back.

"You are coming with us. There are many other sick or old people here. You know we will find a way to do this." From where did I get that confidence? Only God knows. Father called me from the bedroom and I rushed to him. I found him without a shirt and he was trying to tie a package to his body I remembered the pages of Grandfather Ephraim and his scroll of the Torah. I understood. I had no right to tell him what was important and what wasn't.

"Come and help me to tie this up. If I don't make it through this, don't forget to take this package off my body and to tie it around yours. This isn't a request, it is a will."

His voice was determined. If in that situation he still refused to leave the package behind I knew it was as important to him as his life. I helped him. We put on his shirt and a sweater over it and we went back to Mother. Father had two suitcases and a backpack that still had room for bread and sugar. We took all of Mother's medications. I planned to find a wagon to take us to the house. Even though there was an order not to drive Jews, I hoped to find someone to help me take Mother and the bags. Dad made another round of the apartment, closing the shutters and doors. Although I felt the absurdity of his actions, I did not say a word. In such a situation, it is absolutely unnecessary to comment.

A knock on the back door made the three of us jump. I thought it might be the Gentiles who couldn't wait to take all of our houses and everything that was in them. I slowly walked up to the door and opened it. Outside was our neighbor Augur. I was amazed at this courage.

"My wagon and horse are outside. After you use them, leave them behind the train station and I will pick them up later." I didn't have a chance to react before he was already gone. We loaded our meager possessions and went to Uncle Nathan's house. He knew we would not forget them and they were waiting for us ready to leave. I loaded them up and went to my house to bring my family.

My tantrums at the start had helped. I found them now all organized and packed for a journey. My wife sat, with our girl on her knees, ready to go. Toward what, I did not know either. I thought it took about an hour to leave this house. I did not feel sorry for what was being left behind. I was completely focused on my little girl, who was going on the cruelest journey and was only a year-and-a-half old.

Uncle Nathan and my mother, with the little one on her lap, sat on the wagon, next to all the suitcases and parcels, and we walked to the train station. A thin rain was falling non-stop. Our clothes were getting wet and the cool breeze reminded us that winter was at the door. The rain on my face mingled with the tears. Where would they take us? Would we survive?

***

People streamed out of all the streets, each carrying their luggage. Children with small bundles in their hands were dragged behind their parents. Old people leaning on sticks or on one of their family members, patients on stretchers—all crowded into the entrance of the station. The commotion was terrible. Luckily we entered through the back road because Augur had asked us to leave the wagon there. Around the station, Gentiles were also gathered, circling around like vultures, waiting for booty and gloating.

My wife carried our girl in one hand and a suitcase in the other. Everyone else was carrying two bags and backpacks. I carried a big bag on my back, I had a suitcase in one hand, and I was carrying my mother with the other hand. We walked to the front of the train station where soldiers with weapons were waiting to push us into the crowd.

After a few minutes, the Romanian soldiers started shouting out orders and pushing us into train wagons that had just been opened. I lifted Uncle Nathan and then my mother. I took our girl so that my wife would be able to get on the train and then she took her up. We had to move quickly if we didn't want to be hit by the guns. We got on the train. On the floor was a bucket. The soldiers rushed people so they'd get in. Our train wagon was full.

I sat my mother, Uncle Nathan, and my wife down. The soldiers kept pushing people in even though there was no more room.

"There is no more room here. We will suffocate," I yelled from the corner that we were huddled in. The soldiers continued their conversation with wild laughter. The children's cries filled the car, with the parents trying to calm them down in every possible way. Another strong push and we could barely keep standing. The doors were closed with a terrible noise and locked from the outside and we began a terrible journey into the unknown.

The wagon got dark. All of the openings were closed with wooden boards. A few people had flashlights and they occasionally turned them on. We tried to stay standing. Everything started moving. We were terrified, worried, and concerned. We knew that if they kept moving us like that for enough days that none of us would survive. It had already happened to the Jews in Iasi. Everybody knew about it and no one said anything.

"I pee, mother, pee." It was our little girl. The bucket that had been provided for that was on the other side and we had no way of getting there.

"Pee, mama, pee!" the little one yelled and started crying. My wife looked desperately at me and then said to her, "Helika, you can pee in your pants."

The little girl looked at her in disbelief. She probably thought that her mother didn't understand her so she repeated her request.

"Pee, mama, pee."

My wife quietly wiped a tear and whispered, "It is fine. Here you are allowed to go in your pants."

After a minute Helika said happily, "No pee. Helika no pee."

We went through that too.

I looked at my mother. She was shrunk into a corner. She didn't even have room to stretch out her legs. She was praying and her face was twisted. She saw me looking so she put on a fake smile to cheer me up, to comfort me.

The shaking of the train's wheels was cut from time to time by a sigh or the sound of someone crying. Amazingly the children were quiet. My little one usually talked all the time. When I looked at her I saw that luckily she was asleep.

We drove for hours in darkness. I suddenly noticed that the first light of the morning was appearing outside. A new day was born. We had been shut in there for about twelve hours with no food or any way to relieve ourselves. By the smell, we could tell that many of us hadn't been able to wait. The train stopped at a station. We were all alert and tense. The doors opened and we were allowed out. We took deep breaths of fresh morning air. The place was deserted. We were nowhere.

"Relieve yourselves before getting back on the train." The instruction was clear. We were embarrassed but had no time to be. We each took a spot in the field; we lost all humanity or modesty. Tizzy managed to take out a pair of pants for our girl. I helped Uncle Nathan walk to the field. I found a stick that helped him walk and then I carried Mother there.

"Go back to the train or we will shoot you."

We just got off and already we had to return to the smelly train. The pushing started again.

"You are the reason we are on the road. If you die we will have fewer stinking creatures."

They kept kicking and cursing and taking all of their frustrations out on those poor people.

We lost count of the days. We kept going from place to place. Every once in awhile they opened the doors and allowed us to get off. We felt like we were on a death train.

The train stopped and we got ready to get off. We had learned to do it very quickly. We waited, but the doors didn't open. I was able to move two boards to let some air and light in. I looked out. There were many people in the station. I asked them where we were and they said that we were in Chernovitz. My mother struggled to turn around and cling to the opening. I understood that she was trying to see her four daughters. We haven't heard from them for so long. My mother didn't move until we were far away. The pain and the disappointment in knowing she might have lost her last chance to see her girls were all over her tortured face.

**

Our food and water ran out. The babies who were crying started getting weak with hunger. Mothers who were breastfeeding ran out of milk and two men had collapsed the last time we were allowed out. People tried to help them but a shot in the air made everyone stay away. The soldiers solved the problem easily; they shot them as if they were rabid dogs.

The next day, in the early evening, we got close to Otaci, which was a town in Bessarabia, near the Dniester River. The doors opened and we were ordered to get out of the train. Farmers from the area stood along the platform. The soldiers ordered us to get in line and prepare to march. The farmers 'helped' us carry our bags and as soon as we looked away, they disappeared with most of our belongings. We could barely stand but the soldiers made us walk. I supported my mother with one of my hands and carried a suitcase in the other. I noticed that my seventy-year-old father wasn't able to carry his bags but I couldn't help him. My wife was barely carrying our girl. Luckily for us, her two brothers and their wives were helping her parents.

We were walking to a dark town and we didn't know who or what was waiting for us there. We hoped to be able to buy some food. I hadn't eaten in two days. I had divided my food between my mother, my wife, and my uncle. Our legs were trembling, the rain was pouring, and we were dragging our bodies forward. All I could think was, 'Just don't fall.' We walked an endless distance in the mud until we reached what looked like a ghost town. There were no people in the streets. Our order was to settle into the houses and wait for further orders. Each family took a house.

The houses had no doors or windows; the wind was blowing from room to room. Inside, we found shattered furniture and blood stains on the floor, the walls, and the beds. There had been racial cleansing there and no survivors. The writing on the walls told of the horror stories that had taken place.

We entered in one of the houses and were welcomed by big writing on a wall. The Jews that lived here had written in Yiddish, with their blood, "Say Kaddish for us, we walked our final walk."

"Don't look around," I said. The panic was clear in everyone's faces. We had to return to reality and worry about ourselves.

"We will find a way to sleep here and in the morning I will try to find food," I promised.

We found a room that looked good to sleep in and in which, at least, the wind didn't blow. We gathered all of our things. We didn't want to wake up to find ourselves with nothing.

There was so little to take from us. They had taken our honor, they were playing with our lives, and we were desperate, hungry, and dirty. We found some buckets of water and some trees thrown outside the house. We warmed up some water to drink, we washed ourselves a little, and we changed our clothes. We drank warm water with a sugar cube in each cup and felt lucky to be able to stretch out our legs and sleep.

The next day some farmer came to sell us food, and we still were able to buy some. The rain didn't stop. The cold wind got under our skin and to the bones. No one knew what we were waiting for. We tried to gather some strength for whatever was coming next.

Voices of crying and begging came from outside. We hurried out and saw an almost endless line of people being led by soldiers. Most of them were barely clothed; whatever clothes they had were torn and dirty. They had cold blisters all over their bodies. They were crying and begging for food and clothes. They looked like beings from another world. They said they were from Bessarabia, that they hadn't had any time to rest in three weeks, and they were led by foot from place to place. Some of them died on the way and the people talking told us that almost in envy. We gave them some food and some of our clothes. It was impossible to see hungry, naked children begging for dry bread and not give anything.

In the house next to us, stood an old couple, who still looked well. They must have come on the train with us. I couldn't help but hear their argument. The woman was begging her husband to give the poor people some food and he refused and said, "What you give them today can determine if we live or die tomorrow." That sentence was terrible and it was forever etched into my memory. Suddenly I was back in the market in Olmitz, standing in front of that old woman and giving her bread. My mother was telling me, "Sometimes we need to give even if we don't have what to give from." Who was right? "How will we know who is right at the end of the journey?" Either way, I was glad for the little food we had given them. The cold winter season was in full swing and we hurried inside, curling up next to each other and warming up a bit.

We spent another night in that place and kept guessing about the future. We spent our days looking for food and our evening gathered together and guessing what would happen to us.

One morning I was the first to wake up. I covered everyone with coats that had dropped off them during the night. I put my coat over my mother and got up quietly. I thought I heard a bird. In that cold? In that world? I begged God to not let me lose my sanity. But still, I followed the sound. A small bird was standing on the open window singing. Another refugee that didn't have the power to fly away from the cold and the hunger. I took some bread crumbs in my hand and walked to the window. The bird got quiet but didn't fly away. I steadied my hand and the bird slowly started coming closer and started eating from my hand. I looked at her. Such a beautiful thing didn't belong to a world like the one that I was in. She finished eating and flew to a tree. I kept standing still. The bird made some 'thank you' sounds and flew away. Within a second the magic was gone. I was back to nowhere, tired, worried, and hungry.

After a few days, we received an order to move again. That time we were walking in the direction of the Dniester River. They were moving us across the river to Transnistria[15]. They planned to take us on boats and ferries. The farmers told us that a few weeks previously, the soldiers had tried to do the same thing. The weather was bad and the river was crazy. The soldiers had put too many people on the boats and shoved them into the river in the other direction. Most of the people had died before reaching the middle of the river. Bodies were floating. It was a sight that shocked even the farmers who told us about it. The soldiers shot the few who were strong enough to swim across. The river was full of bodies and was dyed red. Fear consumed us; these were possibly our last hours.

I went to my wife and daughter and hugged them tightly and cried. She said suddenly, "Feivel, do you remember that we promised each other to be together forever? I think that forever lasts longer than life." She was so wise. It was as if she'd read my mind. I kissed her forehead, kissed our girl, and looked away from them. Forever, never stop believing in that word of promises, forever.

***

---

15   Between the rivers Niester and Buk, with over 130 Ghettos

We gathered our things and divided them between us. We had a lot less by that time, some things we'd sold, and other things had been stolen. Our silver and gold were sewn to our clothes.

There were many who wanted to destroy us, Romanians, Germans, and even diseases that started appearing. Among those were several plagues. On top of everything, there was a freezing cold. But our little group was holding on. We were still dressed well and we were protected from the cold.

"If you have gold you have to leave it here. You also have to change all your Romanian money to money they use in areas of conquest. A person that will be caught with gold on them will be shot." We decided to save some of our gold and not to change the little amount of Romanian money we still had. The farmers who brought food took most of our money. Their prices were unreasonable, but when people are hungry, there is no price too high for food. An announcer drove by a few times calling people to bring their gold to him.

My mother told my wife, "Give them the gold necklace you have under your shirt. You have to do it for Helika. She wouldn't survive without you."

My wife loved that necklace; it had been my first gift to her. Without any argument she took it off, gave it one more look, and handed it to me to give to the soldiers. It looked so natural.

We got in line and started walking to the river while the soldier constantly pushed us.

"Make sure we stay close to each other," I said. It was obvious but I felt the need to say it. We were walking and barely carrying all of our things, our parents, and our girl. It was an endless line of sad and pathetic creatures. We were very quiet, each lost in their own thoughts, walking silently like lambs to the slaughter.

We reached the banks of the river. The water was convulsing. I started imagining us going through the same thing that had happened a few weeks ago. I was filled with guilt. I should have to hand the little one over to the peasants with all our possessions . How could I not have thought of that? At least I could have saved her from death. Maybe slip away with her now? I did not care if they shot me later. What does it matter how I die? The thoughts were haunting my mind and my eyes did not escape from the rushing, raging river.

We were ordered to wait. "We'll cross the river tomorrow," the soldiers ordered.

The rain stopped, and people started gathering wood along the river. We lit a small fire and sat around it. We boiled water that looked moldy and made tea from water and with sugar cubes, and we hoped the hot, sweet tea would silence our hunger a little.

We arranged ourselves for the night ahead with the girl and the women in the center and the men in a circle around them. We wrapped our heads in our clothes but this was not enough to protect us from the cold wind. It rained during the night, but stopped at dawn. Before the soldiers started rushing us, we managed to make another hot drink. The soldiers were angry and cursed us, saying they were suffering because of us. Some ferries arrived and the people were crammed into them. The first group left as we were waiting our turn. The soldiers started losing their patience because they knew that at that rate they wouldn't be able to get all the people across in one day.

Then a terrible order was given.

"Jump into the water, let your God help you cross to the other side."

The first victims were a family that was standing closest to the river. It was a rabbi's family and he had six children. The rabbi, in his black clothes and with a hat on his head, and his children, with yarmulkes on their heads and Bibles in their hands, didn't know what to do. Some soldiers stood behind them and with laughter and cheers pushed them into the raging water. It was a terrible thing to watch. Romanian soldiers laughing and clapping as an entire family struggled to survive.

There were heartbreaking cries for a few moments but they were over frighteningly quickly. The family disappeared quickly because none of them knew how to swim. For a few seconds, we could hear their heartbreaking screams until they suddenly fell silent. The family disappeared into the abyss. None of them could swim and none of them survived. We froze and this time not because of the cold. A few people began to say Kaddish, and the whole shocked audience stood there saying 'Amen'. Such a burial ceremony could not have been created even by the Devil.

The ferries returned and we managed to get on one. A soldier who pretended to help me get my mother on the ferry took a suitcase out of my hand and walked away. I didn't have enough strength to react. It didn't seem important. We were on our way to the other side of the river, to the area between that river and Bug River, an area that was assigned to Jews.

All of our family made it safely to the other side. We stood and waited for orders. We had got used not to move without an order. Whoever had dared to do so was no longer among the living.

We reached the Mogilev ghetto, a Ukrainian city on the banks of the river. The river washed out the roads and covered them with plenty of mud. The group that had arrived before us, had spread out in the area and we were transferred to a large military camp. Then we realized that they were better off, since they at least had a short break from walking.

***

The camp yard was filled with people in a terrible physical condition. Right at the entrance, we ran into people we knew from our village. Mather from going to them. "Can't you see they keep scratching? They are covered with lice. We cannot help them and we really don't need lice as well."

I had never seen a person who was sick from lice. A man's clothes were torn, he had bare feet, red spots on his skin and looked like a walking skeleton. I noticed that he had no bags in his hands. We knew that the people who had been banished from their homes a few months before, were in much worse condition than us. They were out of food, money, clothes, and power to fight for another day of life.

Near the fence were farmers who sold food. I was careful not to be seen by soldiers so they wouldn't take the little I had left. I reached the fence. Other people were there trying to buy food too. I had to fight to get some milk for my girl. I pushed others away and shoved in closer. I was like an animal fighting for food. I did things I never believed I could do and I was ashamed. On the other hand, I always said that there was no shame when it comes to fighting to keep your children alive.

I returned to my family with some milk and bread. My wife quickly took the milk from me and started heating it up with her hands and her breath. The milk was still too cold so she put the bottle under her clothes, next to her skin. I could see her pain, but putting the bottle of milk on her warm skin was the only way to warm it. We soaked the bread in the milk and gave it to our girl. We had to hurry or the bread could have frozen before it was eaten. Our girl ate everything that was given to her without a word. She looked a little better after living for two days on water and sugar.

I didn't dare to look at the people around me as they were licking their lips and moving their mouths at the rate she was eating.

"What else do we have to sell?" my mother asked. I was surprised by the question. She had been quiet up until that point. She was weak and hungry, but suddenly she was alert and interested.

"We have enough for a long time," I lied. There was no reason to burden her with the truth.

Again, they began pushing us, this time into a building that was already full. There was a terrible smell in the air. We tried to find a place to seat the old men and the women. There were shouts and cries of children. There was a nerve-racking noise in the place. We pushed our way along the wall. People lay there quietly, too quietly. Death was visible in their gray faces. Were they alive or dead? From a distance, I saw a less crowded corner. We got there and sat down. It was a little quieter there.

Next to us, on the floor, laid a woman holding a folded baby blanket in her hands. She rocked the bundle in her arms and sang her a lullaby. Was there a baby in the blanket? Her voice was hoarse and croaking, mixed with tears. Then she lay down all along the bundle. I was afraid she would suffocate the baby. I went up to her and helped her up. The blanket underneath was empty.

"Look how beautiful my baby is," she said to me, smiling through her tears. "I love him so much. He wanted to go, but I did not let him. He's so small." She was crying, laughing, and singing as she stroked the dirty blanket. She was clearly losing her sanity. I wanted to cry and could not. My tears had dried up in the ocean of disasters. I went back to my corner and thanked God in my heart that none of my family had questioned me about what I had seen.

Not far from us was a family we knew. They gave us cold and detached glances. My mother waved to them and for a moment it looked like they recognized her but very quickly a misty look returned to their eyes and they looked as though they were blind. More people who were losing their sanity. Who was better off? I didn't know. Any human creature who survived those terrible days carried it with him forever and mental illnesses stayed with people until their final days.

Thoughts came and went; my mind was racing. I had so many questions and no answers. I didn't know what was going to happen to us. We were very tired. Was there something I could have done? Could I have paid off some soldiers to let us stay in Mogilev? What would have stopped them from taking my money and then shoving me, as they had done in other cases? How long would we last? How close were we to the end?

My mother sensed my distress and tried to comfort me.

"Calm down and we will hold on."

She was direct and to the point. My wife kept the child in her arms all the time and was completely exhausted but she did not utter a word of complaint or anger. I took the little girl from her and she fell asleep in my arms. With a wife like her, I knew we could make it through that hell.

A group of Romanian soldiers entered the large room. They walked among us looking for something until one of them yelled out, "Whoever has a dead body next to him raise a hand."

Many hands were raised. Death was taking control. The soldiers volunteered a few men who looked young and healthy and ordered them to, 'Get the bastards out of the hall."

They were pleased with their phrasing and their laughter was chilling. The place in the hall was slightly spacious. We stretched our limbs and began to prepare for the threatening night. We were not allowed to go out to relieve ourselves and the smell was unbearable.

My mother was very bad. It was hard for her to breathe. If I did not find a way to open the window, she would die of suffocation before morning. Above our heads was a window. I had to open it for her. The soldiers left the hall and locked the front door. That was the moment I was waiting for. I asked my brother-in-law to bend over, stood on his back, and with a strong push I succeeded.

"Are you crazy?" the people shouted hysterically. "They will shoot you because of this. They will shoot all of us because of you!"

At last some fresh air came in.

"Until morning no soldier will enter," I said. "Do not worry if something happens. I will take all the responsibility for myself."

Whether they heard me or not, slowly, silence fell. Darkness and fear silenced everyone. We went through another sleepless night with hundreds of other miserable people.

The doors of the hall opened early in the morning. Soldiers started yelling at us to get in lines out in the yard. Miserable creatures in smelly and torn clothes stood in long lines. The soldiers were pushing, cursing, and prodding with their guns, all of the poor people whose legs didn't obey them. Inside the hall were victims of the night. Men, women, and children were on the floor, lifeless.

"I need a few men to take your leftovers out of the hall. This time you'll be digging new holes, stinking laziness," yelled one of the soldiers. No one volunteered. The next stage was to recruit volunteers against their will.

A few boys were taken to do this work. First, they had to dig a hole near the camp fence. Then they loaded the bodies again on a wagon and threw them into a pit; a mass grave for the animals. We all stood watching the terrible scene. We could almost anticipate as to when our turn would come.

There was a cold wind at our backs, mud under our feet, and we were marching under threats. Our heads were down. We were holding on to the people who we loved so that they wouldn't fall because if they did they would be shot.

I saw that my wife couldn't hold on to our girl anymore. She moved her from hand to hand and my brother-in-law was holding her up from behind so she wouldn't stop. I didn't know what to do. I knew that if I let go of my mother, she would collapse into the mud, but at the same time, I was losing my wife in the crowd of people behind us. I lost eye contact with her and started panicking. I had a few gold coins in my pocket and the time had come to use them. I walked up to a soldier who was sitting on a wagon and shoved the coins into his hand.

"My mother is very ill. Please take her on the wagon."

He looked at me for a long time and I saw the hesitation in his eyes. He already had the gold so with one push he could have knocked me to the ground and ended my journey.

"Get your mother up here," he said. I thought of another thing and knew that if the soldier was human enough I could do it.

"Will you please allow my little girl to sit with her grandmother?"

He didn't answer. I understood from that he didn't object. I ran to my wife, took our girl, hurried back and put her in my mother's arms. I could hardly breathe while waiting to see how the soldier would react. He looked away as though he didn't see what I had done. I got back to the line. The rain kept falling and the mud made it hard to walk. I went to my father. Until then I was always with my mother so I barely thought about him. I took from him the package that he was carrying.

"My hand is numb. I haven't felt it in a long time. If you hadn't come when you did, I probably would have lost it." We kept losing things, losing everything. We worried that at some point we would lose our lives.

We kept walking. The cold was getting worse. The wetness penetrated to the skin. Water soaked through our shoes to our socks and even to our feet. I got some rags from my backpack. During the short breaks we had, we needed to decide between eating sugar cubes and bread and wrapping our wet feet. I decided to take care of my feet at the next stop. I took out some sugar cubes and some slices of stale bread and gave some to each of the family members. In that time they covered their feet with more fabric. The soldiers' instructed us to get up and keep moving.

We were not ready to go. Many continued to walk with one shoe in their hands and continued to chew the bread on the way. The sugar cubes melted in the rain and disappeared. A few shots were heard and another part of the convoy that had remained behind us, were bathed in blood in the mud. Why didn't they shoot all of us, and end this nightmare? We traveled a lot of kilometers this day. We could not go on. The murderous shots were heard more and more often. Those who were exhausted also lost their chance to live. I have no doubt that if I had not managed to raise my mother and the child onto the wagon, our entire family would have been among the dead. People no longer cried, did not shout, did not speak. They walked with their heads bent, their aching feet in the mud, and they tried to hold out until the next stop.

The desire to live was great. The spark of hope did not extinguish even when no one had any chance of being saved, and the survival instinct mobilized incredible forces.

Night came down, and so did the number of people who

were still alive. The winter weather was cruel to us. The wind hit us mercilessly. The evil plan to destroy us was assisted by the elements. Suddenly the soldiers stopped and ordered us to prepare for sleep. There were a few stables in the area. We ran with the last of our power and fell on the hay to give rest to what was left of our feet.

Our family gathered in one of the stables. I put my mother and my daughter to sleep on some dry hay and we looked for more hay to get for the others. Suddenly we heard a baby crying. His mother had left him there, probably from a group that had been there before. No one bothered to bend over. Suffering dulls the senses and the struggle for survival seals the hearts. So many lost their children. So many had lost their human image.

Different moans and cries for help came from different areas of the stables. No one even went to see. We became indifferent. We sealed our ears and our hearts. We didn't have the power to help ourselves and we didn't know who would survive to see the next morning. We got close together to save heat. Did we fall asleep or pass out?

***

Again an order to move. Many didn't survive the night. Many people were crying over their loved ones who didn't survive. I checked to see if my family had survived. Tizzy, my wife, wasn't feeling well. One of her feet was swollen and she couldn't put her shoe on. I wrapped her foot with a few rags. She couldn't carry our girl in that condition. I couldn't carry both her and my mother. The others were barely carrying themselves. I cut Tizzy's coat from shoulder to shoulder. I put our girl into that hole and then I tied her up with a rope.

"That is much better. My hands will remain free so if I find a stick I will be able to use it to walk," she encouraged me.

Our child was so thin. She looked like a few months old baby. She wasn't heavy, but in an endless walk through snow and mud, hungry and desperate, any weight was too much to carry.

"Feivel." It was the voice of Uncle Nathan's wife coming from the other side of the stable. I finished tying my girl so I rushed to her. On the hay was the lifeless body of Uncle Nathan.

"I am staying here. It won't be long before I join Nathan," my aunt said.

"All the Jews get out!" There was a wild cry coming from the stable door. I took advantage of the moments until people got up. I picked up the little baggage my aunt still had, and dragged her toward the rest of the family. She walked like a corpse.It was no different from anyone else in the death convoy.

It began to snow again. It was soft and our feet sank into it easily. Our feet got really wet and I hardly could lift them. I felt that I couldn't carry my mother anymore. We were both close to falling down.

My wife and my father were clinging to me and now all of us were close to the end of the line. I knew that if we did not advance, they would shoot us all. I had to think. I remembered that I still had gold coins in my pocket. I knew that if I die, I wouldn't need them, so I might as well use them.

I took the coins out and went to the soldier who was sitting on the wagon. I shoved the coins in his hand and begged, "I know that you are a good man and that this journey is hard for you too. Please take my mother on the wagon. She is very thin and won't take up much space."

He looked at me with disrespect. He looked at my mother and signaled his approval. I helped her up and hoped to get lucky again and be able to relieve my wife from having to carry our child. I asked him as politely as I could, but when he hit my face with a whip I understood that I better get away. The whip on my cheek was burning like a hot iron.

***

Someone was mumbling to himself, "It is forbidden to look at the snow. It is harmful to the eyes. We will be blinded."

Who cares what happens to the eyes?

From somewhere in the convoy there was a cry of despair, "My girl, don't die. I love you so much. Please, don't die." It was a cry of desperation from somewhere in the line. A curse and a gun shot silenced the sound. The mother picked up the dead baby and hardly carried it in her hands. Only after a few kilometers, she gave up the little body.

The road was hard and people were falling all along it. A woman who was walking ahead of me was carrying a baby. All you could see were two big blue eyes that filled her entire skinny face. Next to her walked two boys. I couldn't guess their ages. Suddenly she stopped, walked out of the line, and placed the baby she was holding onto the snow and bent over to kiss her. Then she said, "Don't worry, my little one. I will come back for you." She walked back into the line, gave a hand to each of her children and kept walking as if nothing had happened. It wasn't the only time a child was left behind. Nothing seemed unreasonable, animals did the same. I didn't judge them. We had been close to leaving our girl in the hands of farmers if we had found someone willing to take her.

Another day passed. We spent another night in barns and many more died. We got used to gunshots every morning; soldiers finishing off the sick, the weak, and the children who could not stand on their feet. When we got out to the cold we saw Ukrainians who offered dry bread in return for anything we could give. People took off their coats, their only shield against the cold, for a few slices of bread. Apparently, it was better to freeze than to starve.

"Mother, I'm staying with you." A voice of a girl was heard from one of the buildings. The mother gathered all the power she had left, and begged her girl to keep going. The girl refused to move and the soldiers didn't wait. Two gunshots put an end to yet another tragedy.

We were walking again. It felt as though the mud had become glue that refused to let go of our shoes. We lost track of the days. All we dreamed of was to get to a dry place, to rest our tired bones, and some day to find work to keep us going. We wanted anything that would restore some of our humanity back. Dreams.

I estimated that half of the people we started with had died. Every once in awhile we heard a gunshot and knew that another human being had died. We became indifferent to it. We didn't even turn to see who the victim was. Another boy was left on the road; another angel was crying with his heartbroken mother. Was it a moment of courage or a moment of insanity? After a few hours of relief, the mother realized what she had done. She stopped and let everyone pass, until the last of the convoy. Even when she was beaten by a soldier she did not move. One shot united her with her little boy.

We arrived at an abandoned train station in a Ukraine area. The soldiers told us that we weren't allowed to leave the area. We were forbidden to go to the village. We couldn't beg for food or money. We must pile our dead outside the station. They turned their wagons around and left. It was raining heavily and we needed to find shelter.

The station had a few rooms in it. Everyone wanted to find a dry place. Nineteen people gathered in one room and we were among them. There was hardly space to lie down on the floor. We placed ourselves next to each other like sardines. The important thing was that we were protected from the rain.

***

My mother felt ill. In addition to her heart condition, she'd contracted pneumonia. I decided to go to the nearby village and try to get some food. I did not know what to offer for the food. I opened the last bag we had left. There were a few clothes for the girl and me, my mother's handkerchief, a piece of silk cloth and a pair of gold earrings. I took the earrings and went out. I knew that if I got caught I'd be lost, but I could not watch my daughter and mother starve to death.

It was evening when I went out to the village. I knew that the sight of me was terrible and frightening. I covered my torn clothes with my father's long coat. It was the only coat that had survived in good condition all this time. The earrings were the only valuable and the last chance we had to survive. I decided to try to save them for the time being, and I hoped that the pitiful sight of me, would help to get something to eat without giving the earrings away. My self-respect had gone long ago, along with the thousands of victims who died just for being Jews.

Next to one of the houses in the village sat a white cat. An idea came to my mind. I picked up the cat and knocked on the door. A little girl opened it, saw the cat, and called out happily, "Someone brought my cat back!" I stayed at the door. A large Ukrainian farmer came to the door. He was shocked by the way I looked.

"What do you want?" he asked in anger.

"I have a little girl too and she is hungry. We haven't eaten in three days. Can you please give me some food?"

The man hesitated. Then he said, "Wait outside."

I stood in the rain and waited. Time passed and I was afraid to knock on the door. I imagined them sitting inside, laughing and eating, while I stood outside. Then the door opened and the farmer handed me a package.

"This is for your girl," he said and closed the door.

I took the food and ran to the train station. I tried to smell what was in the package but couldn't. I felt something hard and prayed it wasn't a stone. When I opened it, it was some bread, a bottle of milk, and a piece of cheese. I fed my mother and my girl first and there were enough leftovers to calm everyone else's hunger too. I thanked the farmer in my heart. It turns out that there are still sane people in this crazy world.

The next day my mother's situation got worse. She wasn't breathing well and her temperature kept going up and down. She called my wife over and asked to eat mamaliga, a Romanian food that was made out of corn flour. We didn't know what to do. We opened our bag again and my wife decided to use the silk to fulfill my mother's request.

It was clear to all of us that it was her last. I decided to go to the farmer who had been so nice to me before. I gave him the silk and he was happy to give me the flour for it. He also gave me a few more things.

My mother got the mamaliga, ate a spoonful, and asked to rest. In a weak voice, she tried to tell me something. I put my ear to her mouth. It seemed to me that she was hallucinating. Her eyes were misty, and she didn't look directly at me.

"Feivel, you see the angels, they're so beautiful, and you play for them so beautifully." Hovering in another world, in my last moments of grace with her, she asked me to play A Yiddishe Mameh again. The words came out of her mouth with great difficulty and then she sank into a faint. The violin! I'd forgotten about it long ago. If only I could hold it to play for her one last time!

Among the refugees was a doctor. His physical condition was poor, but at least we were helped by his advice. I spotted him and he tried to check Mother. He touched her head, put his ear to her chest, shook his head, and left. She regained consciousness. She told me to come closer to her, "I know that it is final, and I have only one request: promise me that I will be buried in a Jewish cemetery, according to Jewish tradition." She took my hand in her hot one and held it to her heart.

"I promise," I replied and kissed her hand.

In the morning my mother was gone. She died as she had lived, quietly, modestly, and without bothering anyone. I went out in to the pouring rain, stood alone dripping water, and prayed for her soul.

***

My mother's voice kept ringing in my ears, 'Promise me I will be buried in a Jewish cemetery.'

I had to fulfill Mother's will. The nearest Jewish cemetery was dozens of kilometers away from Mogilev, in the Kopai Gorod ghetto. If I got caught on the way, they would shoot me. According to the instructions, I had to put her body in the pile of dead near the station. I had no one to consult with. My father sat in the corner, in pain, praying, and crying.

I sat down next to Tizzy. Mother was in front of us, her face calm and all her wrinkles gone. Her suffering had came to an end.

"What do we need to get Mother to the cemetery?" my wife asked.

"We need fabric to wrap around her and boards to make a coffin. The road to the cemetery is long, but first, we need to prepare Mother. We must follow the laws of our religion," I said. My wife got up and disappeared for an hour. At that time I asked people I knew to help me get boards. They looked at me like I'd lost my mind.

"Where do you think you are going? How will you move the coffin that distance? If you have decided to kill yourself, do it here."

I knew I was acting crazy but I couldn't do anything else. I had to fulfill my mother's last request to the fullest.

I remembered I still had the earrings in my pocket. I decided to get boards for the price of one gold earring. I ran to the village. On my way, I ran into a farmer who was struggling to get his wagon out of the mud. He called me to help him. I had no time for that because I had to start moving the body to the town on that day. I was about to return to my running when I saw that on his wagon was a large pile of wooden boards. I stopped and said, "I will help you in return for a few boards," I tried.

"Go away, filthy Jew. You want payment for everything," he said and kept pushing the wagon. Luckily for me, it didn't move. I tried again, "My mother died and I need boards for her coffin." Tears choked me up. I was willing to beg and do anything to keep my promise to my mother. The farmer suspected that I was lying to get wood because wood is a good way to survive in that place. He raised his eyes, looked at me for a moment and said, "Why are you just standing there, miserable Jew, come and help me."

I was stronger than ever before. I pushed with swollen and frozen hands, with my legs, with my body, and with my soul. I cried and pushed. We got the wagon out of the mud and I got my boards. The earring had to wait to save me at another time.

Two men from our town helped me build the coffin. Tizzy got a sheet that served as a shroud. I did not ask her where the white cloth had come from. We did everything right, as mother would have wanted. I had to find a wagon and set out for the Kopai Gorod. Ukrainians circled the area around the railway station with wagons and groceries for sale at exorbitant prices. I asked one of the peasants to drive me with the coffin to the Kopai Gorod and back. He looked at me, puzzled at my request and refused. "If they catch us, they will shoot us both, and if you do not have a pass, you are as good as dead."

He didn't pay any more attention to me. I realized it would be hard to find someone to take me. I went from one man to another, but no one was willing to take the risk. In the distance, I saw an eighteen-year-old boy with a wagon and decided to try my luck.

"You seem like a brave boy. You must know some quick side roads to reach Kopai Gorod. If you take me there and back, I will pay you in gold."

His eyes lit up.

"I know all the roads in the area. I rode the horse all over this area when I was young. Will we return today?" he asked.

"We will leave now and return today," I said.

I took out one of the earrings, and showed him.

"Are you sure it is gold?" he asked.

"I'm sure."

"All right, let's go."

We hurried to the train station. My friends had made the coffin and left it to me to put my mother in it. I picked her up, she was so thin, and she had the weight of a small child. My hands were shaking. I was carrying her body to her burial. Despite the cold, my body was covered with sweat. I steadied my feet so I wouldn't drop her and walked in small steps.

I said goodbye to my wife. She said nothing. We both hoped I would return. I was grateful that she didn't burden me with farewell tears. My little girl ran to me. I bent down and she wrapped her arms around me.

"Where are you taking grandma?" she asked as though I were taking her for a walk.

"Grandma was called to another place and I am escorting her there." What else could I say to a year-and-a-half old child?

We loaded the coffin onto the wagon. Two of my friends offered to go with me.

"We lost our parents on the way and weren't able to pay our last respect. We decided that this way we would be able to honor them." We got on the wagon and went down the road.

The boy really did know all the side roads. We passed fields, forest paths, and deserted villages. All the way we were watching, so if we could see something suspicious in the distance, we'd be able to get away. The main thing was not to meet any soldiers who were everywhere.

We were a very miserable bunch: three people dressed in ragged clothes, big hair, ragged shoes, and, above all, a typical Jewish look. No one would have questioned who we really were. There were many Jews running around from place to place. We were easy prey and whoever killed a Jew became a hero.

From a side path, a rider appeared wearing a soldier's uniform and carrying a weapon. He stopped his horse in front of the cart and turned to the boy.

"Where are you taking those Jews?"

The boy was embarrassed. We froze. The soldier blocked our way. He did not acknowledge us at all, apparently because in his eyes we were already dead.

"Get these Jews off," he ordered the boy. "I have enough bullets to take care of them. I'm sure they paid you for the ride. If you want to go on living, you'll have to give me the money." The boy looked at us questioningly. He didn't know what to do.

When my mother's voice echoing in my head, I jumped out of the wagon and grabbed the soldier's horse. My face turned red and my blood was boiling in my veins. I was afraid, but I knew that if the soldier will notice that, It's my end.

"We're not going to run away, we're just going to bury my mother," I shouted in Ukrainian. I'd lost control of my voice. One of my acquaintances took out a gold coin and handed it to the soldier.

He hesitated and looked around. We were alone within a few miles. Then he took the coin and moved off the path. I jumped on the wagon. The boy whipped the horse, and it started at a gallop. It took a long time for me to recover.

***

We entered the Kopai Gorod ghetto on Friday at two in the afternoon. Many miserable people were wandering the streets, looking terrible, like us. I asked for a rabbi to receive a burial permit for my mother. I had to pay him something and I had nothing to give. Embarrassed, I took off my fur hat from my head. I owed a lot to this hat, which had kept my head warm in the rain and the snow, but it must have been time to part with it.

Outside it was terribly cold. The hat stayed with the rabbi in return for a burial license. I left with the license as I heard the rabbi call after me, "You won't be able to bury her today. There is no one in the cemetery to help you. Come again on Sunday."

I tried to talk to his heart, "I came from Mogilev and the road is dangerous. How would I come again on Sunday?"

"There is no one to dig a grave at this time," was the rabbi's answer. There was no other solution. As I turned to leave the rabbi, he gave me a piece of fabric to cover my head with. "You will need a yarmulke to enter the cemetery," he said.

Many bodies laid on the road leading up to the cemetery and hadn't had a proper burial. The bodies were covered with water and mud. Luckily Mother was in a coffin and in the cold weather I was sure that her body would be alright until Sunday. I left the coffin close to the gravedigger's house. I gave him the license and he promised to have a grave ready for Sunday. I got on the wagon and we drove back to Mogilev.

When we got back, there was a thick darkness all around. It was Saturday night. I found my father sitting and crying, and my wife was taking care of the child. I looked for Yosel, Max, their wives, and Tizzy's parents, but I could not see them anywhere.

"Several wagons organized and they went to Shargorod. We heard rumors that Jews can get permissions to stay there and even get jobs," she explained. Suddenly she noticed I didn't have my hat on. "Did you lose your hat?"

"I gave it to the rabbi to pay for Mother's burial," I answered.

She gave me a slice of bread with cheese and some warm water. I was very grateful and didn't even think of asking where she'd got that treasure from. Before collapsing to sleep, I said, "I had a hard day. I must sleep." I put my head on the hay and immediately fell asleep.

On Saturday I looked for ways to get back to the cemetery the following day. I had hoped to find a wagon with people who had arranged to go to Kopai Gorod and whom I could join. I wasn't that lucky. I couldn't rent a wagon by myself. My possessions were running out and I still owed a friend a gold coin. That time no one wanted to go with me. I had no choice but to get there on my own.

On Sunday I got up before dawn. My father gave me the warm scarf he had had around his head for the entire journey and his coat, which I wore over my coat. It was terribly cold outside. I knew I would make it to the cemetery that day, I just didn't know how.

I remembered the roads we had gone by on Friday and decided to walk the same way on foot. At first, the wind was behind me, penetrating under all the layers and hurting my sore back but also pushing me forward. There was a positive side to it. I wanted to go as far as I could before the Ukrainians woke up. In some places, I had to walk through villages and I was afraid I would get beaten.

I discovered how long the way was, and how tiring when you get when you have to walk. The hours passed and I was still far from my goal. I didn't dare to think about the fact that I had to walk back that day too. I got close to one of the villages. It was in the late morning. Children were playing outside. They had warm clothes on, lucky kids. I tried to walk on a side road, but one of the kids saw me and got the rest of them to throw stones at me. They were five boys with stones so all I could do was run.

They did not give up and I felt stone after stone hit me. A strong, cold wind began to blow and at last, they were driven home. I went quickly. I had to cross through another Ukrainian village, and I did not even have the strength to feel afraid. Only the inner necessity of reaching the cemetery drew me forward.

I got to that village. Since it was a Sunday and it was very cold, the streets of the village were empty. When I was almost outside the village, I heard dogs barking. When they hate and are angry, they are as bad as cruel people. I picked up a stick that was lying on the side of the road. One of the dogs, large and threatening, chased me and came up behind me. I was preparing to crush his skull. I stopped with the cane in my hand, and then, about three feet away, the dog stopped too. I turned and saw a poor creature, its fur plucked, its bones protruding and its tail between its legs. The dog stopped barking and looked at me. I did not move. How similar we were! No one wanted us, we were both hungry, and our bodies were like skeletons. Slowly I turned my back on him and began walking. He followed me a little, turned, and went back to the village.

***

In Kopai Gorod, I went straight to the cemetery. On the way, I ran into a man I knew from Vama. By the look of him, I knew that his situation wasn't any better than mine. I asked him to come with me and help me bury my mother. He quickly agreed. The only man in the cemetery was an eighty-four-year-old man. He directed me to the morgue, to which my mother's coffin had been moved. Many bodies were in that room, bodies of men, women, and children, some in piles, most of them naked. I couldn't help but notice a number of children who were there. Their bones were sticking to their yellow skin, skin that was filled with deep wounds. I had to force myself to look away, to let go of the thought that we weren't far from that situation. I was horrified by the thought of how often I had been close to losing my child.

I was afraid I would lose my mind in this place. The sights and smell were unbearable. My acquaintance fled immediately, and I was left alone with the old man who could barely drag his feet.

I went outside as the man showed me the grave. Strong rain started coming down. I stood there looking around; all I could see were bodies everywhere. The rain was getting stronger and I was alone with my mother's body and with God. There was no one to help me move the coffin. I asked God for the power not to collapse into the grave along with her. I wrapped some fabric around my hurting hands and started dragging the coffin on the muddy ground. The mud stopped me from moving forward. I cried from pain and effort and bit my lips until they were bleeding. I couldn't move anymore. I fell backward into the mud. I sat on the ground. I pulled myself half a meter backward and then pulled the coffin to me, moved again and pulled the coffin again.

I can't say how long it took. It seemed like forever. Then, I was standing in front of an open grave and I had to lower the coffin down. I couldn't just throw the coffin in. I had to lower it slowly, with respect. I couldn't move. I feared for my sanity. With my last strength, I picked up the heavy coffin with both hands. I could barely see what lay ahead of me through the torrential rain. I gathered my last drop of strength, said a prayer, and slowly lowered the coffin into the hole. I collapsed.

***

"Son, get up. You'll drown in the mud." Above me was the old man, holding out a thin, shrivelled hand and helping me up. There was no tool with which I could cover the coffin with earth. I had to do it with both hands. I muttered Kaddish and the old man stood beside me and prayed with me. The rain washed my bearded face with tears. In a world where sanity had become a luxury, in relentless rain, we stood above my mother's grave and we tried to make my mother a jewish burial.

The old man took me to his small room. He didn't let me go until I was completely dry and had something warm and sweet to drink. I thanked him for being so humane. Then he said to me in an excited voice in Yiddish, "Happy is the mother to have such a son."

***

I left and ran on the way back to Mogilev. I was afraid that the darkness would fall and I would not find the way. People threw stones at me and dogs ran after me. I managed to get through all of that. I felt a tremendous satisfaction in having fulfilled my promise and had met an impossible and dangerous task. A few more miles and I'd get there.

I saw a group of soldiers from afar. Were they coming back to take us on another journey? I hid. I wanted to see where they were going. I saw a Ukrainian farmer among them. He pointed at one of the Jews. The soldiers jumped at that man and started hitting him. We had learned not to interfere. We couldn't help; we would just be hurt. There were no more yells. The man had probably passed out. They gave him one more kick and tossed him to the side of the road. I could finally come out of hiding. I went to the hurt Jew and helped him up. We limped inside together.

***

The number of Jews in the railway station got smaller. Most had paid everything they had to get a wagon out of Mogilev. Farmers from the nearby villages chased us away; they sent their dogs after any Jew trying to come near the village. They didn't want to look at us. We were a mess, ill, and we always begged for food. It was very cold. The locals said it was one of the coldest winters they remembered. Snow kept falling constantly and a strong wind was hitting us, penetrating to our bones. Most of us remained with no clothes. Some people wore the flour or sugar bags they stole from farmer's warehouses. A friend of mine was beaten so badly that he needed to be carried from the village to the station. In order to survive, we stole everything we could.

We stripped the dead without feeling. When you are cold and hungry, the instinct for survival triumphs over morality.

Around me lay many sick and dying people. We had to leave immediately before we contracted any disease or died of starvation.

"There are a few typhoid patients in the other room," said Tizzy who seemed to read my thoughts.

"Tizzy, where did you get that sheet to wrap my mother? And how did you get the bread we eat?" I asked her the questions from seemingly nowhere. Tizzy looked at me in amazement. She must have hoped that the pain, the effort, and the grief I was in, would mean I would not ask her. Her face flushed. I knew she would never lie to me.

"When you asked me to bring a white cloth for a shroud, I ran to the village and looked for laundry that was hanging bed linen to dry. It was very difficult to find one in the winter but I finally found one. At that moment, the Ukrainian peasant woman arrived with another load of laundry, I froze in horror, afraid that her husband would come out and beat me or shoot me before I could bring you the sheet. My knees trembled so that I could barely keep my balance. I told her who I was and why I had stolen the sheet. Her voice became soft. She told me that her mother had died a few days previously and the house was a mess. I promised to come back and clean for her. She gave me bread. I went there a few times as I promised her."

I put my arms around Tizzy's shoulders. Every word of thanks was superfluous.

I put a little order to my thoughts. I hoped that Tizzy's parents, her brothers, and their families had found in Mogilev somewhere to lay their heads and some way to earn money. I had to find work immediately; any job under any condition. All our money and possessions were exhausted. It was impossible to survive even one more day in these conditions. I was cold. Beneath the torn coat I wore several shirts, each of which covered the holes of the other.

I had lost the sole of one shoe so I hooked what I had left to a wooden board with the remnants of a rope. Little Helika had lost all of her vitality. She was too quiet as if she was not present. I missed the sound of her crying, her laughter, and her chatter. But maybe it was better? Her silence made it easier for us. In any case, we did not have the strength or the means to amuse and delight her. I remembered how she'd loved the cloth doll that Grandma Frida had sewn for her. I did not know when or where we'd lost it.

***

We decided, together with another family, to leave immediately. We found a wagon, and the driver agreed to bring us to another ghetto. We left at night. We hoped that because of the terrible weather, we would not encounter anyone along the way. We all huddled together to keep our bodies warm. We wrapped the little one in Grandpa's coat.

"Febi, look. It is the ghetto. We have arrived." My wife woke me from my thoughts.

The driver left us near a big building. I gave him a gold earring. He wasn't satisfied, but it was all I could give away. We entered the building; hundreds of people were there and most of them were sleeping. We found a corner and decided to stay there for the night. It was good to have a roof over our heads.

Mogilev was a ghetto with a Ukrainian mayor, but the military government there was under Romanian control. Within the refugees, a Jewish group called Machers had been formed. It was hard to help people with all the poverty, hunger, and sickness that were all around, but at least there was an attempt to help. That group was in contact with the Romanian government in the area and they did the management work for them.

They recruited refugees to clean the ghetto in return for food. They made us an improvised hospital. The doctors that worked there were completely broke and they had no medications to give to patients. Trying to have a natural life in that unnatural world was an impossible mission.

We met Tizzy's family and rented a room together in the home of a Ukrainian peasant. We were seventeen people in a room. There was hardly room to lie down, only the old and the children were left a little more space. Every morning I went out with my two brothers-in-law, Max and Yosel, to look for work. They had come here before us and knew a little more than I did. The snow hit our faces.

I consoled myself with the thought that soon the winter would pass, and it would take with it the typhoid epidemic that had spread and caused many casualties. There was no medicine and the patients were weak and broken even before they became ill. The dead were taken to the streets and a wagon passed and collected them. The piles grew larger by the day. Outside the ghetto, the corpses were thrown into huge pits. All were buried in a large grave. We all became indifferent. Everyone cares only for those closest to them and nothing else existed.

We found work. We were sent out to chop down wood for the municipality. The payment was in food. I got a quarter of bread a day. With that food, I had to feed my father, my wife and my daughter. We had no chance of surviving that way. I lived on melted snow and leftovers I found in the trash. It was cold.

I had to get some wood to keep us warm to heat up water to drink. It was impossible to survive without wood. I spoke with my brothers-in-law and we decided that we had to steal wood. We found a place no one could see and while we were working we would throw a log in there every once in a while.

We worked very hard and while the rest of the workers went to get their bread we organized the wood in bags we kept under our clothes. We were the last ones in the line to get paid. The problem was how to move bags filled with wood to our room.

**

The cold was so terrible that we had to bring pieces of wood quickly. When it was dark, the three of us left walked some distance away and looked for a safe way to carry the logs. On the way, we saw one of the Jewish activists. We could not avoid meeting him.

"What are you doing here in the dark?" The question sounded very friendly. We smiled, and he went on to investigate,

"You're going to get something? The Romanians caught some of our men when they tried to steal from the city warehouses and shot them all."

Exactly what we needed to hear now! I got up and said, "We're going to see if some other relatives have come to the ghetto."

My brothers-in-law looked at me in amazement, but the man was convinced by my creative invention and we said goodbye. Some of the 'Machers' collaborated with the Romanian authorities and their denunciations led to the death of quite a few refugees. In return for the cooperation, they received good conditions, food, and clothing. We were glad we had gotten rid of him.

We reached the place where we had hidden the sacks. Each of us carried a sack and began to stealthily return. We walked slowly, squatting, in the shade of the houses. There was no one on the street and we managed to get the three bags into the room. To our delight, there was no limit. We had wood and we could heat the water. Hot water softens bread at any degree of dryness. We couldn't live for long on food like that. Our work was very hard; we needed to find a way to get more food.

We got to where we'd hid the wood. We prepared three bags, one for each of us. We snuck in one by one and got the bags. The next mission was to get home without getting caught. We walked close to the houses. There was no one in the street; we walked slowly as our eyes searched everywhere to find any sign of people. We got to the house; our happiness was unlimited.

The Ukrainian whose house we lived in, called my wife over and suggested, "You look like one of us. My wife will lend you her clothes. You have to take the train to distant villages and sell my sausages. I will pay you with food."

The offer seemed tempting. The risk was obvious; any Jew who was caught without a permit was shot and thrown off of the train. The fact was that people would leave and never return. Anyone who was caught smuggling food was given an extra punishment before the shooting; murder and cruelty.

I tried to persuade Tizzy to refuse the offer but my arguments did not stand the test of survival. We were hungry. We were almost starving to death.

My wife left the following day dressed as a Ukrainian farmer. The sausages were hidden under her coat and in a big basket that was commonly used by Ukrainian women. The Ukrainian man gave my wife money for the train tickets.

I escorted her to the train station, which was a few kilometers from Mogilev. The train was crammed with peasants who went to sell their wares from village to village. The crowding and the smell were terrible. It was for the best because that way the smell of the sausage went undetected. The train moved, and in my heart, I hoped I would see my woman again. At that moment I regretted letting her go but there was no turning back. I hurried to the town hall. I had to organize the firewood for the mayor and, if I was lucky, I would also find scraps of food in the trash.

I returned from work as usual and saw that there was much commotion in our room. It turned out that one of the men in our room, a forty-year-old man, had got typhoid. Everyone was fighting with the family to take the sick man to the hospital. The family wanted to wait a few more days. They feared that the condition of the hospital would only expedite his death.

I saw that the debate could last forever so I turned to the head of the family and said, "If you don't take him to a hospital right now, we will inform the landlord, and he will throw all of us out. If we tell the health inspector about this there is a good chance that they will finish him off to stop a plague from spreading."

They couldn't really argue with that. He was moved to a hospital that very day. We took out his belongings and burned them. As best we could, we cleaned the room. Fear was gnawing. Who among us had already contracted the dreaded disease?

I couldn't sleep that night. I was tired, but concern for my wife kept me up. I felt guilty. The torture was stronger than my need for sleep. Morning came and there was no sign of my wife. I covered my bruised feet with leftover fabric. I gave the rest of my fabric to my brothers-in-law and we left for work. We were chopping wood again.

We started cutting the trees. My hands were heavy as lead ingots. I could not lift the ax. I felt a terrible dizziness and felt close to collapse. I crawled to where one of my brothers-in-law worked and asked him to cover for me at payment time. No one should know that I wasn't working; such a discovery would be accompanied by a bullet without any double meaning.

I crawled to a small cave at the edge of the forest and lay there. I was feverish and chills of cold and heat shook my body. Typhoid! The thought pierced my mind. I had got infected. I was going to die! I wasn't ever going to see my wife again. If she didn't return, our little one would lose her mother and her father on the same day.

Suddenly I heard a noise from the entrance to the cave. I froze on the spot. I was sure that the foreman had found me and now he would shoot me. I stopped breathing. Then I heard a whisper.

"Feivel, it's me, Yosel. Come, crawl out. Hurry up." I leaned against him, barely reaching the roll call. There I straightened up, walked in front of the man in charge, and was given the quarter of the loaf of bread. We began to move toward our house. From that moment on, I remembered nothing. I collapsed.

When I opened my eyes, I saw a man in a white coat that was torn and stained with blood. I've come to the next world, I encouraged myself. He leaned over me and muttered something. I could not understand what he was saying. I tried to concentrate. Suddenly, I realized who he was. It was the doctor from our town. He was so thin, I hardly recognized him.

"Feivel, you are in the hospital. Your wife's brother brought you here several hours ago. You passed out. You are lucky that I was the one who received you here. At first, I thought you had typhoid. I examined you with greater attention and it turned out to be just a bad case of a cold or maybe pneumonia. Definitely not typhoid."

He stopped talking for a moment. He was tired and weak. Then he said, "I have no medication to give you. The only thing I can give you is advice. Leave this place as fast as you can before you catch something really bad."

Someone walked by and the doctor went quiet. After a few moments, he added, "I haven't started a file on you yet. The moment I turn around you must leave. There is a coat near the bed. Disappear quickly." He turned around and left.

What was I supposed to do? I got one leg down, then the other, and got up. I didn't forget my precious coat. I put it on. I saw bandages in a corner of the room. I looked around and I put some bandages in my pocket and headed out.

The cold weather helped me wake up completely. I was happy to have something to wrap around my feet. It was a short walk to our room. I was there in less than fifteen minutes.

My father and my sisters-in-law Sally and Chela were playing with our girl. Where was Tizzy? How many days had passed since she'd gone? I was so exhausted that even the worry did not prevent me from falling on the straw and falling asleep at once. My sisters-in-law took care of me with cold packs on my forehead and a drink of hot water with sugar cubes. It had been two days and one night since Tizzy had gone and there was no sign of life from her. Now that the heat had gone down a bit, my head cleared, and I could take care of myself.

The Ukrainian man came several times to check. He was afraid that my wife would run away with his food and that we would leave to meet up with her. When he saw that we were all still there he was relieved and asked that my wife bring him his money as soon as she returns. He worried about his money while in my mind I feared that my wife was no longer alive.

***

Tizzy arrived late in the afternoon. She looked terrible. Her eyes were swollen and her hands full of chilblains.

"I managed. I sold all the sausages," she said. "I will go and give the money to the Ukrainian and return the clothes." She did not seem to see us. Not even the child. When she came back, dressed again in her rags, she also brought a package of food. The Ukrainian was pleased with the amount she had brought him and gave her bread, milk, corn flour, cheese, and sugar. He also gave some clothes for our little girl. A miracle. "Look at what beautiful clothes he sent for Helika. They were his little son's." Tizzy pulled out a Chinese-collar shirt and a pair of trousers that were typical of the peasant boys, and out of a newspaper, a pair of small boots slipped out; an invaluable treasure. Helika wanted to wear everything immediately. She looked like a Ukrainian child. Her short hair, which was cut off because we feared lice, suitable to the boy's clothes. She began to dance and sing. She was almost four years old, but looked much younger.

After a warm water drink, we lay down on the straw and fell asleep. My wife didn't have the strength to tell us what had happened to her and no one really had the energy to listen.

The next evening we were together again. Tizzy told us her story.

"The train I took was crowded with farmers and soldiers. Almost every farmer was carrying baskets and packages. A farmer got off at the first stop and I practically jumped into his seat. The place was very small and I almost sat on the man next to me. Sitting was better than standing. I slept for a while. I suddenly felt the elbow of the man next to me.

"Do you have legal papers?" he asked. I didn't have documents that allowed me to leave the Mogilev ghetto. I decided not to answer and instead I tried to get up. As I was about to do that, he grabbed my arm and forced me to sit back down. My world went dark. I had heard a lot about snitches in civilian clothes and it was just my luck to sit next to one. I was shaking all over. I was sure he could feel me shaking.

"Sit quietly. Pretend to be asleep. I will take care of this," he said. I closed my eyes.

All I heard was shouting at farmers traveling without a ticket. I remembered that I had a ticket for the train. With my eyes closed, I reached into my pocket and pushed it into the man's hand. I did not dare move. Time seemed to stop. I was afraid. We've heard about people who disappear and are never found. I felt the man next to me touch me lightly.

'You can open your eyes. All is well.'

You will not believe it; the man spoke Yiddish. This man saved me. I opened my eyes and he smiled. He put his finger to his lips and motioned me to be quiet. The ride continued. All the way I did not say a word, and when he disappeared at the station, I did not have the chance to thank him."

In the meantime, our little girl had fallen asleep. Darkness fell on the room, and the oven spread a pleasant warmth.

Someone shook me. It was so dark that I could not recognize the man.

"Feivel, it's me, Dad. I want to tell you something." What was so important in the middle of the night? "Do you remember the small package with the Torah Scroll?" Without waiting for an answer, he continued, "I took it out, read it, and prayed that Tizzy would come back safe and sound. That little Torah kept her safe."

There was so much happiness in his voice. I wished I could see his face.

***

We kept suffering from lice. Different products that were supposed to get rid of lice started arriving in the ghetto, but none of us managed to get any of them. They were all gone the first day they arrived. We suspected that the Jews in the organization were making money from that too. To relieve the terrible itching, we cut our hair as short as possible and arranged a special ritual to pluck the lice together, like monkeys.

I did not know how I would get the money so we could live. I did not have the courage to steal goods from government warehouses and sell them like some of my acquaintances did.

The winter was close to being over. We were looking forward to it. The typhoid was fading away. The common graves were filled at a rapid pace. We were often recruited to dig more holes for the next dead. Crying was no longer heard. Acceptance of the loss became part of daily life. The clothes from dead were taken to warm up the living.

The disregard we got from the government made it clear that they wanted us dead. They would hit us without reason. They took our bread as punishment. They whipped us so that we would work faster. How could skeletons work?

We held on until we collapsed, then we arrived at the last point of collection, the great pit. I tried to encourage myself with: such thoughts are forbidden. I'll find some work to do. We'll survive. There was no other choice.

Whoever survived the cold had to endure the abuse of those who were in control. There, people lasted for as long as they could and then arrived at the big gathering point, the big hole with the rest of our dead brothers. It was wrong of me to think such dark thoughts. I had to find more work, I had no other choice. We must survive. We had no other choice.

***

One evening, the turning point took place unexpectedly, surprisingly, and amazingly. A familiar person entered the room. His name was Mr. Robinson, and before the exile, he was the president of the court in our region.

I remembered him as a tall man, elegantly dressed, with a respectable position among the Jews and the Gentiles. To reach him, it was necessary to wait in line for a long time. Now he stands before me bent, thin, wearing a worn and dirty suit, the color of his face yellowish-green, his eyes large and protruding.

He came to me and reached out his dry shaking hand, with black fingernails and popping veins. I took his hand in mine and said, "Sit down, Mr. Robinson," and I quickly added, "Your honor."

He tried to smile. He looked embarrassed. His smile revealed a toothless mouth. God was really making fun of us. It was easier to see how we looked by looking at others.

"I live not far from here with my two sisters. We are in a bad condition. I am too weak and old to work here. We have no food or wood. Can you, please, give me some warm water?" We served him warm water with sugar. He only took a few sips and then said, "I will return the glass later. I would like to give the rest of this to my sisters."

As he got up to leave, I saw that he was carrying a violin case. I turned to him and said, "Drink it all. We will give you more for your sisters." He relaxed and sat back down. He closed his eyes and drank slowly. He seemed to be doing much worse than us; at least we had wood.

He recuperated and then turned to me.

"I know that you are a musician. I used to play too when I had hands. You are young; you still have many years to play. This violin is very valuable. It is an Amati. It is similar to a Stradivarius violin." He opened the case, took out a beautiful violin and handed it to me. I took it with a slight shiver. I haven't held an instrument in so long. He kept talking.

"What good does a violin bring? If you could get work playing the violin don't forget me. All I want is a quarter of a loaf of bread and some warm water. I know it is a strange deal, bread in return for playing a violin."

He got up and left. I didn't even get a chance to react. I was amazed by everything that had happened, from the man and from the rare violin I had in my hand. I had taken on a new responsibility and I had to live up to it.

Helika was excited. "My father will play and Helika will dance."

I could not take the bow in my hand. My whole body trembled. I put the precious tool into its case and put it aside.

***

I returned from chopping wood. The bread was divided immediately among the members of my family. We still had some of the food we'd been given from our Ukrainian landlord. The boiled water and the warm room were a lot more than what many other poor people had.

The whole way home I thought about the violin. I looked at my wounded hands and didn't believe I could play. But inside me was the joy of touching the violin, my old love. I asked my wife for some kind of fat to put on my hands, to soften them up. We had no oil to rub on them. I dipped my hands in a bowl of hot water and moved my fingers trying to give them back their flexibility. With anxiety and dignity, I took out the violin of its box.

There were several people in the room. Each was busy with something different. I placed the violin near my neck and ran the bow lightly on the strings. An amazing sound came out. I had never heard a violin make such sounds. I had never been near a violin of that level. I didn't even need to adjust the strings; it was perfect. I closed my eyes and started playing. My world was focused on the magnificent sounds. In those moments I was no longer in the ghetto, I was not hungry, and my clothes were not torn. I was a prince floating in heaven.

I do not know how long I stood there playing. When I opened my eyes, I saw a room full of people listening to me. Sick, hungry, lice-infested people stood around me with happy smiles on their faces, carried on the wings of music to wondrous worlds far away.

"Everybody out!"

The owner of the Ukrainian house shattered the illusion and banished everyone into the street. He turned to me and said,

"You really play well. Do you know how to play Ukrainian songs? I want to recommend that you play at a wedding."

It was a difficult question, but I had to accept this work at any price.

"I play everything," I replied evasively.

"You'll find another musician and I'll let you know when the wedding takes place." One of my acquaintances played the harmonica. We decided to play together and prayed that they would invite us. Two days later, the Ukrainian informed us that we would go to the wedding with him.

The hall was filled with well-dressed people. Most of them were wearing very beautiful national clothes. We hadn't seen such a large group of people in clean clothes and with shoes for a long time. The hall was full of light, the tables were full of food, and children in fancy dress were jovial. In my previous world, too, there were such weddings. An eternity has passed since then.

I thought of the sight of my family, my wife in rags, and my daughter who wanted to sleep at night with the bundle of clothes she had. My friend also looked around as if he could not believe that there were still such abundant and joyful sights in our world.

The Ukrainian came up to us, and told us to start playing.

"You said you know Ukrainian songs," he said, "so start playing."

I nodded. I had heard him humming several times so I had a good base to start with. The rest came to us naturally. We were both experienced musicians. My friend had been in a band with me when we were young. He was a great accordionist. On our horror of a journey, he felt he had to bring his harmonica. He needed to have something for the soul.

The wedding lasted three days and three nights. We played like crazy, any melody was welcomed. The Ukrainians started singing a song and after a few bars, we could play the rest of the song. The violin was playing almost by itself and the harmonica added to and improved every song.

They didn't let us rest for a moment. They gave us a lot of food and we devoured it. We had bread, meat, milk, more bread, and then more bread. We began to feel bad. Every once in a while one of us went out to throw-up and then returned to play. I felt like I was falling asleep and the violin just kept playing. I played and napped at the same time. They did not let us stop.

Suddenly I couldn't hear the harmonica. I looked at my friend and saw that he had fallen asleep with the harmonica in his mouth. I got closer to him and made a splitting sound. He jumped up and started playing vigorously. They were very pleased with us and we each received a large loaf of bread.

We felt really bad. It was not healthy for us to eat so much after a long time of eating almost nothing. We lost our minds at the sight of all that food. We became ill and it took us weeks to get over that sick feeling.

I had bread, and I had an obligation. I had to get the bread to the judge as I'd promised. Even though I wasn't feeling well, I wanted to do it right away. I knew what hunger felt like.

I asked my wife to come with me to help me find the judge's room. We took bread and a bottle of warm drink and rushed to their building. We were surprised to find that all the windows were closed. I knocked on the door and there was no answer. One of his neighbors said to me, "You didn't hear what happened? The three bodies were taken to the mass grave yesterday."

I was shocked. How could it be? I had seen him just a few days previously and had promised to give him food.

The neighbor kept telling us, "Their health had been getting worse. They spent days in that room with no food or heat. We hadn't seen them in days and then a terrible smell started coming out from their room. We found the three bodies on the floor. In their desperation, they drank poison. They were quiet people and we never heard any complaint. Here no one complains. You live or die according to your own efforts."

We came here happily, to bring this poor man some bread. We sat down in front of the door and wept. It was a long time since we had felt tears of pity on our cheeks.

***

We were removed from our work of chopping trees. Hundreds of desperate people stood in front of the town hall until they threatened to shoot at us if we did not leave. Even that one moment of daily bread distribution would not come now. What would I give my family to eat?

Again, I felt despair. Without thinking, I took the violin out of its case and played all the Yiddish songs my mother had loved so much. I remembered the poem, A Yiddishe Mameh that she had wanted to hear on her deathbed. With this violin, the melody sounded magical. The violin wept with human pain, and I could feel the beating of its heart and the excess of its soul under my scarred hands. For a moment I stopped, remembered the man I owed for the privilege of playing this violin. I said the prayer, "God is full of mercy," and accompanied it with a slow, deep, trembling music. May they rest in peace.

"Feivel, there is a party in a village that is a half-an-hour drive from here. They heard you play at the wedding and they want you to play at their party. Are you interested?"

It was my landlord. I would have been willing to kiss his feet just to be hired to play. I was happy to do anything to get food for my family and money to exchange these rags for clothes.

"When?"

"Tomorrow night," he answered and left. After a few moments, he came back and asked, "What other instrument can your friend play?"

"He is a great accordion player," I said.

"Bring him too. There will be an accordion there for him. I will take you in my wagon," he announced and left. I'd heard all I had to. I ran to tell my friend that by tomorrow we would have food for a few more days. It was a true joy.

It was a celebration of farmers who had come to dance and be happy. The accordion was ready and even before I could tune my violin, it sounded wonderful. I remembered the orchestra we'd had and the times when a celebration was a celebration. I found it difficult to believe. We'd also had days of debauchery, joy, and happiness. We started playing together. Ukrainians know how to rejoice. Give them liquor and music and they had the whole world. This time we were careful with food and drink, so as not to overdo it. We drank a little vodka and our joy increased.

One of the men at the party, who loved music, complimented us at every occasion and asked to sing accompanied by our playing. We did not know the song, but within seconds, we connected to it as if we had been born with the melody. He was very pleased and promised not to forget us at the end of the evening.

The night was over, morning came and the crowd kept celebrating. We were tired and foggy but we weren't allowed to move. The party kept on for another day and night and only on the following morning did they get a little tired and returned to their homes.

The Ukrainian that promised to remember us, kept his word. We left with a lot of food and he also gave each of us some money. We returned the accordion, I took my precious violin, and we both took the food we received. We were drunk so we floated easily to the tiny room that was waiting for us. For a moment it looked like a perfect place; a place to put our heads and fall asleep.

***

It was spring; my favorite time of year. The coolness of the evening and the special light of the sun during the day were joyful and refreshing. I thought about the spring days of my childhood. I used to take shortcuts through the fields and enjoy the beauty of the wildflowers. That picture was hidden deep in my memory.

In the ghetto, spring does not look like that. Only the change in the weather and the rays of the sun on our sick bodies foreshadow its arrival. In the fields outside the ghetto, there are pits full of corpses, and the few flowers look to me like the eyes of dead people. I'll never be the same person I was before. Never!

My brothers-in-law entered the room quickly. "They've decided to chop wood in another area. If we hurry, we might get a job."

I was ready within a minute. We ran to the city building to get on the wagons that were going to the new chopping location. My two brothers-in-law got on but I was pushed away by the police.

"We have enough stinking Jews," the policeman said and raised his hand to whip me. Another Romanian, a well-dressed man, caught the whip in the air and said, "That is my servant, how dare you hurt him?"

The policeman moved back and started pleading for forgiveness. He started walking backward without turning his back to the man who'd saved me until he went into the building. I didn't know what to say. I had been saved from being hit. I turned to thank him, but he started talking first.

"Will you be my servant?"

Of course, I agreed. His appearance promised at least food.

"I think I have a fever. I need someone to take care of me. Follow me."

I didn't know where he was taking me but I followed willingly. After a long walk, we arrived at his home. It turned out that he lived alone in a rather large house.

I touched his forehead and it was clear that he had a high fever. I helped him to bed. I had learned various important things in my life. One of them was how to get a fever down in primitive conditions. I placed cold compresses on his head and gave him hot tea to drink. I made sure to keep the room heated at all times.

The doctor came late in the evening and wrote down some prescription pills. I went to get the pills from the pharmacist and returned to the house to help the man take the right pills according to the doctor's orders.

It was late and no one in my family knew where I was. There

was only one explanation for a man disappearing. I asked the Romanian, "Please, let me run home. I will only be gone for half an hour. I don't want my family to worry." I feared his reaction, he could tell me to leave and not return.

"I know you will come back. You have been a great help to me today."

I rushed to the door but he called me back.

"Give me a pen and a piece of paper and wait until I finish writing."

I didn't know what he meant by that. I waited patiently. He finished writing and gave me the note.

"Go tomorrow morning to the city canteen and give them this list. Everything on here is payment for what you have done for me today. I feel a lot better. I will call you again in the future if I need you."

I took the list. I had been living on the road for two years and that was the longest list I had ever seen. I kept reading it over and over until I'd memorized it. It wasn't an ordinary list; it was a treasure that would save lives. I ran home.

I entered like a storm; everyone was back in the room. I stood there and pretended to be on a stage. I recited dramatically, "Tomorrow you will go to the shop and receive: two kilos of sugar, two kilos of yeast, two kilos of corn flour, two liters of milk, two kilos of bread, and some soap. I have more things on the list, but I will keep them as surprises."

Everyone looked at me with their mouths open. Tizzy was the first to return to her senses.

"We couldn't be happier had he given us gold."

It was exactly what I was thinking. I never heard from the Romanian again, but we felt full thanks to him.

***

Rumors about the magical violin started spreading around the Ukraine villages and among the people in the Romanian government. Both the Romanians and the Ukrainians were a culture who knew how to have fun. A thought came to my mind and I couldn't ignore it. The same way they knew how to be happy, they also knew how to be cruel and even how to be killers. We had seen and felt it since the moment we'd left our village.

A well-dressed young man appeared at the entrance and asked, "Who has a violin?" I was glad to see him. More work with music always made me happy.

"I do," I said straight away.

He looked at me in a strange way. Suddenly I recognized him. He worked with the Romanian government. He was in the Jewish police. My happiness faded away. Those men were bringers of bad news. They were willing to sacrifice their Jewish brothers to get good things for themselves. My mood changed and I became defensive.

"We know that Judge Robinson left a violin with you, an Amati. We want you to bring it to the police station."

I hadn't expected that. That violin was the way to stay alive. We all will be starving without the violin. I refused to give it to anyone else. All those things ran through my mind but I had to be careful with what I said.

"The judge gave the violin to me. It is mine now." It wasn't a brilliant response but it was cautious.

The guy smiled at me with disdain.

"If you value your family, you will bring the violin to us today. You wouldn't be able to use it in the hole outside of town anyway." He laughed an evil laugh. He had won. The reference to the hole was clear.

He walked up to my wife, looked at her, and said, "Do you

know what the Germans love to do to Jews the most?" I couldn't believe what I was seeing, he was Jewish too. He kept talking. "If your husband chooses his violin over his family, you should prepare to leave for a German concentration camp tonight. Don't forget your girl."

I was shaking all over. Damn snitch. I would love to break some of his bones. He looked at my little girl. She looked at him and didn't understand what was happening. He took her hand and said, "You are coming with me. We have a special place for orphan children." The little one tore her hand from his and ran to her grandfather. No one moved. He wasn't finished threatening.

"Daughter or violin; it is a hard choice for people like you," he said and left.

I took the violin out. I had to play that magical instrument one last time. It was the music of goodbye to a dear friend. I played a few tunes, but the violin didn't obey me, it was sad too. I packed it in its case and we marched to our final goodbye, to the Jewish police station.

I left the station feeling down. On my way, I thought about the advantage I had over others. My knowledge of music and my talent to adjust to any mood with my music was something I would always be able to use. The music made our lives better. I would never stop playing. I knew I would find a way.

Slowly my head started going back up. I'd not broken down before and I wasn't going to then either. My head was high, my walk was light, and I knew I wasn't going to be put down that day.

***

Several men were gathered outside the house, they looked upset.

"Listen, Feivel. The Romanians caught and arrested six Jews. Some of them are from our families. We have to get the head of the Jewish Council to work to free them. The hungry people were begging for bread on the street. They didn't steal from anyone; they just stood there and asked the farmers for some bread."

I was already upset by what had happened to me and that story just made me angrier. I agreed to go with them to speak with the head of the council. They refused to let us in and claimed that he was very busy. We started yelling and cursing them for being against their own people. They hesitated and we took advantage of that and pushed our way in. The head of the council was a smug man and he welcomed us in with a fake smile. We asked for his help about the six people but all he had was excuses.

"You know begging for food isn't allowed. They were breaking the law. We would have to teach them a lesson. There won't be anymore begging in this city. This issue is handled by the authorities and it has nothing to do with you." He saw the shock on our faces and he added, "I will see what I can do."

He turned his back on us. To him, that conversation was over. I was filled with anger. Before leaving I took a chance and said,

"Have you ever heard about hunger, sir?"

He didn't even turn to see who was talking. We left the place and we knew that as soon as we had, he'd forget us completely. Those people were doomed. He wouldn't do a thing to save them.

The next day we heard that four men, a woman, and a child had been shot for begging. We bowed our heads down in their memory.

***

One day a priest came to our house. He delivered a letter from my sisters in Chernovitz, some money, and some clothes. He told us about what had been happening there.

"The situation in Chernovitz has been very bad. When the Russians left, thousands of Jews were slaughtered. The rest of them were gathered in ghettos and it was terribly crowded. They got the Jews there by promising to send them to work. Many saw that as a chance to get out of the ghetto so they volunteered. They were all sent to Transnistria and over the Bog River. They went through the same things you have and only a few came back. The rest were killed by the Romanians and the Germans." He stopped talking. We gave him a warm drink and some bread and waited for him to keep talking.

"A short time ago, they decided to get more Jews out of the city. The police had a list of names and they went from house to house, capturing whole families. The fear of banishment was big because the rumors had already spread about what had happened the previous time. We, the people of the church, helped many Jews escape from the police. Your sisters, for example, managed to find shelter in a basement and weren't sent away. I hope that they are still doing well. Your sister Anna looks like one of us so she helps us take care of lost children in the church. She has fake identification and she can go around easier and gets food for her family. Their financial situation is good, but there are times that even money can't get food." He grew tired from talking.

"We are very grateful to you. Mostly for letting us know that my sisters and their husbands are safe. We haven't heard from them in years. Thank you for what you have brought to us. You are a dear man."

He got up and went on his way. We thought that my sisters would be spared the troubles of war but they weren't. Jews were being chased everywhere. We started wondering if it would stay that way forever?

I had different jobs from time to time. I took every job that was offered to me. One day a junior officer told me to deliver wood to his house once a week. I made sure to be on time and I was there every week. One day I heard him play a cello. I couldn't resist so I waited until he finished playing and then I knocked on the door. He opened the door surprised.

"You already took the flour I promised you for the delivery," he said in anger.

"The cello," I said.

"What about the cello?" he asked. My clothes were dirty so he wasn't about to let me into his house. He was going to close the door before I had a chance to answer. I rushed to say, "I play the cello." The door opened again and he showed signs of interest.

"A Jew with a cello?" It seemed to him to be a strange combination. I didn't answer.

"Clean up a little. Wash your hands, take off your smelly shoes, and come in." I did as he asked and in a minute I was in. I remembered the cello I'd got from my brother Herman when he'd visited us from America. I'd left that cello behind when I left home.

"Show me your hands," he ordered. Then he handed me the cello and asked me to play. He didn't stop me for a long hour.

"You play very well. Come into play when you deliver my wood."

"I would be happy to," I said. I understood that my show was over so I turned and left.

I got a job with a Romanian engineer. I was in charge of managing his accounts. I'd done the same work in the army so it was right for me. The pay was minimal. When there is no choice, even a little is a lot. I managed to buy some used clothes for my family and myself. The clothes were torn so we only wore them inside the house.

One morning, on my way to work, I was caught by Romanian soldiers and Jewish police and was thrown in jail. It turned out that there was an order to catch ninety young Jews and send them to do hard work in Germany. My wife heard about it and she rushed to the engineer to tell him that I was in jail. Unfortunately, he wasn't in town that day. She became really afraid. She knew I could be saved just so long as the shipment of people hadn't been made yet. She heard my stories about the officer with the cello. She had no other choice, so she went to speak with him.

I was on the jail floor, sad and hungry, and I fell asleep. My mother appeared in my dream. She was kicking me and yelling. I heard her say, "You will not go. You won't get away."

The strong pain in my ribs made me jump to my feet. I didn't know if I was awake or still dreaming.

The officer was in front of me aiming a gun at me and whispering for me to be quiet even though he was going to hit me. I didn't really know what to do. He hit me with the back of his gun and with his fists and he yelled, "You criminal, you thief! You stole money from my house. You filthy Jew, I will kill you. I'll shoot you like a dog. You are not going anywhere. I will finish you. Do you think you can just go to Germany and that I won't find you?" he kicked me again.

The Romanian soldiers stood there enjoying the show. Another Jewish criminal was caught. He turned to the soldiers and said, "You will not take him with you. I won't let you save this thief. I will be the one to kill him after I finish torturing him." He stopped talking and looked to see the effect of his words on the soldiers.

"Move out of my way." Amazingly enough, they did. He pushed me forward and in a few minutes, we were out. We kept going until we were far enough from the station to not be seen. He turned to me.

"Run home. Your wife is waiting for you."

With two broken ribs and one broken leg, I ran as fast as I could. Salvation had come from an unexpected source.

My mother had saved me once more.

**

The fight for existence was hard to bear. People around us kept dying from hunger and disease. The dirt was hard to control despite attempts to clean the ghetto often. Tuberculosis, the lice, and other illnesses killed without mercy.

No one could guess how long we would be able to last like that or what was waiting for us in the future.

The Ukrainian who'd been pleased with my music came back and asked me to play at his daughter's wedding.

"They took away my violin," I answered shortly and with sadness.

"I will find a violin for you," he answered.

"I am willing to pay for the violin. I have to keep it for practice." It was an excuse.

"If I find you a violin will you play at the wedding? I did treat you well the last time." I remembered it well.

"I will try hard for you. I noticed you know a lot about music." The compliment hit its target. He inflated like a rooster.

"Tomorrow we will find a violin." He decided and left.

The next day he came and took me to another Ukrainian who had a violin for sale. He helped me bargain and I left with an instrument. I had my own violin; no one could take it from me. As soon as I got home, I went to try it out. I needed a moment to adjust; it wasn't easy to switch from an Amati to a plain violin. But it was mine and I loved it. It was a friendship that would last a lifetime.

I played at the wedding with my accordionist friend and everyone was pleased. After the wedding, the Ukrainian man gave me a few coins and said, "Half of the violin is on me," he said and smiled kindly at me. I was grateful to him. We also received what was left over from the wedding food. We had enough food for a long time.

***

One evening there was a knock on the door. Lately, they had been dragging people, mostly men, from their rooms. They were taken to work in distant places. Every knock on the door was frightening. I looked around and knew I had to hide. I had decided to jump from the window, but before I could move the door burst open and two Romanian soldiers came in. It was as I had expected. I hadn't been quick enough and I was about to pay for it and maybe with my life.

"You are coming with us right now," they said.

My wife started crying and my little girl ran to me and asked me to pick her up. I took her in my arms and gave her a kiss. She said to the soldiers, "I am coming with Father." The soldiers smiled. I didn't know that those creatures could smile. My wife stopped crying because it wasn't helping anyway. She turned to the soldiers and begged, "Please don't take him from us. We have suffered so much. What do you want with him?"

One of the soldiers went to my girl. He patted her head and said, "She is a cute girl. We are taking him to play for us. We will bring him back in one piece in the morning."

Her sigh of relief could be heard from a distance. I took my new violin and went with them.

The drive to the location of the party was long and I spent it talking with one of the soldiers. He was in a good mood so I got some useful information out of him, "Very soon, German soldiers will be coming through here. The SS soldiers retreated, and they might be cruel to any Jews they encounter on the way. You should hide. I am a socialist, but I have to follow orders or I will be punished."

I'd heard all I needed to hear. I decided to think about it later.

We arrived at a large hall filled with soldiers. Easy women were walking around serving the soldiers. Drinks were flowing and tables were full of food. They arranged a stage for me, made of turned over boxes. They placed me on it and told me to play. It didn't matter what music I played as long as it didn't stop. It took me a little time to tune the violin but as soon as I did I played for twenty-four hours without stopping. They didn't let me rest. I made several attempts to take a break, but every time I did I heard the calls of, "Music! Where is the music?"

I played everything I knew how to play. I even played Jewish religious music and they danced to it without knowing. It was my private revenge.

As the soldiers had promised, they took me back the next day with some food and blankets that were tossed around the room. We could turn them into good coats for the following winter.

**

My wife came home with a bag of groceries. She was happy with the purchases she had made. Some of the women, the ones who still had power in their legs, would walk for ten kilometers out of the city to buy at the cheapest prices. With the little money I'd given her, she'd bought enough food for a week. She'd bought corn flour, onion, lard, cheese, and some apples. Each apple was split into four pieces. We smelled each one first and only after that, in small bites, we ate our piece.

Even though some of the refugees were doing better still the number of deaths was growing, and every day there were more orphans in the ghetto. The children looked like old men. They were skeletons with wrinkled skin, swollen stomachs, and thin gray hair. All the children who had lost their parents were placed in a long shed and lived at the mercy of other people. Women would volunteer to take care of them. They would try to feed them food that was made of warm water and bread or watery corn flour porridge.

My wife decided to help too. She took some food with her. The things she saw there completely broke her spirit. She hadn't believed that anything could get to her but she was wrong. There were naked children in the cold with bare feet, walking around dirty and hungry. Some of them couldn't move. They'd lost all feeling in their limbs, and their bodies and minds had frozen. The dirt and diseases made the place an indescribable horror. Small lifeless bodies were taken out on a daily basis. No one was there to cry over the dead and the miserable. The living kept fighting for every breath and every breadcrumb.

There were talking about moving us to Bucuresti, but so far nothing had been done. The Jewish Machers knew about the horror in the children's shed but didn't do a thing about it.

Our daughter was three-and-a-half-years old, and there was still no sign of the war being over. We were so tired, so broken. Life seemed like a burden too heavy to carry. Refugees who arrived at the ghetto told us frightening stories about the methods of killing in the places they'd come from. They had slow ways and fast ways, but the end result was the same; death to all Jews. It was clear that if things stayed the same there would be no one left. Even the strong would fall; it was just a matter of time.

We each took any job we could find; picking potatoes, gathering corn, lugging wood, and clearing bodies. Women did some of the work. The jobs were hard, but we still fought to keep working. These jobs paid very little money or a small amount of food.

**

We heard yelling in the streets. "The Germans are coming!" We didn't know whether to run and hide or to go to the street. Where had they come from? I looked through some cracks in the boards that were blocking our windows. Only four Germans were walking down the main road. They looked the way we had when we'd arrived at that place. Suddenly I understood.

"The Germans have started drawing back!" I rejoiced. "There might be an end to this war."

We started seeing the great German machine going down. Soldiers were wearing ragged clothes and begging for food and water. No one went to help them. We feared them, but we couldn't feel sorry for them. They were murderers. Where had they been when we'd begged for water? Probably on wagons, wearing shiny boots, and holding a whip that they weren't afraid of using. I ran my hand across my face. I remembered the feeling of being hit by a whip. I would carry the scar from that for the rest of my life.

The engineer I worked for, called me to help him pack his things. I knew what he and others like him were afraid. All the people who'd taken advantage of us because they'd had the support of the Germans were suddenly afraid of Soviet soldiers. It was clear that the Soviets would be there soon. I knew that it would be our salvation and we might get a chance to return to our old lives. That night the engineer and all of his friends left town. Among them were Romanians, Ukrainians, and Jews.

We started fearing something new. We knew that troops of Germans might be coming through our ghetto and they might take every piece of clothing and food we had. This would be their last chance to take revenge.

In a short time, we saw convoys of German soldiers retreating and it was clear that there was nothing to fear. They passed through in small groups. It was the shabby remains of a crumbling, crushed army.

***

It wasn't long before the Russians came. We cheered them on. We gave them food, water, and alcohol. We wanted to hug them. We cried and laughed for joy. Anyone who was able to walk found him or herself outside. There hadn't been such happiness in our world since the beginning of the war. Most of the Russians kept moving and only a few officers and some soldier troops stayed.

After several hours we heard that everyone had to go to the center of town. We were sure it was good news.

After everyone arrived a general got up on a truck and started speaking, "Our war against the Germans isn't over. There is still resistance and we have to fight Hitler until the last of his soldiers. I know what he has been doing to you; I am Jewish myself. You have to draft and join our good cause. All men under the age of forty will be going out to help finish off Hitler's army."

It wasn't what I had been expecting. There were all these sad people standing there, filled with lice, sick, and wounded in their bodies and minds. They wanted to make us soldiers now? What could our bruised hands do to help fight a war? It was a very sad joke.

Russian soldiers instantly surrounded us. They sent the women and the old men home, and kept us without a way to escape. It was a horrible surprise. The soldiers lined us up and wrote down our names. I showed my hurt feet to the soldier who came up to me. He didn't even look at them. His job was to write the names. I gave a wrong name. When he asked for documents I told him that I'd lost them. There were no more questions. All of a sudden trucks appeared. They started pushing us onto the trucks. Were we in the hands of the Germans or the Russians? By behavior, there was no difference.

The trucks took us to Mogilev. We were placed in closed camps. When they did another checkup they told me that I was a runaway and that I had to wait for a trial. It was too much for me. They allowed us to wander around the camp during that time. I knew I had to run away or I would never get to see my family again. I went to speak with the guard at the gate.

"Do you know you have a very important job here?" He didn't seem very smart and I'd got him curious.

"Why do you say that?"

"You guard the entrance and exit of the camp. Everyone has to go through you, even officers. They see you first. I always wanted to be a guard at a gate but I was never smart enough." I saw him sitting taller. He brought his chest out and straightened his hat.

"Do you want a cigarette?" I asked.

"I would love one. I'll smoke it when I finish my shift." He reached out to take the cigarette. I started looking for it. I knew I hadn't had a cigarette in three years, but I pretended to be disappointed when I couldn't find one.

"I must have left the pack somewhere. I will go out to a store near here and get us both cigarettes," I said trying my luck.

"I can't let you out," he said aggressively and walked away.

"You are right. You can't be sure I'll come back." I pretended to think and then happily said to him, "I have a solution. I know that I'm coming back but to help you be sure I will take my coat off, the only one I have, and leave it with you." Before he had a chance to react I took my coat off, put it in his hand, and left the camp. I'd bought my freedom with a lice-infested torn coat.

I had to return to my family quickly. I knew they must have been going crazy with concern. I didn't have anything to pay a Vassily with and I was afraid to sneak onto trains. I couldn't take any more risks so I had to walk many kilometers to Mogilev.

It took me a day and a night of walking to arrive. I was surprised to receive food from the locals. They didn't even ask questions. I would knock on the door and ask for food in Russian. They would bring out bread and meat or cheese and close the door. I didn't understand what had brought on the change but I didn't starve and that was all that mattered.

I got home. The Russians had stopped looking for men to draft and they left town that morning. Suddenly we didn't have any masters. We had to decide what to do. After years of having others tell us what to do the new situation seemed unnatural.

We gathered all of our money and bought a horse and a wagon. We decided to go to Chernovitz, to my four sisters.

***

We were back on the road. My father was weak and he complained about blurry vision. I figured that it was because of his age and the fact that he hadn't been eating well. I promised him that my sisters would take care of him and that he would feel better.

He took care of our girl during the drive. In fact, throughout the whole war, a special bond had formed between the two of them. In difficult days when we didn't have food to give our girl, and there were plenty of those, she would curl up near her grandfather, hold his hand and ask, "Grandpa Moshe, play 'grandma made porridge' with me." Then she would lick her lips as though she was enjoying her porridge. After a short time, she would fall asleep from weakness. Even during the drive, on a wagon with a horse, she moved from her mother's arms to her grandfather's arms, curled up, and fell asleep.

We only drove at night and stayed hidden during the day. We were afraid that the Russians would catch us. Men our age would get sent to the front. Even at night, we made sure to take side roads.

In the morning, as we were looking for a place to park for the day we came across two Russians who were on foot. They were carrying weapons.

"Get off the wagon," they ordered. I knew we couldn't show signs of weakness or fear. We knew that we were practically dead without the wagon so we couldn't lose it.

"We have weapons in those bags; we got them from Germans we killed. Can't you tell that we are partisans?" I leaned over one of the bags as if I were about to pull out a gun.

"Partisans?" one of them asked as he walked off the road. The other man moved after him. We rushed our poor horse and left the place. They must not have realized the lack of logic in the story. By the time they understood we were far away.

***

We arrived at Chernovitz. The city was half ruined. Russian soldiers were everywhere, walking around as though they were kings. Very few citizens were outside. We'd hoped to find a city that had returned to life. We knew that Jews had been chased out of there too, but the situation was better than in South Bukovina. There wasn't complete banishment. Those who had been allowed to stay were moved to the ghetto on the edge of town. They were able to get food and clothes and even though the conditions weren't very comfortable, each family still had a private room. My wife's parents and her brothers had found a large room in the ghetto and they'd stayed there. We kept going to where my sisters lived. They'd never dream of seeing us there.

While we were searching, I ran into one of the clerks from the mill I'd worked in. He was happy to see me and said, "I have been moving from place to place for the last year. Hiding, stealing some food, and moving on. They hit me and sent their dogs after me and I am wounded all over my body. I came here two days ago. I hope to find a place to rest my head here; I don't have any energy left."

I felt sorry for him and said, "We are going to my sisters' house. If they have room for you, you can join us there." After everything we had gone through I still believed that we were lucky.

My sister Dora opened the door and burst out, shouting with joy at us. There were tears of joy in the eyes of all of us. For years we hadn't known the fate of my sisters and they had not heard about us. Dora looked from one to the other and asked where Mother was.

"We will tell you everything once we recuperate. Now we can barely stand."

She took control of the situation.

"First thing you must do is have showers. We will throw away all of your dirty clothes. I will give you some of our clothes. After that we can hug a little," she said with a happy smile. Taking a shower with running water was a dream come true. We had gone a long time without a decent wash, clean clothes, and a nice warm home. While we showered, the rest of my sisters came home. We felt so good being clean and well dressed.

We told them about everything that had happened to us during the time we were away. The first thing we told them about was how we lost Mother and we all wiped away a tear of pain. We wanted to keep telling them stories, but we were too tired.

We sat at a table covered with a white tablecloth, ate on plates of china and drank in glasses. The food was wonderful and we enjoyed every bite.

We lay in the beds offered. What a wonderful smell; that of clean sheets! We covered ourselves well and had a quiet, peaceful sleep.

***

There were loud knocks at two in the morning. We woke up in a terrible panic. A few minutes passed before we realized where we were. The knocking grew louder until my sister got up and opened the door.

Two Russians in uniform stood in the doorway. They pushed her aside and came up to me.

"You have to come with us immediately. Everyone in Czernowitz has to register. Are there other men in the house?"

One of the soldiers moved from room to room. They found the man I had brought here, my former clerk, and ordered him to get dressed immediately.

"They only arrived yesterday, tired and sick." My sister tried to help me. "Feivel, show them your legs and your wounded hands."

One of them looked and said to her, "They'll be back in an hour."

We got dressed and went with them. Dora knew where the collection was and what awaited us.

We arrived at a big military camp to find out that the Russians had put on a rather large hunt that night. Whoever didn't hide well enough was caught. There were about three thousand men there. We were placed in lines and they started taking our names. At that point, we were very much awake. They tried to find out if we'd come with other families to take their addresses. We informed them that we arrived alone and that we didn't know anyone but my sisters. They took us out to a large yard, where we sat on the cold ground and waited. A man who was sitting next to me never stopped crying.

He looked at my face in amazement and asked, "Do you not know where we are being taken tomorrow?"

"No," I replied honestly.

"We will be sent to the front, friend. You see, yesterday we left the filthy ghetto we were in because of the Germans, and now they are sending us to fight on the front and be killed because of the Russians."

I was amazed. "They said they would keep us for only an hour and send us home."

The man stopped crying, to laugh at my stupidity. "Did you believe them?" he asked, mocking my innocence. After my long experience in the ghetto, did I still believe what I was told? I did not want to accept the possibility that this was my last stop.

After all the hell we'd gone through, was it not time for us to come back from there? In a whisper, I begged, "Mother, get me out of here."

The men next to me gave me a suspicious look. A person who talks to himself could be dangerous. He got up and went to sit somewhere else.

***

In the morning they gave out warm drinks and told us we had to get in lines inside the camp. We weren't allowed to talk to the people who were outside. We formed lines and in between were soldiers with weapons. Whoever stood out of line was pushed into his place by the back of a gun.

I saw my wife and my daughter standing outside next to the gate. My sister Anna was standing near them. I was standing in the line closest to the gate. I heard my wife talking, but I didn't turn my head. I didn't want the soldier next to me to suspect that she was talking to me. I just listened.

"We spoke to anyone we could and they all refused to help. You probably know that you are being sent to the front. You will first go to another military camp and only after that will you get on a train. We will walk with you for as long as we can." I could hear her clearly. She didn't allow herself to be controlled by her emotions even though it might be our final hour. I felt relieved even despite the situation. I even had a small sparkle of hope. I knew that my wife and my sisters would do anything to help me, even if it meant risking their own lives. The clerk who'd come with me was there during that conversation and heard every word too.

We were divided into groups of hundreds and the officer yelled into a microphone.

"We are moving to another camp. You are not allowed to leave the line in any case. From this moment you are soldiers and all the laws of the army apply to you. If you leave the line or talk with anyone you will be shot. Each group will leave the gate when ordered to. These armed soldiers are instructed to shoot anyone who doesn't obey."

Lines of rows began to leave the main gate and go out into the street. Each row was surrounded by armed soldiers. We were very tense as we waited for our turn. I had to pay attention to any possible means of escape. To go with the line to the second camp meant dying.

Our line was instructed to leave. We first passed by the fence. My sister Anna stood there shouting, "Do not worry, we'll get you out of line." The noise was terrible, and no one else knew who she meant. Women, mothers, and children stood along the fence, shouting to their loved ones and crying. Three thousand enlisted men, and at least the same number of people standing and shouting from the outside, created a terrible commotion and general hysteria.

We were a few steps from the gate. My heart was beating very fast. Just a few more steps and we would be on the street. At that moment, several women who had husbands in my line, jumped at them in an attempt to give them packages with money and food. The soldiers started yelling. One woman jumped on her husband's neck in tears. Two soldiers went and tried to take her away, and when they couldn't do it, they shot her and she fell at her husband's feet.

Those moments of chaos were enough to get my sister to come up to us. She grabbed my arm in one hand and the clerk's arm in the other and said, "We do not look back. We walk slowly, we walk leisurely, and we do not run away."

It was hard to stop my legs from running. We knew we might be shot in the back, but maybe an angel was guarding us this time too? We reached the corner of the street, turned right and started running to the first destroyed house. My sister left and we both stayed there until dark. Thank you, God. Thank you, Mother. Thank you for keeping us alive.

***

I knew I couldn't stay in my sister's house. I was a risk to everyone there. My wife and child were in danger too.

Anna managed to get my wife and child forged papers, and found them a hiding place in the attic. The place was big enough for all three of us. My wife, thanks to the false papers, could go out and bring us food. I was never allowed to leave. The Russians hunted for every man under forty. They learned all the methods used by the Jewish boys to escape and were assisted by informers. I spent three months in that attic.

One day, Tizzy returned from the street trembling.

"When I showed them the false papers, an acquaintance from our town passed by and called me by my real name. The soldiers began to suspect me, and I almost fainted. The acquaintance realized that he had made a mistake and started running in the opposite direction."

She fell onto the chair, still horrified.

"It's time to go home," I said firmly. I asked Tizzy to look for a wagon Vassily to take us to Dorohoi.

I grew a mustache to make my identification difficult. From time to time, one of my sisters sneaked into the attic and we talked. They decided that father would stay with them. He had gone through too much turmoil for a man his age. She had to see that his eyes were taken care of, since he found it difficult to see. Walking the long distance in the snow was the reason for his blindness.

My wife met a wagon owner who had agreed to take us to Dorohoi. We prepared ourselves and obtained farmer's' clothes. The boots I found were too large for me, but the costume I wore and my curly mustache gave me a Russian look. Our little girl could still wear the clothes she'd got from the Ukrainian landlord. We were ready to go back to Romania.

Vassily, the driver, did not want to take the risk, so he waited for us outside the city.

We set off with a small package of food and the violin. We wanted to cross the border into Romania at night because the guard was thin on resources and with some luck, we would not be noticed. But luck was not on our side. At the last moment, a Russian guard stopped us. We tried to explain ourselves and bribe him.

We found ourselves in the Russian Border Police prison. In the morning an officer arrived and told us, "You are being accused of espionage. We will take care of you tonight." He turned to me and to Vassily.

My wife, my daughter, and the wife of the wagon Vassily were given certificates enabling them to return immediately to Czernowitz. I parted from the girl and my wife. I did not believe I would make it this time. But when we embraced, Tizzy told me, "It's not time to say goodbye forever." I hoped she was right. A soldier came in and took out the women and the girl.

We weren't in the mood to talk to each other. Each of us settled into his thoughts. I stood by the window and looked out. It was a beautiful morning; there wasn't a cloud in the sky. In front of the window was an old pine tree. I could see drops of dew sparkling in the sun. The picture didn't fit my mood at all. Suddenly I noticed a Russian officer walking past the yard. I was sure I knew her. She was at a Ukrainian wedding where I'd played. She'd been standing near the musicians singing Russian songs. I had told her then that she had a nice voice. I couldn't believe I was seeing her there of all places. I made some noise to try and catch her attention. She looked in my direction and her eyes opened wide. She couldn't imagine seeing me there either. She came to the window.

"What are you doing here?" she asked.

"We tried to get across the border to Romania and we got caught. Can you try to get us out of here? We are being charged with espionage. You know what will happen to us. You are my only hope, please." I knew that she would try, but I didn't know how powerful she was.

She came to our cell in the evening with a tray of food.

"It doesn't look good. The officer in charge is very strict. He was mad at me for interfering, but I didn't give up and I got him to promise to come to talk to you tomorrow and you can tell him the whole story. I can't tell you what your odds are."

The next morning the officer called me. I saw immediately what affect my friend's influence had had. He would listen to me for a long time.

"I know you will make the right decision," I said, adding, "I would like to entertain you with a little music. I have a violin here and I love to play Russian music."

His eyes lit up. He was very pleased with the offer. I also had some money from my sister. I offered him a suggestion. "Officer, I would be happy to invite you to eat at a small inn in the nearby village. I will take the violin with me and you will have a special evening." There was no hesitation in his decision.

"I am ready to go."

The whole inn celebrated and honored the officer who'd brought along his musician. I played all the Russian songs I knew. I played with all my heart. I played to save my life.

I was called to the officer's office in the morning. He was in a good mood and gave me a friendly smile.

"Stay here. We will arrange an orchestra and you can run it." That wasn't what I needed. How do I get out of here as long as his mood is high? I replied with great caution, "I would be happy to do so but my parents are very old and they are alone in Romania. I have to get to them. They need my help."

"I will give you passports so you can return to Chernovitz." He was about to leave. He stopped at the door and turned around. "You are a talented musician. I will remember that night for a long time."

My magic violin seemed to soften the tough officer's soul. I no longer missed the wonderful Amati violin. I embraced my simple violin, which once again had saved my life.

On my way out I met the officer and thanked her.

"In about two weeks, eight wagons will leave for Romania to

bring food to our battalion. If you offer them a proper sum, they will get you across the border." She looked around, said goodbye, and disappeared into the next building.

We contacted the soldiers who agreed to take us across the border. They asked for a lot of money, we promised to return in two weeks with that sum. I knew I could depend on my sisters for the money I needed.

We got back on the road, this time in the direction of Chernovitz. As soon as we got out of the base, I saw the two women and my child. It turned out that they had been hiding in a deserted building opposite the prison and waiting to see what would happen to us. We were together again. Another danger that had threatened us had passed.

***

Our stay in Chernovitz was short. My sisters got us more clothes and tools to help us get settled in the new place. I also received from my sister Dora the address of a lawyer in Dorohoi. She said he'd help us find an apartment and possibly a job.

We returned to the building across from the jail. We wanted to be sure that we wouldn't miss the wagons to Romania. Besides the violin, we had several packages. We knew that we couldn't miss our opportunity. The wait was longer than we imagined but we didn't lose our patience. We had only one goal.

The wagons were being organized to go. Each one was carrying a large amount of hay, the horse food for the road. The soldiers got the money they asked for and we got on our way. During one of the stops, we saw the soldiers looking at us and whispering. We didn't like it at all. One of them came to talk to us.

"We are going to leave you here if we don't get more money. The decision is yours." He turned around and returned to his friends.

We had no choice and gave them what they wanted. Until we reached freedom we were in their hands.

We entered into the city Dorohoi. The soldier stopped the wagon, and while I was helping Tizzy get down, he hit the horses and took off with our belongings. I ran and managed to jump on it and threw out all our bundles. The soldier panicked and stopped.

"I did not see that you had things there," he tried to explain. I was angry but realized that I had no chance of winning in a confrontation with the soldiers. I jumped down and waited for my wife and child to join me. I consoled myself by knowing that I hadn't allowed him to run away with all our possessions.

We immediately went to the address that I'd got from my sister. The lawyer's wife opened the door for us. She greeted us coolly but politely. "We have a warehouse in the yard. You can stay there until you find a room to rent."

We felt safe and satisfied. We were close to our hometown. The lawyer's wife gave us food while we stayed there. We didn't have any demands and were happy with what we got.

We did not dare go out and look for work. We waited for the Russians to leave. After many discussions between us, we decided to remain in Dorohoi for the time being.

I made a fateful decision and it was time to talk to my wife about it. One evening I said, "Tizzy, I've gone through two wars in this country. My father and my brother fought for foreign people. I don't even want to talk about what we got in return. I think it is time we go home."

My wife looked at me in amazement. What were I talking about? For her, home was in Gura Humora, Bukovina, the town where she was born and where she spent her whole life. By the sparkle in my eyes, she realized that I was thinking of somewhere else—about the shared dream we'd had before we'd gotten married.

"Home, my darling, to our Palestine." We felt the need to hug. A warm sensation filled us both. That was the warmth of hearts that were missing the real thing, the home we'd never had. A small country with enemies from outside and foreign domination inside, but with the advantage that no other country in the world has; it was ours!

Embracing and full of hope and anticipation, we fell asleep.

***

With the lawyer's recommendation, we found a small but nice apartment on the main street. I got a job in a warehouse of old equipment. The work was hard, but I'd forgotten how to complain a long time ago. I was happy to have a way to provide for my family.

My wife bought a loom and started making vests and scarves. They sold very well.

We sent Helika to a Jewish school where she learned a few words in Hebrew. She especially liked singing songs in the new language she did not understand. We asked her to sing softly so the neighbors would not hear. We still did not feel safe enough.

Dorohoi was a rather pleasant town. After everything we'd gone through, it was finally a place where we could start living a normal life. We worked, we took walks in the park, and our girl was in a place that contributed to her development. We felt that we were starting a blessed new path in our life.

Many of our friends had also arrived there and our home had become a happy meeting place for friends. I decided to set up an orchestra for fun and for a living. Soon I had an orchestra with four musicians. In the evenings we practiced a program for parties and weddings. I managed to get a cello and played alternately on it and on the violin.

What a joy to play again! The lawyer made friends with us and came to hear music for "the soul," as he put it. One day he told me that the police were looking for an employee who had very nice handwriting and suggested that I apply. The work in the warehouse was exhausting and I wanted to have the strength to perform in the evening so his offer seemed very good to me. I passed the test and got the job. I was given a police rank and overnight I became a major. I was the only Jew who worked for the police at the time. I did not know exactly what was required of me, but that did not bother anyone.

Our orchestra was ready to perform and we had to choose an appropriate name. The proposal Freedom for the Homeland was accepted with unanimous enthusiasm. We bought new clothes so that our appearance would be respectful and professional.

Between me and Tizzy, there was no more talk about Gura Humorului. Our plans took on a completely different direction.

Between the police work and the performances with the orchestra, I also began to be active in the Zionist movement. Many activists came into our house, they mingled with the musicians, and we thought that this did not arouse any suspicion.

***

One day, one of the activists burst into my house excitedly. "Feivel, you have to help them." I waited for him to explain. "The two guys who were here yesterday did not have any documents and the police caught them." I asked how they had been caught, and he replied, "In one of the houses there was a meeting of our activists. Apparently one of the neighbors informed on us. The police arrived and managed to arrest the landlord and the two young men.

"How can I help them?" I asked.

"You are in the police station every day. Try to find out how much it would cost to release them and we will raise the money." I knew I was taking a risk by asking about two political prisoners without documents. On the other hand, I knew that everything could be bought with money, even the freedom of those two young men. And indeed, we paid a lot of money and added a new pair of shoes. They stayed in our storage room, which was big enough until a way was found to smuggle them out of the city.

After a few days the clerk from the mill, an old friend of ours, showed up at our door with his wife. They were having financial problems and didn't have a place to stay. Our storage room had space so they took it.

That friend suggested I buy a wagon and two horses and he would pay back half of the investment and we would share the profit. I had money so I willingly agreed. His wife helped my wife with housework and made the threads for weaving on a loom.

After six months I noticed that money was missing from our house savings. We had a special place where we stored the money and everyone in the house knew where it was. I suspected that my friend was taking the money. I marked the bills I placed there. I didn't want to embarrass anyone with false suspicion.

After a few days, money went missing again. I checked my friend's pockets and found the marked notes. My disappointment was very great. I had helped this man. I had given him a place to live for free, and this was his thanks? I could have gotten him arrested. I decided to talk to him.

"I know you stole money from this house. How could you be so ungrateful?" I asked. I was so hurt and insulted by his behavior. He began to apologize, to try and wriggle out of it and accused his wife of inciting him. How does a person descend to such a low level to steal from his friend, and does so not from deprivation but from mere greed? I did not want to talk to him anymore.

"Take all your stuff and leave right now. I never want to see you again. I thought I was helping a friend and I found out I had a lowly thief in my house."

They left our house that very day. In our bedroom, I found some money he left.

***

My four sisters came, with their husbands and my father, from Czernowitz. We were very happy to see them. My father looked much better, even though his eyesight hadn't improved. He didn't complain; he had learned to live with his disability. They all settled into a large apartment in the city and the men worked. It was good to be close to the family; we missed those days. From a letter we'd got from Tizzy's parents and brothers, we learned that they had managed to return to Gura Humorului and that they had started working in the mill as partners. I admired their determination. I knew that I would never invest in building a life in a foreign country so that others would harvest its fruits.

Our band was a success and we kept getting more work. I saw an old neighbor at one of my shows and he asked me if I was a member of the Communist Party. I was amazed at the question and realized I was in a predicament. Anyone who wasn't a communist was a problem to the government. He promised to come by my house so we could talk.

***

Recently we had been very cautious in meetings of activists of the Zionist movement. I took advantage of my work at the police, and secretly signed immigration documents for Palestine. I knew how much I endangered my family and myself, but I had to contribute my share. The members of the central committee in Bucuresti gave us instructions for action, through special emissaries.

The Communists ambushed us everywhere. Each member endangered his life with his Zionist activity.

One Friday we did everything as usual. Our daughter was doing her homework. My wife was in the kitchen making soup for Shabbat. A few friends sat with me in the room talking about our plans for the future. We all wanted to emigrate to Palestine, but the way there was still blocked. Suddenly, one of the activists burst into the house and came straight to me. His breath was quick and sweat covered his brow.

"You must leave Dorohoi at once. They are onto you."

I did not understand what he was saying.

"Who is on to me?" I asked.

"They discovered in the police what you've been doing. I do not know who betrayed you. If you do not leave as soon as possible, they will arrest you and you will never come back. I have a vehicle outside, I will get you out of the city and then we'll decide what next."

I called my wife, "Tizzy, we have one hour to leave this town." She wasn't surprised.

"I heard the story from the kitchen. What should we take with us?" she asked calmly, as though we were taking a short vacation.

"No luggage should be taken," one of the members said. "You have to look like you're going for a few hours' walk."

Once again, to leave a house that we'd managed to sort out. Again persecuted and wandering. But did we have a choice?

"Everyone will wear a few layers of clothes. There is no possibility of taking suitcases. I can only take the violin." I stopped for a moment with the smell of burned food growing stronger in my nose. "Tizzy, you have to turn off the stove. Everything will remain the same. If someone breaks in, everything should look as if we've left for a short family trip.

Friends, you need to leave and let us organize."

Our friends hugged us warmly. They all had one blessing. "We will see each other soon in our country."

We had no time to lose. I called Helika, explained to her that we were going for a walk and that she should not talk to anyone about it. We took the rest of our money, put on the layers of clothes, I took the violin next to me, opened the violin case and said to Tizzy, "Do you have anything to put in the strings box?"

"My scissors should fit in that space," she replied. Now we were ready for the next journey; a journey to our home, to our country, to the light.

***

Our friend was waiting for us in the car. I saw how tense he was. He too was taking a risk by driving us. We were constantly risking our lives and hoping for a better future.

We drove for an hour-and-a-half until we reached a remote village where we boarded a train to Bucuresti. We knew that we would receive help, guidance, and travel visas from the activists of the Zionist leadership. I had an address in Bucuresti for initial assistance.

We weren't alone. It turned out that hundreds of families had sold everything they had and were waiting for a chance to go to Palestine. We stayed with a Jewish family in the city. The waiting was nerve wracking. The information was clear; the British didn't allow Holocaust refugees to enter the country.

Some of the immigrant ships that approached the shore were returned to their countries of origin. Others were caught and their passengers transferred to camps in Cyprus. When the word "camps" was mentioned one's body was covered in cold sweat.

The governments of Romania and Bulgaria had received specific instructions from the British to prevent Jews from leaving for Palestine. In order to circumvent the orders, they tried to be smart and to inform them that the refugees were staying there only as a transit station to South America. No one spoke of immigration to Palestine.

Meanwhile, many refugees gathered in Bucuresti. Obviously, one ship would not be enough for everyone. After two months of waiting, we took the train to Bulgaria, to the port city of Varna. There were two ships that looked huge in our eyes. One was called Geula and the other the Jewish state. They put us on the second ship. All in all, we counted four thousand and fifty-two refugees who wanted to get home.

The first immigrants were housed in the cells inside the ship. We arrived among the latter and stayed on deck. The crowding was terrible. If you raised a hand, you hit the man next to you. But no one complained, the people smiled at each other, and returned saying, "Whoever travels on a ship called the State of Israel is already in the State of Israel." For us it was not a word, for us it was a vision.

The entire mood in the ship changed once we got to the territorial waters of Israel, which were controlled by the British. Two British warships escorted every ship, one on each side. We started preparing a welcome for the illegal owners of our country. We collected tin cans and placed them in strategically planned areas. The young men improvised weapons. The plan was to go down to the belly of the ship and leave the women, children, and old men on the deck. We planned to jump on them when they got on the ship. We didn't even think about what would happen later. We just didn't want them to take control of the ship.

We also prepared rooms with bandages and plenty of water for young children under four years old; we needed to take care of them after the British threw gas bombs. They took Helika too. Even though she was seven years old, she looked like every other four-year-old child. Everything was organized and we felt like true freedom fighters.

The critical moment came. The ships of war on both sides sprayed tear gas at us. Our eyes burned badly and we could see nothing. Within a few minutes, the British soldiers boarded the ship, lined up in rows across it, splitting the deck and separating us. People lost contact with their families and began to make a lot of noise. We, the men in the belly of the ship, were waiting for a signal from the observer on board, but no signal came. We heard only noise and shouts from above.

We decided to go up and fight with our sticks, but when we came up, we discovered to our surprise that the British had already taken over the whole ship. They were waiting for us with ready-made weapons. That was the end of our war.

Things on the ship calmed down. The soldiers put sacks with fresh bread on the ship's deck and just the smell alone drove us crazy. Long queues formed, and I, too, with Helika on my shoulders, waited in line for bread. One of the refugees lost control of himself, began to run wild, and forced himself forward to get there first. When he reached the bag of bread, he attacked the English soldier and tried to grab the bread from his hands. The frightened soldier raised the club he was holding, beat the poor man on the head, and wounded him. The blood flowing onto his clothes brought us back to places we so desperately wanted to escape and forget. My daughter began to pull me out of the line and yelled, "I do not want bread! I want to go to Mother!" Of course, I did not give up. After they evacuated the wounded man, no one dared to push. It was a shame that this was the start of our way to a sane life.

There were many children on deck, and as usual, they began to play around. The fear of the soldiers faded away. They tried their best to be nice and help, but we did not accept any help from them. More bags were loaded onto the ship and large packets of chocolate were pulled out. The soldiers gave them to the children but they did not understand what those dark cubes were.

Children who'd grown up in the Holocaust did not know the look and the taste of this sweet. One of the soldiers approached my daughter and handed her a packet. The girl, who knew of the struggle against the British, glared at him, climbed onto a pile of suitcases, and ostentatiously threw the precious delicacy into the sea. Then she straightened up and began singing in Hebrew, "We brought Shalom Aleichem."

All the people on the deck turned their eyes to the thin girl with very short hair and eagerly joined her singing. The children imitated her and a shower of chocolate bars was thrown into the sea. Only a few of them tasted it and quickly threw it into the sea.

In the evening we approached the shores of the country. The city of Haifa was stunning. Mount Carmel was illuminated as if all its lights had been turned on especially for us. We stood, thousands of people—men, women, and children—and looked at the lit city with tears in our eyes. This time it was tears of happiness and hope.

"A French doctor will come to the ship. Anyone who has medical problems will come to him and he will determine which of you needs immediate medical treatment, and they will be taken by boat to Haifa. All others will be moved to a camp in Cyprus."

In the instructions I received in Romania, my colleagues told me to do everything possible to reach the camp Atlit.

I didn't know why, but I decided to do as I was told. I called my daughter, "Helika, listen well. Most of the people will be taken to a different place that isn't a part of our country. We need to find a way to stay here. The only way is to get the permission of the doctor who is coming. You need to convince him that you are ill. After all, you have always been our actress." I smiled and remembered all the shows she had put on for us. I had to admit that the girl was talented.

The doctor arrived. Due to the crush and the big number of people waiting for his inspection, he was seated on the deck. My wife and daughter were waiting for their turn. The doctor also spoke a little Romanian and there was no problem communicating with him. I stood aside. I did not want to miss my child's performance. Their turn arrived and Helika began to cough in a shrill voice and held her stomach. Before the doctor had even asked how she was doing, she had already prepared the diagnosis.

"I have a severe cough. I have a sore throat. It's hard for me to breathe, my stomach aches, and I have a high fever." Her face wore such an unhappy expression that I, too, almost felt sorry for her. The doctor turned to my wife, while the little girl did not stop coughing, to find out if she had a problem too. The answer was short. "I'm pregnant," she said, and then added, "I'm also bleeding." The doctor, who under these circumstances was unable to examine her, gave a letter confirming our transfer to Haifa.

When we got to Haifa my wife was no longer pregnant and my little one was feeling much better. It was too late to send us to Cyprus so they moved us to a refugee camp in a place called

Atlit. It was exactly where I wanted to go. We were welcomed at the gate by an old friend.

"Be ready tonight, you will go on a mission with us."

I didn't know what he meant but it was clear that I would learn quickly.

The English soldier put me in a hut with forty other men. Tizzy and Helika were placed in a similar place with women and children. We were floating with joy. I remembered the training I'd gone through several years previously. I remembered the happy nights we'd had after working, all the singing and dancing that the Israeli instructor had taught us. We'd made it. And it was our final stop. We would spend our 'forever' here. Here is where we would learn how to fill our time with life.

The instructions were explicit: it was forbidden to leave the hut during the night. Here, too, they threatened to shoot any unidentified figure. Nevertheless, I slipped out of the hut and my friends took me to a hiding place where they explained to us the planned operation. "We managed to smuggle a few kilograms of explosives into the camp. Our goal is to sabotage the British equipment and undermine their safety—"

"How did they smuggle the explosives in here?" I stopped the guy in the middle of the explanation. Everyone looked at me and smiled.

"First rule, here we do not ask questions," he replied. After hesitating, he added. "This time I will answer you. A box, containing the explosives, was put between the wheels of a British military vehicle that was parked in Haifa."

So simple and so clever.

***

I met a special kind of people in the camp. Proud men and women who'd fought for the liberation of the homeland. I thought that such a kind of Jews would never have been taken to the crematoria.

I met a woman whose name was Hannah. She was imprisoned here for sabotaging an English convoy. Who ever heard of such a thing in the Diaspora? When I asked her for how many years she had been sentenced, she accompanied her answer with a ringing laugh. "Until I run away and come back after another sabotage operation."

A British soldier came over and went to talk to her. They spoke English, a language I did not understand. The conversation seemed very friendly but it was clear to me that tomorrow she could kill him without hesitation. An enemy remains an enemy.

We stayed in Atlit for five months. They transferred the political prisoners to closed prisons and we were released to the Jewish Agency.

I'd hidden one lira and a hundred dollars in the heel of my shoe. I had got the money from my sisters.

All I had was a violin, a wife, and a child. With that, I started my life in a country that still wasn't free of British control and Arab hatred.

We got a room in an apartment in the town of Rehovoth. In it were three iron beds, three blankets, and we also received money, thirty-six liras. We shared a kitchen with two other families. To us, it was like living in a palace.

We heard about an upcoming vote in the United Nations regarding the question of Palestine. We listened attentively to the fateful vote. The decision was made; we had our own state. We went out into the streets with all the people. We sang, danced, and hugged anyone who approached us. People were standing on the street and blessing.

"Thank God we lived to get to these days."

We were out of our minds with joy; it was a rebirth for us.

***

My father came to Israel with my sisters. My little girl Helika was the happiest in the world. She finally had her grandfather back. He stayed in our house.

One evening, Moshe, my father, came to me holding a small package. He said, "Do you remember the yellow pages and the small Torah that you helped me wrap around my body before we were taken to the ghetto?" His eyes had lit up. How had it been preserved with all the tribulations we'd gone through? It was a miracle.

He kept talking. "The time has come for this package to move to your hands. It passed from generation to generation and has kept our family safe." Father said excitedly, "The fact that we are here, in the Land of Israel, is the best proof of this. Now it is in your hands. Keep the scroll of the Torah, and pass it on to your son in due course." He stopped for a moment. "Now I'll tell you what my father told me when he gave it to me: A day will come, and this story will pass on, printed on new white pages. People will read and understand how such miracles that happen to us could really happen."

With awe and trembling hands, I took the package.

EPILOGUE

In front of the television screen, on the treadmill, walking at a rate of six kilometers per hour, my body temperature rose, and I start feeling a strange wetness on my hands.

Suddenly, without thought or preparation, I knew the name of the book I was about to write starting that very day, that moment.

I sat next to the computer and written pages started filling up one after another with hundreds of words. I was writing quickly and almost uncontrollably. At that moment I realized that my late father was directing my thoughts and my hands and was helping me write our family's amazing story.

Some truths are hard to believe; some we can't grasp.
I experienced that wonderful floating feeling and it was how my book was born.

Thank you, Father

I WAS THERE

A journey in the footsteps of my book, *Waiting for a miracle*.

After writing this book I felt a strong desire to visit all the places mentioned in it. I wanted to see their real existence and see what they looked like. I had no real memories from there. Everything that was written came from images I had drawn from the depths of my subconscious, from the stories of my parents, and from what had grown up in me mysteriously. I felt as though I was there in some mysterious way.

So I followed 'the yellow pages' that had given birth to this book and I experienced amazing things in those places I described. It was hard for me to believe what I saw.

I started my journey in the town where I was born, Gura Humorului. I had an old photograph of my parents' house. I went to every elderly person I met and asked for help in locating the address.

A twelve-year-old girl grabbed my hand and promised to take me to the house in the photograph. I floated after her and the thoughts darted in my mind at a dizzying speed. Here, in this town, my parents had been born. In the waters of this river they'd bathed; on these streets, they'd walked, laughed and planned their future. Here they'd been happy and joyful.

"It's the synagogue of the Jews. It's closed all the time," the girl remarked. My father had told me that his Bar Mitzvah celebration was held here. I went through years of history, skipping back and forth in time, and I could not believe that my family had lived right here a few decades ago.

"This is the house." The girl stopped. I was standing in front of the house identical to the photograph I held in my hand. A house more than a hundred-years-old stood there, three floors tall, and very strong. I could hear my late father telling me that it was the tallest house in the area.

From the yard, just as I had imagined, a family came out and a little girl was in the mother's arms. All the others were carrying packages and suitcases. Everyone looked afraid except for the baby who was laughing and pulling her mother's scarf. The little girl was me, a year-and-a-half old, on October 1941, on the way to the unknown.

The twelve-year-old pulled her hand out of mine. "You're hurting me," she shouts and moves away from me.

I came back here, after more than sixty years, and I experienced the departure as if I'd remembered it.

From there I walked along the road to the train station, just like before. The station was renewed; the trains were terrifying with their sirens, but I felt nothing. I was petrified.

Progress and time had physically erased all traces of the past but from my soul, they would never be erased.

Tuesday was market day in the town and I wanted to see it. Many people were out on the streets trying to find things they needed for a good price.

In one chapter of the book, I had described a hungry old woman to whom my father, who at that time was ten years old, had given a loaf of bread.

Suddenly she was standing in front of me. I saw her, the sad old woman standing at the entrance to the market in Gura Humorului, holding a knitted tablecloth.

I was thrown back to World War I, with my father's family who had fled to Moravia and sold everything to survive. Of course, I bought the tablecloth and paid double the price I was asked for. For a moment I turned my head from the old woman to fold the tablecloth, and when I looked up, she disappeared. Was she an angel or was she a poor woman who was afraid that I would ask her for change.

I met the last Jewish woman still living there, Becca Fiol. She invited me into her house, apologized for the poor small room, and barely managed to put her sick old body onto the chair.

When she began to speak, with amazing clarity, I forgot all the questions I'd wanted to ask her. Miraculously, she knew that I am the daughter of Tizzy Doliner Wininger.

She and my mother turned out to be childhood friends. The woman knew every member of my family and remembered names, events, and shared experiences. I saw Becca's extinguished eyes come to life, as memories of the beautiful distant past of her youth.

I owe this woman a thank you for giving me back briefly my young mother, full of life and plans; that pre-war mother.

From there, I went through Vama to Campulung Moldovenesc. I found the synagogue. The horror that took place there on the Day of Atonement, Yom Kippur, 1941, came back to me. I saw the rabbi being led away like a horse attached to a wagon by thugs. Everything was painfully real.

Today, grass was growing at the entrance to the synagogue in which a Jewish foot hadn't stepped in a long time.

I went on to Vatra Dornei. My father, as a student in Campulung Moldovenesc, had fled to play with the orchestra he had organized. They'd played on a stage in a park in the city center. I got there, and shivered as if cold despite the hot weather. My eyes wandered from person to person. I looked for my father, the young boy with blue eyes and blond hair. Suddenly an orchestra began to play that music. I burst into terrible tears and fled to my hotel room.

The places, sights, and the excitement wore me down, but I wouldn't give it up for all the money in the world.

I went back there alive, in spite of our enemies. I did it for my soul, for my parents' souls and in the memory of all the Jews who went along the same path and never came back.

Blessed be their memory.

Wininger Family Tree from 1830

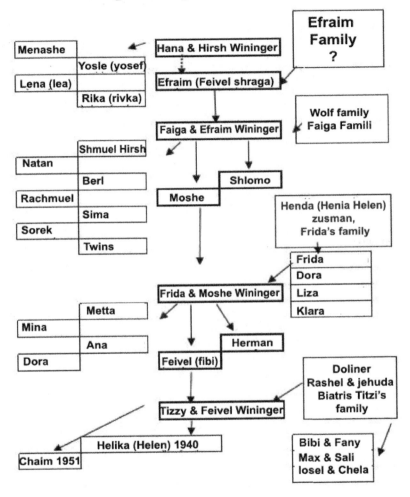

Printed in Great Britain
by Amazon

20325192R00210